When The Night Falls

By C. K. Bennett

The Night series

When The Night Falls

Memento Mori series

Heart of Stone

WHEN THE NIGHT FALLS

C.K. BENNETT

First published by Midgard Press 2023

ePub: 978-82-93952-06-0
PB: 978-82-93952-03-9
HB: 978-82-93952-23-7

Cover and artwork by C. K. Bennett

Find out more about the author and their books at **https://ckbennettauthor.com.**

Connect with the author on Instagram: **@ckbennettauthor**

CONTENT WARNING

This series explores themes of love, trust and jealousy in relationships. It includes scenes and flawed characters that some readers may find disturbing and/or upsetting. Additionally, it is largely character-driven, not plot-driven, and contains sexually explicit scenes. It is intended for mature audiences only. Reader discretion is advised.

ACKNOWLEDGMENTS

While I may have embarked on this book on my own, it was only through the unwavering support of my husband, A, that I saw it through to completion. The year 2022 proved to be a formidable challenge, brimming with unforeseen trials and tribulations. It was your steadfast presence, A, that lent me strength and kept the flame of my resilience burning. Life with you does not merely make everything possible – it makes everything worthwhile. If I've made any one right decision in my life, it was choosing to spend my life you.

I owe a massive debt of gratitude to Darla Cassic, my literary other half, who seems to share more than just half my brain. Our compatibility is as baffling as it is extraordinary – my sincerest thanks for sharing this remarkable journey with me.

Finally, I wish to extend my heartfelt thanks to you, my readers. The truth is, I was on the brink of stepping away from writing in 2022. However, your unwavering support and encouragement reignited my passion. Your kindness and dedication are unparalleled, and it has been an absolute pleasure to write for such a remarkable group of people. Thank you for being there, for existing, and for gracing me with your boundless kindness.

To my faithful readers.
Thank you for always believing in me.

There is always some madness in love.
But there is also always some reason in madness.

– Friedrich Wilhelm Nietzsche

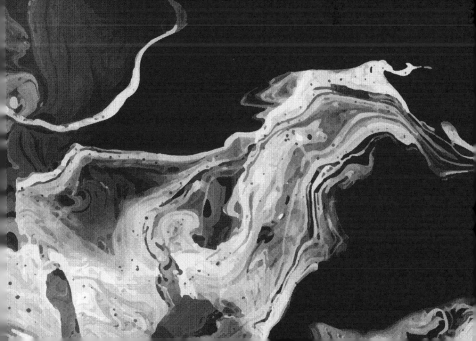

PART I

12 April 2019

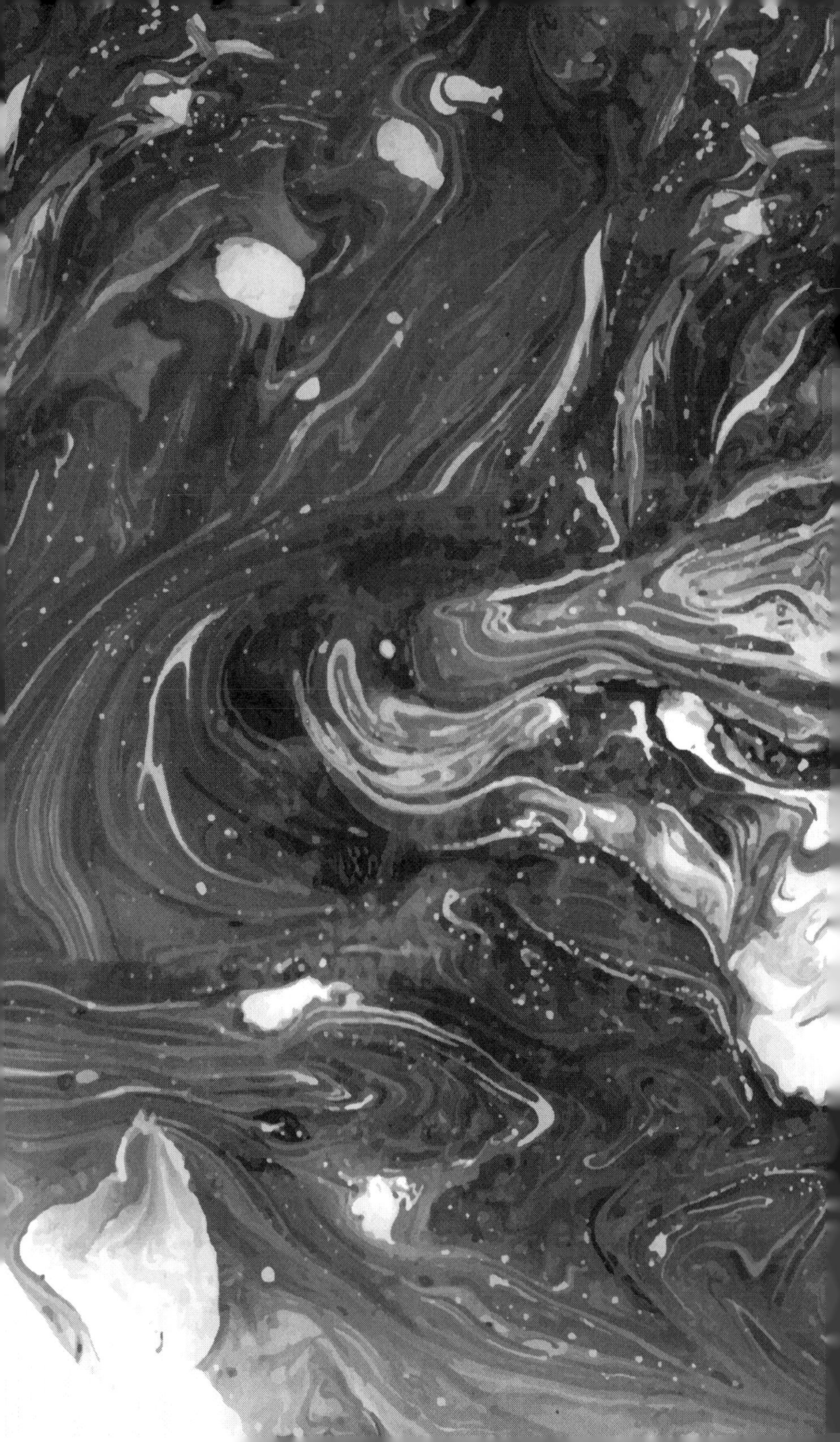

1

GOOD TERMS

'It should be here,' I told Olivia as I turned left, into a small alley, to find the secluded bar. Looking up, I saw a white and gold sign that was shaped like a hexagonal prism, though cut in half, which overhung a green door. Disrepute, it said. It was a members' club, but it welcomed walk-ins. Still, to be on the safe side, I had booked a table a few days in advance.

I halted in front of the entrance, where Olivia and I were greeted by a polite man who opened the door for us. We journeyed down a narrow staircase and came into an underground cavern with a barrel-vaulted ceiling. It was still relatively early on a Friday night, so there weren't that many people here yet. Our arrival attracted a few glances, but none of them lingered; at least we didn't stand out.

We left our coats in the cloakroom before the staff showed us to our table and handed us the cocktail menu. As I sank onto the settee, I gazed around. The interior was reminiscent of the sixties, with plush colours and lots of velvet furniture, but the music was contemporary – electronic lounge music.

I straightened my back, trying to look more sophisticated than I was. The average age of the clientele was a little older than we were used to. Most of the people present looked like they were well-established men and women in their thirties and forties, so I doubted that students frequently went here.

Olivia wrinkled her small nose as she sat beside me, her plump, light-pink lips forming an uncertain line.

'Was this the place Jason recommended?' she asked.

Jason was one of my best friends and had become my flatmate just a few days ago.

'Yes.'

She leaned closer. 'It's very posh, isn't it?'

'You sound surprised.'

'Well, I'm worried I'll stand out.'

I studied her from head to toe. In her deep-red dress, Olivia resembled a magnificent rose. If anything would make her stand out, it was her beauty, and that alone.

'I wouldn't worry if I were you. You definitely look like you belong.'

A heartfelt smile spread across her face. 'Really?'

'Yes. You look stunning.'

She put her hand on her ample bosom, seemingly touched by my compliment. 'Thanks, Cara, but so do you.'

I shrugged and reached for the pine green menu on the small table in front of us. The velvet cover was adorned with the letters D.R.P. in gold.

'Should we have a look at the menu, then?' I asked.

Olivia scanned our surroundings once more and leaned closer again. 'Well, are you sure lawyers frequent this place?'

'Judging by the look of it, I'm positive.'

'It's just that I'd hate to waste my time here if it isn't the case.'

'Nice pun.'

She chuckled.

I said, 'This was Jason's recommendation, and since his father established a law firm, I took his word for it. Mentioned something about his brother favouring this place as well, and he's a solicitor, too, from what I've gathered.'

I hadn't met any of Jason's family members; he no longer lived with them, so the opportunity hadn't presented itself yet. I was aware they were extremely wealthy, thanks to Jason's father being the founder of Day & Night LLP – a firm offering legal services – and that they were a busy bunch, since each individual had a demanding job that took up most of their time, but that was as far as my knowledge about them went. I didn't even remember their names, aside from his father's – John – and I only remembered his name because he was a big shot in the legal field. As for

Jason's mother and brother, he usually referred to them either as 'Mum' or 'My brother', so I hadn't managed to commit their names to memory yet.

That reality was about to change, though. Now that I had secured a vacation scheme at Day & Night to be completed over the summer, and had moved into Jason's flat in Notting Hill, his family had made it a priority to meet me, so they had invited me for dinner in two weeks. I was looking forward to that. I had wanted to meet Jason's family for a while now, especially since he had already met mine several times.

As I returned from my thoughts, I could tell that Olivia was on the fence. 'If you're having second thoughts, we can always find a new place, but let's give this one a fair chance first, yeah?'

She tucked a lock of her light-blonde hair behind her ear as she continued to assess our sumptuous surroundings. Her hesitation was blatant.

I sighed. Olivia could sometimes be impossible to deal with. If she didn't get her way, she transformed into a whiny brat that I couldn't be bothered to babysit. It didn't help that I was already beginning to suffer from a guilty conscience at the constant thought of my neglected coursework, and seeing as I was a law student in my third year at UCL, it was not a matter that I took lightly. Besides, my reasons for being here were purely selfless. I wasn't the one who had wanted to go out tonight. She was. So, if she was going to be a pain in the arse, I would leave her to prowl on her own. But I had already warned her of that, so she had been surprisingly compliant today.

Finally, she directed her attention to me. 'Fine. Let's give it a chance.'

I groaned. 'Took you long enough.'

'Yeah, sorry. It's just been so long since we've had a girls' night out that I want everything to be perfect.'

My lips twisted with amusement. 'Like you're actually here to spend quality time with me,' I said with a note of sarcasm.

'Hey, I'm here for that too. It's just that, ever since I broke up with Colin, I haven't had sex.'

I couldn't help grinning. 'What, so you've had a dry spell for three months? Poor you.'

Three months without sex? I'd be going insane. No wonder she had been so eager about this night.

She gave me a scowl. 'Yeah, well, unlike you, I haven't got a fuck friend. I need to satisfy my libido somehow.'

'Vibrator not doing the job?'

'Not even close. I need skin-to-skin contact – I need a man.'

'And preferably one with a heavy wallet at that.'

A chortle escaped her. 'Hey, you know I'm not like that. I just thought it would be nice to find a lawyer since I'm a law student and all that. We'd have something in common.'

'Aside from sexual desperation, you mean.'

She shoved my shoulder. 'Stop teasing me.'

'Sorry.' I laughed. 'I couldn't help myself. Anyway, we're in the right place, then.' I shook my head. 'I still don't understand how you managed to persuade me into joining this.'

Olivia snorted. 'Cara, even though you may come across as aloof, you've actually got a fairly warm and large heart in there – that's how I managed to persuade you. A heartbroken best friend isn't something you're able to ignore.'

'Lesser of two evils, perhaps.'

'What's that supposed to mean?'

I smirked. 'Maybe tending to your needs is my way of making you shut up sooner.'

She scoffed. 'If that's your attitude, you'll make a rubbish parent.'

Amused, I focused on the menu. 'I suppose it's a good thing I don't want children, then.'

Did I want children? I always said I didn't, but Mum always told me that the right man would change my mind. Since I was one for keeping an open mind, I didn't argue with her on that. She had wisdom in her years that I could only dream of. My perspective today was no guarantee of tomorrow's.

'Have you settled into your new flat yet?' Olivia asked.

I looked up and saw that her eyes were wandering. Another smirk surfaced on my mouth. She surely wasn't wasting time locating a target. Well, I appreciated that. As soon as she sealed the deal with someone, I'd be heading home.

'No, I've been so busy with coursework that I haven't had time to unpack much. I had to search for a whole hour before I found this dress.' I glanced down at the purple material. It was my favourite cocktail dress because it clung to my figure like glue. Although I wasn't voluptuous – I didn't have big breasts like Olivia – I had relatively wide hips, and years of hard work at the gym had got me a round, perky bum, which this dress accentuated beautifully in my opinion. 'But I've booked a date with Jason tomorrow to finish unpacking.'

Jason and I had met at a pub three years ago, where a live band had been performing songs by Arctic Monkeys – one of my favourites. Our encounter had been perfectly coincidental and, in retrospect, rather comical. I was returning from the bar with a new round of drinks for my younger sister Phoebe and myself when a drunken idiot bumped into me, and the impact made me spill the pints I was holding over Jason, who was walking past me just then.

I was mortified, but, thankfully, Jason didn't fail to notice that it hadn't been my fault. After telling off the lad that had bumped into me, he offered to buy me a new round. I was so charmed by him at that moment that I struck up a conversation with him, only to learn that he also studied at UCL, although he wasn't on my course. Instead, Jason was about to finish his second year of studying medicine back then.

After a few minutes of effortless and invigorating conversation, I invited him to join my sister and me. Since he was there with a couple of mates, he brought them along, and ever since that fateful moment, we had formed an irreplaceable and platonic friendship.

These days he was much like an elder brother to me, so when his flatmate had decided to move out to live with his girlfriend, Jason had asked me to take his place. I hadn't hesitated to accept, even though it had made Olivia sad. Before then, I had been living with her and two of her friends from college, but I had never really got on with the other girls, hence why I had been eager to move in with Jason. Besides, Olivia and I were still studying together, and we had been best friends for as long as I could remember. It wouldn't matter if I didn't live with her anymore – we would never drift apart – and she knew that as well as I did, so she had forgiven me for wanting to move out.

'I think I'll have an espresso martini,' I said and glanced at Olivia with a smile, but it faded as soon as I recognised the look on her face.

Already?

Looking in the direction of her gaze, I saw the profiles of two men seated at the bar. They were frowning angrily at one another while they spoke, seeming to be in a heated debate about something.

The next thing I noticed was how attractive they were. Late twenties, perhaps? Early thirties? Both had neatly trimmed stubble and short hair that was immaculately groomed. The man I found most handsome was brown-haired, the other dirty-blond, like Jason. But I'd always had a kink for dark and tall.

'Which one?' I asked.

'Brown-haired.'

'Let's head over, then, shall we? I'll mind his friend.' I ascended from my seat, confident. I always had been.

Olivia seemed hesitant. 'Cara, maybe not. They don't look like they want to be disturbed.'

I scoffed. 'So what? You won't know unless you try, Livy – and I can handle rejection. Can't you?'

Her warm brown Bambi eyes turned to me, and they were filled with a vulnerability that I hated to see. Colin had really done her in, hadn't he? When he cheated on her time and again?

'Livy' – my tone was unusually strict – 'Colin is a bastard who never deserved you, but just because he is, it doesn't mean every man is. You can't give him that power, and you shouldn't let your past ruin your future.'

Olivia inhaled deeply and gave me a firm nod. I was slightly surprised at how quickly she absorbed my pep talk. She must really be desperate, I thought. Either way, I gave her no time to change her mind. I strutted over to the two men while Olivia trailed behind me.

The dirty-blond man noticed me first, and the look on his face stroked my ego. He turned his whole body toward me, his thin lips parting. Just like his brown-haired friend, he had a strong, lean build.

'Hi,' I greeted and held his gaze as I presented my most lascivious smile. His deep-set eyes were big and a warm shade of brown, like melted chocolate. I loved chocolate.

I tilted my head, studying him. He was gorgeous.

When he didn't respond, I continued, 'I'm sorry to interrupt your conversation, but my friend and I were wondering if we could buy you guys a drink.'

'We're not interested,' a dreadfully sensual voice intervened.

I looked over and locked eyes with the man Olivia had laid her favour with. They were light-blue and strangely familiar. Dark brown eyebrows ran in nearly straight lines above them, and the shadow they provided amplified his alluring and mysterious aura.

Had I met him before?

A frown formed on my face. I could have sworn I had seen him somewhere.

At that moment, I was so preoccupied with trying to put a name to the face that I neglected the chance to admire it, but Christ, had I ever seen a man more striking than him? Prominent cheekbones highlighted the shape of his strong, square jaw. It was clenched, I saw, but I gave no thought as to why.

Below a proportionate, straight, and masculine nose rested a pair of full, delectable lips. They pressed together, forming a brooding line, while he continued to study me in his annoyance. He was easily the most physically attractive man I had ever encountered, and he wasn't remotely interested.

'Where are your manners, man?' his friend scolded. Then his eyes darted back to mine. 'Please excuse him. He can be a tad too blunt sometimes.'

Puzzled, I persisted in staring at the dark-haired stranger. I must have met him before. I was certain I had seen him somewhere. But would I have forgotten an encounter with such a beautiful man? I doubted it. Where had I seen him, then? Was he a celebrity?

'I'm sorry – have we met before?' I blurted out in my bewilderment.

His eyebrows arched and a condescending chuckle slipped out of his mouth. Sardonic amusement oozed from his riveting features.

'Honestly, you're interrupting our conversation, and you couldn't be more original than that, Miss? At least you could have compensated with a better chat-up line. I'm disappointed. And as I said, we're not interested, so move along, would you?'

Bewitched by the sound of his sensual voice, it took me a few seconds to process the content, but once I had, I frowned, offended. His friend groaned and shook his head, clearly despairing of his companion.

Could they be gay partners?

Since I was struck by mild shock at his impertinence, I asked, 'I beg your pardon?' Then, as soon as it subsided, I snapped back, 'I was being serious, you utter twat.'

His eyebrows furrowed while he gazed up and down my body – twice. When he met my stare again, a crooked smile crept across his tempting mouth. From the way his eyes had devoured my body, I eliminated the option of him being homosexual. Only a straight man could regard me with such a gleam in his eye.

'Perhaps we've slept together,' he said. 'But if we have, you weren't worth remembering.'

I gasped. What a complete arsehole!

To think he had piqued my interest earlier . . . What an insolent way to treat another human being. His arrogance was off the charts. Who did he think he was? So yes, I had interrupted them, but there was a polite way to reject me. There was no need to step on my dignity.

Rigid, my stare transformed into a pure glower. 'As if I'd ever get so lost and desperate that I would wind up in a bed with *you*. You're a sorry excuse for a man. Tell me, was it the lack of your mother's affection that made you grow up to treat random women like shit?'

He blinked at my ruthless insult, perhaps a little gobsmacked. Beside me, his companion burst into laughter. Olivia's existence was lost on me, but, knowing her, she was probably a breath away from withering.

'I can assure you that my mother and I are on good terms,' came the handsome man's calm reply.

I folded my arms and scoffed. '*Too* good, I wager. Heading home to spend the night in her bed, then? That why you're not interested?'

Olivia gasped and clasped my hand. Observing their shocked facial expressions, she said, 'Please excuse us.'

'Excuse *us*?' I echoed disbelievingly as she tugged me away from them. 'Didn't you hear him just now? How bloody rude he was?'

'I thought you said you could handle rejection,' she retorted.

I flushed with a blend of anger and embarrassment. 'I can, but that was being unnecessarily mean!'

'Well, choose your battles, then! He's obviously not worth our attention.'

A valid point. I tried to simmer down, but it was difficult. Looking at Olivia, I saw that she was trembling with irritation. She was clearly rattled, just like the two men. Well, that was something I quite excelled at – rattling people. It was definitely a flaw, but then everyone had flaws, I consoled myself.

Olivia steered me down onto the settee again and dumped her body next to mine. Folding her arms, she glared away from me. 'Cara, honestly! "Have we met before?" What was that?'

My lips protruded. 'I'm sorry,' I said, hoping to reconcile. 'I honestly thought I'd seen him before. Worst part is that I still think I have.'

She frowned and stole a glance at the men. Mirroring her, I saw that they were laughing, clearly at my expense. Well, they could laugh all they wanted. Personally, the only thing I found laughable was how attractive I had initially found them to be. Instead, they were ugly people with nasty tendencies. Looks could be so deceiving.

Olivia faced me with a puzzled expression. 'Yeah, you know, now that you mention it, he does look a bit familiar.'

'Right?'

'Yeah.'

Where had *we* seen him, then?

I sighed, wondering if the encounter with them had ruined my chance for a pleasant night. 'Well, whatever. Order us a round, please, would you? Strongest cocktail they've got.'

Olivia's subsequent chuckle assured me that I was already forgiven. 'Sure.'

I watched her graceful gait as she returned to the bar like she hadn't a concern in the world. Olivia had always been great at rising above things. Less could be said for myself. I had much to learn from her in that regard.

The dark-haired man turned his head toward Olivia. It was obvious from how consciously he regarded her that he desired her attention. But, with her chin raised high and her gaze fixed straight ahead, Olivia refused to acknowledge him. The satisfying view made my lips twitch into a devilish grin.

If only Jason had been here. Right about now, he would have laughed his lungs out and patted my back repeatedly, but he'd had coursework to do, which I had respected. Nevertheless, I could have used his moral support, so I decided to send him a text.

20:58

You didn't warn me about dickheads when you told me about this place x

Thought that was a given? You wanted a place with lawyers. You can't have one without the other x

You twat. I'm not a dickhead

You're not a lawyer

Yet x

I just accused a man that Livy wanted to get off with of sleeping with his mum. Doubt your coursework is more entertaining...

Lmao you did what?

Did he deserve it?

100 %

By the time Olivia returned, it felt like only a minute had elapsed. As she placed an espresso martini on the table, I looked up from my phone and found her smiling. I grinned back, putting my phone aside. She had brought me my favourite cocktail.

'Next round's on me,' I said.

'I didn't pay for it.' She pressed her lips together in a poor attempt to restrain a smile.

'What?'

'The guy you insulted did. Asked for your name, too, but I didn't give it to him. Gathered I'd leave that choice to you.'

My jaw dropped. Had he really bought me a drink? After all that?

On impulse, I looked in his direction. Spellbinding blue eyes met mine, and I was immediately captured by them. Wearing a complacent smirk, he raised his glass at me and gave me a wink, causing his friend to snigger beside him as he shook his head.

'Seriously? What's his problem?' I grumbled and broke out of his spell to focus on Olivia. Sinking into the spot beside me, she raised her cosmopolitan to her mouth.

After a sip, she said, 'I think you changed his mind, acting the way you did. While I waited for our drinks, you were all he asked about. I told him nothing, though.'

Bemused, I blinked at her. 'You had a conversation with him?'

Olivia frowned. 'He insisted on paying for our drinks, Cara. What was I supposed to do?'

Ignore him? I would have.

'I'm so sorry you had to go through that.'

She laughed. 'You can have him,' she said with a grin, her tone clearly implying that she harboured no bitterness and genuinely meant to give me her blessing. 'He put me off with his attitude. His friend, though – Andrew – he seems nice. He apologised on William's behalf. William's the arsehole.'

I scoffed. 'Thanks, but no thanks. I'd rather he pissed off.'

Olivia chuckled and scanned the room again, probably to locate new targets. Meanwhile, I stared at the cocktail Mr Arsehole had bought me. I wanted it, but it felt wrong to accept it, so I just kept staring at it, conflicted.

'Oh, for heaven's sake, Cara.' Olivia rolled her eyes. 'It's a free drink. Consider it an apology. Drink it.'

'You do realise that if he sees me drinking it, he'll consider himself excused?' I shook my head. 'I won't allow that. I'd rather buy my own.' I stood up.

'He's going to speak to you, then. Is that what you want?'

'Who says I've got to reply? I might as well return the favour – "not interested".'

As I went to the bar, I glanced at Olivia over my shoulder. She was grinning at me, shaking her head.

I had nearly reached the counter when I felt Mr Arsehole's eyes on me. It demanded every ounce of my willpower not to meet them. To signal that I did not want to be approached, I arrived as far away from him as possible.

I flattened my hands on the dark surface of the counter, searching for a bartender, but both were busy serving other customers. Mr Arsehole continued to stare at me, and it made me feel uneasy. Hyperaware of myself, I put my elbows on the bartop, held my head between my hands, and studied the wall of myriad bottles straight ahead.

Suddenly his bare and muscular forearms entered my peripheral vision. Out of the corner of my eye, I saw them resting on the counter beside me. He had rolled up the sleeves of his white shirt, and the grey waistcoat that he wore on top clung to his robust anatomy, serving as an unfair reminder of his tantalising masculinity.

I recoiled a small step.

'Miss, I'm sorry about earlier. You're right, I was very rude.'

I refused to acknowledge him; I pretended not to have heard anything.

'If you'd give me a second' – he must have realised that I wasn't going to respond – 'I'd like to explain why.'

Just then, a bartender spared me from having to reply to the imbecile. Blond with green eyes, he looked quite Nordic. A warm grin decorated his mouth when our eyes locked.

'What can I get you, Miss?'

Judging by his strong accent, I thought he might be Swedish.

I smiled back. 'An espresso martini and a gin and tonic, please, thank you.'

Nodding, he extended to me the payment terminal he had just typed into. I was just about to grab it when Mr Arsehole beat me to it. Snatching it away from me, he inserted his own card.

'No!' I objected and stared at his large hands. Prominent veins branched across the back of them, and a few climbed a small distance along his fingers, although they stopped long before they reached his neatly trimmed nails. They were undeniably male hands, and they were a beautiful pair at that. The experienced look of them wasn't something

I would forget anytime soon. During a brief moment of weakness, I wondered what it would feel like to have them caress my naked skin.

His eyebrows arched at my harsh tone. Wearing a lopsided smile, he said, 'Now that I've got your attention—'

'You had my attention earlier, Oedipus, and you wasted it.' I snatched back the device.

'Oedipus?' he echoed with a titter of amazement. 'How astute.'

I rolled my eyes and was just about to withdraw his card when his loud sigh made me look at him.

'If you withdraw my card,' he said, 'dear Philip will have to restart the whole process. Do you really mean to make his job any more difficult than it needs to be? Just because you can't swallow your pride?'

I could hardly fathom the audacity of this man. I had never met someone quite so irritating in all my twenty-three years of life.

When I looked at the bartender, whose name I supposed was Philip, I saw a flash of humour cross his face.

'You should have a sign on the door that warns of arsehole clientele,' I told him.

He pressed his lips together and winked at me. Then, while looking at the pest beside me, he asked, 'What have you done, Will?'

William chuckled. 'Well, I acted like an arsehole, naturally.'

Philip frowned. 'That's unusual.'

'Yes, she caught me at a bad moment.'

'Then you ought to apologise to the lady.' He jerked his head in my direction.

'I'm trying, but she's not letting me.'

'Try harder.'

William faced me again. 'Andy, my mate, has got a girlfriend. Or . . . he used to. They split up just today, but I expect it's only temporary. So you've got the wrong end of the stick, love,' he said. 'I'm the nice guy. Now, unless you'd like to get in the middle of that, I reckon I did you a favour.'

I pursed my lips, despising the fact that I found his reason valid. Then again, it could be a lie. I didn't know the man. And if it was the truth, he could still have treated us more respectfully.

'Why should I trust what you're saying?' Scepticism coloured my tone.

William gestured to the payment terminal just as it started beeping. We had run out of time.

'Let's settle this first,' he said as Philip grabbed the device to start over. 'May I buy your drinks for you?'

His gaze was penetrative, and the sight made a lump gather in my throat. I hadn't noticed it before, but the man was rather intense. Everything about him was.

I swallowed, nodding.

'Thank you.' He gave me a look of wonder. Puzzled, I frowned back.

'So . . .' he said while tapping his card against the machine, paying contactless. I blinked. Why hadn't he done that in the first place? 'What's your name, then?'

'Oh, so you actually *are* interested,' I quipped as I watched Philip perform his magic. 'How funny. I haven't been bullied by a boy who fancies me since primary school.'

Stealing a glance at William, I saw his mouth bend into a grin. An incredulous laugh slipped out of it. In front of us, Philip pretended not to exist, although he failed at concealing his amusement. From his pursed lips, it was obvious that he was struggling not to laugh. Seeming to realise the same, he walked away to finish my drinks further away from us, probably to give us some privacy.

'Yes, well, I'm glad I could treat you to some nostalgia,' William said.

'More like trauma.'

Glancing over again, I noticed that William had turned slightly away from me to hide his reaction. From my limited view of his face, I saw that his grin persisted, but he was now biting on his lower lip while looking at the floor as though he could barely contain himself.

'Listen' – he turned to face me properly – 'if it's not obvious already, I seriously regret my behaviour. I hadn't thought you'd be so . . .' His eyes narrowed faintly. 'Intriguing.'

I snorted. Did he really consider *that* to be a legitimate excuse for his behaviour? What if I hadn't been intriguing? What then? Would he have considered his conduct justified?

He was obviously a conceited idiot. Why was I wasting even a breath on him?

Condescension was etched on my face when I finally turned toward him. Even though I was wearing heels, he towered over me. Since I felt small and vulnerable this close to him, I wondered how tall he actually was. Taking my own height into account, and adding it to the fact that I was wearing heels, I reckoned he was at least six-foot-four, maybe five. He was strong, too, which I could tell from the way his shirt and waistcoat strained against his broad upper body.

'Who would have guessed?' A wry smile flickered across my mouth. 'How to seduce an arsehole: accuse him of sleeping with his mother. Turned you on, did it? The idea of her?'

Frightened, I turned rigid when he suddenly leaned toward me. Hardly an inch separated our noses. He was so close that I could smell the alcohol on his breath as it fanned against my face. In my momentary fear, my eyes locked with his, and I was immediately hypnotised by their dominating gleam.

Perhaps this wasn't a man to be trifled with. He didn't come across as the sort of man who allowed others to walk over him. On the contrary, he looked to be in the habit of performing that deed himself; I felt walked over. To be honest, under the burning heat of his gaze, I felt vanquished.

'*You* did,' he said firmly.

2

THAT'S MORE LIKE IT

His bold reply took me aback. I hadn't anticipated that he would be so direct, but I couldn't deny that it was strangely refreshing. Suddenly I grew nervous. My heart started pounding.

'Well . . .' I drew in a deep breath, mustering courage. 'You got what you wanted – something original.'

His lips tucked into a smile. 'Without a doubt. Is your name as original as your personality, though?'

The astute method he employed as he made a third attempt to fish out my name impressed me. He was obviously a cunning man, so I reminded myself to practise caution. All the same, it amused me that he wasn't one to give up.

A vague smile nested on my mouth as I shook my head. 'I'm afraid I'll have to disappoint.'

'How so? It's not Electra, is it?'

I couldn't suppress the giggle that escaped my lips, because the reference was remarkably shrewd. Electra was, in some ways, Oedipus' female counterpart. William had clearly read his fair share of Greek tragedies, too.

Momentarily inspired by the current theme, I decided to lie. I wasn't naïve enough to trust him on a whim, so I didn't feel like giving him my real name. Besides, he hadn't proved himself remotely deserving.

'No, but you're not far from it, actually. It stems from Greek.'

'Really?' He looked intrigued.

'Yeah. Name's Cassandra, but everyone calls me Sandra.' I was incredibly amused at my own ingenuity. By choosing that name, I had sort of given him my real one. He only had to cut out the middle and he would end up with Cara, but I doubted he would ever realise that.

'Sandra,' he echoed with a nod. 'Well, I'm William, as you may have already gathered, but you can call me Will.'

'Or Oedipus. Tomato tomato.'

Amusement twinkled in his eyes. 'So you're a fan of Sophocles and Greek tragedies, then? Or are you merely a disciple of dear Mr Freud?'

His evident intellect irritated me somewhat because it led me to like him more than I wanted to. He was retaliating with precisely the same sense of humour and with force equal to my own. It wasn't often that I encountered people who could keep up with my sharp wit, but this man seemed to be up to the task. Despite his lack of affability, he clearly stored a quick and well-functioning brain behind that annoyingly handsome face.

I was still contemplating whether to reply when Philip interjected, 'Here you go, Miss,' and presented two lush cocktails. 'An espresso martini and a gin and tonic.'

'Thank you.' I was about to grab them when William beat me to it.

'I'll give you a hand,' he said as an explanation.

'I've got two already. Three aren't required, as you can see.'

He chuckled. 'You've got quite the witty mouth, haven't you?'

'Well, at least one of us has got some wit,' I said. 'Poor man can't even count right.'

William shook his head but persisted in carrying my drinks away. With a pout on my face, I trailed after him. How had it come to this? I hadn't meant to attract him earlier. Had I known my insult would prove so counterproductive, I'd have bitten my tongue.

'Andy,' he called and jerked his head in the direction of Olivia's lonely figure. Surprise flashed across Andrew's face. His brown eyes widened as he stood up from his seat.

When I fixed my gaze on Olivia, I found her smirking. The sight elicited a groan from my mouth. Unlike Andrew, she wasn't the least bit surprised, and I didn't appreciate it, because it spoke of her expectations of me.

'It's Olivia, right?' William asked when we reached her.

'Yes, but everyone calls me Livy.'

'Livy,' he echoed as he put my drinks on the table. 'Well, Livy, would you mind if Andy and I joined you?' he asked politely and stretched back up. His sudden gallantry made my eyebrows furrow. How was it possible to host both a gentleman and the Devil himself in the same vessel? Flummoxed, I watched him.

'Not at all,' Olivia said with a dazzling grin.

'I mind,' I declared.

William turned toward me with a sardonic smile. 'You don't get a say, I'm afraid.'

'Says who? You?' I snorted.

He faced Olivia while pointing his thumb at me. 'Is she always such a handful?'

Olivia studied me with clear humour in her eyes. 'Takes one to know one?' she said cheekily. As thanks for the support, I wanted to kiss her entire face like an excited dog.

William laughed. 'I suppose I deserved that.'

I rushed to grab the available seat beside Olivia on the small sofa so that I wouldn't be forced to sit next to William. After I had left my purse on the floor beside my feet, I leaned closer to her and whispered, 'I don't know what he wants, but my name's Sandra, okay? Short for Cassandra.'

Olivia pursed her lips. 'He wants you, but all right.'

I scoffed and continued in another whisper, 'Andy split from his girlfriend earlier today. Just thought you should know – unless William was only telling a lie.'

She nodded.

'Well, then, Sandra . . .' William fetched a chair over. 'Now that you're done whispering about me, why don't you tell me a bit about yourself?' Descending into the chair, he sat at a right angle from me. Intimidated, I recoiled toward Olivia.

That was what he was: intimidating, and immensely at that.

'I'd rather not.'

He chuckled. 'Are you students? You look a bit younger than the average woman here.' His eyes shifted between Olivia and me.

'We are,' Olivia said, and I was immediately alarmed.

Worried she would inadvertently expose my real identity, I hurried to say, 'Livy's studying law at UCL.'

William and Andrew gazed at one another.

'Are you?' Andrew asked her.

Catching on to my deceit, Olivia cast me a quick glance. Nevertheless, she proceeded with honesty. 'Yes. I'm in my third and final year now.'

'I see. And how do you like it?' Andrew asked as he brought a stool over to sit across from her.

'I love it, but it's very demanding.'

A chuckle escaped both men and, again, a message I couldn't quite decode passed between their eyes.

'What's funny?' I asked.

William directed his attention to me, and it looked like he was struggling to suppress a grin. 'Well, both Andy and I are lawyers, so it's just a bit charming to hear a student's perspective.'

Points for Jason. Lawyers did in fact frequent this place.

'Are you barristers?' I asked.

William shook his head and folded his hands together. 'Solicitors. Corporate kind.'

'I see. So you're colleagues, then?'

'Yeah.'

'And how's working with corporate law? Is it compelling?' I had a personal interest in whatever he had to say now. Like William, I aspired to be a solicitor rather than a barrister, regardless of whether the latter weighed heavier in matters of prestige.

William smiled, and I thought it was because I was finally expressing signs of interest.

'It is. Initially, I wanted to specialise in human rights, but my father swayed my mind. I'm glad he did.'

'Probably wise,' I said. 'You don't seem to excel at dealing with anything human.'

Andrew chortled, tossing his head back. 'The mouth on this one. She fires so many shots.'

William blew his cheeks out. 'I wonder if she'll ever run out of ammunition.'

I captured William's gaze, smiling crookedly. 'Keep acting like yourself and I doubt I will.'

'There she goes again.' Andrew guffawed. 'This is priceless.'

As I looked diagonally across the table, I caught Andrew's eye. Seeing an opportunity to taunt William, I deliberately gave him a seductive smile and asked with feigned interest, 'How about you, Andy? Have you always wanted to practise corporate law?'

His laughter quickly died at my behaviour, his gaze darting in William's direction. 'I was never really sure until I completed the LPC.'

'But I'd like to know more about you,' William said and leaned forward to demand my attention.

I frowned. 'You can't always get what you want.'

He peered at me, eyes narrowing faintly. 'Since you specified that Livy is a law student earlier, I think it's fair to assume you're studying something else. Otherwise, you'd be more likely to say, "*we're* studying law". And considering the nature of your insults earlier, I'm going to take a guess and say psychology.'

A giggle surged out of me. 'Well done, Sherlock.'

He didn't look convinced. 'No,' he murmured as he analysed my reaction. 'That was too easy – I was wrong. It's something else, isn't it?'

Olivia nudged my arm. When I looked over, I saw disapproval in her features. William had clearly managed to stir her sympathy to some extent, and now she was asking me to share her sentiment.

I sighed and returned my gaze to William's. 'I study medicine,' I lied. I knew enough about the coursework from Jason to be able to make it convincing.

William's eyebrows climbed up his forehead. 'Really? Here in London?'

'No, in Edinburgh. I'm only visiting Livy for the weekend.' Another lie.

William's eyebrows lowered again, a crease forming between them. 'Oh. Edinburgh.' He looked at the table, turning quiet.

Andrew gave him a look that I didn't understand, but it seemed to carry a hint of compassion. 'Well, medicine,' he said and focused on me, picking up where William had left off. 'That's impressive. Decided what to specialise in?'

I shook my head. 'Not yet.'

William leaned back and stared at me as if he were observing every corner of my soul. His gaze was remarkably piercing – penetrative, as if he could catch a glimpse of my core with a mere glance. It made me wonder if he had already discerned all my lies.

'Well,' William eventually said, 'the mother I love to sleep with is an oncologist.'

I blinked. 'Oh. Well, that explains everything. You've clearly got a type.'

He gave a mirthless chuckle. 'And you clearly embody all the characteristics of said type.'

'Just my luck.'

His eyes gleamed. 'Anyway, are you in your third year as well?'

I groaned. 'Is this an interview or something?'

He turned to Andrew with a grin. 'She's lovely, isn't she?'

Andrew smiled winsomely. 'She is.'

Taken aback, a blush emerged on my cheeks. Were they mocking me, or were they being sincere? Olivia sniggered beside me, clearly at my expense.

William faced me again. 'I'm worried I might have fucked up my chance completely,' he said, although he seemed to be speaking to Andrew still.

'You have,' I assured him.

'How do I change your mind?'

I scoffed. 'You're the lawyer. Shouldn't you know how to sway one's opinion?'

I heard a strange sound then, like a strangled laugh. I glanced sideways. Andrew was looking anywhere but at me, trying to fight back a massive grin.

'You're quite right,' William said, summoning my attention again. I fixed my gaze on him, and I could have sworn his eyes were aflame with something I had no experience dealing with.

'I'll start with this,' he said. 'We've definitely not met before. There's not a chance I wouldn't remember you, for several reasons.'

Sceptical, I raised a brow. 'Such as?'

'Aside from the obvious?'

'What's obvious?'

'Well, the obvious is that, physically speaking, you're absolutely stunning, but then that's rarely enough to capture my interest, much less my memory. You see, beauty isn't in short supply in this world. However, *your* beauty is in a league of its own. It's completely unforgettable.'

A wave of heat crashed over my face.

'What's not so obvious at first sight,' he went on, 'is your admirable integrity, alluring personality and keen intellect. Simply put, you're stunning in every way.' He shrugged. 'Ultimately, you're totally bewitching, and quite impossible to forget.'

My breath caught in my throat at his climactic declaration. I stared at him, trying to process what he had said, but my brain was malfunctioning.

Olivia quickly nudged my arm. Recovering my wits, I gave William a genuine smile. His earlier insult, where he had accused me of not being a memorable encounter, had angered me. It was the way he had phrased it, as if I were an escort offering my services. But his compliments assuaged my resentment somewhat.

'That's sweet of you to say,' I replied. 'But I meant what I said earlier –

you do look familiar. Livy thinks so as well.'

Frowning, he looked at Olivia. 'Do I?'

She nodded. 'No idea why, though. Have you been on telly?'

He chuckled. 'Not to my knowledge.'

'Newspapers?' I asked.

William cocked his head. 'Once or twice. Work-related, though.'

I narrowed my eyes. 'How old are you?'

He grinned. 'Now who wants to know?'

I rolled my eyes.

'Tell you what,' he said, 'for every question you ask, I get to ask one as well.'

'No deal.'

'Oh, come on. What have you got to lose?'

'My dignity.'

He burst out laughing. I wouldn't get an answer from him anytime soon.

'How old is he, Andy?' I asked. Hoping to resemble a puppy, I pouted at him, but his ensuing scoff proved my efforts ineffective.

'Sorry, love, you're on your own.'

I sighed. It was worth a shot.

Wearing a sly smile, William gave his friend a nod of gratitude and said, 'Looks like Livy's finished her drink.'

Grinning, Andrew stood up. 'I'd be delighted to buy you another,' he said to Olivia.

'I'll come with you.' She pushed herself out of the sofa.

My heart missed a beat. Was she blind to the fact that this was precisely what William had intended? Or did she mean to go along with it? Was she going to abandon me to the care of this dreadful man? This horribly intriguing person that I did not want to succumb to?

'Don't leave me,' I pleaded.

Visibly amused, she met my gaze. 'You're a grown woman, Sandra. You'll be all right. We've all seen that you can fend for yourself.'

From the faint pinkness in her cheeks, it was obvious that she wanted time alone with Andrew, but it would cost me severely. William had piqued my interest to the extent that I considered it morally wrong. He wasn't right in the head. He was rude, and he was bloody attractive.

Lethal combination.

As I continued to entreat her with my eyes, William said, 'Yes, I wonder what you're scared of.'

I looked at him. 'I'm not scared.'

'Then why are you objecting?'

'Because I don't want to be left alone with you,' I said as Olivia and Andrew went to the bar without further ado.

William's eyebrows furrowed. 'Am I that terrible?'

I pressed my lips together.

'I'd just like to get to know you better,' he said, shrugging. 'Isn't that what you wanted in the first place? I mean, you approached us first.'

'Specifically your friend,' I reminded him.

He tilted his head and, even though he concealed it well, I thought I recognised hurt somewhere deep within his eyes. I must have bruised his ego.

'Oh, so that's what this is?' he asked flatly. 'I'm not cutting it?'

Was that the impression he was getting? Since it was far from the truth, my conscience suffered. Averting my eyes, I grabbed my gin and tonic. As I raised it to my lips, I quickly said, 'No, that's not quite it.'

He leaned forward again to attract my gaze, and when he captured it, he scoured it thoroughly. Folding his hands between his thighs, he twiddled his thumbs.

'So . . . I do make the cut?' he asked then, ever slick.

I couldn't fight my smile. 'There is no "cut" to make, Will. I'm not here looking for anything if that's what you mean.'

'Then how come you approached us to begin with?'

My eyes darted in Olivia's direction, but since I didn't want to expose her, I quickly looked away again. Alas, William didn't fail to notice my wandering attention. As soon as he turned his head to observe Olivia and Andrew at the bar, he said, 'Right. I get it now. You were winging her.'

He looked at me for confirmation, but I merely stared back so as not to reveal anything. Suddenly a grin claimed his mouth. I frowned in puzzlement.

'It's been a long time since I've gone on the prowl,' he said, 'but if I'm not wrong, you approached him because she was initially interested in me.' He leaned back. 'What a textbook performance. Didn't work, though.'

I had to give it to him: the man was remarkably perceptive. His aptitude for reading social situations was outstanding. Even so, he still hadn't detected my lies, or at least it seemed that way.

I scoffed. 'Doesn't matter. As soon as you opened your dreadful mouth, her interest shifted onto your friend instead.'

William laughed wholeheartedly. 'I'm not even slightly upset. She's not my type.'

'You mean she doesn't remind you of your mother?'

He rolled his eyes. 'Either way, she's clearly not interested anymore, so there's nothing holding you back. You've got a green light to get to know me.'

'I'm sorry, didn't you hear what I just said? I'm not interested in anything other than helping Livy out.'

He surprised me when he suddenly stood up. 'Right, well, if that's the case, I'll just head over to them if you don't mind. Shame if that sabotages Olivia's chances.'

'Wait, wait – fine!' I raised my hand to halt him. 'I'll entertain you.'

Releasing a satisfied sigh, he sank back down and folded his hands above his crotch. 'That's more like it.'

I desperately wanted to tear the smug smirk off his face. 'You're insufferable,' I grumbled.

'You're only upset because I've outwitted you.'

'Why are you so determined to get to know me?'

'Because you've seriously piqued my interest.'

Again, his directness took me aback, and just like earlier, my heart began to pound. Each thump pressed against my ribcage to the extent that a keen eye could probably see it.

I was starting to realise that my body wanted something quite different from my mind.

'I commend your grit, at least,' I muttered and put my drink back on the table. Folding my arms, I hoped to hide my vigorous heartbeat.

Another smirk climbed to his annoyingly kissable mouth. 'Thanks. I'm quite pleased with that attribute myself.'

He moved off his chair and grabbed the vacant spot beside me on the sofa. I stiffened when he draped his arm over the back of it, behind my shoulders. It wasn't that I minded the intimacy. On the contrary, I seemed to enjoy it more than I was willing to admit.

'Listen, let's start over, yeah?' he said. 'I realise it's a poor excuse, but I've had a rough day at work and, to make it worse, Andy and Chloe have been together for an entire decade. She's practically my sister, so when I heard the news – two minutes before you arrived – I was very upset. I just wasn't in the right frame of mind to handle you well. I'm very sorry. I truly am.'

'I still think you were unnecessarily rude.'

He wrinkled his nose. 'Well, I tried to just be direct at first, but then you persisted and I got impatient, so I thought being rude was the best way to make you go away as quickly as possible. We were seriously in the middle of an argument.'

'Were you able to sort things out at least?'

He shook his head. 'We agreed to talk about it later.'

I nodded, wondering what the issue was. I refrained from digging further, though, because it was none of my business.

He brought me closer then. As I softened against his warm body, the scent of him struck me hard. He smelled intoxicating. Drugged, I inhaled the fragrance deep into my lungs. I picked up testosterone, something dark, something sweet, and plenty of challenge.

My Achilles' heel.

'You smell amazing,' I blurted out without thinking. 'What fragrance is that?' Indeed, he smelled remarkable – even better than Jason did.

He shook against me, laughing, and leaned forward to grab one of my drinks.

'Stick around, and perhaps I'll tell you. And you smell amazing yourself.' He leaned back again. 'On another note, you've got three of these to finish.'

He raised my espresso martini toward my mouth, and he did not stop until he had placed the glass to my waiting lips. Consequently, my lips parted not because of the cold and solid material against my skin, but rather because of his surprising gesture. Wearing a smug smile, he tilted the glass and carefully poured a portion of the cocktail into my mouth.

I watched him the whole time, overwhelmed by his sensuality. I had never met a man quite so slickly domineering before. I had an inkling he was in the habit of getting his way.

He lowered the glass to allow my swallow, and he watched me intensely as I did. The expression on his face was strangely erotic. Was he imagining me swallowing something else?

'I guarantee you, Sandra, that had we slept together, I would not have forgotten. So, where you might have seen me before, I don't know – but I wish it were in bed.'

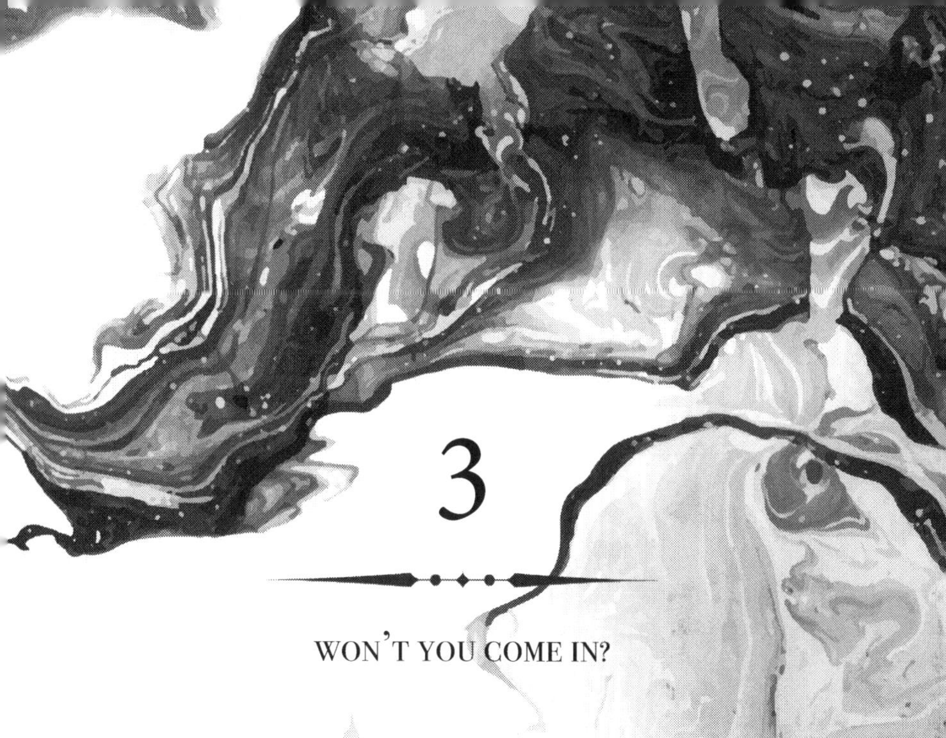

3

WON'T YOU COME IN?

His statement expelled the air from my lungs, but I couldn't take my eyes off him. He had me trapped in his gaze.

Astonished, I asked, 'Are you always this crude?'

'Sorry,' he apologised insincerely and put my cocktail back on the table. 'I can't seem to think straight in your presence. My tongue travels before my mind.'

The edge of his mouth tucked up to form a crooked smile, and I recognised it as the one he had already presented several times. It was unique to him, and a testament to his cunning and calculating persona. The shape of it whispered tales of his intellectual conquests, of how sublimely he outwitted any opponent. Anyone could have been fooled by the invincibility it exuded, and yet, despite this, I thought I detected a hint of veiled vulnerability, and it intrigued me.

'Anyway,' he interrupted my analysis, 'though I haven't been acting my age, I'm twenty-eight. How old are you?'

Since I saw no harm in sharing this detail about myself, I said, 'Twenty-three.'

'So you're in your—'

'Ah-ah,' I interrupted. 'My turn.' I pointed at my chest and his eyes followed. It occurred to me then that I had directed his gaze straight to my shy amount of cleavage. Immediately, heat flooded my face, causing a crimson blush to penetrate my faint layer of make-up. I hurried to lower my hands to my lap. William seemed equally bothered, his gaze veering to Olivia and Andrew.

Was it possible that he harboured at least a modicum of respect for me? I had just provided him with a golden opportunity to ogle my breasts, but instead, he had hastily looked elsewhere. It increased my faith in him. Perhaps he wasn't so terrible after all.

'First impressions,' he muttered. 'They can be surprisingly difficult to disprove.'

I chuckled. 'Spoken like a true solicitor.'

He gave me a vague smile. 'Your turn, you said. What would you like to know?'

Where to begin? Glancing at Olivia and Andrew, I was reminded of his companion. They seemed like good friends, and that made me curious. 'How long have you known Andy?'

'My whole life. My turn.' He grinned. 'What are your interests, aside from medicine?'

That was a substantial question. 'Er, I have eclectic tastes, so I find that question too vast to answer. You'll have to filter it down.'

'What do you spend your spare time doing?'

I scoffed. 'Spare time? What spare time?'

'Have you got a boyfriend?' he suddenly tossed at me.

I stiffened. 'That's none of your business.'

A lascivious gleam entered his arresting eyes, and it captured me wholly. All I wanted was to explore the dancing blue depths. In so many ways, he seemed like a promise of pleasure. Given his level of self-assurance, I couldn't imagine that he would disappoint between the sheets, so why did I deny myself the chance to explore his potential?

His smile turned crooked again. 'I assure you, darling, it is.'

Unsure of what he meant, I looked briefly away. I had a vague idea, but I wanted to be certain. Frankly, I wanted to hear him confess it.

'And how is that?'

'Because I'd like to see you again.' His smile faded. 'So, if you've got a boyfriend, I'd prefer to know. I'll have to reconsider my tactics, then.'

I gaped. 'Reconsider your tactics?' I echoed disbelievingly. 'Are you trying to say that if I do have a boyfriend, you won't respect it?'

'No, I'll respect it – physically.' Glancing away, he murmured, 'But I'll try and tempt you to leave him.'

'You're ruthless,' I said. Was he drunk?

'Which you need,' he claimed with a smirk.

I frowned. 'You don't even know me.'

'No, I don't, but I've got a vague idea of what I'm dealing with.' He shrugged. 'My intuition tends to serve me well.'

I blinked at his cockiness. 'Are you drunk, Will?'

His brows furrowed. 'What makes you think that? No. I've had two cocktails.'

'Because your head is messed up.'

'You've messed it up.'

I snorted. 'That's ridiculous. What a cheesy line.'

'Better than "have we met?", though.'

I glared at him, and he glared straight back. Eventually, he tilted his head and watched me as though he were trying to solve an enigma.

'If you'd actually had a boyfriend,' he said with narrowed eyes, 'I doubt you'd allow me to keep my arm round you like this, much less let me pour your drink into your mouth. Then again, you could just be a partner prone to cheating, but I seriously doubt you're the type. You seem too righteous.'

I leaned forward and grabbed my espresso martini. 'I don't see why we're even entertaining this question. You said you'd prefer to know because you'd like to see me again, but in case you've already forgotten, I live in Edinburgh.'

'Sure, but for now you're still in London. How long are you staying?'

'Will,' I shook my head, 'I'm not going to set aside time to see you. I'm here to spend time with Livy.'

'Who is obviously interested in getting laid.' He jerked his head in Olivia's direction. Looking over, I saw her laughing at something Andrew must have said. 'I'm sure she'd appreciate it if I took you off her hands, at least for tonight.'

Though it had been on the cards, his proposal still took me by surprise. I faced him, and his eyes were ablaze – two blue flames, wild in their craving for me.

Under the dim orange light, he resembled something of the divine. A Greek god, perhaps, and I was only a mere mortal. How was I supposed to resist such celestial temptation? I was submitting to his power more by the second.

I struggled to fathom the reality that I had only met this man mere moments ago. Our chemistry was clearly off the charts.

When I had spent too long contemplating his offer, his impatience got the better of him. 'Listen, we can either spend all night bickering, or we can spend this ridiculous energy in my bed. It's up to you.' His tone was clipped while his gaze burrowed into mine. 'Either way, you would be doing both yourself and your friend a favour by joining me back at mine.'

Pink and breathless, I looked away from him. This man surely didn't beat around the bush. He hadn't even kissed me yet, and now he was suggesting sex? What sort of a scene was he into? No-strings-attached, I reckoned. That notion filled me with relief, because I didn't have the capacity for romance at this point in my life.

To buy more time, I raised my drink. 'I'm not nearly drunk enough for this,' I said and filled my mouth with the liquid courage. Amused, William watched me drain the remaining contents.

'I fancy my women responsive, Sandra, so please keep the intake to a minimum.'

'You're speaking as if I've agreed,' I said and put my empty glass on the table.

Just as I was about to grab my next drink, a large and unfamiliar hand clasped my jaw. Turning my face toward him, William leaned in until our noses touched. Only then did he pause his advances.

My breath abandoned me, my heart throbbing with bittersweet delight. It was begging me to give in, to allow myself a night I would never forget. Besides, it wasn't like I hadn't had a one-night stand before. Hell, I often preferred them. The less they knew, the better.

I wasn't at a point in my life where romantic companionship was even remotely appealing. It was far too time-consuming a venture. I had my studies to mind, my ambitions to realise. I was a millennial woman, and fiercely independent at that. Intellectual pursuits were my main priority.

However, I was still a sexual creature. I had needs. While I had a friend – Aaron – to fulfil them, my casual arrangement with him allowed me to have one-night stands, which I occasionally indulged in. Tonight, William wanted me to treat myself to another one. So why was I being so difficult? Because he had been an arsehole at first? What did that matter if I wasn't going to see him again? Plus, he had apologised, and now he wanted to make amends – properly.

The light-blue colour of William's eyes struck through my defences as he gently released my jaw. Trailing his thumb across my cheek, he buried his hand in my long, wavy brown hair.

His voice was as mollifying as a lullaby when he said, 'I want you to know that if you decide to join me, I'll have no expectations. I'd be happy just to talk all night.'

My heart throbbed again. Seduced by the sensual promise that basked in his eyes, I gave him a faint nod.

'I'm going to kiss you,' he warned.

Utterly at his mercy, I swallowed. I couldn't move another muscle. He had me completely spellbound.

'Okay.' It was barely a whisper that escaped my mouth.

A lopsided smile claimed his lips, and then he pressed his soft mouth to mine. I marvelled at the taste of him. Only seconds into it, I knew he was the best kisser I had ever encountered. His lips moved tenderly across my own – gently at first, until his lust overruled his resistance. With his hand in my hair, he brought me closer, his other arm coming around me.

He pressed me tightly against him, kissing me like I'd never been kissed. It set my heart on fire. No words could ever match the immense feeling. Kissing someone had never felt so right. The mere motion of his lips overwhelmed me. He made me feel like the most precious thing alive, as if he couldn't bring himself to stop until he had devoured all of me. Craving more, he pushed his tongue into my mouth to explore the rest of me, and I welcomed him with eagerness.

The space between my thighs tingled, and I realised why this particular kiss affected me so. For the first time in my life, kissing someone didn't feel like a mandatory part of seduction. I actually wanted this – I wanted to kiss him. I was desperate to.

But he pulled away far too soon. Breathless, he looked at my drinks on the table and said, 'We're leaving. Non-negotiable. I'm not wasting another second.' He clasped my hand and stood up, dragging me up with him.

'I – okay.' I searched for his eyes. Something was off about him. His gaze was fleeting, and he looked a bit lost, even dazed.

It surprised me. He didn't come across as the kind of man who would react so profoundly to a mere kiss. Taking his expertise of the art into account, I was confident he had kissed his fair share of women.

Was it possible that the same flame that had spread through my system like wildfire had also ignited in him?

He started toward the exit, meaning we would have to pass the bar where Olivia and Andrew sat chatting. Olivia studied us, seemingly confused. Was it the look on my face? It had to be.

'We'll be off,' William announced and released my hand to wrap his arm around my waist.

Olivia laughed. 'Sandra, you devil. I knew it.'

'Devil indeed.' William shot me a look that I didn't understand.

Concerned, I asked Olivia, 'Will you be all right by yourself?'

There wasn't a chance I would leave her behind if she didn't approve. If that meant losing my one shot at a sensational night, then so be it. My duty as her best friend would always come first.

She eyed me knowingly. 'Yes. You, on the other hand, I'm not so sure about.'

'I'll take good care of her, Livy. You have my word,' William said, suddenly the gallant man again, rather than the greedy, libidinous and domineering man I had just been kissing. I quite fancied them both.

'You'd better. I know who you are, should she happen to disappear by the morning,' Olivia threatened.

'She might be sleeping until dusk, seeing as she won't be getting much rest tonight, so don't be concerned if she doesn't answer her phone first thing in the morning,' William replied.

Andrew chuckled beside my gaping blonde friend. 'He's a bit of a character, but you get used to him. Tad blunt is all.'

'Just a tad,' I said under my breath.

'Get your minds out of the gutter,' William said, looking between them. 'I didn't specify *why* she won't be getting much rest. For all you know, we'll be talking all night.'

Olivia raised a brow. 'Sure. *Talking*. With your bodies.'

'That's generally what people use when they talk, yes.' William grinned.

Olivia rolled her eyes. 'You're definitely a lawyer.'

William chuckled. 'Anyway, it was lovely to make your acquaintance, Livy. I hope we'll meet again.' He leaned in and pecked her cheek. 'You're a sweet girl. Again, I'm sorry about earlier.'

'Y-yeah. Me too.' She met my eyes with evident concern, and I knew why. 'I hope we'll meet again,' he had said. I hoped it was only his courteous side speaking, because as far as I was aware, this was a one-time thing. Had I jumped the gun by assuming that no-strings-attached was mutually understood?

'I'll see you later, Andy,' William continued to his friend, who responded with a perceptive smirk.

'Yeah. Have fun.'

Without replying, William dragged me toward the cloakroom, and his impatience was clear from his strides.

'Do you live nearby?' I asked.

'Yes,' he said. Then I heard him murmur, 'And thank fuck for that.'

§ § §

'Have you got the time?' I asked when we had walked along the streets of Soho for a few minutes. Raising the hand that was holding mine, William eyed his watch. I swallowed as I recognised the brand – a Rolex.

Glancing at his profile, I realised that he oozed upper-class wealth, and I wasn't enchanted by it. Rich people could sometimes be dreadfully arrogant with their aristocratic tendencies. But, since I wasn't one for prejudice, I wouldn't let his probable fortune define my impression of him. Besides, Jason came from a wealthy background as well, and he was as close to an ideal human being as could be.

'Ten to ten,' William said and tugged me closer.

'Ten to ten? I was only there for about an hour?' I was astounded. Had he managed to seduce me that fast? How licentious of me – and I wasn't even tipsy!

Seemingly amused, he looked at me from the corner of his eye. 'If it's any consolation, I didn't leave you much choice.' He rounded a corner to enter Wardour Street.

I frowned at myself. Was I really so desperate for him that I couldn't last much longer than an hour? Poor Olivia. I hoped I hadn't ruined her evening.

'Do you think Andy will take good care of her?' I asked, worrying. 'I feel like I'm being a bad friend.'

'Again, I didn't leave you much choice.'

I halted promptly. 'We ought to head back.'

William chuckled. 'I disagree. You're honestly doing her a favour.'

'But what if I'm not? What if Andy rejects her and she ends up alone tonight?'

From the wrinkles that formed across his nose, I got the impression he could understand where I was coming from but, for selfish reasons, felt disinclined to oblige.

When he didn't reply, I withdrew my hand from his grasp. 'You said yourself that you expect Andy will get back with his girlfriend. Don't you think he'll reject Livy because of that? He's probably not ready to sleep with anybody else, especially so soon after spending an entire decade with his ex.'

A sigh poured from William's mouth and his shoulders sank. He studied me for a while.

‘I’m tempted to lie because I’d like to be alone with you,’ he confessed. ‘But, at the same time, I wouldn’t want it to bite me in the arse later on, so I’ll be honest. Andy’s unlikely to sleep with your friend. He’s still in shambles over Chloe.’

I huffed. ‘Right. Well, then . . .’ I dropped my gaze to my feet. Had we really met our end already? It seemed so abrupt. ‘It’s just, I’d like to be alone with you too, but I don’t think it’s right to—’

‘I get it,’ he said. ‘You’re a good friend. I’d have done the same.’

I looked at him, my lips protruding. Since I was unsure about how to proceed, I resorted to admiring how beautiful he was. I could hardly believe I was about to turn him down. Then again, for the sake of friendship, there were few sacrifices I was unwilling to make.

‘I’ll walk you back,’ he said after a short silence.

‘That’s not necessary.’

‘I insist. London’s not safe at night, especially for women like yourself.’

An idea occurred to me then. ‘You know what?’ Reaching into my purse, I fished for my phone. ‘I could always just call her.’

‘A perk of the twenty-first century,’ William joked and earned himself a smile.

I hurried to locate Olivia’s number. While she was slow to pick up, at least she did.

‘Hello? Is everything all right?’ she asked.

‘Hi, yes. Don’t worry. Quick question, though.’

‘Yes? Did you forget to bring condoms?’

‘What? No.’ I frowned. ‘Listen, are you absolutely sure you won’t mind if I—’

‘Oh, for heaven’s sake. We’ve already been over this.’ I could hear her eyes roll.

‘It’s just that—’

‘Are you still with him?’

‘Yes.’

‘Then don’t keep the poor man waiting!’

‘But Livy, there’s something you ought to know first.’

‘What?’

‘I don’t think Andy’s interested in the same as you.’

She was quiet for a beat. Then I heard her murmur to somebody, ‘I’m so sorry. Please excuse me for a minute.’

A few seconds of silence elapsed before her voice returned.

'Hello, Cara?'

'Yes, I'm still here. Did you hear what I said?'

'Yes, but so what?'

'What do you mean "so what"?'

'Why should that matter?'

'Well, wasn't your aim tonight to . . .' I paused and stole a glance at William. Lowering my voice, I continued, 'Find a man?'

'Oh my God. Cara, I'll have plenty of opportunities to find a rebound in the future. I love you for caring so much, but I wouldn't dream of getting in your way. Besides, I'm genuinely enjoying myself. Andy's a really sweet guy, and he's actually hilarious. To be perfectly honest, I started friend-zoning him even before you called to warn me.'

Unsure of her sincerity, I asked, 'Really?'

'Really. In fact, it dawned on me while we've been chatting that I don't need to sleep with a stranger to reinstate my status as a single woman. What I need is an actual connection with someone. A one-night stand isn't going to provide that, and it isn't going to help me get over Colin, either. Frankly, I think sleeping with Andy would've made me feel like shit. I'd feel used again, which is the last thing I need right now. Only a new, genuine connection is going to help me get over Colin.'

Impressed with her rationale, my eyebrows arched. 'Points for introspection, Livy. I'm glad you've got such a healthy mind.'

'Are you being sarcastic?'

I tittered. While I had a habit of being sarcastic, I wasn't now. 'No. I'm being sincere. I'm impressed.'

'Thank you! Honestly, I'm a bit impressed myself if I can say that.'

'You can.' I chuckled.

'Well, then. With that out of the way, you can stop worrying about me. I'll be fine. Get back to your man. I'll want to hear every single detail in the morning.'

'Okay. Speak soon, then.'

'Yes. Love you.'

'Love you too.'

As soon as I rang off, I gave William a grin and stuffed my phone back into my purse. 'She doesn't want him that way either, apparently.'

His responding grin far outmatched mine. 'Problem's solved, then, I take it?'

'Seems that way.'

'Brilliant. She say why?'

'Well, like Andy, she's recently split from her partner as well.'

'I see.'

'Now, then. Where to?'

'Right this way.' He reached for my hand again. As soon as our skin made contact, my heart contracted in the most peculiar way. I couldn't remember having experienced a similar sensation in all my life. It was almost painful in its intensity.

'Besides,' I said once we started walking, 'I've no idea what it's like to endure a break-up, so I'm sure Livy appreciates speaking with somebody who understands, even if they don't go into it.'

'You've never had a boyfriend?' William asked, sounding shocked.

I shook my head. 'Nor am I looking for one.'

'Why not?' His tone was slightly odd, as if he was feigning nonchalance.

'Because I don't have the time that's required for a happy one.'

'Please elaborate.'

I grimaced. 'I'm very dedicated to my studies,' I said. 'So, firstly, I can't afford to be preoccupied with a man, as I'm sure it would divide my attention. Secondly, he wouldn't deserve to get only leftover scraps of my time, which is what would happen.'

Glancing up, I thought William looked quite impressed with my reasoning.

'Is that the real reason you're reluctant to see me again?'

Once more, his directness caught me off guard.

'You're very forward,' I said.

'Don't digress.'

My heart slowed as I gazed blankly ahead. He was putting me on the spot, and it wasn't comfortable. I worried my honesty would change his mind, but I decided to share it anyway.

'Yes.'

I could, of course, have resorted to a lie, but I wasn't in the habit of mistreating people. If his feelings were under threat of being toyed with, he deserved to know. I would have wanted as much for myself.

'I see.' William nodded. 'And it's never occurred to you to let your suitors be the judge of that?'

'Of what?'

'Of whether they'd be content with only "leftover scraps" of your time.'

Facing him, I stopped walking for a split second. 'I – no. Why should I? Wouldn't that involve inviting the risk in the first place?'

He shrugged. 'I suppose. Then again, the reward you'd reap would be invaluable.'

'But the odds of achieving that are astronomical.' I shook my head. 'I really don't think it's the best tactic.'

'And there's no way I can convince you otherwise?'

I noticed that he was consciously keeping his gaze from meeting mine.

I sighed. He might be the most alluring man I had ever met, but I was a rational woman; I knew meeting him again would be sealing my doom. He was a little *too* alluring.

I could manage one night without getting attached to him, but another was a different story entirely. My attraction to him was too immense to ignore. I had never been so captivated by another individual before, and surely not so fast. It made me fear his power over me. If we met again, I didn't trust that I would be able to resist growing fond of him; I didn't trust myself not to give in to temptation. I would want to explore more of him – every alley of his enigmatic mind, and every fibre of his mouth-watering anatomy.

I couldn't have that. Not now. I didn't have the capacity for it. I was a top student. Becoming infatuated could ruin that, and I wasn't about to take the risk. Moreover, I wasn't interested in making a commitment to someone when I knew I would fall short of their expectations. And, even in the event that I didn't, my reverence for them would tell me that they deserved better than what I could offer.

'I'm afraid not.'

William chuckled, but it was a mirthless sound. He stopped walking and faced me. 'Well, I'll try either way. For starters, I both admire and respect your dedication to your studies. If you agree to meet me again, you'll find that out for yourself. I wouldn't dream of getting in the way of your education.'

Somewhat surprised, I stared up at him. 'I appreciate that, but I'm afraid it's out of your hands. You can't decide how I respond to something – you could get in the way even without meaning to, because I'd simply care about you too much.' I shrugged. 'I'm sorry, but this is how I've handled it my whole life, and I'm not inclined to change my ways for you.'

His jaw flexed as vague irritation swelled in his features. Letting go of my hand, he glared away.

'I must admit, I'm a bit shocked your sole intention tonight is to use me for your own sexual benefit. What the hell is that all about?'

Guilt flooded my body. Unsure of what to say, I fell silent.

'Please don't tell me it's due to some discreditable idea of feminism, because that's nothing short of toxic feminism, and you're doing every feminist – myself included – a great dishonour and disservice by acting like it's not.'

'What do you mean by that?'

He looked at me. 'I'm asking you if you feel justified in objectifying men because some of us treat women that way.'

I inhaled sharply. He couldn't have been more wrong. With eyes that sought acquittal, I replied vehemently, 'No, of course not. It's got nothing to do with that – I don't mean to objectify you. I just assumed that sex with no strings attached was mutually understood and agreed upon.'

'Well, you assumed wrong,' he retorted. 'I mean, for fuck's sake. I thought I made myself clear when I said I'd like to see you again.'

My lips quivered. I could scarcely believe I was having such a candid argument with a stranger.

'Well, I'm sorry. I do' – I paused and gestured to him – 'fancy you. I'm just not interested in anything more than one night.'

He was silent for a beat, contemplating. This was it, I realised.

'I suppose I'll just have to fuck you so well that you'll change your mind,' he finally asserted.

Air stormed out of my lungs like somebody had just punched me in the gut. I doubted I would ever get used to the shocking, yet somehow arousing, effect of his vulgar tongue. Frankly, I wondered at that moment just what else his tongue was capable of.

'But if you don't mind my saying,' he continued before I could catch my breath, 'I think you're being ridiculous. Law isn't an easy path of education either, and I completed my degree at Cambridge. Even so, I still found time for romantic endeavours. That should speak volumes.'

I gaped. He had studied at Cambridge? No wonder his intellect had impressed me earlier.

Smirking, he put his forefinger below my chin and closed my mouth.

'Something to consider,' he said. 'You can gape later, when we're naked in my flat.'

The mouth of this man rendered me speechless. It must have earned him a slap or two.

He didn't bother waiting for my response. He started toward the entrance of an elegant white building with warehouse-style windows. A Starbucks dwelled on the ground floor. Was he a regular there?

I looked down the busy street, seeing herds of people outside a great number of pubs. It must get noisy here during the weekends, I thought.

He entered a code on a keypad to unlock the front door and stepped aside to let me enter. As if I had walked into a past era, I gazed around the splendid reception area, where marble made up the floor and walls.

'Nice building.'

He didn't reply. His hand on my back, he ushered me to the lift and pushed the button. The doors opened immediately. On a keypad inside, he pressed the digits of a code again. As we watched the doors slide shut, I mentally thanked myself for having shaved earlier that day.

Gravity tugged at my gut as we rode up, but it was nothing compared to the magnetism the man beside me exuded. He seemed electric, and it was making me increasingly nervous. Looking over, I saw that he was completely composed. Was I the only one struggling to resist sexual urges? It seemed that way, and it bruised my ego so much that a pout dominated my face.

'I hope you're not a Patrick Bateman,' I said, hoping to lighten the atmosphere. Out of the corner of my eye, I saw his lips twitch.

'An American psycho? How could I be? I'm not a Yank.'

'Ha-ha.'

He grinned. 'I'm afraid the only thing I've in common with Mr Bateman is a taste for the finer things in life.' To indicate what he meant, he lowered his hand from my back and gently patted my bum.

A second later, we arrived at our destination – the top floor. The doors parted and revealed a vestibule, where a dark brown entrance door interrupted the wall straight ahead. With a gentle shove, William encouraged me to approach it.

Here as well, a code was required to unlock the door. He entered it quickly. Turning the handle, he revealed a marvellous and spacious flat. Complementing the front door, the floor was made of dark brown wood. Surrounding it were cream-coloured walls decorated with a fair number of contemporary paintings. The interior was undeniably modern with a touch of old-fashioned moments.

He stepped in first to hold the door for me, and when his eyes met mine again, they were lit with desire alone.

'Please, Sandra, won't you come in?' he asked, and his voice was an invitation in and of itself.

4

SATISFIED?

I walked in with my breath stuck in my throat and was just about to remove my heels when William clasped my wrist and tugged me harshly toward him. As I slammed into his strong body, the little air I had left was knocked out.

'I'd rather you kept those on,' he purred and dipped down to engulf my mouth. Wide-eyed, I mellowed against him, utterly at his mercy. The effect this man had on me was beyond my comprehension. I felt like a snake hypnotised by its master's flute.

He shut the door while his mouth demanded possession of mine. My heart missed a beat at the sound of it being locked. I was both literally and figuratively trapped, yet I harboured no desire to escape. Then, was I truly trapped? Perhaps I was suffering a mild case of Stockholm syndrome, because I was surely in favour of my captor. The taste and scent of him was intoxicating. How had it come to this? I definitely hadn't been expecting his attention earlier tonight, and yet here I was, about to explore every bit of his tantalising body.

He didn't waste a second. Impatiently, he plunged his tongue into my mouth and reached for the sash of my coat, unravelling the knot. He spread it apart, arms circling my waist as he pressed me against him.

Without breaking from his mouth, I shrugged out of my coat and let it fall to the floor. The instant it landed, he pinned me forcefully against the wall. I groaned into his mouth, and he smiled at the sound. The anticipation was thick and dense in the air between us, and it revealed itself in how increasingly erratic our breathing became.

'You know . . .' he said as he moved to leave soft kisses on the slope of my neck. 'Despite the sorry excuse for a man that I am, you seem to find yourself so lost and desperate that you've wound up in my bed after all.' He raised his head, smiling conceitedly as he stared into my eyes.

My eyebrows furrowed with slight irritation. 'Is that supposed to arouse me?'

'No.' He chuckled. 'But it certainly aroused *me*.'

A small smile curved my mouth. 'So degradation is your kink?'

His eyes gleamed. 'Women who are challenging is my kink.' He seized my jaw, holding it firmly, and ran his thumb across my lower lip. '*You're* my kink.'

Suddenly he thrust his crotch against me, making me gasp. His erection strained against the lower part of my abdomen while his big hands trailed down my waistline and gripped my hips.

'The shape of you should be illegal,' he said admiringly and leaned slightly away to get a better look. A heartbeat later, his gaze struck mine like a bullet.

Caught by his allure, a groan leaped over my tongue. I flung my arms around his neck and brought his tempting lips back to mine. As the delectable flavour of him exploded in my mouth, I closed my eyes to savour it. Like an addict, I craved more of the drug-like sensations he evoked. Under his influence, I felt ecstatic.

Expertly, his tongue teased mine with gentle flicks. I had already noted his remarkable way of kissing, but that didn't prevent it from mystifying me. How was it possible to be so tender, and yet simultaneously so forceful? He wasn't eating my mouth, yet I had never felt so devoured. His lips moved according to the bliss-point, the brink between too much and too little.

Needing air, I pulled away. 'Where did you learn to kiss like that?'

He smirked. 'Unfortunately for me, you weren't there.'

Heat streamed into my cheeks, turning them pink. Just when I was about to reply, he distracted me by dropping to his knees.

Puzzled, I looked down. 'What are you doing?'

He put his hands over the pale skin of my bare knees and brought them over his shoulders. I almost let out a squeal, thinking I was about to fall backward, but, thankfully, the wall behind me served as support.

Inwardly, I commended his original move. It made me even more curious to know what scenes he could orchestrate. So far, he hadn't proved particularly conventional.

At the sound of my muffled squeal, he grinned up at me, and the look in his eyes completely paralysed me. Through long dark lashes, he watched me intensely. Held by his wilful gaze, I didn't object to his next advances. Slowly but confidently, his hands smoothed up my naked thighs, warm and soft. Then they moved inward. His touch left tingling sensations in its wake, making me pant loudly. Raw arousal flooded my veins the closer he drew to my nether lips, my heart thundering in my chest.

Only then did I realise the state of my black lace thong. Blushing scarlet, I stared bashfully at William as he drew closer to it. Not once did he break eye contact.

When his slow fingers reached the fabric of my wet underwear, he placed the pad of his thumb precisely against my pulsating clit. Acute and sharp, the sensation shot up my spine and all the way to my nose. My back arched away from the wall, my hands gathering in his dark brown hair.

My eyes shut.

Holy shit.

'Ah,' I groaned as he rubbed it gently.

'Sandra . . . You're drenched,' he said smugly.

Opening my eyes, I was caught once more by his smouldering stare. He had beautiful eyes. They resembled a serene ocean surrounding a warm paradise. How ironic. He was anything but that.

'Please. Take me already,' I pleaded breathlessly and dragged my hands through his hair. It was soft and thick between my fingers.

'Oh, I'll take all of you, darling. *Hard*.'

I tensed up, my vagina throbbing furiously.

Keenly attuned to any response, he observed me intently and pushed my dress upward, revealing my bum. He smoothed his hands across the firm curve of it and, carnal in his methods, squeezed my cheeks before he gave my right side a quick, harsh spank. I hissed, the sting of his palm burning a mark on my skin. I nearly flinched away from him, but his hold on my hip prevented me.

'That's for being a bloody pain in the arse earlier,' he said roughly and gripped my underwear. 'Now, how much do you care for these?'

Confused by his question, I looked down. It was difficult to keep up with him. I was much too aroused to stay focused on anything but his hands on me.

'I'll just have to find out, then,' he murmured.

Shocking me, he ripped my lace thong to shreds between his strong fingers. I gawked at him, overwhelmed by his arousing action.

He discarded my split underwear by the front door and leaned in, ever so slowly, to trace the inner side of my thigh with soft kisses.

'Do we need protection?' he asked as he trailed the tip of his nose across my skin.

'I'm clean,' I assured him breathily. 'Are you?'

'I am.'

I swallowed, wondering whether to trust him. 'Good. But I'd prefer if we used a condom either way.'

I tensed as his lips grazed closer and closer to my bundle of nerves. Just before he reached it, my hand formed a fist in his hair to halt his advances.

Seeming to notice my reluctance, he said, 'I'll respect that, but the scent of you is driving me mad, so I'm willing to risk it. May I?'

I blushed at his vulgar statement. I wasn't used to verbal lovers, but William appeared to be one. Though, surprisingly, it only made him more alluring.

If I went along with this, I would finally discover just what else his tongue was capable of, and that idea was slowly but surely seducing me.

'If you give me anything, I'll have your balls on a platter,' I said.

The cool breath of his chuckle spread across my wet lips. I clenched my teeth, struggling to hold on to my self-control.

'I've no doubt you will, but I won't give you anything other than bliss.'

I looked at the ceiling, contemplating whether to succumb to temptation. The desire to feel his tongue on me was too powerful to ignore. I badly wanted to assess his talents with it, especially since I was confident it would bring me pure ecstasy. Besides, it seemed unlikely that he would lie about being clean just for a chance to please me. In the end, what he intended to do was entirely selfless. He wouldn't derive any physical pleasure from it himself.

'Fine. But I'd still prefer to use a condom later on, to diminish the risk.'

'That's a deal, love. I can't wait to taste you,' he said lustfully and placed a gentle kiss on the spot just above my clit.

For quite some time, he continued to circle it with soft kisses. Rigid and enthralled, I watched his head between my thighs. This teasing was driving me insane. I had never endured such agonising lust before; he was far too tantalising. If he didn't act soon, I would have to take matters into my own hands.

'Will,' I prompted.

Again, he chuckled against my dripping lips, his breath fanning across them. I inhaled sharply and squeezed my eyes shut.

'All in good time, darling,' he said and pressed a tender kiss directly on my throbbing bud.

God, it felt good. My legs tensed. The friction was divine.

'Again,' I begged.

Then, a slick and warm sensation revolved around my clit, expertly sensitising it. It was his tongue, and it was astounding. My mouth formed a circle, my breath abandoning me as the slick sensation sank lower, lapping over my lips and licking up my juices.

'Mmm. Even better than I'd imagined,' he said, and I could hear the grin in his voice.

What an unbelievably erotic man. Blushing at his words, I opened my eyes to watch him. He held my gaze, giving me a playful wink as he moved closer again.

'Oh,' I whined as his tongue drew slow circles. He avoided making direct contact, and it was driving me wild. My blood felt like it was on fire.

'Please, Will.'

Finally he listened, yielding to my demands. As he swept his tongue directly across my clit, my head jerked back into the wall, but the pleasure he provided numbed out the pain. Resolutely, he increased the speed of his flicks, and his pattern was out of this world – a combination of up and down and around.

He was blowing my mind, masterfully crafting a sensational orgasm within me. Never in my life would I forget the climax I was about to reach. I was certain.

The tension raged through my veins. My whole body flexed as I struggled to withstand it. It centred in my lower abdomen, growing denser and larger. When it verged on becoming unbearable, I cried out his name.

Determined to drive me over the edge, he persisted. My toes curled first. Then my shudders started.

Oh no.

'Ah!' I gasped as the most powerful orgasm I had ever experienced flooded my body. Convulsing away from the wall, I crouched over him and tugged his beautiful hair, overcome with relief and a sense of liberation.

Oh, my God.

While I floated on sheer bliss, he shoved my legs off his shoulders. Then he grabbed my waist and hoisted me up against the wall. Only vaguely did I hear the undoing of a belt. I was much too sated to pay attention to my surroundings. But when the crest of his erection swept across my soaked folds, I could no longer ignore them.

'Condom!' I chided and opened my eyes to glare at him. I was religious about my practice of safe sex.

With a look of disdain on his face, he frowned back. 'What do you take me for?'

Confused, I gazed down at his erection and blinked with surprise. He had already sheathed his length in the latex.

I stared at it. I had never come across such a perfect dick, both in length and girth.

'R-right.' I swallowed.

'Satisfied?'

Meeting his eyes, I gave him a lecherous smile. 'Almost.' I lowered my hand and traced the length of him with my fingertips, all while I held his gaze. 'Get inside me and I will be.'

Lust and wonder danced in his eyes while he chewed on his lower lip, his mouth curving into his increasingly familiar crooked smile.

'Careful what you wish for,' he said. Pushing his hips forward, he reached between us and aligned himself with my entrance. As he coated the tip of himself in my wetness, he said gruffly, 'You'd better muster your strength. By the time I'm finished with you, you won't be able to walk.'

My mouth watered at his carnal warning. As I stared into his striking eyes, my heart palpitated in the same alien manner that it had earlier that night. It was a sweet sensation, but it was also devastatingly profound. I couldn't fathom the nature of it.

Indeed, he was devastating, but before I could contemplate my strange heartbeat further, he thrust powerfully into me.

I whimpered, but he didn't stop. He shoved past my walls until he reached the very end of me. It hurt, albeit faintly. Gripping his broad shoulders, I clawed his shirt and the skin beneath it.

'Shit,' he breathed out, 'you feel fucking amazing. The pressure of you—' He cut himself off by demanding my mouth. While kissing me as though I were his salvation, he withdrew from within me.

'Be gentle, please,' I said against his lips. 'You're very big.'

I felt rather than saw his responding smile.

'You'll survive,' he said smugly and pushed forcefully into me again. His thrust was of such strength that I was pushed slightly up the wall.

I hissed into his mouth and locked my legs around his waist. 'Fuck.'

He started a punishing rhythm – in and out, and so bloody deep, but the friction was nothing short of exquisite. This man was clearly an expert in the art of fucking.

'Oh.' I panted. My brows furrowed as I sank into the intense look in his eyes. I could barely believe my good fortune. I must have been accumulating some amazing karma as I consoled Olivia through her heartache. Nothing else could explain this uncanny encounter. Then again, I had never believed in karma.

I was just lucky. It was that simple. To express my gratitude, I would savour this beautiful man.

His large hands began to roam across my body, exploring and caressing every curve. Ruled by zeal, he gripped the fabric of my dress above my breasts and dragged it downward, liberating the aching mass.

He grinned at the view. 'Just when I thought you couldn't get any more perfect.'

He lowered his head and engulfed my left nipple with his mouth.

My face flushed at his sensual compliment, and more again when he harshly sucked my erect nipple. Groaning, I buried my breast deeper within his possession, relishing the delicious sensations that rippled through my body.

He was well on his way to obliterating all my defences. Would one night with this man truly be enough? I worried it wouldn't. Truly, if this was what it entailed, it was tempting to submit to him.

Moving away from my breast, he kissed his way across my sternum and up my neck, reaching the line of my jaw, all while he continued to fuck me into oblivion against the wall. We hadn't even made it to his bed, I realised.

Upon a particularly perfect thrust, I gasped and hugged him against me. He had struck precisely against my front wall, a spot that was especially sensitive. Seeming to notice this, he repeated the same motion, again and again.

'Oh my God,' I mouthed, because I lost my breath.

'Come on, love,' he growled. 'Give in to me,' he commanded, his authoritative tone making my walls clench around him.

Holding my breath, I squeezed my eyes shut and felt the tension border on unbearable. A few more of those thrusts and I would come undone whether I wanted to or not.

I wailed, my toes curling again.

'No,' I whined. I didn't want to climax so soon.

Burying his hand in my hair, he tugged my head back. 'Yes,' he panted and ploughed harshly into me.

Fuck!

Immediately, I was sent over the edge again, reeling straight back into bliss.

I pushed against him, desperate for space. I was so overwhelmed that I feared I would implode. My entire body was convulsing, but he confined me to him, strong arms becoming a cage.

'Stop, please,' I squeaked, heaving for air.

'You're exceptionally sensitive,' he said, his voice full of wonder. He wasn't the first to tell me that, but that didn't make it less true. I had always been like this. Maybe that was why I enjoyed sex so much. I rarely had it without coming at least once.

'Yeah, well, for better and for worse.'

He chuckled and, to my relief, ceased thrusting. He brought us away from the wall and carried me into his living room. Locating his dark brown dining table, he lowered us onto it and propped himself on his forearms on either side of my head.

We stared at each other in silence. While I couldn't speak for him, I was overawed by the chemistry between us. I had never experienced anything like it, and certainly not with a stranger. The mere magnitude of it was uncanny. Was this the sort of encounter that would only happen once in a lifetime, if at all? Was I currently staring at the Right One, or was he just another fool among the crowd of imposters? My gut whispered he was different, but I was scared to listen in case it was wrong.

With a look of amusement, he pushed up and leaned back, but he remained buried inside me, which my vagina was hyperaware of; it throbbed around his dick.

'Your sexual stamina could use a remedy,' he said as he started undoing the buttons of his waistcoat. Offended, I gave him a scowl.

'Fuck you.'

'You are. Right now, as it happens,' he fired back, thoroughly amused, and thrust gently into me again.

'Ah,' I complained and looked grumpily away from him.

He laughed. 'We'll just have to practise, I suppose.'

'In your dreams.'

'There as well, I'm sure.' He smirked. 'But I have to say, after watching you come – twice already – I'm less inclined than ever to let you leave this place without any intention of seeing me again. I could honestly watch you come for a lifetime without growing bored.'

My face grew hotter. I refused to discuss this with him. I wasn't changing my mind. He surely drove a hard bargain, though, in more ways than one.

Something soft dropped on the floor. I looked back at him, and my heart jolted at the view. He had taken off his shirt.

I stared at his powerful torso, salivating. The man was clearly no stranger to the gym. He was easily the fittest man I had ever slept with. I could wash my clothes on his stomach, for heaven's sake, and his pecs were bigger than my boobs.

I couldn't resist ogling him. While his muscles were prominently defined, they didn't look unnatural. They were athletic and proportionate – exactly my taste.

Groaning, I turned my head and tucked my face into the palm of my hand. This wasn't fair. I didn't deserve this. Why were my willpower and dedication to my studies being put on trial like this?

'Either way, we're nowhere near finished,' he said. Gripping my arm, he dragged me off the table and slipped out of me in the same go.

Towering in front of me, he leaned down and pressed a sweet and extended kiss to my swollen mouth. Then, as suddenly as he had kissed me, he whirled me around and reached for the zip at the back of my dress. As it came undone beneath his skilful fingers, I studied my surroundings. He evidently had excellent and expensive taste. I wasn't sure I had ever been in a flat with an interior design this elegant. It was dominated by darker shades that gave it a masculine atmosphere, which made me doubt that he had a female housemate – if he had one at all.

On my left, a set of stairs led up to another floor. His penthouse had to be even bigger than I had initially thought. It was a lot of space for just one man.

'Do you live alone?' I asked as my dress fell to pool around my ankles.

'No. My girlfriend will be back tomorrow night.'

My heart faltered. It hadn't occurred to me to ask whether *he* was single. I had taken it for granted that he was.

Plagued by dread, I slowly turned my head and looked at him over my shoulder. A sardonic smile welcomed me.

'Dickhead,' I insulted him, annoyed. He was pulling my leg.

He laughed, his eyes creasing with mirth. 'Yes, darling, I live alone. Do you?'

'No, I've got a flatmate – best mate.' I looked around. 'You have similar taste, actually. He'd have loved this place.'

He frowned. 'He?' he echoed. 'You mean you live with a man?'

'Yeah.'

'That's a bit unusual, isn't it?'

'Maybe.' I shrugged. 'He's like a brother to me, though.'

'Poor guy.' He tittered. 'Is he aware you think of him that way?'

'Of course, it's a mutual thing.'

He looked sceptical. 'I'm sure. You haven't slept with him, then?'

I laughed at the preposterous idea. 'Of course not.'

'I can't imagine he'll be happy with my future visits.'

Visits? What did he mean 'visits'? Had he forgotten that I apparently lived in Edinburgh?

I was about to ask what he meant when he put his hand on the small of my back and pushed me forward, tenaciously. Spread flat across his dining table, I felt his nails claw down my back.

'Mm. You are a sight to behold,' he said and left a soft kiss on my shoulder blade. As he stretched up to his full height behind me, he smoothed his hands across my buttocks.

'This' – he squeezed – 'is more enticing than I could possibly express.'

I swallowed a lump in my throat and closed my eyes to prepare for his intrusion. Soon enough, he rubbed the tip of his erection over my slit, lubricating himself in my fluids. It was a careful action, and yet the sensation made me shiver. I was overly sensitive now. I would be coming again in record time.

'Ready?' he asked, his voice low and seductive.

'Yes.'

He pushed into me with a lengthy groan of satisfaction. Searching for something to hold on to, I spread my arms and gripped the edges of the table. He grabbed my hips upon his steady retreat, and I perceived it as a warning. His next shove wasn't going to be merciful.

But his subsequent thrust proved me wrong. Unlike earlier, he was deliciously delicate in his treatment this time around. He didn't plough into me. Instead, he settled into a steady rhythm that massaged my front wall in the most pleasurable manner. In all fairness, this pattern was far worse, because it seemed to trigger me much faster.

'Oh my God,' I moaned and propped my upper body on my

forearms. Using his hold on my hips, he dragged me to meet each of his thrusts, making him reach so blissfully deep.

I had never been penetrated so well.

'You like that?' His voice was sexier than any other I had heard, and especially when he used that tone. It made him irresistible.

'Mm, yes. Don't stop,' I said breathlessly.

His warm mouth placed a loud, hungry kiss on the spot between my shoulder blades. As the tip of his nose trailed up to the nape of my neck, he said sensually, 'If I could, I'd fuck you for ever, darling. You feel *that* good.' And then, a single harsh thrust.

I whimpered and shook my head. Would I survive this?

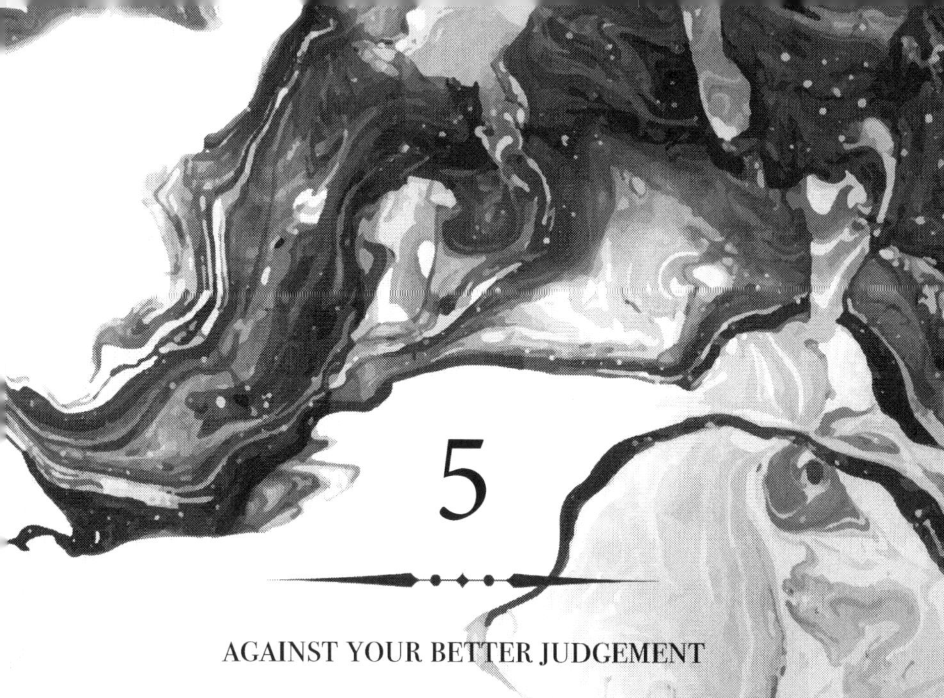

5

AGAINST YOUR BETTER JUDGEMENT

Inexorably, he continued, seemingly determined to ruin me. But, all of a sudden, he pulled out and grabbed my arm. After turning me onto my back, he knelt between my legs and tucked them over his shoulders. My face flushed when I understood his intention.

'No. Please.' I sat up and clasped his jaw. 'I'm satisfied. I just want you to come.'

Soft laughter spilled from his mouth as he gripped my wrists and locked my arms by my sides.

'Well, that's not what I want.'

'Will.' I writhed against his hold of me, but he was much too strong. I tried to close my legs, but his mouth had already reached me. Pleasure bolted through me at once, merciless in its force.

'Shit!' I cried out as his tongue continued to torment me. Crouched over him, my toes curled again. Breathing erratically, I felt the tension rebuild within me, impossibly strong. A tearless sob escaped and I failed to inhale again. All I could focus on was the unbearable tension that engulfed my entire body. Desperate for release, I tried to break away, but he wouldn't have it. While maintaining his grip on my wrists, he smothered my legs with his arms to hold me in place.

And then it unfurled. Shuddering against him, I wailed his name and collapsed onto him, limp as a corpse. Only vaguely did I hear him chuckle.

Gently, he moved me onto my back. My eyes had been shut, and when I opened them, he was hovering above me. A soft expression dwelled in his features, and I hoped it included sympathy. He brushed a lock of my hair behind my ear, his eyes roaming across my flushed, dewy face.

'Women as beautiful as you shouldn't be allowed to wear clothes,' he suddenly said.

Unimpressed, I only frowned back. What an unbelievably shallow compliment. As if it ought to be a beautiful woman's duty to please the male eye. As if an attractive woman shouldn't be allowed to decide over her own body.

Confusion crossed his face. 'What?'

'That was a shit compliment, even though I know you were only trying to be nice.'

'What? How was it shit?'

'It sounded a bit sexist.'

He gaped with disbelief and then shook his head.

'For the record, I'm not a male chauvinist. I find sexism outrageous. Besides, you're living proof of how amazing women are.' With a pleading gaze, he said, 'If you give me your number, I'll prove to you all of the above.'

My lips twisted with amusement. Damn it. I didn't want to be smiling right then. It was giving me away, and I worried it would encourage him, that he would misread a smile as actual interest.

'No.'

He sighed, his head dropping. 'At least give me your Instagram handle, then.'

I groaned, despairing of him. 'No, Will.' Reflecting on his persistence, I realised this had been a mistake. 'I should leave.' I sighed and tried to shove him off, but he wouldn't budge. 'Will.'

'Fine,' he grumbled. 'Have it your way.'

Since he didn't move, I wasn't sure what he meant. 'Sorry?'

Lifting his gaze, he studied me for a brief moment, his lips snapping into a tight, brooding line.

'When you leave tomorrow, that's it. But I'm going to have you all of tonight. If you're still determined not to meet me again after that, I'll respect it.'

I swallowed. 'All right.'

He leaned away and dragged me with him. Then he bent over and heaved me across his shoulder. Wide-eyed, I stared at the floor beneath my head as he walked off with me, wondering what I had set into motion.

'What are you doing?'

'I'm ensuring my end of the bargain,' he muttered and kicked open the door to another room. He stepped into the darkness of it and dropped me off his shoulder.

I squealed in fear of meeting the floor, but confusion silenced me the instant my skin met soft material. His bed?

He shut the door and turned on the lights. He was grinning at me, clearly amused by my squeal.

'What, did you think I'd resort to violence?' he asked.

'Maybe. For all I know, you could still be Mr Bateman in disguise,' I said, my lips protruding.

That made him laugh. 'I'm not. I'm just a man who's hopelessly interested in you.'

I smirked. 'I'm sure your mother would be jealous had she heard that.'

He shuddered. 'What? No. Way to kill the mood.'

I raised a brow and directed my gaze to his ever-present erection. How potent was he? Seriously.

'You don't seem affected.'

'That's thanks to the glorious view.' He gestured to me.

I looked away, observing my new surroundings. His bedroom was really quite big. Three doors led into it, and we had arrived through one of them. What was hiding behind the other two? A bathroom, I assumed, as well as a wardrobe, or perhaps a private office?

'Even for a successful solicitor, your flat's rather big,' I said. 'And seeing as you're only twenty-eight, I'm struggling to understand how you could've amassed such a fortune already.'

'Well, you'll never know, and you've got yourself to blame,' he quipped and approached the bed. 'Shame you're not a gold digger, Sandra. I'd have you on your knees in a heartbeat if you were.'

I faced him. Unimpressed, I stared at his lopsided smile while he reached for my heels and peeled them off my feet. Once he had put them on the floor, his mouth dived for my calves, and then he kissed his way upward, slowly.

He really was remarkably sensual. It demanded all my willpower not to submit to his wish about meeting again.

I wondered if I would regret it. Then again, if I did, I knew where he lived. He, the poor man, didn't even know my real name.

While I had been worrying, he had made his way to my throat.

Covering it with soft, amorous kisses, he elicited another groan from my mouth. Meanwhile, I seemed to have wrapped my limbs around him subconsciously.

His mouth roamed across my moisture-laden skin, his hands closing around my upper arms. Then he turned me onto my stomach beneath him. I fixed my eyes on the black headboard of his bed and felt him lift only my derrière.

'I'll be coming with you this time, but it won't be the last,' he warned.

Without further ado, he thrust into me, pushing forward until he reached the very end of me. Hissing, I ground my teeth and fisted his bed sheets so hard that my knuckles grew numb and white. As he made his retreat, he leaned over me, and the intimacy of his action struck me hard.

Strong as a fortress, he hovered above me while his lips blessed my neck. Making his way toward my ear, he said, 'This is going to get a bit rough, love. Tell me to stop if I'm hurting you.'

My eyes widened and I swallowed. Just what did he have in mind?

Sneaking his hands under my body, he found my wrists, locked them within his grip and dragged my arms back, successfully lifting my torso from his colossal mattress. When he thrust again, I realised what he had meant. I barely managed to stifle a whimper. He was using my arms to balance out his weight. With each thrust, he dragged me toward him, and it made him reach a depth that no other man had.

How it was possible to fuck anybody so well was beyond me. He must have been designed to pleasure women into insanity. Though it hurt faintly, it was undoubtedly a pleasurable pain. Never in my life had I been dominated like this, and I relished it. Granting him power over my pleasure was easily the best decision I had ever made, sex-wise. He knew exactly what to do. He was introducing me to a whole new dimension of sex, and I feared I would never be satisfied with anything less again.

A bottled-up cry spilled out of my mouth as he continued to slam into me. This tension was intolerable. I couldn't last much longer. It was far too powerful. *He* was far too powerful, and so my shivers started.

Oh no.

'Not yet,' he chastised and released my right forearm to spank me. The sting of his palm made me hiss. What he had done was counterproductive, because my drenched, quivering walls clenched down on him as if to reject him, but he forced past them all the same.

'Don't you dare,' he growled. 'We're coming together this time.'

The sound of our flesh parting and meeting echoed through the room as the most erotic thing I had ever heard.

'Please,' I begged, shaking my head. A whole night of this was out of the question. I wouldn't last. I was sure.

'Nearly there,' he consoled me and released my left arm as well, but he grabbed my hips to hold me in place. Desperate to release at least a portion of the tension, I tugged my own hair while I silently pleaded for him to come.

Finally, his thrusts switched rhythm. They grew slower, but harder.

'Fuck,' he groaned, and I could hear that his teeth were clenched. He dug his fingers into my buttocks, nails clawing them. 'Come for me,' he commanded, and I instantly obeyed.

I shuddered through my intense climax, lost to the world. He closed over me immediately, confining me to him. With strong arms wrapped around me, he performed his final thrust and spilled himself within me. Falling limp in his arms, I heaved for air. I barely noticed that he rolled us onto our sides, where he withdrew from within me.

We recovered in silence. Though I couldn't speak for him, I was not only recovering from my row of orgasms, but also from shock. I had never had better sex, nor met a man more compelling.

His eventual sigh broke the quiet. While squeezing me against him, he planted a firm kiss on my neck and nuzzled his face in the crook of it.

'I'm gutted you don't want to do this again some other time,' he said.

I didn't reply because I couldn't find my voice.

An invisible fire in the form of his hand travelled up and down the curve of my waistline.

'You're so damn stunning. Do you know that?'

I cleared my throat and turned to look at him. Wearing a smile, I said hoarsely, 'Now that's how you give compliments, William.'

He smiled lopsidedly. 'I'm a quick learner.'

I tittered. 'You're conceited, is what you are.'

'Really?' He frowned. 'And how would you know? You hardly know me.'

'Cocky, at best,' I teased and faced away again.

'Well, you're rather annoying.'

'And yet here I am.'

'Against your better judgement.'

I laughed. 'If you'd like me to leave, I will.'

He tensed against me. 'Don't.'

'All right, then.' I turned over and smiled at him. 'All part of the deal,

I suppose.'

He propped himself on his arm and studied me for a while.

'Sandra, I'm curious.'

I wasn't sure I wanted to oblige, but I did anyway. 'What?'

'You don't seem to be particularly inexperienced in terms of sex. Frankly, you come across as being on the liberal end of the spectrum.'

I frowned. 'Okay?'

'Well, it makes me wonder how often you do this sort of thing. I realise it's none of my business, but . . .'

I smirked. 'Well, how often do you do it?'

'Random one-night stands? Every leap year, maybe.'

I watched him disbelievingly, but there was no hint of a lie in his eyes.

'I don't believe you. I mean, with your talents, as well as stamina, you must be getting your fill somehow.'

He chuckled. 'Right. If I answer, will you?'

I narrowed my eyes. Again, he drove a hard bargain. I was desperate to know now. 'Yes.'

He looked away. 'I have regular sex, but with the same partner' – his eyes darted toward me – 'usually.'

'Elaborate.'

He scratched his stubble, looking contemplative. 'I'm not in a relationship, but I've got an agreement with another woman. A sexual one.'

'Right.'

We were in similar situations, then. I had Aaron for that. But, regardless of my arrangement with Aaron, I didn't shy away from the occasional one-night stand. The only condition was that I used a condom so that Aaron wouldn't have to, but I would have done it anyway. Collecting sexually transmitted infections was not a hobby of mine.

'Your turn,' William reminded me.

'Well, same as you, I suppose. Though, when it comes to one-night stands, I might do it a couple of times a year, all depending on the person, really. I don't go all out to sleep with a stranger.'

'Like I did tonight,' he said with a leer.

'Right.' I grinned, but my amusement quickly vanished when something occurred to me. 'Is your partner going to mind?'

He scoffed. 'She hasn't got a right to know.'

'That's not an answer.'

He sighed. 'I'm not sure. It's implied that I'm allowed to do this sort of thing, but predicting a bruised ego can be difficult.'

Right. That made sense. In fact, that was exactly the reason Aaron and I had agreed not to mention other partners to one another.

Suddenly William frowned. 'Wait, did you say "same as" me? You've got a regular partner?'

I blinked, surprised at his sudden display of disapproval. 'Yes?'

Gripping my jaw, he glared into my eyes. 'Then what's the problem? Clearly, you do have time. Reject that wanker already – you can reserve that energy for me.'

My jaw clenched in his hold. 'Of course I won't do that. The arrangement I've got with Aaron is perfect. I hardly ever give him a thought. He's so low maintenance that he might as well be air, and I have a funny feeling you won't be, Will, but it's not your fault. It's just that you're new. Aaron's familiar. New, right now, is bound to mess with my head for a while, and I don't want that.'

He groaned loudly and collapsed onto his back beside me. 'You have got to be kidding me.'

His dramatic reaction made me pout. 'I'm not, I'm sorry.'

'How about this, then. Give me your number and I promise I won't reach out to you till you've completed your exams, so in about two months.'

I frowned with frustration. It became apparent that I would need to be brutally honest with both him and myself. After drawing in a deep breath, I mustered up the courage to put myself in a vulnerable spot. I had never been this transparent with a mere stranger before, but William surely made it difficult to avoid.

'William, I'm sorry, but you're not casual sex material. You're *boyfriend* material. I'm a bit too compelled by you. Meanwhile, Aaron doesn't intrigue me that way at all. He's just there, platonically.'

'I can't believe this,' he moaned. 'Are you seriously saying I'm *too* interesting?'

I grimaced. 'Well, yes. Basically.'

'This is honestly unbelievable. It's completely backwards.'

I could understand why he would see it that way, but I didn't agree.

'Depends on what the goal is. Mine is to avoid distractions. I want to keep a strict focus on my studies and my career, so I prefer to stay away from things that can get in the way of that. I'm very sorry, but I have to be rational about this. What I'm doing is damage control.'

'Fuck it,' he muttered. 'I'm done.'

I tensed. 'As in you want me to leave?'

'No, but I'm forfeiting. It's clear you won't change your mind.'

Sighing, I lay down on top of him. On his chest, I folded my hands under my chin and held his gaze. It hurt to look at him now. He had better be worth rejecting.

'I'm sorry.'

'I'm over it,' he said, sounding nonchalant.

'I'll give you a blowjob if you want, for compensation.'

'I'd prefer if you kept quiet, I think. The more you talk, the more I like you.'

I smiled. 'I don't know what your partner is into, but I don't tend to speak much when I'm performing fellatio. It might have to do with having a dick in my mouth, but what do I know?'

I pushed myself up and trailed soft kisses down his torso. The slabs of muscle flexed beneath my mouth, making me grin. Was he ticklish?

Reaching down, he buried his hands in my hair and dragged me back to his face.

'What are you?' he asked as he stared into my eyes. 'The Devil?'

My lips twitched into another smile. 'It's your night. I'll be whatever you want.'

'Mine, then,' he said, and my heart throbbed. Had he really just said that? Once again, the strangest feeling seared into my chest, but I couldn't fathom the nature of it.

'Oh, but you already are,' he said and claimed my mouth.

Irked, I pulled away. 'I'm not.'

'You just said it yourself.' He grinned. 'I'm "boyfriend material".'

'You're also an idiot.'

He chuckled. 'My degree begs to differ.'

'Cambridge.' I rolled my eyes. 'Quite the card that is.'

'Yes.' He tucked his arms under his head. As he lay beneath me, his eyes were riveted on my face. 'I hope I'll forget you.'

His brutal words made me grimace. 'What? Why?'

'Because if I don't, I'll go mad.' He wrapped me in his arms and flung us around. 'But for now, I intend to take full advantage.' He reached for his nightstand. When I saw him withdraw another foil packet, my eyes widened. Already?

'I assure you, though,' he said, his face grave. 'I won't give you a single reason to ever forget *me*.'

§ § §

An internal alarm woke me up. When I opened my eyes, the black and unfamiliar nightstand prompted me to remember where I was. One after the other, memories of last night flashed through my mind until there was an abundance of heat in my face. I smiled in spite of it, for it had been dreamlike.

There wasn't a sound around me, not even of a body softly drawing breath. Was he still here? I remembered I had fallen asleep in his arms sometime after midnight, but nobody was holding me now.

In case he was still present in the bed, I turned carefully and slowly, but he was nowhere in sight. Relaxing, I groaned and rubbed my face. I despised the inevitable next phase: the awkward conversations and forced small talk that always occurred the morning after a one-night stand – unless I had snuck out before the guy woke up. There was always that dreadful question hanging in the air and spilling between the lines: what's next? Should we go back to being perfect strangers, as if we hadn't just enjoyed each other more intimately than most, or should we embark on a journey that was bound to end in tragedy once I failed to live up to his expectations?

Considering what a paradigm shift William represented in my expectations of men, I lingered in the bed for a while longer, hoping it would help me reinforce my resolve. I would need every drop of it to stick to my rules and leave without any intention of a reunion.

Gazing around, I wondered what time it was. Last night, I had brought my purse into his bedroom, so I reached down the side of the bed and took out my phone. As the screen lit up, I saw that it was half ten and that I had two missed calls from Jason, as well as a text from Olivia that had been received just a minute ago. Since I had plans with Jason today, I decided to call him before I did anything else.

'Morning, love,' he answered after a single ring.

'Morning,' I replied hoarsely and cleared my throat.

'Glad you're not dead.' He chuckled. 'Whose bed did you fall asleep in?'

'The bed of the guy I insulted.'

'No way. You're joking.'

'Am not.'

Laughter burst out of him. 'Oh my God. Course you did. Was it worth it?'

'Yeah, actually. Best I've ever had.'

'Really?' he asked, sounding amazed.

'Really.'

'Damn. Will you stick to your rules, then?'

I sighed. 'That's the plan.'

He was quiet for a beat. 'You don't sound too happy about that.'

Somebody knocked on the door, and my heart contracted with a thrill upon the sound.

'Yeah, I know. But listen, I've got to go. I'll be home soon, all right?'

'Later, then.'

'Yeah.' I hung up. 'Yes?' I called out.

The door swung open, revealing the gorgeous man I had managed to seduce last night. I must have been wielding some black magic. Nothing else could explain this. For better or for worse, he was exactly my type, both physically and mentally. Dressed in beige trousers and a simple white shirt, he leaned against the doorpost and smiled.

There wasn't a chance I could keep myself from blushing.

'Morning,' he said and tucked his hands in his pockets. 'Sleep well?'

'I did. You?'

'Same.'

'Have you been awake for long?'

'About an hour.' He shrugged. 'I've made you breakfast. If you'd like to shower first, there's a bathroom through that door.' He jerked his head toward it.

My eyebrows arched. I hadn't expected this level of hospitality.

'Thanks. You're very kind.'

'You'll find fresh towels on the shelf beside the shower. There's shampoo and conditioner for women there as well, should you want to use it.'

I grimaced. 'Why have you got that? Is it your regular partner's?' If it was, I wasn't inclined to even touch it. It would feel wrong, like I was trespassing on her territory.

His smile transitioned into a grin. 'No. I shopped for it this morning when I went out for coffee.'

'Oh.' My blush intensified at his thoughtfulness. 'That wasn't necessary, but I appreciate it.'

He shrugged again. 'I left a T-shirt for you as well. If there's anything else, let me know. I'll just wait in the kitchen.'

As soon as he closed the door, I pushed the duvet aside, climbed out of the bed and went into the bathroom. It was like walking into a spa that smelled of citrus. It was spacious too – he even had a bath.

It was tempting to stand under his rain shower for ages, but I was quick to step out because I wanted to respect Jason's time. He had reserved the whole day to help me unpack, so I ought to get home as soon as possible.

As I looked in the mirror, I was happy to see that there wasn't much make-up left on my face. The remaining traces were nothing the wipes I kept in my purse couldn't get rid of.

When I had finished rinsing my face, I put on the plain white T-shirt that I found on a shelf beside the bath. The size of it made it work like a dress, and since I no longer had any underwear, I was grateful for that. Grabbing my towel, I wrapped my hair and decided to face reality.

I walked out of William's bedroom and was hit by the smell of bacon. London buzzed in the background through a window he had opened in his living room. As I ambled toward the kitchen, I looked at the front door and noticed that my knickers were gone. He had probably thrown them in the bin.

Heading past the staircase, my eyes landed on his square dining table. My vagina tingled at the memory it evoked, even despite how sore it was. It would need at least a week to recuperate. He'd had his way with me three times before he had let me sleep.

Passing a big, black-leathered sofa group, I turned a corner and came upon the door to his kitchen. It was open, and the scent of bacon was concentrated there. I sucked in a deep breath for courage and walked in. William sat at the island table, reading on his iPad.

'It smells amazing,' I said as he looked up. When I saw a pan of scrambled eggs, saliva amassed in my mouth. While I was certain they would be no match for Jason's recipe, I could hardly wait to fill my mouth.

'Oh my God, you've pulled out all the stops, haven't you?' I said as I hesitated to hop onto the stool beside him. Seeming to notice, he smiled and patted the top of it as an invitation.

'Please,' he said when I had sat down. 'Help yourself.'

Hungry, I scanned my options and was about to grab a scone when I noticed the Starbucks cup standing next to my plate. My eyes zoomed in on the black ink on the side. *Electra*, it read, making me laugh. I pointed at it and faced William.

'Is that for me?'

Smirking, he reached for his own cup and turned it so I could see the name. *Oedipus*, it read, and it made me laugh again.

'You're certainly something else,' I said.

'Glad you've noticed.'

I got the feeling there was another dimension to his response. However, since I didn't want to ruin the mood by introducing the conversation that would ultimately lead to rejection, I pretended not to have registered it and grabbed a scone.

'I wasn't sure how you take your coffee, so I opted for a regular black. If you'd like any milk or cream, it's in the fridge,' he said while I helped myself to some scrambled eggs.

'Like I'd have the nerve to complain,' I said amusedly.

'What's your regular order, though?'

'At Starbucks?'

'Yeah. Or just in general.'

'Flat white. But I often opt for black as well. Depends on my mood.'

'I see.'

'And you?' I had no use for this information, but I thought it polite to ask anyway.

'Black, nothing added. Always.'

'So you're not a tea person, then.'

'No, I like tea now and then. Usually black, though. But I prefer coffee.'

'Same.'

I raised a forkful of scrambled eggs to my mouth. The moment the flavour exploded on my tongue, my eyes widened with disbelief. It tasted precisely like Jason's, if not even better.

Observing my reaction, William asked, 'Everything all right?'

I paused chewing and frowned at him. Stowing the eggs in my cheek, I covered my mouth and said, 'This is delicious. What's your secret? I've never tasted better scrambled eggs in my life.'

A grin formed on his face before he fixed his gaze on his iPad again. 'I'm glad. It's my mother's recipe. If you agree to see me again, perhaps I'll share it with you.'

My heart sank. It was clear that he was waiting for me to announce my decision, and he wasn't going to like it. But there was simply too much at stake. I had no guarantee we would turn out to be compatible, and I wasn't willing to explore the possibility when I already had countless obligations to mind that were crucial for my future.

I put my fork aside and folded my hands on my lap. 'Will, I've already told you, I don't have the capacity for anything other than a one-night stand, especially now with my exams round the corner.'

His jaw clenched and he locked his iPad. Shoving it away, he faced the windows and stared out at the rooftops of London. 'And as I've said, I'm willing to compromise. Focus on your exams. Once you're done, let me know.'

Unsure of what to say, I kept looking at him. Eventually his impatience got the better of him and he faced me again.

'Why won't you just give me a chance?' he asked. 'That's all I'm asking – a single chance to prove myself worthy of your attention.'

'I've already explained why.' Groaning, I put my elbows on the island and buried my face in my hands. 'Is it really so hard for you to understand that I'm just not interested in anything more than this?'

'Yes.'

I sighed.

'And it is,' he went on, 'because this sort of chemistry isn't commonplace, and you've admitted that you feel the same way. Otherwise you wouldn't have called me "boyfriend material", would you?'

I looked briefly away, regretting that I had been so candid with him last night. I should have kept my mouth shut to make this easier for us both.

A certain lie I had told him marched into my mind then, and I intended to make use of it. Perhaps reminding him would moderate his zeal.

'Will, I live in Edinburgh. There's no chance we'd work out.'

He frowned. 'Don't be so pessimistic. Edinburgh is just a flight away,' he argued, shocking me.

I gawked at him. 'Are you implying that you'd be willing to fly to Edinburgh only to see me again?'

'Yes. One hundred per cent.'

Stunned, I could only stare at him.

'I realise how crazy that sounds,' he said and waved a hand in the air. 'But what I'm trying to say is that I'd like to keep in touch.'

'You mean like long-distance dating?'

He shrugged. 'Why not?'

My heart was hammering like never before. I would never have thought him to be such a romantic. Indeed, what an unbelievably grand, romantic gesture. And the worst part was that he didn't even know my real name.

Full of guilt, I found myself on the verge of giving him my real identity, but I bit my tongue before I could. He was obviously very interested in me, so giving him that information could make things complicated. He would be able to contact me then, and I didn't want that. This way, I could ensure a clean break. And, if I changed my mind, I could always seek him out, because I knew where he lived.

He peered at me. When I didn't say anything, he sighed and gazed out the windows again. 'I see it as a win-win situation. You said you're reluctant about dating because you don't have time for it. Well, I obviously won't be able to demand much of your time while you're in Edinburgh. And, like you, I don't have much time to spare either. I'm an ambitious man, so I spend most hours of the day at work anyway. It would be mutually beneficial. Don't you see? Our needs are compatible. What's it going to cost you to keep in touch while you're in Scotland? I just don't understand how that's asking too much.'

After a while, he added, 'Had you said it's because you don't fancy me that way, I'd of course respect it. But that's not the case, is it?'

Conflicted, I swallowed a lump in my throat. The solution was simple – all I had to do was say that I didn't fancy him that way – yet I couldn't bring myself to utter the lie.

'No,' I said. 'It's not.'

He groaned loudly, tossed his head back, and stared at the ceiling in despair.

I studied him for some time. I had totally misjudged him last night. He wasn't an arsehole in the slightest. In his own way, he was instead a rare breed of a gentleman. Considering how rarely he indulged in one-night stands, he didn't seem like a man who chased skirts merely for the thrill of it. On the contrary, he seemed rather fastidious about whom he blessed with his time and attention.

And here I was, wasting it.

'I'm sorry, Will. You deserve better.'

He sighed and reached for his iPad. 'Well, I agree. I deserve at least a chance.'

I nodded. 'I really am sorry.'

He fell silent.

I stared at my plate. I had lost my appetite. 'I should go.'

He stiffened. 'At least finish your breakfast.'

I shook my head. 'I've lost my appetite. I'm sorry.'

'Don't apologise.' His tone was saturated with remorse. 'I'm sorry I pressured you.'

I slid off my stool. 'I don't mean to be ungrateful, but I really think I should go.'

He gave me a vague nod and grabbed his phone from the table. 'I'll call for a taxi.'

'Thanks.'

I went into his bedroom and collected my things. When I was about to take off his T-shirt, he came in and insisted that I should keep it. To go along with it, he gave me a pair of white Calvin Klein boxers since I had no knickers to wear. I chuckled as I pulled them on, but they served the purpose. In fact they were quite comfortable – like wearing hotpants.

I had just finished combing my hair when he arrived in the doorway of his bathroom and announced that the taxi had arrived.

'I'll walk you down,' he said.

In the lift, the journey from his penthouse to the ground floor felt to last an age but, oddly enough, it still seemed too brief. We stole glances at one another the whole time, both appearing restless in our demeanour, but neither of us said a word.

Out on the street, we approached the black cab that was parked along the kerb. Taking advantage of his long legs, William strode to reach it first and opened the door for me.

'Thank you,' I said and halted in front of the open door to face him. 'I had a wonderful time.'

The smile he offered took my breath away. It would have turned most women into blind fools. Wearing that, he could do whatever he wanted and get whatever he desired, apart from me.

Hesitation radiated from his behaviour when he lowered his head somewhat. Realising what he wanted, I smiled and stretched up to meet him. His warm mouth moulded against my own, but it felt different this time. There was a vulnerability behind the motion of his lips, as if he was holding back to protect himself from harm, when what he truly wanted was to consume me. While part of me wished the moment would last for ever, a larger part told me to pull away.

'You know where I live,' he said and cupped my face in his hands. 'So if you change your mind, you'll know where to find me.' He stole another kiss, and when his lips parted from mine, I was mesmerised by the urgency in his eyes. 'Do change your mind,' he implored.

I gave him a faint smile and turned away. With a sigh that came straight from my heart, I headed into the car. William shut the door for me and tapped on the window on the front passenger side. Curious, I leaned over to see what he wanted. The driver rolled down the window and, through it, William extended a few notes to cover the fee for my trip.

'Drive safely,' he stressed.

'Of course, sir,' she replied.

'Thanks. Have a good day.'

'You too.' With that, the driver rolled up the window and pulled out on the street.

'Where to, Miss?' she asked.

As I gave her my address, it was tempting to glance through the rear windshield, but I didn't. A grimace covered my face while I wished William all the best. Right man, wrong time, was what it was. So, in the end, he wasn't really the right man at all. Had he been, he would have arrived later, when I would be ready to commit to someone.

6

SOUNDS LIKE YOUR TYPE

DURING THE TRIP, I OPENED OLIVIA'S TEXT.

You alive? x

Just left. Can I call you? x

A moment later, she called.

'Hi,' I greeted.

'How was it?' Olivia wasn't beating around the bush.

Heat prickled my cheeks. 'He was brilliant, all around.'

'I knew it! You had so much chemistry, Cara. I've never seen anything like it. I'm so happy for you.'

'Yeah, I guess we did,' I said while studying my nails. Were there remnants of his skin still underneath them? I remembered clawing down his back several times.

'Did you have sex?'

'Several times.'

'Oh my God,' she said excitedly. 'How was it?'

'I don't even have the words, Livy. He's . . .'

'He's what?'

'He's . . . unsurpassable.'

She inhaled sharply. 'I bet he is. I'm almost jealous.'

I chuckled.

'What are you going to do, then? How were things this morning?'

'They were a bit awkward, mainly because I rejected the chance to see him again.'

She groaned loudly. 'Cara, why? Why would you do that? If you liked him, why not give him a chance? I seriously don't think you'll ever come across a better match in your life.'

I didn't reply.

'So you didn't tell him your name, then?'

'No.'

'Gosh. Poor man. Honestly.'

I huffed. 'Yeah, he was quite remarkable. I wonder if I'll regret it. Then again, I have enough to worry about as it is, so I'm sure it was for the best.'

'Just don't come complaining to me when you end up alone.'

I looked out the window. 'Well, there's a difference between being alone and being lonely. I doubt I'll ever be discontent with being alone. You see, I really enjoy solitude. It's my best friend. We get on so well.'

She groaned again, and I knew that if she had been here, I would have seen her eyes roll.

To change the subject, I asked, 'Anyway, how was your night?'

'I had such a blast.' I could hear the smile in her voice. 'We left the bar after a couple of hours and went to play table tennis. Some random lads joined us, as well as a couple of girls, and it just turned out to be a really fun night. I made so many friends I'll probably never see again.'

Her last statement made me laugh. 'I'm glad.'

'Yeah. But you know, Andy did tell me something after you left last night, about Will.'

Dread made my chest contract. 'What did he say?'

'It's nothing bad, but I just think you should know.'

'Know what?'

'Apparently, Will's not one to have one-night stands. Andy was quite shocked about it after you left. Mentioned it had been years since it last happened.'

I had already inferred as much, but that didn't prevent my heart from clenching in that same unfamiliar manner. All I could think was that it was the last thing I needed to hear.

'Are you saying this to make me feel special? Because I don't require an ego-boost.'

'Oh, Cara. I think you know why I'm saying it. Just something to consider.'

I pressed my lips together. 'I'd rather not talk about him. I need to think. I'm extremely confused.' And conflicted.

She was quiet for a beat. 'You need to think?' she echoed, and her shock was audible. 'Meaning you might actually give him a chance?'

'Don't get your hopes up.'

'Too late.'

I groaned. 'Anyway, I'm nearly home now. Speak later, yeah?'

'Yeah. Tell Jason I said hello when you see him.'

'Will do. Love you.'

'Love you too. But you are an idiot.'

§ § §

When I opened the front door, Jason was exiting the bathroom, wearing nothing but a towel around his hips. With his dirty-blond hair and light-blue eyes, he resembled Apollo himself, especially with that towel that could have doubled as a fustanella. Any other woman would have grabbed the opportunity to ogle his impressive physique, but since I had already seen it countless times, I hardly noticed.

'There she is.' He smiled. 'How are you feeling?'

'Tired.'

'I bet.'

'Livy says hello.'

He frowned, looking as if he had suddenly recollected something. 'What happened to her last night?'

'Well, the guy I slept with was there with a friend, so she spent the rest of the night with him. Went to play table tennis apparently.'

'Sounds like fun. They end up in bed?'

I shook my head. 'No, she wasn't feeling it, and neither was he. Like her, he was fresh out of a relationship.'

'But I thought the whole reason you went out last night was to find her a rebound?'

'Yeah, but she's changed her mind. Told me a one-night stand isn't going to help her get over Colin, so she'd rather wait till she makes a new genuine connection with someone.'

Jason looked impressed. 'Good for her.'

'Yeah, I thought so too. Anyway, I'm sorry for making you wait.'

He scoffed and waved his hand at me. 'No worries.' Folding his arms, he tilted his head and smirked. 'Well?'

'What?'

'Did you stick to your rules, then?'

I sighed as I undid the sash of my coat. 'Yeah.'

He shook his head in comical despair. 'Poor man. Was he gutted?'

Upset at the reminder, I pouted. 'Quite.'

He clucked his tongue. 'Again, poor man. I'm so glad I've never fancied you that way. You're as unattainable as they come.'

I snorted. 'Don't be silly. Besides, I'm not sure you would have liked him much, so you shouldn't feel bad for him. He was very forthright, and opinionated.'

Jason was far too liberal and easy-going in his nature to genuinely appreciate a stubborn, cocky man like William. If there existed a person who could make Jason lose his temper, I was confident that William would be that person.

'Sounds like your type,' Jason said teasingly.

I chuckled. 'Definitely was.'

Jason's eyes widened then. 'What are you wearing!' He laughed.

Glancing down at myself, I sensed my embarrassment reveal itself in my face. 'He tore my knickers apart. Gave me a pair of boxers to compensate, as well as a T-shirt.'

'He did what?' He continued to laugh, but he sounded more shocked now.

'Yeah, he was something else.'

'Jesus Christ, what a brute. Were they expensive?'

'No. Besides, it was honestly quite arousing.'

Disbelieving, Jason shook his head. 'What else did he do? Who is this guy?'

'I don't want to talk about it.'

His ensuing smile was sympathetic. 'You never do.'

I nodded. 'Just easier to leave it in the past that way.'

'You know best.' He gestured to the mountain of boxes standing outside my bedroom door. 'Anyway, shall we crack on with it, then?'

'Yeah.'

§ § §

The following Monday, I walked into Bentham House alongside Olivia, where we had planned to meet Aaron in the social hub before our lecture on Advanced Contract Law. It was the only module I had in common with her now that we had completed the compulsory ones of the first and second year. While she was ambivalent about the module, I found it nothing short of riveting, and the same applied to Aaron, which wasn't all that surprising when considering that Aaron and I had selected all the same ones. While Olivia preferred areas of public law, Aaron and I favoured private law.

As we entered the social hub, I scanned the people present until I spotted Aaron next to a girl named Cassie. I had nothing against her, but I had a feeling she disliked me, and I suspected it was because she had developed feelings for my regular bed partner. Aaron denied it, but I was quite sure I was right.

'She doesn't dislike you,' he would always say, 'and she doesn't fancy me that way.'

'Ah, Cassie,' Olivia said. 'Of course.'

I chuckled. Olivia absolutely could not stand the poor girl since she had heard her gossiping about me in one of the common rooms two years ago. I hadn't minded because I was aware that I came across as aloof and tended to make a terrible impression on people.

'Retract your claws, Livy,' I joked and adjusted my bag on my shoulder.

'I can't believe he doesn't see it. She's so taken with him, it's almost painful.'

'He insists she isn't.'

Olivia raised a brow and faced me. 'Would you be cross if he ever sleeps with her?'

Dumbfounded, I replied, 'It's far too early in the morning for this, but no, of course not. He can sleep with whomever he likes. We're not in a relationship.'

'What if they start dating?'

'Then he'll have my blessing.' I shrugged.

While it was true that a small part of me worried that he would suddenly fall in love with someone else, it was only because I would ultimately lose him as a bed partner then, and I didn't think I would ever find another Aaron. He was the ideal fuck friend, so I would be upset if I lost him before I was ready for it to happen. But I had been aware of that risk ever since the beginning of our arrangement, so of course I wouldn't be so selfish as to get angry over it. If he fell in love, I would be the last person to stand in his way, because while I didn't love him romantically, I loved him as a friend, and that meant that I would put his happiness first.

'You're so rational it should be criminal,' Olivia said.

'Hardly.'

'Do you even have an ego?'

'A huge one,' I joked.

'Oh, he's seen us.' Olivia turned her head and gave him a smile of acknowledgement. When I looked over, he was walking toward us.

Tall and lean, Aaron Myers was easy on the eyes. He had very short and curly black hair, and I had a habit of clawing it whenever he claimed my body. His eyes were nearly black, and they regarded me with tenderness as he approached. Below them, he had a strong nose with a slightly wide bridge, and full, dark brown lips that I loved to kiss. His stubble was longer than usual, though – it was almost a beard now. He clearly hadn't trimmed it in a while.

I smiled as I studied his handsome face.

Aaron was one of the cleverest men I had met, and I had always adored his introverted nature. He was one of those people others loved to be around because of his innate calmness and tolerant attitude. He would always listen in silence and contemplate what people had to say before he would offer unique insights and impressive reflections.

We had met during our first year at UCL at a social event that the university's student union had organised to provide students with an opportunity to make friends and start networking. He had been seated with a group of lads, but I had noticed him stealing glances at me while they talked. When I finally caught him, he didn't look away. He gave me a demure smile instead, which I immediately reciprocated. Excusing himself from the others, he approached me, somewhat shy in his demeanour. I was easily the more socially confident one, and he seemed to appreciate that, because once I started talking, he didn't express any desire for me to ever shut up.

That night, we ended up in bed together, and from there, our casual arrangement had been set into motion. In fact, one of the things I fancied most about sleeping with Aaron was that his schedule was aligned with my own, so finding time for a sensual round was never much of a challenge. We had done it in the toilets on campus several times, generally whenever we required a quick break from studying. Another bonus was the fact that Aaron wielded skills that were far above average. He was keenly attuned to my needs and always prioritised them, just as I made a point of prioritising his.

But the expertise of a certain man I had met last weekend forced him into the shadows. William possessed what I considered to be an X-factor. Aside from his outstanding talents between the sheets, there was something remarkably compelling about him, but I couldn't put my finger on precisely what it was. He was just so assertive and self-assured, seemingly unshakable. I admired his apparent resolve about things. He knew what he wanted, and he didn't hesitate trying to seize it. Like a breath of fresh air, he had been exceptionally stimulating. That was just it, he was exceptional.

'Hiya,' Aaron greeted and successfully distracted me from the dangerous lane of thought I had entered. I reminded myself not to think of William. It wasn't fair to Aaron, and it wasn't good for my sanity. William was the past. Aaron was the present.

But would I keep it that way?

'Did you have a nice weekend?' he asked and managed to steer me right back onto the thought of William.

'It was quite dull, to be honest,' I lied. Olivia cast me a glance, but I ignored it. 'I finished unpacking most of my things, but I had to order a new wardrobe from IKEA since there wasn't enough space for all my clothes. Bought a desk while I was at it.'

Aaron chuckled. 'I'm not even slightly surprised. Jason help you out?'

'Yeah.'

'Good of him. You could've asked me, you know.'

'I know, but I wanted some quality time with him.'

'How about you, Livy?'

'My weekend was great. Spent it with my mum.'

'Weren't you and Cara going for a drink on Friday?' he asked then, but she didn't so much as twitch.

'We did.' She smiled. 'Was great fun, but we decided to head home early because of exams coming up.'

'Responsible of you,' he said amusedly. 'I take it your plan to find a rebound failed, then?'

'I cancelled the quest,' she said with a chuckle.

'Oh. How come?'

Since I had already heard this part, I zoned out of their conversation and started toward the lecture theatre. I was adamant about sitting at the front, which was why I always arrived early.

§ § §

We were having lunch with a few other classmates when my phone notified me that I had received an email. I wasn't usually one to look at my phone when surrounded by my friends, but since I wasn't particularly involved in their current discussion, I decided to take the liberty.

My heart leaped to my mouth when I identified the sender. It was from Day & Night LLP, where I was set to complete a vacation scheme this summer. Alarm ruled my body as I rushed to open it. I hadn't expected to hear from them during this time, so I was worried it contained bad news. While I waited for it to load, I prayed to the god I didn't believe in that they weren't going to terminate my contract.

The text showed up, and I was at first met with a polite greeting from Theresa Ainsley, who was the woman I had been both interviewed and hired by. As I read on, I was pleasantly surprised.

'You okay, Cara?' Aaron asked. He must have noticed my apprehension.

Lifting my gaze from my screen, I said, 'More than okay. I'm brilliant, actually.'

Everybody grew quiet around me.

'What's up?' Aaron asked.

'I've just received an email from Day & Night.'

'And?'

'Well, one of their paralegals is pregnant and is going to take maternity leave this summer, so they've asked whether I would be interested in extending the length of my work experience placement. They've offered me to shadow one of their solicitors instead, as a paralegal slash legal assistant. Essentially, they're offering me to be a trainee for a few months.'

Aaron's lips parted and Olivia gasped beside me.

'You're kidding!' she exclaimed.

'I'm not.'

'No doubt due to your excellent marks. For how long, though?' Aaron asked.

'Three months.'

'Three months!' Olivia echoed, astonished. 'That's amazing! That's bound to be a positive contribution to your CV, Cara.'

'I know. I'd be a fool not to take the offer.'

'You have to take it,' Aaron urged.

'I will, I will,' I said with a smile. 'If you'll excuse me, I need to write back.'

'Well, there go our plans for the summer,' Olivia said. 'Can't say I'm upset about it, though.'

I chuckled. 'Me neither.'

§ § §

It was nearing time for dinner when Olivia decided she had revised enough for the day. Shortly after she had left, Aaron leaned back in his chair, and I felt his eyes on me.

'Have you heard back from Day & Night yet?' he asked.

Looking up from my laptop, I met his eyes and nodded. 'Yeah. I've got to sign a new contract, so I'm stopping by on Monday next week at ten.'

'I'm very happy for you, Cara. This is big.'

'It is, and I wouldn't have managed it without you.'

'What do you mean?'

I raised a brow. 'You know what.' I focused on my screen again. 'My marks wouldn't be half as good without your help.'

'You're giving me too much credit. You're helping me just as much.'

'Our brains were made for each other.'

'They were,' he said, and his tone was conspicuously fond.

I thought our conversation was over, but since I sensed him continuing to observe me, I asked, 'What?'

'Have you got any plans tonight?'

My blood slowed in my veins. I knew where he was going with this, so I kept my eyes on my laptop.

For the first time, I dreaded sleeping with him again, and it wasn't because I felt like I was keeping him in the dark. I had faced him the day after sleeping with someone else several times before, and it had never posed a problem. Not once had my conscience suffered. Besides, for all I knew, he could have scored last weekend as well.

The truth was that I dreaded sleeping with him again because William had left a lasting impression. I hadn't yet recovered from the power of his attention, so a quick fix with Aaron wasn't something I had the mind for. Moreover, I didn't want to ruin my experience of Aaron's talents in bed. But if we slept together so soon, it would inevitably result in that.

'I'm sorry, but I'm just not feeling up to it today,' I said.

'Fair enough.' He nodded and focused on his textbook again.

Even though I knew I could only delay it for so long, I released a quiet breath of relief.

§ § §

On Monday the 22nd of April, I was about to sign my new contract. I was tense as I waited for Ms Ainsley in the grand reception area of the Day & Night building on Cannon Street, but she wasn't the one to collect me; a middle-aged man exited the lift and called my name.

'Miss Darby?'

'Yes?'

His piercing light-blue eyes, which were the first thing I noticed about him, locked with mine, and something about them struck me as familiar. Scattered throughout his dark brown hair were silver strands, but his cheeks were neatly shaven, making him look years younger than he probably was. He was one of those men who made age his friend.

As he moved toward me, I admired his elegance. He had a level of class I could only dream of managing. Mirroring his grin, I wondered who he was. Was he the lawyer I would be shadowing?

'It's a pleasure to finally meet you. I've heard great things,' he said as he halted in front of me. He extended his hand, and I was quick to take it. His grip was firm, and I appreciated that.

'Have you?'

'Yes. You must be wondering who I am.'

'Well, we've not met before, have we?'

'No, I'm afraid not. I'm John Night, Jason's father.'

I gaped, awestruck. Was I really looking at the legend himself? To what did I owe this honour? I doubted it was normal for a CMD to welcome insignificant trainees like this, so why the special treatment? Was it because I was his son's flatmate?

'It's an honour to meet you, sir,' I said.

'Please, call me John.'

'Then you must call me Cara.'

He smiled crookedly. 'Theresa told me you were here, so I thought I ought to welcome you myself. It's a shame we haven't met till now. I know Jason's very fond of you.'

'I'm very fond of him too.'

'I'm glad to hear that. Anyway, thanks for being motivated to move things around on such short notice. I hope you didn't have to cancel any plans for the summer.'

'I'd happily cancel my entire social life for this opportunity, John.'

He chuckled. 'Then you'll make an excellent solicitor when the day comes. Are you anxious to start?' He ushered me past the security gates and toward the lifts.

'Definitely.'

He put his hand on my back. 'You'll fit in perfectly, I'm sure.'

'I hope so.'

'How was my son this morning?' he asked as we entered a lift. He pressed the button for the tenth floor.

'Groggy, but grateful for the breakfast I served him in bed.'

'He has mentioned that you're an excellent chef.'

'Has he?' I asked, surprised.

'Yes. Hasn't he told you?'

I smiled and shook my head. 'Must have slipped his mind.'

'He's probably just too busy devouring your cooking to think of commenting on it,' he said amusedly. 'Wherever he lost his manners, I don't know, but I'm sure my parenting is free of any blame.'

I laughed, grateful to discover that John was a man with a sense of humour.

'My office is on the top floor,' he said, 'but yours will be on the tenth floor, with the M&A department. That's where the solicitor you'll be aiding has got his. If ever there's anything at all, don't hesitate to stop by.'

I nodded.

'You'll be shadowing my eldest son during your time here, so he'll be in charge of overseeing your work. He's a good man, I like to think, and one hell of a solicitor. I couldn't be prouder of his achievements. Hopefully you'll learn a great deal from him.'

My eyebrows climbed up my forehead. I would be shadowing Jason's elder brother? I hadn't expected that.

'If he's your son, I'm sure I will,' I said sincerely.

The lift stopped at our floor and the doors parted, revealing an open-plan office which closed offices surrounded. The contemporary interior design was dominated by pale colours and looked expensive. Down the corridor on my right, I saw a break room, fitted out with fancy furniture and decorations of various shapes and sizes. Was that huge olive green thing a beanbag?

I noticed a small kitchen then, and my eyes focused on the coffee machine beside the kettle. I would probably be using that a lot.

John put his hand on my back and guided me past the curious eyes of a few future colleagues of mine, then further toward a dark brown door. The office behind it seemed to be rooted in the corner of the building. I wondered what the view from it was like.

John gave me a wink as he raised his hand and gave the door three gentle knocks. 'He may bark, but he never bites.'

A short, nervous laugh escaped me.

Then, a strangely familiar voice called from inside, 'Come in.'

I frowned. I was certain I had heard that voice before, but where?

John opened the door and stepped aside. I looked at the man in the room, and then my throat constricted, my heart missing several beats. He was staring at the screen of his desktop Mac, seemingly absorbed, and clearly hadn't seen me yet.

Panicking, I glanced at John.

'After you,' he said.

I walked in and froze after five paces, overcome with emotion. Confusion, despair, as well as fear and unbelievable joy, were searing into my heart, causing it to twist rather painfully.

Trepidatious, I watched as Jason's brother finally lifted his gaze and looked at me. His eyebrows leaped up his forehead and his eyes widened beneath them.

Totally stunned, William stared back at me.

7

HAVE WE MET?

For a moment, all I saw was his naked body, both on top of and within me, while he pleasured me into the celestial.

I could scarcely believe my eyes.

This was why I had thought he looked so familiar back then. He was Jason's elder brother!

I recoiled a step, struck by the overwhelming power of his gaze.

Ever since the morning in his flat, I had tried to consign my adventure with him to the depths of my memory, but every night, it had come back to haunt me. I had wondered so many times if I would ever see him again, but I had always assumed it was up to me to decide whether I would. Not even in my wildest dreams had I imagined it would happen like this.

Yet there he was, in the flesh, regarding me with total disbelief. The odds of this happening were astronomical, and it made me question my own convictions. Did coincidences truly exist, or was everything written in the stars? If so, what tales did they hold of my future? And why on earth had they included *him*?

'Will, this is Cara Jane Darby, the new trainee,' John said. 'She's also Jason's flatmate, as you know.'

Paralysed, William kept staring at me. I didn't blame him for struggling so hard to compose himself. Not only had I arrived like lightning from a clear blue sky, but I was also being introduced under an entirely different name.

'Yes, I know she's stunning, but it isn't polite to stare, William,' John said, obviously trying to make humour out of his son's puzzling behaviour.

William charged up from his seat. 'I'm so sorry. For a moment I thought I recognised you,' he apologised to me, but I could tell from the gleam in his eyes that he did in fact recognise me.

Hearing his voice, I realised how much I had missed it. Deep, authoritative and oddly soothing, it whispered of sensual pleasures. How strange it was, to find myself having missed a person I had only encountered once before.

Marvelling at the beauteous view of him, I stopped breathing as he made his graceful approach. Only he could hypnotise me like this. I simply couldn't look away.

'It's a pleasure to make your acquaintance, Miss Darby. I'm William, but you can call me Will like everyone else. I'm looking forward to working with you. I hear your marks are impeccable. I'll personally ensure that you'll get to put theory into practice during your time with us.'

He extended his hand. I directed my gaze to it, feeling the blush mount in my cheeks. I remembered how it had dominated me. A particular memory, of when he had used his grip on my arms to balance the weight of his forceful thrusts, flashed through my mind.

This was outrageous. What was I supposed to do? I couldn't work here, under the leadership of a man who had fucked me into oblivion. How was I supposed to look him in the eye without being reminded of that? How were we supposed to take each other seriously, as professionals, when our current acquaintanceship was composed of carnal indulgence? Would we be able to overlook it? Start anew?

I wanted to cry. This was the worst possible thing that could have happened. I had worked so hard to prove myself eligible for this placement, and now I had quite literally fucked my chance at it. Not only that, but William was also the only man I had ever seriously considered dating, and now he was turning out to be my future boss and my best friend's brother.

'Murphy's law,' Dad whispered in my mind. 'Anything that can go wrong, will go wrong. In other words, whatever can happen, will happen.' Well, I was currently witnessing evidence of that theory. Lesson learned, Dad, albeit too late.

'Y-yeah.' I broke contact with William's eyes and grabbed his familiar hand. His grip was firm around my own, as if he was worried I would disappear if he ever let go.

'Well, I'll leave you to it,' John said and glanced at his watch. 'I've got a meeting in less than two minutes. If there's anything I can help you with, Cara, let me know, but I expect William will take good care of you.'

'Of course,' William said, and there was a faint smile on his mouth when he finally released my hand.

John gave my shoulder a supportive squeeze before he went to the door. I stiffened at the sound of it drawing shut behind him.

'Well, then, *Cara*,' William said, emphasising my real name, and walked back to take a seat on his black desk. He folded his hands above the crotch of his light-grey trousers and studied me with the same crooked smile I had tried so hard to forget.

'Have we met?' he asked, and it knocked the air out of my lungs. The bastard was using my own words against me. How dare he toss that line at me right now?

'I'm quite sure we have,' he said, his eyes narrowing. 'I could have sworn I've seen you before. Have you been on telly? In newspapers?' Not a hint of sympathy was present in features. Choking with emotion, I couldn't dodge even an ounce of his wrath. All I could do was stare at him.

He looked briefly away, nodding. 'Right, it's coming back to me now. I know where I've seen you. It was in my bed, wasn't it? While I fucked you senseless? Yes, I believe so. Now that I think about it, how could I forget? Must be your lies that have got me all confused.'

I took a sharp breath and averted my gaze. Stringing together a single coherent thought proved impossible. I had never been so shocked.

'Please, have a seat.' He gestured to one of the two black chairs in front of his desk. As I fixed my gaze on them, I noticed that his office was rather big. Against the wall on my right stood a white leather sofa, along with a coffee table made of transparent glass.

Incapable of ministering any muscle of my body, I remained in the same place. Seemingly impatient, William leaned back and fetched a document from his desk.

'I gather you're here to sign this contract.'

My gaze dashed to his and I swallowed a huge lump in my throat. It might well have been my heart. Though, since it was currently thundering like a furious storm within my chest, perhaps not.

'I . . .' Averting my eyes, I adjusted my purse on my shoulder.

'You?'

'This is . . . I'm sorry, I'm just . . .'

'Shocked?'

I still couldn't bring myself to look at him, so I only nodded. The mere sight of him was unbearable.

'Cara, take a seat,' he ordered, reminding me of his domineering attitude.

Obeying, because I didn't know what else to do, I approached the chair that stood furthest away from him. As I went, I sensed him observing me with interest.

I was about to sit when he slid off his desk and descended into the chair beside mine. Freezing, I met his eyes and watched him recline. He smirked up at me and gestured to my chair again, triggering me to mentally curse his confidence.

After I had slowly found my seat, he turned his chair toward me and asked bitterly, 'Is it Cara? Or do you prefer going by Sandra?'

I pursed my lips. 'I didn't think I'd see you again.'

'I realise that, and yet here we are.'

Grimacing, I inwardly begged my heart to calm down. From the speed of its beats, I had to be shortening my lifespan.

'I don't quite think that this is a good idea,' I said.

He was quiet for a second. 'What? The placement?'

I nodded.

He scoffed. 'Don't be silly. This isn't an opportunity you should cast aside merely because you've coincidentally fucked your boss, and it's far too late to apply for a spot somewhere else. I can guarantee you won't get it. The competition is intense.'

My breath rasped in my throat at his blunt phrasing and I blushed blood red. I had almost forgotten about his vulgar tongue.

He leaned forward, toward me, and it perturbed me. The tension between us was thick and dense in the air, and it made me feel like I was suffocating. Having him so close wreaked havoc on my emotions. Suddenly I made no sense to myself. All I knew was that I wished he would back away so that I might be able to think clearly.

His eyes focused on my blank facial expression. 'I seem to remember you having a dreadfully sharp tongue. Have you lost your bravado?'

'Are you at all able to be quiet for longer than a second? I need to think!' I snapped, growing increasingly annoyed with his scrutiny. I was trapped in a clusterfuck of a situation, and he wasn't allowing me any mental room to sort it out.

'I honestly can't believe you're Jason's flatmate. All along, you've been within my reach. I'm furious,' he said.

Horribly uncomfortable, I tensed in my seat. At the very best, this was wildly inappropriate, and if he was still adamant about getting me into bed with him, things were going to end in chaos.

He sighed and tossed the contract on his desk. 'When Theresa told me who she'd hired for the position, she mentioned a girl named Cara, studying law. Not Sandra, studying medicine, in fucking *Edinburgh*.' He leaned back. 'At least I've got your number now.'

'What do you want me to say?' I retorted defensively.

'I'd like an apology.'

'Well, I'm sorry, Will. It wasn't personal.'

He nodded and clenched his teeth.

My eyebrows furrowed. 'You have to see why this won't work.'

He glared at me, and I nearly withered under the heat of it. 'I don't. You'll only be here for three months. Had it been indefinite, we'd be having a different conversation, but it's not. We're also adults; we should be able to work our way round it.'

'How do you think John would react if he knew? Or Theresa?' I said sceptically.

He grimaced at the mere idea.

'Exactly,' I said and crossed my arms.

'There won't be any reason for concern unless we behave in a way that warrants it. If you can manage, I guarantee I will too.' He shook his head, and I thought he looked a bit sad. 'I'd hate to see you waste an opportunity like this, especially when knowing it would be my fault.'

My chest tingled. I hadn't expected him to be primarily concerned about how this could affect my future.

I took a deep breath. 'Listen, if we're going to do this, I'd like to make one thing clear. I will not have sex with you again. Do I need to explain why, or are you on board with that?'

I couldn't believe what I had done. Never in my life had I managed something so outrageous before. I had slept with my best friend's brother. Not only that, but he was also going to be my boss for three months. The part of me that had wanted to meet him again had been completely obliterated in the wake of this. I could not get romantically involved with this man. He was completely off limits.

I wondered whether I ought to tell Jason, but immediately decided that I wouldn't. Since it had only been a one-night stand, I thought he would be better off not knowing. Informing him was simply unnecessary, as it wouldn't happen again.

Aloofness spilled from William's eyes while his heart-shaped lips formed a straight line. Added together, his expression made it impossible to guess his thoughts.

'With all due respect, Cara, who says I'd want to?'

My breath hitched. Right. I hadn't thought of that. For a moment, I considered myself despicably conceited. He was the professional between us. Of course he would abandon the idea now that our circumstances had changed. On top of that, he had just discovered that I had lied to him when we met. I wouldn't blame him if the revelation had changed his opinion of me.

'Right. That should make things easier.' I managed to sound stoical, but behind my pretence, I was hiding an awfully bruised ego. Being a woman that William Night desired was the most significant boost I'd had in a long time. At the same time, I had meant for it to turn out this way, so why did I feel so upset? My feelings weren't justified.

'Good. Anyway, we can't really afford to spend more time on this matter,' he said. 'I'm a busy man, and people are counting on me to perform according to schedule. On that note, you should prepare for three intense months.'

It hadn't been necessary to tell me that. I was strapping up for the most challenging three months I would probably ever have to endure, and it wasn't strictly due to the tasks I would be delegated. It was also because I would be facing intensity in the flesh for the better part of ninety days.

I nodded as I guided myself into a more professional frame of mind.

William grabbed the contract and leaned toward me. Now close again, the scent of him struck me with merciless force. Immediately, I was sent down memory lane and into his bedroom, where his alluring scent was etched into the walls, and where his naked skin caressed and guided mine.

I was certain my pupils were dilated when I looked at the contract, though I could barely make sense of a single letter. I was much too distracted by my lust for the testosterone-bomb beside me.

I realised at that moment that there were two sides to this. I was divided. One part of me wanted to fuck him for eternity. The other was adamant about remaining sensible, and sensible did not favour erotic thoughts of William Night when taking our new circumstances into account.

But I wasn't deluded. There was no point in denying that I was drawn to him like a moth to a flame. To claim anything else would be an absolute lie. My whole body tingled where I sat, aching for his sexual attention. He was the sexiest man I had ever encountered, both in mind and body, and he was my best friend's brother, as well as my future boss. Really, he was Satan in a Sunday hat.

Fuck.

He started speaking again, and like a siren, his voice summoned me to my doom. 'Your tasks will mainly include that of a paralegal's. Although I'll be your supervisor for the span of the placement, Elisabeth will be teaching you the basics the first few days. She's a full-time paralegal, close to your age – twenty-five – and very kind and patient. I'll make the introductions once I've guided you through the contract. If you have any questions, don't be shy. Tell me to stop, and I'll explain the implications to the best of my ability. Understood?'

He was awfully authoritative, and although I didn't like to admit it, it had a direct line to my libido. When I had thought things couldn't possibly get any worse, he proved me wrong. William, when focused and professional, was devastatingly attractive. As he was right then, I could watch him for a lifetime, endlessly aroused and fascinated.

When I failed to answer, he looked at me. Utterly susceptible, I looked straight back. Suddenly his eyes widened. Had he guessed my thoughts?

'No, Cara. Do not look at me like that.'

'Like what?'

'Like you want me to claim you across my desk, right now.'

My mouth dried as my breath left me. Though outrageous, the idea made my knickers grow damp. I would have loved every second of it, I was sure – until he surrendered his domination of me to remorse.

'What?' I said feebly.

'You heard me.' He charged up from his seat. Walking around his desk, he reached for the black telecom and raised the handset to his ear. Then he pushed a button and said, 'Ellie, could you come in here for a sec? I need you to do me a favour.' He rang off. Locking eyes with me, he clenched his teeth.

I frowned in confusion, wondering what his thoughts were.

A few seconds later, Ellie, I presumed, knocked on the door.

'Come in,' William said and sank into the seat of his stylish, grey desk chair.

Turning my head, I watched a woman walk in. She had dark brown skin, her curly hair styled into twists that stopped just below her breasts, and she had the sort of smile that would make you turn your head after her on the street.

'You must be Cara,' she said, and she had a voice that would suit a lullaby. What a remarkably soothing voice. Cooing was likely a constant for her.

A little chubby in her anatomy, she came over and extended her small hand. She was quite a short woman, but her breasts were huge. They strained against her dark blue satin blouse, and I couldn't help but catch a glimpse of her cleavage while I sized her up.

Eager to escape the heat of William's attention, I clasped her hand and ascended from my chair. In my heels, I was at least a head taller than her.

'That's me, yes.'

Her smile transitioned into a full-blown grin. 'I'm Elisabeth, but please, call me Ellie.'

'Ellie,' William said, 'please see to it that Cara finds a space where she can read through her contract. I've got work that requires my immediate attention.'

'Of course, Will. Whatever you need.'

'Thanks. Did you manage to contact GreenPark for me?'

'Yes. I've sent you an email about it. The appointment should already be synchronised with your schedule.'

William looked at me with a smirk. 'Watch and learn.' He gave Ellie a fond wink.

'Certainly. But Mr Night' – it felt incredibly weird to address him that way – 'what shall I do once I've signed?'

He frowned at how I had addressed him, but I had done it deliberately to create as much psychological distance between us as possible. It was purely a defensive mechanism to remind me of our professional relationship.

'I told you to call me Will, Cara.' He extended the contract to me across his desk. 'If you've any questions, take notes and bring them to me once you've finished reading through. If you don't, simply sign and hand it over to me.'

Nodding, I walked over, but with each pace, the electric current between us grew more intense. Our gazes met as I grabbed the contract, and no words were required. I understood precisely what his eyes meant to convey.

He wanted to fuck me again, and he wanted to do it now.

Shocking myself, I realised that if our circumstances had been different, I would have succumbed to the desire.

I turned my back to him and said, 'Thank you, Mr Night.'

I thought I heard him curse under his breath, but I wasn't sure.

8

MOMENTARY LOVER

Ellie was guiding the way to a vacant desk when warm brown eyes met mine across the room. The owner was walking straight toward us, seemingly on his way to William's office, but he came to an abrupt halt just before he passed. Visibly confused, his attention flickered between Ellie and me.

Could this day get any worse? If he learned that 'Sandra' and I were the same person, it was only a matter of time before rumours about my previous encounter with William would flood the office. As their latest trainee, that was the last thing I wanted.

Ellie paused to regard him. Meanwhile, Andrew kept studying me with a bewildered expression on his face. Exerting every ounce of the self-discipline I had harnessed over the years, I managed to remain composed. While feigning obliviousness, I returned his gaze with eyes that claimed innocence.

'Sandra?' he asked, sounding surprised. 'What are you doing here?'

Ellie came to my rescue. 'Sandra? This is Cara Jane Darby, our new trainee.'

Perplexed, Andrew's eyes did a sweep of my body. Faint pink coloured his cheeks and he frowned. Clearing his throat, he lifted his gaze to mine. I gave him a small smile, sympathising with his confusion.

'Sorry, I must have confused you with someone else,' he said embarrassedly. 'I could have sworn you were her.'

Ellie giggled.

'No worries,' I said.

He offered his hand. 'I'm Andrew Thompson, but everyone calls me Andy.'

Nodding, I clasped his hand and gave him another small smile. 'Cara.'

'Are you showing her around, Ellie?'

'Sort of.'

His attention shifted onto me again. 'Why not William? I thought he was supposed to be her supervisor.'

He was slick! I was certain he had only asked to observe my reaction. Thankfully, my face didn't even twitch.

I said, 'He had work to do. He seems delightful, though.'

Andy tittered. 'He seems delightful? First time I've heard that. "Delightful".' He glanced at something behind me. 'Just remember that where other people might end a sentence with a question mark, Will usually finishes with a full stop. It's just who he is and always has been, but as long as you're aware of that, I'm sure you'll be fine.'

I was almost tempted to say, 'No shit, Andy. I've already gathered as much,' but I refrained.

Ellie chuckled. 'I haven't briefed her on what to expect of Will's general behaviour yet, so thank you for taking care of that.'

Andy gave me a wink. 'I've got your back, sweetheart.' Looking at Ellie, he asked, 'So he's busy right now? I've got something I'd like to run by him, preferably before his meeting with the lawyers from Lightning Charge this afternoon.'

'He's always busy, but he hasn't got anything other than paperwork until then. I'm sure he could spare you five minutes if it's urgent and you ask nicely.'

'Great, thanks.' Steering his eyes back to mine, Andy grinned. 'Pleasure meeting you, *Cara*.'

'You too.'

As he walked away, he shook his head, and I had a suspicion as to why. I feared he would ask William about me in only a few moments. If he did, I prayed William would either tell him a lie or ensure his silence some other way.

'Seems you've got a replica out there,' Ellie said and started walking again. 'But I'm sure her freckles aren't as adorable as yours.'

Her compliment made me flash her a grin. I had always been grateful for my freckles, and they were in fact Aaron's favourite part of my face.

My smile faded as I thought of him. Now that I was bound to encounter William time and again, I was certain it would wreak havoc on the dynamic between Aaron and me. It had taken me a week to recover from my session with William, and Aaron had spent it growing worried about our arrangement. How was I supposed to manage this time around?

By not flirting with William, I thought. I was motivated to manage that for several reasons: for the sake of my placement, for the sake of my friendship with Jason, for the sake of my arrangement with Aaron, and last, but certainly not least, for the sake of my sanity, my education and finally my career.

'Here we are.' Ellie brought me out of my thoughts and motioned to a vacant desk.

'Thanks,' I said, perhaps too eagerly, but I was in dire need of privacy.

I would have to call Olivia as soon as I left. She was the sole person I could confide in about this, and I was desperate to talk to someone. I would use her as a soundboard to air my thoughts. Perhaps then, I would be able to make sense of this dreadful mess.

As I went over my contract, I found nothing I would like to discuss. Unsurprisingly, it was faultless. I hadn't expected any less of a law firm. However, I couldn't help but read the contract with William's voice in my head, because I could imagine that he had penned it. Authoritative and impatient, his otherwise sensual voice barked every single word at me. It caused a constant grimace to cover my face as I read through.

Bloody hell, he was everywhere – even in my head. I felt like I was suffocating.

'Cara,' he called. That wasn't where I was in my contract? My head snapped up when I realised he was actually speaking to me. Turning, I discovered him behind me, slightly bent over my shoulder.

I immediately recoiled toward my desk. 'Shit, you scared me.'

'Not my fault you're so oblivious to your surroundings.'

'I was concentrating.' My gaze flitted to his brown leather shoes. 'I hadn't expected Bigfoot to move so quietly.'

Amusement danced in his eyes before he briefly closed them to refocus.

'I've got ten minutes to spare, should you want to go over your contract now.'

'I was just finishing.'

'Then let's continue in my office.'

A normal person would have said, 'Right. Shall we continue in my office?' But of course, he was everything except that.

Ascending from my seat, I collected my contract to heed his command. As I started walking, his hand landed on my back. I immediately stiffened. Did he think I required a compass to find his office?

'I can walk on my own,' I muttered.

Devoid of emotion, he quietly said, 'I'd prefer not to walk behind you. My eyes keep landing on your beautiful bum, and I'd hate to sexualise you like that.'

My cheeks grew hot and red. I charged into his office and watched him shut the door.

'You can't speak to me like that,' I said. 'I was actually considering signing, but you just reminded me why I shouldn't.'

'Calm down.'

I gaped. How could he, as an able lawyer, possibly find his comment justifiable?

'Calm down? Are you actually telling me to "calm down" when what you just said clearly constitutes sexual harassment under the Equality Act of 2010?'

His eyes widened with shock, and the sound of his sharp inhalation satisfied me deeply.

'Do you tell Ellie that you prefer not to walk behind her since you'll sexualise her if you do? As if that's acceptable behaviour?'

He blew his cheeks out and gripped his hips. 'No.' He had the grace to look ashamed of himself. 'You're right. It's completely unacceptable, I'm sorry. It won't happen again.'

'It better not.' I folded my arms.

We stared at each other in silence. Finally, he let out a loud sigh.

'Honestly, Cara, I truly am sorry. I didn't mean for it to come across that way. It's just . . . Well, there's really no excuse, but I've got my roles a tad confused today. Give me some time to adapt and I promise I'll do better. Seeing you again wasn't something I expected, and certainly not here. It's messed with my head, especially because it's you. I just need to readjust, to start regarding you as a colleague, rather than as my . . .'

I could tell he was searching for the appropriate label by his fleeting gaze.

'One-night stand?' I filled in.

His eyes shot to mine, and the sudden certainty they contained made it clear that my suggestion hadn't resonated with him.

'I was going to say momentary lover.'

My cheeks prickled at his phrasing. He obviously thought our night together had been more meaningful than the label 'one-night stand' typically implied, and I found consolation in that, because I felt the same way.

'Yeah, well, you're not alone in that,' I said. 'How do you think I've experienced all this? Not only have I managed to fuck my best friend's brother, but he also just happens to be my new boss. And yet I still manage not to sexualise you – outwardly, anyhow.'

I wished I hadn't added the last part, but my mouth had spoken before my mind caught up.

William's eyes glimmered, his stare growing so intense that I whimpered. Why had I said that?

A smug smile crept across his lips as he propped his back against the door. Folding his arms, he studied me until I felt ready to expire.

'Outwardly, you say?'

'Mr Night.' Impatience filled my tone. I was not a woman to be trifled with right now.

Smirking, he said, 'I admire your resolve, Cara, but why do you insist on calling me Mr Night?'

'It's all part of the resolve you so admire.'

'What?'

'I'm creating psychological distance between us, and it's working, so I've no intention of stopping.'

He burst out laughing then, and I found it awfully mocking.

'Fuck this,' I grumbled and dropped the contract on his desk. I wasn't going to sign it. This would never work. The man wasn't taking me seriously at all, and I found it extremely offensive. I was serious about this placement. That meant that I was determined to put our sensual past behind us, but he kept insisting on reminding me of it. He wasn't treating me like every other employee at all, and that wasn't something I found acceptable. I wanted to be treated like anyone else in this firm, like we had never shared a bed. I couldn't fathom why he would assume it was all right to do anything else.

My action murdered his laughter. With the eyes of a hawk, he watched me approach him as he stood in front of the only sensible exit, but if he didn't move, perhaps the windows of his office would become sensible options too.

'Cara.'

I hated when he used that tone, because it exuded power not even I dared question.

'Sign the contract.'

I reached for the handle, but his hand intercepted. Grabbing my wrist, he dragged my hand away, and then he completely shocked me. Entwining our fingers, he fixed his gaze on them and held my hand most affectionately.

Overwhelmed by the intimacy, I followed his stare. My heart bashed on my ribcage until I wondered if it would explode within me. It felt like my whole body was vibrating.

What the hell was going on with me? Was this truly just lust or was I infatuated with this man? No, I couldn't be. I hardly knew him.

'Sign the contract, Cara.'

Speechless, I kept staring at our hands. I was trying to make sense of my feelings, but it was impossible. I just couldn't seem to grasp the extent of his influence. All I knew was that I had never felt this way before, as if I was about to burst with sheer delight, and he was only holding my hand.

'I promise I'll be good to you,' he said and, much to my regret, let go.

Paralysed, I watched him get my contract from his desk. As he came back, he withdrew a pen from his pocket and gave me a grave look.

'I won't let you waste an opportunity like this, and I'm not saying that because I want to get in your knickers. I'm saying it as one solicitor to an aspiring one. We'll work it out. We'll just have to communicate. This is a strange situation, but we're both adults. We'll work our way round it. Please don't squander your potential just because you happen to have shared a bed with me.'

I swallowed, hypnotised by his power. Still paralysed, I merely stared at him, undecided. I just couldn't decide!

Sighing, he grabbed my shoulder and made me face the door. Next, he shoved the pen into my hand, retreated a step, and held the contract against the door.

'Three months, Cara. You'll survive, and you'll be thanking yourself, and me, for the rest of your life.'

He resembled the Devil, urging me to sell him my soul in exchange for perpetual success. Was I really going to take that deal?

I looked at him for some time, contemplating, until I finally decided that he was right. This placement would most definitely assist my career, and I wasn't about to waste it over an issue like this. Like he had said, we were adults. We would work our way round it. If his behaviour escalated into being truly intolerable, I reminded myself that I could always notify the HR department, though I hoped it wouldn't come to that. Seeing as he was Jason's brother and John's son, I would rather avoid going to such measures, but if he didn't stop sexualising me, I would have to. And so, since my career was in fact at stake, I finally decided to sign the contract.

My hand was shaking when I put the pen to the dotted line, but it stilled with revived confidence as I began to write my signature. As soon as I finished, he snatched the document away. Air stormed out of my mouth as I embraced my new reality.

I had signed. I was trapped with him now, for three long months.

'There,' he said, audibly pleased.

My body was rigid while my eyes followed his. He walked around his desk, where he stored my contract in the top drawer.

'Now, then.' He exhaled and slumped down in his chair. Grinning at me, he spread his arms in a jovial manner. 'Will you have dinner with me today?'

Grinding my teeth, I glared back. 'Are you taking the piss?'

'Not at all.' He chuckled. 'Seeing as you'll be stuck with me for the better part of three months, I reckon we should get to know each other better. Dressed, this time.'

There he went again. I would never admit it out loud, but the man had wit. All the same, I didn't appreciate the reminder it contained this time around. Despairing, I looked away and shook my head.

'You're unbelievable. Unless there's anything else, I'd like to leave now.'

'It's a harmless dinner, Cara.'

Nothing involving that man was harmless.

'See you later,' I said and opened the door.

'Tell Jason I miss him, will you? Ask him if I can come over this week.'

'Ask him yourself,' I replied without thinking, then I froze.

Jason. I had almost forgotten about him. Thank goodness William had reminded me.

Shutting the door, I turned back around and crossed my arms.

'Speaking of Jason, I'd rather he didn't find out about us.'

William's smile grew cunning. 'Is that so?'

'Can you promise you won't tell him?'

Bringing his pen to his mouth, he chewed at the end of it and studied me for some time. 'Depends.'

'William, seriously.' I was reaching the end of my tether. 'How do you think he'd react if he found out? He'd be awkward around the both of us to say the least, and I'd like to avoid that. God knows, he might even get angry with me.'

'Have dinner with me, then. If you do, I won't tell him.'

I gripped my hips. 'Are you listening to yourself? You're abusing your power. This is blackmailing.'

A smug chuckle slipped out of his mouth, irritating me.

'You know, you really are a right arsehole,' I said.

He raised a brow. 'Says the woman who deceives like it's second nature to her.'

That hurt, especially because it was deserved. I had lied to him when we met, and now I was asking him not to tell Jason about us.

I opened the door, my chest aching. 'Do what you want, then, but if you have any regard for my feelings, you won't tell him.'

'Wait, wait.' He sighed. 'I won't tell him, Cara. I promise.'

I scanned him, unsure if I could trust him. 'Really?'

'Really.' He nodded gravely. 'I was only taking the piss, I'm sorry.'

I pressed my lips together and turned to walk out.

'Hold on, I'll walk you down,' he said. 'I'm about to have lunch.'

I didn't wait. I headed straight toward the lifts. Andy and Ellie were waiting just in front of them. To my regret, William managed to catch up with me by the time the doors opened to let us in, and his pace grabbed the attention of both Andy and Ellie.

'Christ, Will, you must be starving,' Ellie said.

'Tight schedule.'

During the brief journey, Andy traded regular glances with William over my head. They sent each other lopsided smiles, but Ellie paid them no attention, which made me think that the two men behaved like this on a regular basis. It wasn't surprising when taking into account that they were best friends, but it annoyed me nevertheless, because I was certain I was the cause of their current amusement.

Stealing a glance at William in the mirror, I wondered if he had intentionally misled me earlier – when he had implied that he didn't want to sleep with me again. In the end, his statement had been rather equivocal. 'Who says I'd want to?' didn't erase all room for doubt. He hadn't actually denied anything. Had he deliberately phrased it that way to misguide me? To buy himself more time to analyse how to proceed? In fact, he might only have said it to retaliate for a bruised ego.

The possibility intrigued me. Had he truly abandoned the idea of me, or was he only weighing up which route to take in order to win me over?

The impression I had of him was that he was not inclined to cease his pursuit when he had his sights set on a prize. He was far too stubborn. Last time we met, he had ardently tried to persuade me to give him a chance. The question remaining was: was I still the prize?

'Oh my God, I just recalled – do you know what Andy did earlier?' Ellie whirled around and faced William. Laughing, she said, 'He thought Cara was somebody else, so he called her Sandra. You should've seen him. I've never seen him quite so confused.'

'Did he?' William replied, and it was clear from his tone that he was highly amused.

Too curious to stop myself, I stole another glance at him. He met it with a gleam dancing in his eyes, and I immediately grasped that they had talked about it behind closed doors.

Fuck.

When we reached the ground floor, Ellie and Andy exited before William and I did. William grabbed my arm, stalling me, while the others kept on walking.

I faced him.

'Andy knows,' he said.

'You told him?' I snapped, both irked and defensive.

He glared back. 'He's a fucking lawyer, Cara – he's not dim. Of course he recognised you.'

'Shit,' I whined and stamped my foot.

Blinking, he dropped his gaze to it. 'Did you really just stamp your foot?'

'William! If Andy spills, it's only a matter of time before everyone knows!'

His grip tightened on my arm. 'He won't tell anyone. He's my best friend, and he's got my back. Always.'

'Tell anyone what?' an exceptionally gorgeous woman asked as she entered the lift. With thick raven hair that cascaded down to the middle of her back, she took my breath away. Her upturned, dark brown eyes met mine, and her plump, pinkish-beige lips tucked into a vague smile beneath her small nose. She turned her attention to William. Once she saw him, her smile stretched into a grin.

'Mind your own business, Vi,' William said and dragged me out with him. Casting a glance at her over my shoulder, I saw her fold her arms over the ample chest of her slender and curvaceous figure.

Intrigued, I asked, 'Who's that?'

'Violet Rodriguez. She's my partner for a transaction I'm currently working on.'

'She's gorgeous,' I said. When I looked back at William, he was staring at me with an unreadable expression on his face.

Returning to our conversation, I asked, 'Do you swear Andy won't tell?'

His jaw flexed. 'Yes. But don't be surprised if he gives you any funny looks. He laughed until he cried earlier, in my office.'

Well, at least someone was enjoying the chaos of our circumstance. Sulking, I looked at the exit of the building.

'I suppose I'll be seeing you around, then,' I said.

'I guess, yeah.'

A day ago, I would have kissed him goodbye. Strange to think of that.

'Later, then. Enjoy your lunch,' I said and looked up. My chest tightened at the expression on his face. He was watching me with a strange sort of longing in his eyes.

He merely gave me a nod, and I felt his gaze on my back as I walked out.

§ § §

'He's your boss!' Olivia shouted down the phone, totally shocked.

Trying to remain calm, I asked, 'What am I supposed to do, Livy?'

'Christ, Cara! Is Jason aware?'

'Of course not,' I said. 'Had it been serious between Will and me, then I probably would have told him, but forgive me if I don't feel like telling my best friend and flatmate that I completely sexually exploited his elder brother.'

'Yeah, don't tell Jason. I wouldn't want to know if I were him. But how did Will react when he saw you?'

Once I had given her the scoop on my day, she huffed out a long, loud breath. 'Shit. You're in it now, aren't you?'

'Livy,' I whined. 'That's not helping. And the bastard even tried to blackmail me into having dinner with him today – after I'd signed, and he'd promised to behave. Said he'd tell Jason about us if I didn't accept.'

'That's outrageous! Please, don't tell me you agreed.'

'Of course not.'

'I can't believe he tried that.'

'Me neither. I'm livid.'

'He must be really taken with you.'

'I don't care. It's completely out of the question. You'd think he'd realise that when *he's* the professional between us.'

'Yeah, he was out of order. I'm so sorry, Cara. I honestly don't know what to say. I hope for your sake that he won't tell Jason.'

'He promised me he wouldn't.'

'Well, then I hope he'll keep it. But, aside from the shock of meeting him again in the role of your boss, have you considered what this means now that you're living with Jason?'

'Yes,' I whined again.

'We both know Jason's very close with his brother. To be honest, it's a wonder we hadn't met him sooner.'

'I know.'

'And now that you've just moved in with Jason, you're bound to see Will a lot more, even before you start work.'

'I'm well aware of this, Livy.'

'Sorry. I wish I could be of more help, but I've honestly got no idea what to say. It's a huge mess for sure, of epic proportions.'

I sighed. 'Well, I appreciate the moral support.'

'It's the least I can do. I feel like you've been my acting psychologist for the past three years. About time I return the favour. Anyway, are you on your way here?'

I closed my eyes and stopped walking. 'Fuck.' I had completely forgotten that I was supposed to revise with her and Aaron today.

'Yeah, Aaron's here. Do you think you'll be able to act normal?'

I briefly considered whether to go home instead, but I decided against it since Jason was likely to be there. His shift at the A&E department at the hospital didn't start till two o'clock.

'Well, it's not like heading home would be any better. Honestly, between the two of them, Jason's the one I'll have the hardest time facing.'

'Yeah, I get that. I wish there were something I could do.'

I sighed. 'Thanks. I appreciate the sentiment. Anyway, I'm sure I'm just overreacting. It's not like anything's changed. Will and I aren't going to have sex again. The only thing that's different now is that I will inevitably be seeing him again, and that's what's messing with my head. I've never been in this situation before. I've never had to face Aaron while knowing I'm in touch with one of my previous bed partners, and I've definitely never had to face Jason while knowing I've fucked his brother.'

'Yeah, that's enough to mess with anyone's head.'

'Right? And you know, the worst part is that I feel like I'm keeping them in the dark about something when, really, it's actually none of their business.' I rubbed my forehead. 'Gosh, listen to me. William has promised not to say anything, so there's really no reason I should treat this as a problem.'

'Again, Cara, your rationality astounds me. I wish I were half as level-headed as you.'

I released a mirthless laugh. 'Honestly, I'm all talk and no trousers right now. Truth is I'm still all over the place.'

'But the fact that you're aware of that obviously means you're slowly coming to terms with things. As you said, you've had quite a shock. Let it settle first. Once it subsides, I'm sure you'll be able to go about your business as usual.'

Her words fuelled my motivation to get over this sooner rather than later. 'You're right. Of course I will.'

'That's the Cara I know and love.'

'I don't know what I'd do without you, Livy. Thanks for listening to my rant, and for existing.'

She laughed. 'Right back at you, darling. I'll see you in a bit, then.'

'Yes.'

§ § §

I thought I deserved an Oscar for how well I handled facing Aaron. There was both a positive and a negative side to that, because while it enabled me to maintain harmony, it also meant I was a skilled liar. The latter wasn't something I took pride in – I despised dishonesty – but I reminded myself that there was a difference between being honest and being open, and there was no need for me to be transparent, which meant being both. If I was confronted by either Aaron or Jason, I would tell the truth without hesitation, but to tell them unsolicited? I couldn't see what good it would do other than relieving my conscience.

It was nearing nine o'clock when the three of us decided to leave the library. Olivia had stayed behind for longer than usual, and I suspected it was because she had wanted to help me carry the burden of entertaining Aaron after today's events. She would never know how much I appreciated that.

By the time we parted ways, Aaron was still in a delightful mood. It was clear that he didn't suspect a thing. I hoped I would handle facing

Jason equally well, but part of me doubted it. There was something about my friendship with Jason that was completely unique, because I genuinely regarded him as a sibling. Total transparency was something I had practised in his company ever since we met. To look him in the eye, while knowing how his actual sibling performed in bed – as well as against the wall, or on the dining table – wasn't something I looked forward to because of that. But I would have to, and I hated it. This was the first time ever that I was keeping something from him, and I prayed it would also be the last.

Slight panic grabbed hold of me when I unlocked the front door and discovered him right behind it. From his outfit, I could tell he had just come home from work.

He turned toward me, looking surprised. 'You're home late.'

'Yeah. I was at the library with Aaron and Livy.'

He knelt to untie his shoes. 'I see. Have you had dinner?'

I walked in. 'Yeah. How was your shift at the hospital?' I closed the door behind me.

'Hectic, as usual.'

'I can only imagine.'

Apprehensive, I scanned his body language for any sign of veiled anger or disappointment, but came up empty. He didn't look like he had the slightest clue. Had William kept his promise?

All of a sudden, a knowing smile claimed his mouth. With a mischievous twinkle in his blue eyes – eyes that were insufferably similar to his brother's – he met mine and stretched back up.

Maybe William had told him after all.

'I heard you met my brother,' he said and slowly took off his shoes.

Had William told him that?

To hide from his gaze – and potential wrath – I faced the wall as I untied my coat.

'I did. Impressive man.'

A short laugh escaped him. 'Really? You'd call him impressive? Perhaps I should have warned you, but he can be a bit of a dick sometimes. You get used to it, though, and if anyone can hold their own, it's you.'

'Good to know.'

'Anyway, I wasn't aware you'd been hired for the job as *his* legal assistant. Dad told me just today.'

So it was John he had spoken to. I found relief in that.

'Neither was I. Safe to say I was surprised.'

'Well, you'll have plenty of time to get to know him before you start. We tend to hang out at the weekends to watch football together. He was actually meant to come over last Friday, but I had to cancel because I was asked to take a shift at the hospital.'

Since I could only imagine the shock that situation would have made for, I counted my blessings. Jason would certainly have learned the truth had it turned out that way, so I thanked the heavens for small mercies, because thus far, he seemed unaware.

'Right. Looking forward to it.'

'I actually think you'll get on really well.' Far better than he knew. 'You're sort of similar in a lot of ways.'

'Yes, I got the same impression when I met him.' After hanging up my coat, I grabbed my bag and headed for my bedroom. 'Anyway, I'm knackered, so I think I'll go to bed.'

'Mind if I have a shower first?'

'Go ahead,' I said and shut the door between us. I walked straight to my bed and collapsed on top of it. What a day. It was tempting to never leave my room again. At least here, I was safe.

Or was I? With Jason as my best friend, would I ever truly be rid of William?

9

SKIN OF THE NIGHT

By Friday, I was no longer anxious about William's inevitable presence in my life. The process of coming to terms with it had been aided by the fact that I hadn't heard a word from him since Monday, and Jason hadn't shown any signs of being aware of our one-night stand either. Clearly, William had kept his word so far. Besides, considering how busy Jason currently was with work at the hospital, I doubted I would be seeing his brother much. Jason barely had time to catch his breath between shifts. The A&E department was clearly no joke. I had never seen him this exhausted.

'Shit,' I muttered when I eyed the time. Lifting my head from Aaron's bare chest, I sat up in his bed and put my phone aside. 'It's half six already. I should go.'

'You might as well sleep over.'

I brushed my hand across his torso, caressing his soft brown skin. 'No, I didn't bring my things.' I climbed out of his bed and picked up my clothes from the floor. 'Besides, I've got to assemble my new wardrobe and desk. I'm in dire need of a quiet place to revise, and I can't be bothered to head for the library every time, especially with our first exam coming up next Friday. I'd save so much time reading at home.'

'Course you can't,' he said amusedly.

Turning, I caught him admiring my state of undress.

'What do you mean by that?' I asked and pulled my blouse over my head.

He met my eyes as a smile climbed to his kiss-swollen mouth. 'That you've always been a devout subscriber to efficiency. I'm sure you'd buy a new microwave if it meant you could save ten seconds heating your meals.'

A laugh snuck out of me. 'Well, who would want to lie on their deathbed knowing they'd wasted hours that could have been minutes waiting for their meals to cook?'

'People who don't permanently live in the future.'

'I can live in the moment.'

He didn't look convinced. 'If that were true, you'd stay the night.'

My shoulders sank. 'That's not fair.'

He sighed. 'Maybe.'

Pushing himself up, he climbed out of the bed and reached for his boxers on the floor. 'Mum was wondering if you'd like to come for dinner on Sunday.'

It had been over a month since I last saw his mother Mary-Anne, so I was slightly disappointed that I would have to decline. Mary-Anne was one of few role models in my life – I admired her resilience as well as her strength – so I adored spending time with her.

I had met her for the first time over dinner two years ago, and I had learned then that Aaron's father had been both an alcoholic and an incorrigible gambler, so Mary-Anne had eventually been forced to leave him when Aaron was only four. He hadn't been present in Aaron's life since then, but I was vaguely aware that he had taken out substantial loans during their marriage to settle his gambling debt, and that he had also spent a considerable amount of the sum that Mary-Anne had set aside to finance Aaron's eventual education on his troublesome habits.

With barely a penny to her name, Mary-Anne had raised Aaron to be the exemplary man he was today. Through hard work as a waitress, she had given him the most comfortable life she could. Her story inspired me, and so did her character. In fact, upon meeting her, I had quickly realised where Aaron had inherited his patient and constructive nature from, although Mary-Anne was slightly more forthright than her son.

As I pulled on the black, low-denier stockings that I had worn under my grey pencil skirt, I cast Aaron a glance. 'I'd love to, but Jason's parents have already invited me for dinner that day. If she's got time next week, tell her I'd love to come then instead.'

'Right, I'd forgotten that. I'll ask her.'

'Good.'

He pulled on his boxers and sat down on the bed. Reclining onto his forearms, he watched me get dressed.

'So I won't be seeing you anytime soon, then, now that you'll be revising at home.'

'Jason's working on Monday. His shift starts at two, so you could always come over and revise at my place then.'

He nodded. 'I'd like that.'

'Mind if I invite Livy?'

'Not at all.'

'Shall I invite Cassie as well?' My tone was playful, but truthfully, I asked because I wanted to check if I was on the brink of losing him to her.

'Don't be a tit.' He rolled his eyes, and that was all the reassurance I needed.

§ § §

With a screw in my mouth, I was sitting within the frame of my new wardrobe, listening to Foals, when I heard a key being inserted into the front door. Frowning, I put the manual screwdriver aside. Was it half-past eight already? Reaching for my phone, I saw that it was only eight.

Leaving the screw on the floor, I called, 'Hiya. You're home early.' I stood up. 'How was work? I'd planned to cook dinner for you, but I started assembling the wardrobe that I ordered from IKEA,' I said as I walked toward my bedroom door. 'So I thought we could just order something since—' I gasped when I turned toward the front door. It wasn't Jason.

'What are *you* doing here?' I asked, my heart pounding. Heat flooded my face, and I dared not imagine its new colour. Adrenaline heightened my senses, making me hyperaware of his presence.

William was the last person I had expected to see, so I hadn't been remotely prepared to endure the power he exuded, nor had I been prepared to regard the gorgeous view of him.

It really wasn't fair that anyone should be so attractive, especially when considering our circumstances. In his navy suit, he looked nothing short of edible. To think I had seen him stripped of it, naked in all his glory – I could hardly believe it.

All at once, the anxiety I had managed to overcome since Monday recovered in full.

A crooked smile of amusement emerged on William's mouth, and the sight evoked the memory of how lovely it had felt to kiss those lips.

'I'm thrilled to see you too, Cara. I've missed you.'

I hadn't thought my cheeks could become any hotter, but he proved me wrong.

'Work was fine, thanks for asking,' he went on. 'And don't worry about dinner. I'm charmed you planned to cook for me, though.'

'You're such a knob,' I grumbled, but that only made him laugh.

'Sorry.' He raised his hands as if to claim innocence, and I saw a keychain hanging around his forefinger. 'I didn't mean to startle you. I'm here to watch the match with Jason.'

'Match?'

'Chelsea's playing at eight. I've come straight from work, so Jason said to let myself in. He should be home soon, though, so you won't have to endure me on your own for long.'

'You've got a key?'

He stored the keychain inside his suit jacket. 'I've had a key ever since he moved in.'

My eyebrows arched. 'Good to know.'

'He didn't tell you I'd be coming over?'

'No. Must've slipped his mind.'

'He's been rather stressed lately.'

'Clearly.'

Unsure of what to do with myself, I folded my arms and glanced over my shoulder. 'Well, make yourself at home, then, I suppose.'

'Thanks.' He shrugged out of his jacket and bent to loosen his brown leather shoes.

'I'll be in my room if you need anything.'

Still bent over, he turned his head and looked up at me with a smile.

'Really? I'd have thought you would bolt the door.'

Chuckling, I turned toward my room. 'Don't push your luck.'

'Is that Foals I hear?' he asked then. Surprised, I froze in the doorway. Did he share my taste in music as well? If he did, I wasn't sure I would ever discover a single flaw in him.

'Might be.'

As he stretched up to kick off his shoes, he gave me a winsome grin. 'You're into rock?'

'Among other genres.'

'Which is your favourite?'

I swivelled to face him. 'By Foals?'

'No, genre.'

I shrugged. 'Probably rock.'

'And here I thought you couldn't get any more perfect.'

At this rate, red was becoming the permanent colour of my face.

'Do you have a favourite band?' he asked as he took the liberty of coming closer.

'What's it to you?'

'Oh, come on, Cara.' He smiled and delved his hands in his pockets. 'You already know the answer to that.'

My heart raced when he stopped in front of me, awfully close. It felt like an electric current charged between our bodies, begging me to close the gap. I wondered what would happen if I did. Would he push me away or would he press me against him?

'Do I?' I smiled back.

'Yes.' His tempting mouth spread into a grin, his hypnotic eyes glimmering above.

'I'm not sure I do.'

He shook his head and turned his profile to me, still grinning. 'Well, I spent a whole night getting to know a woman named Sandra. Don't get me wrong, she was perfectly charming, but there's something about the real you that I find even more . . .' He met my eyes again. 'Riveting.'

I inhaled sharply. Were we flirting? It certainly felt like it. If we were, I knew we ought to stop, but I just couldn't help myself.

I pursed my lips, trying to suppress my smile, but it was ineffective. 'Is that so?'

'I'm afraid so, yes.'

My face was unbearably hot, and it didn't help that he kept staring at me, keenly observing my reactions.

'Well, I'm sorry to say that I'm actually much more boring than Sandra is.'

His smile turned crooked. 'I'll be the judge of that.'

I averted my eyes, trying to keep my feelings in check, but it was futile. They ran amok within me, filling my chest with exhilarating sensations.

'What's your favourite band, Cara?' he prompted, and when I looked back, his gaze radiated furtive amusement.

I swallowed, but my throat remained tight. 'It's hard to say. I've got several, and I can't choose between them. Though, right now, the band I listen to the most is probably Arctic Monkeys.'

'Excellent choice.'

'How about you?'

'Well, I feel similarly, but Pink Floyd is the band I always return to, so perhaps I should go with them.'

I chuckled. 'Old-school. Nice. They're at the top of my list as well.'

'Really?'

'Really.'

He looked elated. 'Then I propose you come over to my place one day. We can listen to old vinyl records together over a glass of wine.'

'Of course you'd propose that.'

'Is that a Yes?'

I laughed. 'It's a definitive No.'

'Gutted,' he joked, though I suspected he was slightly serious.

'You're relentless.' Still smiling, I shook my head and entered my room.

Lingering in the doorway, William scanned the chaos on the floor. 'I see you've abandoned Sandra to become Bob the Builder instead.'

The amount of wit his tongue ceaselessly whipped around was outstanding, and it had a direct line to my sense of humour. Before I knew it, I was laughing my head off. The joke was just so unexpected, and so apposite.

'William, oh my God.'

'You've got an adorable laugh,' he said then, and it shut me up at once. Something fluttered in my chest, and I could feel myself blushing yet again.

Smiling, he leaned against the doorpost and studied the neat pile of folded clothes in the corner of my bedroom. Wondering what was so interesting about it, I looked over and realised that his T-shirt was lying at the top.

'You can have it back,' I said and gestured to it.

He shook his head. 'I've no need for it. Besides, it looks better on you.'

My eyebrows arched and my lips parted, forming a disbelieving smile. He was so damn slick.

'I'm guessing that's supposed to become a wardrobe,' he said and jerked his head toward my project. I didn't fail to notice that he changed the subject before I could insist on giving back his T-shirt. He obviously wanted me to keep it, but why? Was he simply being generous or was it something else?

'Yeah.'

'Need any help?'

I sat down within the frame of the wardrobe and gave him a sceptical look. Upper class as he was, I doubted he had ever done similar work.

'Do you even know how to use a screwdriver?'

From the expression that crossed his face, it was apparent that I had offended him. 'Of course. It's not exactly rocket science, is it?'

'Well, I appreciate the offer, but I'm good, thanks.'

'All right, then, Bob. I'll leave you to it. Give me a shout if you get stuck.'

I strangled a laugh. 'Won't happen.'

Part of me definitely preferred him gone, but another wished he would stay for ever.

When I heard the characteristic sound of a crowd cheering on their team, I realised he had switched on the TV. Hyperaware of his proximity, I contemplated whether to shut the door between us, but I decided against it. I was desperate to maintain some level of control over his whereabouts so that I might predict a sudden arrival.

On edge, I focused on my labour, but when half an hour had passed, the music that played in the background had swept me away into a state of mindfulness. Activities like these were thoroughly therapeutic. For the first time in weeks, I hadn't given my exams a single thought within the span of thirty minutes. Even William's presence had faded into the background.

But my state of relaxation soon transformed into frustration, because apparently, several screws were missing. I searched the floor for the assembly instructions. That was when I noticed a pair of feet in the doorway. Right in front of them, I discovered the document.

My heart missed a beat and I lifted my gaze. How long had he been standing there? Our eyes collided, and I saw humour basking in his.

'Sounds like you've fucked up,' he said and reached down for the assembly instructions.

Since I wanted to present myself as capable of the task, I said, 'I haven't. A few screws are missing.'

He eyed me dubiously, opened the instructions, and skipped a few pages until he located the step I was currently stuck at.

'Give me that,' I demanded. 'Don't you have a match to watch?'

'Half-time,' he said and approached to assess my work. Squatting next to me, he studied the various screws still in the bag and extracted one to compare it with the illustration in the instructions.

'There are enough screws, all right,' he said. 'You've merely put them in the wrong holes.'

Mortified, I snatched the document from his grasp. 'How would *you* know?'

'I've got an eye for identifying holes,' he said, looking at me sideways.

Meeting the lecherous gleam in his eyes, I replied, 'Me too, especially arseholes.' My quip earned a chuckle.

'Here' – he motioned to the screwdriver behind me – 'pass me the screwdriver.'

I shook my head as I studied the instructions. 'I'd rather cast it into the fire.'

His eyebrows arched. 'Is that a *Lord of the Rings* reference?'

Since it had been exactly that, my lips pursed. 'Maybe.'

His head tilted while he studied me with a sense of wonder in his eyes. 'Honestly, where have you been all my life?'

Snorting, I closed the instructions and left them on the floor. William had unfortunately been correct.

'In hiding,' I said. 'And I'm still not happy about being found, because I was never lost.'

He tittered. 'Love, you're so lost you don't even realise it.' He leaned past me to fetch the screwdriver. He lingered there for a second, and his closeness caused a bolt of ferocious electricity to course through my heart. Mindful of the memories his scent was likely to provoke, I held my breath and leaned slightly away.

'Am not,' I said, but didn't object when he began to remove the screws, because the sight of his beautiful hands distracted me. Steadily and patiently, they removed one screw after the other, and I thought at that moment that I must be going insane, because the view was oddly arousing. They moved so capably, so confident in their work. Those hands could make anything come undone.

In the dim light, his dark brown hair glistened faintly. My eyes journeyed along the tidy waves of it, down to where their darkness gently kissed his paler skin as they cradled his ears and neck.

As my gaze strayed further to admire the rest of him, that alien feeling crowded my chest again. It made me feel so full, like I hadn't sufficient space to contain it. It was dense and heavy, yet I felt lighter than air.

Transfixed, I studied his beauty as though it were the most impressive constellation ever to have fallen into place. Indeed, he seemed out of this world. Like stars upon the sky, each gorgeous feature of his body connected to form a celestial masterpiece.

He was undoubtedly a work of art, and I marvelled at how many secrets each detail veiled. I wondered what his thoughts were, how far the alleys of his mind stretched, how vast their content. Could they be endless? He seemed like the embodiment of the entire cosmos – the skin of the night.

'The Devil's in the detail, darling,' he suddenly said and glanced at me out of the corner of his eye. 'Something to bear in mind, especially if you mean to practise law.'

Since I was still mortified at my display of incompetence, I folded my arms and looked away. 'I'm just tired after revising all day. I've never encountered this problem before, and I'm a veteran when it comes to assembling IKEA furniture.'

It seemed like he was just about to respond when somebody unlocked the front door. Shooting up, I panicked at the thought of Jason discovering his brother in my room. A moment later, I remembered that the scene he would come upon was entirely innocent, so in the end, there was no cause for concern.

'Hello?' Jason called as I heard a bag land on the floor.

'Hi, Jason,' I greeted, but I didn't sound half as calm as I had intended.

'We're in here,' William said.

Hearing Jason's footsteps, I took a deep breath and begged myself to remain composed. I had never been around the two of them at the same time before, and the reality of it was straining my conscience, because it intensified the notion that I was keeping Jason in the dark about my sensual history with his brother.

When he appeared in the doorway, I forced a smile.

'What's happening here?' he asked as he observed the mess on the floor.

'I'm just teaching your brother how to assemble a wardrobe,' I said.

William froze, a blend of amusement and astonishment on his face.

'Yes,' William said and looked at Jason. 'You see, I put the wrong screws in the wrong holes. I'd say it's because I'm tired after work, but the truth is that I was just too stupid and stubborn to realise it.'

My mouth fell agape at his playful insult, but before I could reply, Jason chuckled and said, 'Sounds like you,' to which William responded with an underwhelmed expression.

Speaking over each other, I said to Jason, 'I love you,' just as William replied, 'No, you halfwit.'

In perfect synchrony, we turned toward each other, but I was the first to speak. 'I win.'

A chuckle slipped out of him and he shook his head. 'Fake it till you make it, I suppose.'

'Glad you seem to get on,' Jason said, grinning, and crossed his arms.

William returned his focus to my wardrobe. 'You're late.'

'Yeah, I know. Chaos at the hospital today. Fridays, you know. I've been keeping track of the match on my phone, though. Doesn't look like I've missed out on much.'

'You haven't,' William said. 'Anyway, have you had dinner?'

'No, I'm starving.'

'Same.'

'Have you had dinner, Cara?' Jason asked and removed his shirt.

I shook my head.

'Should we order something, then? I'm in the mood for sushi.'

'When are you not?' William and I replied in perfect unison. Since I felt him gazing at me, I resisted the urge to look in his direction.

'Right.' Jason curved a brow and flung his shirt over his shoulder, his eyes flickering between us. 'Why don't you place the order while I shower? Half-time's nearly done.'

'I'm busy slaving around,' William said. 'Cara, would you be so kind?'

I frowned. 'I would, but given the size of you two, I've no idea how big of an order I should place.'

'Order for a family of six,' William said.

'Yeah, six is good,' Jason agreed.

Six? Jesus Christ.

'Right, okay.' I picked up my phone from the floor.

Not only had Jason finished showering, but the match had also started again by the time William handed over the screwdriver.

'Please don't fuck up my work,' he said amusedly.

'While I appreciate your assistance, kindly piss off,' I replied with equal humour.

'If it suddenly collapses in a few weeks, you'll be the culprit, not I.'

'It won't.'

From the gleam in his eyes, I could tell he was about to ridicule me, but Jason's sudden cry came to my rescue. 'Fuck! Are you kidding me?'

The look on William's face made me giggle. His eyes were wide with horror.

'Fly, you fool,' I joked, and it earned a smirk as he caught the reference.

Following his hasty exit, I got back to work with a smile.

10

THE WAY OF THE WORLD

CHELSEA LOST, AND I DIDN'T NEED TO SEE THE RESULT TO KNOW THAT, because William and Jason's constant whining made it obvious. The only thing that finally shut them up was the dinner that arrived, which William insisted on paying for.

'You're students,' he said dismissively when Jason and I tried to object. 'If you'd like to contribute, you can set the table.' He closed the front door once the delivery guy had handed over our dinner.

Jason shook his head. 'It's useless to try and argue with him,' he said to me. 'We won't win.'

'You definitely won't.' William turned and faced us with a smirk. 'I argue for a living.'

I chuckled at his witticism. 'First you help me out with my wardrobe, and now you're buying me dinner?'

His lips twitched, and there was a glimmer of humour in his eyes. 'Is the strong, independent woman triggered?'

I laughed. 'Full-on quaking.'

'Well, you might as well get used to it. I'm all for gender equality, but I won't let it get in the way of basic chivalry.'

I looked at Jason. 'I thought you said he could be a bit of a dick?'

'He doesn't know what a dick looks like,' William said. 'He hasn't got one.'

I chortled.

Jason grabbed William's shoulder, and his grin was splitting his face apart. 'Proof enough?' he asked me.

I shook my head, still laughing. 'I'll set the table, then.' I turned to go into the kitchen. 'What would you like to drink?'

'Just water for me,' William said.

'Same here.'

When I came into the dining room, they were discussing the stock market.

'The tech sector?' Jason echoed as I put a plate in front of him on the pale wooden table.

'Yeah. I bought some shares in three different companies last night,' William said.

'Who tipped you?'

'Nobody.'

Jason nodded. 'Well, I'll look into it.'

'Do you pay attention to the stock market, Cara?' William asked as I gave him a plate across the table.

I shook my head. 'I'm busy enough as it is.'

'That's a shame. It could be worth your time.'

'Maybe, but I know next to nothing about it, so I wouldn't know where to start.'

'There are plenty of guides out there, not to mention advisers at the bank.'

'True. I keep a relatively decent sum in a mutual fund, though. Does that count for anything?'

He smiled. 'That's a good place to start, yes.'

'That's the money from when you worked at Starbucks, right?' Jason asked as I pulled my phone out of my back pocket and put it on the table.

'Yeah,' I said and sat down beside him.

'You've worked at Starbucks?' William asked, curious. My thoughts travelled to the one at the ground floor of his residential building, though I hadn't worked there.

'Yeah, before I started studying law.'

He seemed to hesitate. 'How come? Were you unsure about whether you wanted to study anything?'

'No, it was all part of the plan. My parents are covering my tuition fees, but I still have to cover the cost of living, and since I didn't want to get distracted by a job while I was studying, I decided to work full-time for a couple of years before I started. This way, I don't have to take up a loan, nor do I need a job on the side, so I can dedicate all my time to my studies to ensure better results.' I looked between them. As children of wealthy parents, they had probably never had to worry about the same.

William looked impressed. 'That's some wise thinking, especially for a person so young.'

'Thanks.' I beamed.

'And who gave you the idea to put it in a mutual fund?' he asked as he blended a rich amount of wasabi in his soy sauce. My eyes widened. He clearly loved spicy food.

'My mum. She's an economist.'

'Is she?' He sounded pleasantly surprised. 'What's her name?'

'Lillian. She inspired my sister, actually.'

'You've got a sister?'

'Yeah. Phoebe.'

'Is she younger or older?'

'Younger. She studies business at Columbia in New York.'

'Your parents have made some clever children, I hear.'

I chuckled. 'I could say the same to you.'

'Mine failed with one out of two,' he said and looked at Jason.

Jason merely showed him the middle finger.

'Anyway, how does Phoebe like New York?' William asked as he brought a few pieces of sushi onto his plate.

'She loves it.' I sighed.

He tilted his head. 'Why the sigh?'

I shrugged. 'She's got a girlfriend there, so sometimes I worry she won't move back.'

'I see. Well, I can't say I blame her – New York is fantastic, and I'm sure her girlfriend is too – but I hope for your sake that she will.'

I nodded.

'What about your father? What does he do?'

I peeked at Jason, fearful that he might find William's curiosity a little conspicuous, but he didn't seem remotely suspicious.

'Jamie is a sixth form philosophy teacher,' Jason said as he helped himself to some sushi. 'Lovely man.'

'Really? I love philosophy.' William smiled.

I wasn't surprised to discover that. He had given me the impression he was learned on the subject the night we'd met. But I smiled back all the same.

'Do you?'

He dipped a piece of sushi in his soy sauce. 'Yeah. I read plenty of books on it in my spare time. Nietzsche is one of my favourites.'

'Ah.' I crossed my arms, amused. 'I haven't read Nietzsche.'

'You should. It's hard, but it's seriously rewarding.'

'Dad says the same.'

'He's probably read all his works.' He filled his mouth. After swallowing, he went on, 'I'm reading him chronologically. I just finished *Thus Spoke Zarathustra.* Plan is to start *Beyond Good and Evil* this summer.'

Suddenly my phone rang on the table. Eyeing the screen, I saw that it was Aaron. My heart jammed in my throat and I tensed. When I looked up, both Jason and William were peeking at my screen. It took all my self-discipline to raise my hand as if I wasn't fazed and press the lock button to silence the ringing. I knew I had mentioned Aaron's name to William, but I hoped he didn't remember.

'Is Aaron coming over tonight?' Jason asked as he raised a piece of sushi to his mouth.

I stole a glance at William, but he wasn't looking at me. Instead, he seemed strangely fascinated with his plate.

'No.'

Jason nodded. 'Well, feel free to answer him.'

I shifted, feeling uncomfortable. 'It can wait.' I grabbed my chopsticks.

Jason looked at William. 'Aaron is Cara's . . .'

Shut up, Jason, I almost said.

William raised a brow when Jason trailed off. 'Boyfriend?'

Jason chuckled and shook his head. 'Sort of, only Cara doesn't date.'

'Oh.' William finally looked at me. 'Why not?'

I swallowed and averted my gaze, trying to recover my equilibrium. Why was he asking me this again? I had already explained why.

'Well, because this is my only chance to be selfish,' I said and met his gaze.

'By "selfish" you mean . . .?'

Feigning nonchalance, I brought a few pieces of maki onto my plate. 'That I want to take advantage of my freedom while I still can. As soon as the time is right for finding a man to settle down with, my personal aspirations, like my career goals and things like that, will have to take a backseat. He'll be my main priority then, and I'm not ready for that to happen just yet.'

'Right.' He took another bite.

'I just feel like I can contribute to this world with more than my ovaries, or the role of a girlfriend.'

A faint smile bent his lips. 'Are you trying to say that finding love isn't really your goal in life?'

I shook my head. 'I wouldn't phrase it like that.'

'How would you phrase it, then?'

'It's more precise to say that finding love isn't my only goal, and as of now, it definitely isn't my main goal.'

Jason gave me a smirk. 'But it will be later? Your main goal?' His playful tone elicited a chuckle from my mouth.

'Perhaps. At least I won't dismiss the idea. But for now, I really love law, and I think I can be good at it. I'd like to practise it for a few years, nurture my passion for it, before I consider other aspects of my future.'

William cocked his head, studying me. 'You are quite the anomaly.'

'What, because I'm a careerist? Aren't you the same?'

He scratched his cheek. 'Not really. I'm ambitious, yes, but I'm not mainly concerned with advancement in my profession.' He shrugged. 'I think that applies to most people, to be honest. I mean, it's my impression that people in general tend to be searching for a partner to settle down with. That's why your lack of interest in it seems a bit . . . unusual to me.'

'Well, our situations are different, so maybe that's why you can't relate. You've already got your foot in the door, so you can afford to consider stuff like that. I haven't. I still have to claw my way in. Plus, you're John's son. That's bound to give you more leeway.'

Jason snorted. 'I'm sorry, Cara, but that's bullshit. Will has worked extremely hard his whole life to get to where he is. In fact, he has to work twice as hard as everyone else in the firm *because* he's Dad's son – he constantly has to prove that he was hired for his abilities and not because of nepotism. Honestly, being Dad's son just raises people's expectations of him. They don't cut him any slack, and Dad least of all.'

The ghost of a smile flickered across William's lips as he watched Jason, and there was clear gratitude in his gaze.

'He's just super family-oriented,' Jason went on as he lifted a piece of sushi. 'He's wanted a big family for as long as I can remember.'

Feeling remorseful, I focused on William. 'I'm sorry. I didn't mean to belittle your efforts.'

'No worries.' His smile oozed forgiveness. 'I get your point, anyway.'

I sighed. 'Basically, I just think there's more to this life than chasing love. It's so primitive. Procreation? Really? Is that all there is?' I shook my head. 'It's not – not to me. There is the option to make the world a better place for those already in it, there are intellectual challenges, there's personal growth – really, the meaning of life doesn't have to be about reproduction, and certainly not exclusively.'

The curve of William's brows told me that he had not anticipated the conversation to take such an existential turn.

'No, I agree,' he said. 'Procreation doesn't have to be the sole meaning of life. But without it, there'd be no life. So, in the end, without life – without reproduction – there'd be nothing to add meaning to.'

I tittered. 'Valid point, but still, I said "exclusively".'

I watched as his familiar crooked smile surfaced on his mouth, and this time, the vulnerability it veiled was clearer than ever. 'I'm assuming now that, by "reproduction", you also mean love.'

'Well, I suppose you can love without reproducing. But, genetically, we're wired to fall in love in order to ensure reproduction – that's my understanding, at least. Anyway, what I'm trying to say is that there's so much I want to explore before I go down that route, so I need things to happen in a specific order. First, I establish my career, and after that, I'll probably be open to finding a partner.'

William swallowed another bite of sushi. 'So it's about self-realisation.'

'I guess you could call it that.'

The corner of his mouth tugged up briefly. 'You're surely at the top of Maslow's hierarchy of needs.'

'Yes. I'm privileged that way.'

William gazed away for a moment, looking contemplative. 'Have you ever been in a relationship before?'

I frowned. He already knew the answer to that. 'No, but what's that got to do with anything?'

'Well, it just sounds like you're severely overestimating what's required of you.'

'What do you mean?' Jason asked.

William met his gaze. 'That having a relationship doesn't have to equal stunting your professional life. When two compatible people are together, it usually works out with little effort. Compromises are made and, frankly, it offers a support system that might even help you prosper and reach levels you otherwise would not. I just don't think it's necessary to choose one or the other. It's possible to do both. You can have a relationship without it jeopardising your career, as long as it's with the right person.'

Jason faced me. 'He might be right,' he said, shrugging. 'He speaks from experience.'

Did he? I looked at William, curious.

'Anyway, back to Nietzsche,' William said, and I chuckled. He clearly wasn't interested in discussing his romantic life.

Never in my wildest dreams would I have imagined this interaction to unfold the way it did, but we remained at the table for a good while, talking about everything between heaven and earth. Jason and William shared heart-warming stories about their childhood together, and I adored listening to them. The strength of their bond was truly something I admired, because it was even deeper than mine and Phoebe's.

Tales from William's days as a student were particularly riveting, because his inexorable drive was clear between the lines. We dived into politics, too, and I was amazed when I learned that William and I shared the same view on almost everything. From there, the conversation travelled to music and art, films and literature. We even discussed celebrity gossip, although none of us boasted much knowledge on that.

The whole experience was so intense that I caught myself wondering once more if I would regret not pursuing anything more with him. Our chemistry was more apparent now than ever, and I wasn't blind to it.

But he was still Jason's brother.

And he was still going to be my boss.

In other words, he was totally off limits.

Pursuing him was a terrible idea for so many reasons. So why couldn't my heart seem to agree?

'You should take it,' Jason said when Aaron called again, his tone strict. 'It might be urgent.'

'Yeah, you're right.' I sighed and excused myself from the table.

'Hello?' I answered as I walked into my bedroom.

'Sorry, were you asleep?'

The sound of Aaron's voice made my chest ache with guilt. He hadn't the faintest idea that I was currently having dinner with one of my previous bed partners, and he definitely didn't know that I was enjoying every second of it. I felt like I was cheating on him, even though I wasn't.

'No. What's up? Is everything all right?'

'Yeah, sorry. I just spoke to Mum, and she asked whether you'd like to come for dinner next Friday.'

'Oh, that's great. Tell her I'd love to.'

'I'll ask Livy and Tyler if they'd like to come too.' Tyler was Aaron's flatmate of five years.

'Great.'

'How's the wardrobe coming along?'

I looked at it and wrinkled my nose. 'Well, it's not done yet, but I plan to finish it tonight.'

'I could always come over and help you if you like.'

'I appreciate that, but I'm all right.'

'Well, feel free to call me if you change your mind.'

'I doubt I will, but thanks.'

'I'll tell Mum we're coming next Friday, then.'

'Yes.'

'Don't stay up too late.'

'I won't.'

'Good night, love.'

'Good night.'

I rang off and huffed. Part of me wanted to hang out with Jason and William for a while longer, but seeing my unfinished project had reminded me that I still had exams coming up that needed my attention; I needed my desk for revising.

I went back to the dining room to let them know.

'I need to get back to my project,' I said and grabbed my plate.

'No worries.' Jason nodded. 'Aaron all right?'

'Yeah.'

'Good.'

'Well,' William said, 'we should do this again sometime.' He smiled, but it didn't reach his eyes.

'We should.' I reciprocated his smile. 'You're lovely company.'

His eyes widened slightly, as if he hadn't expected me to say that. 'So are you.'

I turned around to leave, and I felt his eyes on my back as I walked out.

Though I wasn't usually one to eavesdrop, I kept my bedroom door slightly ajar so I could overhear their conversation. I couldn't help myself; William piqued my curiosity like no one else. For the most part, it wasn't that rewarding since they mainly discussed football and work, but when the time was nearing eleven o'clock, it took a different turn.

'I should probably think about leaving soon,' William said.

'You heading to Violet?' Jason asked, and I didn't like the way my heart reacted. It clenched and twisted before it sank in my chest. Given what time it was, it was likely Jason had referred to a woman who played a particular role in William's life – a sexual role.

The name echoed in my mind. Violet. I vividly remembered a beauty named Violet at his workplace. I had encountered her in the lift with William just when I had been about to leave after signing my contract. He had said then that she was his partner for a transaction he was currently working on. Was she his partner on other fronts as well? Was *she* the regular bed partner he had mentioned?

At first, the possibility intimidated me, but when I realised where my thoughts were headed, I frowned at myself. First of all, I had no claim on him, and secondly, I had no plans to ever sleep with him again. Ultimately, this information shouldn't have bothered me.

But somewhere deep within, it did.

Just my ego, I thought. Get a grip, Cara.

'Yeah,' William finally replied, and my heart sank even lower.

'Why the hesitation?' Jason asked.

'Well, my head's got a mute button reserved for your voice, so I just wasn't listening at first.'

'God, you're such a tit.'

'Anyway, yeah.'

'How are things going with her?'

'What do you mean?'

'Has anything changed since we last spoke about her?'

I should not have been as relieved as I was when William laughed.

'Changed?' he echoed. 'Are you asking whether things are evolving into a relationship?'

'Considering your reaction, I gather they're not.'

'Not even close. It's just sex, J, and always will be.'

'What does that mean for Francesca, then?'

Freezing, I stared blankly ahead. Francesca? William was involved with yet another woman?

Somewhat repelled, I wondered how long his list of lovers actually was. Disappointment came next. For some reason, I hadn't thought him a womaniser. I had thought him above that. The impression he had given me was that he was fastidious about his choice of partners. Clearly, I had been naïve to think that. Then again, considering his unconventional charm and attractive appearance, it shouldn't have surprised me that he had a queue of women just waiting for scraps of his attention.

For the first time, I experienced a moment of pure gratitude that I had rejected him. To have to battle for his attention wasn't remotely appealing. I wouldn't settle for anything less than a man who recognised my worth from the outset and treated me accordingly. To fight to persuade him to pick me, to urge him to see that he should favour me above the rest – my integrity would never let me sink so low. Just like every devoted woman, I deserved to be treated like I was the only woman in the world for him when it came to matters of romance.

Groaning, I asked myself why I was even entertaining this lane of thought. A relationship with William was out of the question, so why should his conduct with other women matter to me? I should have been happy about this. He had just reinforced my resolve about not pursuing anything more with him. And yet, despite this, disappointment still dominated my feelings, and I scolded myself for it. Who did I think I was? I had no right to be disappointed that he was seeing other women.

'Why should my arrangement with Violet have anything to say with regards to Francesca?' William replied, sounding confused.

'So you plan to see her again, then?'

'I haven't decided yet.'

'Because she's Kate's friend?'

Who on earth was Kate? Yet another lover?

'For example.'

'What other reasons are there?'

'Well, she's not my type – too sensitive and emotional.'

'Yeah, that's a bad match.'

'And she seems rather keen, so I'm worried I'll end up hurting her.'

'How shockingly empathic of you.'

'Besides,' William said, 'there's another girl I haven't told you about.'

My heart climbed to my throat. Was it *yet* another girl, or was he referring to *me*? Panicking, my gaze dashed to the door, and I dared not even breathe for fear of drowning out what would come next.

Would he break his promise?

'What?' Jason sounded surprised. 'Who?'

'I met her last Friday, at Disrepute. We slept together, but she rejected me the next morning. Said she's not interested in dating, and I'm still a bit gutted about that, so it wouldn't be fair to Francesca if I start seeing her when I'm still hung up on someone else.'

My pulse pounded in my throat. Though I hadn't met him last Friday, but rather the Friday before that, I got the feeling he was referring to me. The similarities were too conspicuous. It couldn't be yet another girl, could it?

'Are you being serious?' Jason asked disbelievingly.

'Yeah.'

'But you don't do one-night stands.'

'Yeah, well, I made an exception.'

'Shit. You must have really liked her.'

'I do.'

'Damn,' Jason said, astounded. 'What's her name?'

'Sandra.'

I gasped. Dropping the screwdriver, I sat back on my heels and stared at the door with shock. Had I actually just heard that? He couldn't genuinely be that affected, could he?

Trying to make sense of it, I considered my own feelings. I had already acknowledged that he had left a lasting impression, but I hadn't thought I could be guilty of the same. I had thought he was just joking earlier – when he had said he found me 'riveting'. I hadn't realised he was being entirely serious.

'Well, Sandra clearly doesn't know what she's turning down,' Jason said, sounding unimpressed.

'Yeah, it blows.'

'Have you tried hunting her down?'

'I did, but the mission failed. Besides, I think I should respect her decision. All I need is some time to get over it, because she was . . . Well, let's just say that I seriously doubt I'll ever meet someone like her again.'

'And she rejected you solely on the basis that she's not interested in dating?'

'Mainly. She studies medicine in Edinburgh, so there was that issue as well. Apparently, she just didn't see us working out.'

He was definitely referring to me, and it completely obliterated the disappointment I had experienced earlier.

'Well, I hope for your sake that she'll change her mind,' Jason said, audibly displeased.

'Same. Anyway, I need to get a move on. It's getting late, and Vi's a bitch about tardiness.'

Jason laughed. 'In general, or specifically when it comes to this sort of appointment?'

'Both.'

'Well, keep me posted on Sandra, then, yeah?'

'Sure, but you need to stop living vicariously through me when it comes to women, J. You ought to get your arse on the market.'

'There's no time for it.'

'You sound just like Sandra now.'

'Damn. I guess it's a curse haunting every med student.'

'Well, on the bright side, by not sleeping around, you won't tempt anyone to chase the unattainable the way Sandra did.'

'That's exactly why I'm avoiding it. I'd hate it if I ended up hurting someone.'

When I heard them start to clean the table, I dashed to my bedroom door and closed it before either of them could walk out and notice. Not much later, someone knocked.

'Yes?'

William opened the door. Our stares collided, and I wondered if he could tell that I had overheard every word as he confided in Jason. From the piercing power of his gaze, I got the impression that he knew, but since his lips formed a brooding line, I wasn't certain. If he truly suspected me of having heard him, I would have expected him to present his typical crooked smile, as its cunning shape would have revealed that it had never been unintended.

'I see you're nearly done,' he said and studied my new wardrobe.

I nodded. 'Only the doors left.'

'Good job.'

'Thanks.'

His eyes homed in on my bed then. Without asking, he walked over to it and picked up my textbook on Advanced Contract Law.

'If it isn't Contract Law,' he said, flipping through the pages. 'I selected this module in my third year as well.'

'Did you?'

He nodded, but his attention remained fixed on a page. 'Which modules are you taking, exactly?'

'Advanced Contract Law, Company Law, Commercial Law and Law of Taxation.'

'Private law is your forte, I hear.'

'Of course. That's why I should fit right in at Day & Night.'

He looked up then, and the smile he offered was small but sincere. 'You certainly will.' He shut the book and dropped it on my bed. 'Well, give me a bell if you ever need any help while you're revising for your exams.'

'That's very kind of you.'

He shrugged. 'I'd be delighted to help you out in whatever way I can.'

His statement evoked the memory of when he had insisted that he would never get in the way of my education should I opt to give him a chance. He seemed to be recalling the same memory, as his gaze lingered on mine for a moment.

'Anyway, just thought I'd say goodbye. I'm heading off. Good luck assembling the rest of your' – he glanced at the box containing my desk – 'furniture.'

I gave him a smile even though I wasn't comfortable knowing where he was headed.

'Thanks for your help,' I said. 'I'll have you to thank if my wardrobe *doesn't* collapse.'

He chuckled as he went to the door. 'Let me know if it does.'

'You know I won't,' I said playfully and trailed after him to see him out.

While Jason and I watched him put on his shoes, the younger brother asked, 'Sunday, then?'

'Yeah.'

'You're coming for dinner on Sunday?' I asked, enthused.

'Well, yes, but I think Jason was referring to the gym.' William's eyes flickered to Jason's while he grabbed his jacket.

'I was. Speaking of, how about you join us, Cara? You're a gym rat just like us.'

'You lift?' William asked.

A chuckle slipped past my smirk. 'Yeah.'

'Impressive. Too few women do.'

'I know, it's a shame.'

'She mainly trains lower body, though,' Jason said. Suddenly he grinned and looked highly amused. 'All those squats and hip-thrusts have made her bum a magnet for attention, in the gym or otherwise. I've witnessed it first-hand.'

'Which is why I like to cover it up when I'm training,' I said as blood sprang to my cheeks.

A carnal memory seemed to flare in William's eyes when they landed on me. 'I'm sorry you have to go to such measures in the first place.'

I shrugged. 'Me too, but such is the way of the world.'

'So you'll join, then?' Jason asked, but I hesitated.

'Come on.' William smiled. 'It's important to work out when you're revising for exams.'

I knew I should avoid spending time with William whenever it was possible without raising suspicion, but part of me was eager for his company. Not only that, but I also felt I had to earn back some of the respect I had lost when he caught me failing to assemble my wardrobe. I wanted him to find me competent because, for some ridiculous reason I couldn't quite understand yet, I wanted to impress him. Besides, it wasn't like we would be able to do much talking. We would be there to train, not have tea.

Finally, my desire to see him again capsized my reason. 'Okay, I'll join.'

William's smile broadened into a grin. 'Great. Looking forward to it. Sunday, then.' He opened the door.

'Yeah.'

'Have fun with Violet.' Jason gave him a wink.

Without looking at me, William said, 'I'd rather it was Sandra, to be honest, but such is the way of the world.'

His bold declaration shocked me. I barely managed to remain composed while he closed the door between us. Either he already knew I had eavesdropped, or he had said it to make it clear that he had mentioned me to his brother. One way or another, he obviously wanted me to know that he was still interested in me.

'Sandra is this girl he met recently,' Jason explained as he locked the door after him.

'I see.'

He turned toward me with a grin. 'Anyway, that went well, didn't it? I knew he'd like you.'

All I managed for a response was a faint smile, because my feelings were colliding into an unsolvable mess.

'I'm so glad you get on,' he said. 'My two favourite people in the whole world. What a trio we'll make.'

'Me too.' I nodded. 'Anyway, I should finish my project.' I went back to my room.

11

HUNT OF A LIFETIME

WILLIAM

One cannot choose with whom to fall in love. It is entirely primal and has been ruled by instincts as long as humankind has existed. Had I been a victim of the delusion that we had such a thing as free will, I would have believed that you could only choose whether to pursue or not. But I wasn't. I knew full well that my reaction to her existence was embedded in my DNA, and that it was encoded in my genes that I would pursue her despite her rejection.

However, I was a strategic type of suitor – the calculating kind. Some would even say cunning. Unlike those who went straight for the kill, I preferred to lure my target into my web. In order to do that, I had to know my prey – how it operated, how it thought, how it could be seduced and finally overcome.

Indeed, the beginning of love is very much a hunt – thrilling, rapacious, and utterly instinctual. All at once, the brain and the body have turned toward one person, the senses have sharpened to perceive even the slightest sign of their existence.

However, when falling in love, you never recognise it at the very moment it happens. In retrospect, it's easy to identify the moment which triggered the realisation, but one cannot recognise it in the exact moment when love first begins to manifest. Because of that, I was entirely unaware of just how profound my feelings were on the verge of becoming. In fact, as I glanced at Cara across the gym, I thought all I was guilty of was fleeting interest or a rude curiosity that was based on primitive, reproductive urges.

I hadn't realised that the process had begun, that with each second that ticked by, I was gradually losing myself in her, that my sense of self was slowly waning to create room for her, in favour of her. Instead, I was under the impression that I was mainly looking to sway her mind to repair my bruised ego. I was bitter that she hadn't found my offer sufficient enough, bitter that she had been able to remain sensible despite my ardent efforts to stir romanticisms in her, and I was bitter that she didn't seem as preoccupied with me as I was with her.

I simply hadn't grasped that how I reacted to her soft voice delivering sharp remarks was a sign of love manifesting, that her seductive eyes and the total fire they contained had instead lured *me* into their heat; nor did I, at the time, fathom the reason why I would gladly have made a fool of myself merely for the chance to hear her laugh.

Oblivious to the truth, I mistook genuine affection for an injured ego and assumed it was only my vanity that urged me to change her mind. I had no idea that it was the prelude to love. I was convinced that if I managed to change her verdict about us, I would finally be able to exorcise her constant presence in my thoughts. I was aware it was a cynical motivation, but to spare my sanity, I considered it a necessary evil.

However, I was still contemplating which route to take in order to achieve my goal. Thus far, I had settled on the tactic of trying to befriend my foe, because if I did, I could perhaps locate her weakness and eventually exploit it.

The trouble was that I had never encountered an enemy quite so strong before. She seemed impossible to read, like she existed in a language entirely foreign to me. There was a mystery to her, like the suspense of a tale I had never heard before and couldn't predict the end of.

She was whole all on her own, and frankly, I admired her for that. She didn't need anyone but herself, much less me. She wore her independence like armour, and it protected her to a fault. So then, how does one defeat an enemy boasting such a brilliant defence?

The Trojan way, I supposed. I would have to trick her into letting me past her walls, and once inside, I would make them crumble one by one until only she remained. Then, at last, my mind would be free of her – my ego restored.

Perhaps the extent of my determination should have encouraged me to suspect that something about my fascination with her was beyond the ordinary; had I truly not cared for her, then her rejection wouldn't have injured me as badly as it had.

But I didn't suspect. Instead, I had gone blind and was desperately groping in the dark.

After a final pull-up, I released the bar and landed on my feet. I glanced over my shoulder, but I was far from the only one to look in her direction. Jason hadn't lied: she was indeed a magnet for attention. Had she been mine I might have enjoyed it, but she wasn't.

While I knew she was perfectly capable of managing on her own, their hungry gazes still irritated me. From the little I had learned about her thus far, I was certain this was a far cry from the attention she appreciated. Why else would she feel the need to cover up her derrière with that oversized black jumper whenever she did squats?

I also inferred a dimension of disrespect from their ogling. Her jumper might as well have been a sign begging her admirers to look away, yet they all turned a blind eye to it and objectified her anyway.

I found their behaviour repulsive and uncivilised, and it summoned a strange urge to protect her from their sexualising stares, so without further thought, I grabbed my bag and bottle of chalk and approached her. I hoped my presence by her side would intimidate at least some of the men to look away. Their eyes would avert for the wrong reason, but at least she would be spared from their ogling for now.

'Eighty kilos – not bad,' I said.

'Just finished my last set,' she replied breathily, and I had to smile at the sight of her flushed face and damp skin. It all looked so familiar.

'So you won't be needing the rack?'

'No.' She wiped her forehead with her arm. 'Dumbbell rows next.'

'I'll take over this, then. Deadlifts.'

'I'll help you remove the plates.'

'You can leave two of them on.'

After giving her a nod of gratitude, I wondered what to say. It had been obvious from the moment she arrived with Jason that she was here to train, not chat. It was also plausible that she was deliberately trying to avoid me, but that didn't align with my goal, so I had to stall her somehow.

'Did you finish assembling your furniture on Friday?' In my hurry, it was the only thing I had thought to say, but after hearing it, I wished I had remained quiet instead. What a dry start to a conversation. I hoped she wouldn't think me boring for that.

'My desk? Yes, I did.' She tilted her head and smiled, and the view was enchanting. 'Thanks for helping me out.'

'Anytime. So your wardrobe still hasn't collapsed, I take it?'

She chuckled as she pulled a plate off the barbell. 'Not yet. Did you have fun with Violet?'

Her bold question took me aback. Unsure of where to look, I gazed around and noticed that Jason was watching us from the bench press area. When I recovered from the surprise, I turned my attention back to her and scoured her features for any sign of resentment, but I discovered nothing. She looked perfectly unfazed.

I sensed my bitterness beginning to fester. It was obvious that I had meant nothing to her at all, and that I would be flattering myself if I assumed anything else. There wasn't a spark of envy in her, not a fragment of jealousy.

'Not quite as much fun as I would have had if she'd been you,' I shamelessly confessed, because I hoped to provoke a reaction from her.

But none came.

'Is she the partner you mentioned?' she asked while removing another plate.

I studied her intently. 'Yeah, why?'

'I'm surprised you're comfortable sleeping with a colleague.'

I thought I detected a hint of resentment in her voice, but perhaps it was only wishful thinking on my part. It might well have been general disapproval, which would make sense in light of her stated reservations about sleeping with a colleague.

'I'm usually not, but I can make exceptions. Something to bear in mind.' My tone was playful, but we both knew I meant it, which was probably why she didn't respond with anything other than a scoff.

I wondered again whether she had overheard my conversation with Jason the other day. I had meant for her to hear it, but I wasn't sure she actually had. The door to her bedroom had been closed before I knocked. If she had, I wondered what her thoughts were. That Jason had decided to probe into my recent sexual endeavours so thoroughly wasn't something I had anticipated, so I had tried to shine a light on the fact that I would much prefer to spend time with her than them. But her favour still seemed far from my reach, so now I doubted she had eavesdropped at all.

'Impressive weights you're doing,' I said to help myself think of something else. 'I saw you hip-thrusting two hundred kgs earlier.'

She gave me a smirk. 'Scared I'll put you out of business?'

Her cheek never failed to entertain me, but she always seemed to forget that I was rather a proficient player in that game myself.

'We both know I'm a capable thruster. I can still hear you moaning my name in my sleep. Quite the melody, that was.' I hadn't been able to resist. There was something about teasing her that felt entirely necessary. She reminded me of an angry chipmunk whenever I flustered her, because her voice reached octaves so high that it frankly impressed me – and amused me.

Her mouth dropped open, and the fresh colour in her face contended with even the brightest of reds.

'You!' she spluttered, high-pitched as predicted. 'Stop reminding me already,' she continued, glorious in her anger.

I was sure my grin matched the Devil's. 'It was only a joke, Cara. Just taking the piss while I still can. Can't be doing it once you start work now, can I?'

'You shouldn't be doing it now, either!' she said in a harsh whisper, clearly irate. Her hands had curled into fists by her sides. Her anger didn't intimidate me in the slightest, though. On the contrary, it tempted me to continue.

'But you look so lovely with that colour in your cheeks – especially since I'm the one who put it there.'

'You are unbelievable.' She sounded despairing, and I realised I had shot myself in the foot when she undid the belt around her waist, grabbed her bag and stormed off.

As I gazed after her, I caught Jason in my peripheral vision. When I looked over, he shook his head at me.

'Don't be a dick, Will!' he shouted across the gym, which earned us some curious glances from the few not listening to their own music.

I didn't bother replying.

§ § §

In the changing rooms, I was facing my locker when Jason asked, 'What did you say to Cara earlier?'

'Nothing, really.'

'Didn't seem like nothing.'

'Made a bad joke, that's all.'

'About what?'

'Nothing I'd like to repeat. I mean to apologise.'

'You should.'

I glanced in his direction and gave a faint nod as I reached into my locker for my shirt.

'Were you flirting with her?' he asked then, but since I had expected the question, my equilibrium remained intact.

'No,' I said with ease, but what I actually wanted was to tell the truth. In fact, I wanted to tell every single person in this room – the whole fucking world – that I had slept with her, only so I could deprive her of the excuse – the poor and pathetic excuse – which was but one among the several ridiculous excuses she had used to reject me. At least then, I would have been one step closer to achieving my goal – she would no longer have been able to hide behind the erroneous conviction that people would care about whom she invited into herself.

But I had made her a promise, and I intended to keep it. Besides, I could only befriend her if she remained unaware of my antagonism. I couldn't imagine she would want anything to do with me if I told Jason prematurely.

I frowned when I realised that I ought to be questioning why it should matter whether I had been flirting with her or not.

'Why?' I asked, and his potential answer filled me with dread. Had we, unwittingly, shared a woman? 'Is there something I should know?'

It bothered me that he decided to put on his jumper at that precise moment, because it made me wonder if he had done it deliberately to veil his reaction, or whether it was merely because he didn't care all that much for the subject. Was it genuine or feigned nonchalance?

'What do you mean "why"?' he asked, but his voice was muffled. 'Are you asking whether I fancy her?' he continued as soon as his head popped out.

'Do you?'

Something strange happened inside my chest as I considered the idea. There was a contraction, and for a moment, I stopped drawing breath.

'Not really. She's hot, though, really hot. Or perhaps beautiful is a better word to describe her. I've never been able to decide – she's a good blend.'

'Have you slept with her?'

Jason laughed. 'No, we're not like that. I'm only saying she's attractive. Hardly think that's worth fucking up our friendship for – pun intended.'

I faced my locker again, and it demanded some effort to remain composed. He hadn't really denied anything – not as clearly as I would have preferred, anyway – and I couldn't keep probing him about this without raising suspicion.

Would he have slept with her if offered the chance?

'You don't agree?' he asked.

'On what?'

'That she's attractive?'

I hadn't the faintest idea why, but the question pissed me off.

'Jason, she's your best friend. Quit sexualising her.' What I said gave the illusion that I refused to speak further on the matter for moral reasons, but the reality was that I wasn't exactly sure why I wanted him to shut up. Perhaps it was because I felt nauseated at the possibility of him being sexually interested in her. The disgusting images were already feasting on my mind. Or perhaps it was because I wanted her for myself but didn't want to take her from him. He was my brother, after all – the person I cherished the most. If he wanted her too, would I be able to let her go for his sake? Would he even desire her if he learned the truth about our past?

Now more than ever, I felt the strain of keeping the truth from him. I wished she hadn't begged me not to tell. I wished she would have understood that, while Jason might have disliked the news at first, he would have come to terms with it within the span of a mere day – I was certain. Unlike me, he simply wasn't capable of holding grudges. But now that she had demanded my silence, I couldn't break it without self-sabotaging.

Jason's eyebrows leaped up his forehead. 'Damn, someone's triggered. I wasn't sexualising her, I was admiring her. There's a difference. Christ.'

'She's well fit,' a random bloke commented behind us then. 'The bird with the black jumper covering her arse, right? I'd do her in a heartbeat.'

That sort of crass, macho behaviour was exactly the reason why women often felt hostile toward our gender. Like them, I had no patience with it. But that was only one among several reasons why his statement roused great ire in me.

I refused to acknowledge him. If I did, I worried I would inadvertently get myself into a fight. If there was one thing I had learned over the years, it was that my mouth was quite adept at getting me into serious trouble. It had earned me a black eye on more occasions than I cared to count, especially on the football pitch during my teenage years. So, with difficulty, I bit my tongue and faced away.

Jason appeared to notice my riled state, so he merely gave the bloke a nod before he turned his back to him as well.

'What's put you in such a foul mood?' he asked very quietly.

I lost it. 'Men who constantly sexualise women, as if their primary purpose is to please us, as if their personality and intellect are of secondary importance. I wish they'd understand that, by behaving that way, they're doing us all a great disservice.'

'Are you talking to me, mate?' the bloke asked, sounding menacing.

I turned toward him, my muscles tensing as my stance grew hostile. I hated violence of any sort, but if he attacked, I was prepared to defend myself.

'Well, since you ask, you must have identified with the men I'm referring to.'

His brown eyes lit with anger, and I could tell he was considering whether to strike me. Judging by the look of him, I was confident he had steroids to thank for the size of his muscles. I was still stronger than him, though, and much taller. He would be no match for me. Studying me from head to toe, he seemed to realise the same, so he took a step back and clenched his narrow jaw.

I growled, 'Why do you think she was wearing a jumper to cover her arse?'

He pressed his lips together but said nothing.

'And yet you sexualise her anyway,' I spat.

'Will,' Jason intervened, grabbing my shoulder. 'Calm down.'

'Sorry,' the lad murmured. 'I meant no disrespect.'

'Try thinking next time, yeah? With something other than your cock.' I turned away from him and grabbed my bag. 'I'm finished,' I said to Jason. 'I'll wait outside.' Giving the lad a final glare, I headed out.

I was surprised to find Cara there, leaning against a wall with her phone in her hand. In my experience, women tended to be slower than us when it came to changing and getting ready, but I supposed this was just yet another rule she was an exception to.

I knew I owed her an apology, so I drew in a steadying breath before I approached. I had barely managed three paces by the time she noticed me, and the look she gave me told me I wasn't forgiven yet.

The instant I reached her, I said, 'I'm sorry about earlier.'

'You're honestly such a knob.' She shoved her phone into the front pocket of her jumper. 'I'm trying to put it behind me.'

'Pun intended?' I joked, hoping to lighten her mood.

She gaped, and soon enough, an incredulous chuckle poured out. 'Okay, that was funny, but I'm being serious. You've got to let me move on.'

I knew she hadn't meant to injure my feelings by saying that, but she did, nevertheless.

'I'm having a hard time doing it myself. Perhaps that's why I keep bringing it up,' I said frankly.

I thought I detected sympathy in her eyes, and she looked about to say something, but right before she could, Jason interrupted.

'Fucking hell, Cara,' he said upon reaching us. 'I told Will just now that I find you beautiful, and he went and accused me of sexualising you. Do you feel sexualised? Because my conscience is seriously suffering right now, so I'd—'

'Jason – what?' She frowned, and I had averted my eyes by the time she searched for them. 'You call me beautiful every day,' she said, and I considered that to be valuable information. 'Of course I don't think that.'

'Right, good.' He huffed with relief. 'Will got me thinking, you see. Actually, he nearly got into a scuffle with another lad just now, defending you.'

Though my intention hadn't been to defend solely Cara, but rather women overall, I was grateful he told her that. Perhaps hearing this would make her consider me in a favourable light.

'He did what?' Cara asked, astounded. Feeling her eyes on my profile, I looked over to meet them.

'Yeah.' Jason nodded. 'This random guy declared – unsolicited – that he found you hot, and Will lost it. I'm honestly quite proud.'

I knitted my brows. Important details had been left out. I didn't want Cara to get the impression I was prone to violence either, because I wasn't.

'It was the way he said it,' I defended myself. 'He sounded primitive. It pissed me off, especially when you' – I gestured to her – 'were wearing a jumper to hide your bum. It might as well have been a bloody placard, and he ignored it. I wasn't looking for a fight – I despise violence. I'd never hit someone first. I merely meant to rebuke him.'

Cara's deep-blue eyes grew warmer, almost inviting. Seeing it, I forgot everything else. The effect it had on me was far more severe than I had been prepared for. This wasn't normal, I thought, perplexed.

'Thanks, Will,' she said, and I hated the smile she wore. She was supposed to grow weak for *me,* not the other way around. Yet, when I looked at her, I could sense that my strength was waning.

I gave her a vague nod. Looking between her and Jason, I found my situation quite intolerable. With too many thoughts to sort out, I started toward the exit.

'I'll see you later.'

§ § §

There was quite the deluge outside, but I decided to walk home in spite of it, hoping to clear my head. After fifteen minutes, I had got no further with sorting out my thoughts, so, eager for a distraction, I took my phone out of my bag and checked my messages. There was one from Andy and one from my good friend Alexander Winton. The three of us had been a trio ever since primary school, although I supposed Jason was an uncounted member of it as well.

I opened Andy's first.

> Omw to Alex. Join?

Instead of replying, I opened Alexander's message.

> Andy's coming over. You should come. I'm sure he's going to complain about Chloe, and you're much better than I am at putting him in his place

Groaning, I halted to reply to Alex.

> You'll have to manage on your own. I've got dinner plans with the fam. Just tell him he's being an idiot. He knows it's true, deep down

Poor Chloe. I truly pitied her.

Over the years, both Alexander and I had grown to regard her as a sister; she wasn't just Andy's girlfriend to us. Because of that, we had taken her side in the aftermath of their split. Besides, we both knew it was only a matter of time before Andy would come crawling back to her, because his love for her was undying. Their issues weren't based on a lack of love, but rather on a difference of opinion on how to proceed in the future.

Chloe desperately wanted to conceive, and she was growing short on time. Four years ago, she had been diagnosed with endometriosis, which was a condition that could affect her fertility. The older she got, the slimmer her chances of conceiving would become. Like Andy and Alex, she was twenty-nine now, and she had waited a whole decade for Andy to become mature enough to be a father. The trouble was that

Andy still didn't feel ready. The idea of children frightened him. He had voiced concerns about whether he was fit for the role at all and frequently hid behind the excuse that he wanted to focus on his career for a while longer, which – understandably – Chloe had grown impatient with.

All she demanded was a clear answer – did he want to have children anytime soon? If he didn't, he had to let her go. But Andy did want children. He had told me several times. He just wasn't quite sure he was fit for fatherhood at this point in his life.

It was quite the dilemma, but I was convinced Andy was overthinking it. As soon as he held his baby in his arms, he would settle into being a father without trouble.

A message came in from Francesca then, and I was reminded that I still hadn't replied to her last text.

> Sorry if this seems clingy, but are we meeting tomorrow or not? I'd like to know so that I can make other plans if you've changed your mind x

'Fuck,' I muttered and resumed walking. I had marked her text as read, something I always did because I favoured transparency, but now it had cost me the time I otherwise could have spent contemplating her offer. I would have to reply soon.

I wondered if Kate knew about us. We hadn't spoken all that much since the end of our relationship five years ago. As I thought about it, I couldn't remember having spoken to her at all during the past year. She lived in Lancaster now with her new boyfriend, whose name was Matthew – an engineer like her.

Kate and I had met during my final year at Cambridge. We were only bed partners when I first met Francesca – Kate's best friend from childhood. It wasn't until I was about to move back to London to complete the LPC LLM at the University of Law that Kate and I agreed to try a relationship.

At first, things were stable between us, and I often went back to Cambridge to visit her. But, as time went on, my career demanded more and more of my time. In the end, our relationship fell apart, but I hadn't tried to save it either.

Following our split, I hadn't thought I would meet Francesca again, and I certainly hadn't imagined that I would ever end up in bed with her – I had never found her interesting.

Then, by some coincidence, I encountered her at Disrepute a few weeks before I first met Cara. Violet was there as well, but she left early to meet Clive – a man she was currently seeing unofficially and had yet to make up her mind about.

Nevertheless, Violet's departure that night made way for Francesca and me to rekindle our past friendship. She told me she had recently split from the boyfriend she'd had when I was with Kate – Oliver, who I had met a few times – and that she had plans to move from Southampton to London in the near future.

As the evening progressed, she found the courage to ask me out on a date, but I was hesitant to accept. Though Kate and I were no longer together, I still had tremendous respect for her, so I would never think of courting one of her closest friends, and I especially wouldn't when knowing I had completely broken her heart. It would only have rubbed salt into the wound, and I wanted to avoid that.

But when I asked Francesca if she still kept in touch with Kate, she explained that they had drifted apart and were no longer close, so I didn't see any harm in going on a date with her.

I didn't expect much from it, but it turned out to be endurable, and I even went so far as to end it with her in my bed. As she recovered beside me, her naked body damp with sweat, she confessed to lusting after me even while I was with Kate and she with Oliver, and that she had been infatuated with me back then.

The news upset me at first because I did not appreciate the disloyalty it implied toward Kate, but upon remembering that she was no longer part of our lives, I put it out of my mind. Besides, Francesca had never acted on it, and I could hardly hold her human errors against her. We were all guilty of having thoughts and feelings that would be considered immoral if acted upon, but that was the critical distinction – they required the act in order to be punished as immoral.

We had met six more times since then because – and it was an awful thing to admit – her presence in my life had become a matter of convenience for sexual purposes. Though she wasn't the brightest, she was a pleasant person – she could even be funny sometimes – and she was capable of arousing me, so I had seen no reason to end it. Recently, however, I had sensed that her attachment was becoming stronger than I was comfortable with. While she was perfectly charming, I didn't want to pursue a romantic relationship with her, because our chemistry had never been effortless. Unlike Cara, she didn't fascinate me in the slightest, and I considered initial fascination a requirement when it came to my romantic endeavours.

There I went again. Cara, Cara, Cara – as if I hadn't a life of my own, as if she was the only person worth my attention in the entire world.

I now compared every potential candidate to her. She had become the standard I sought, and nothing else would suffice. I no longer enjoyed Violet's moans of pleasure because they weren't Cara's, and I seemed unable to admire Francesca's beauty because it wasn't Cara's.

The reality of that angered me to the extent that I acted on emotion and replied to Francesca that I would be delighted to see her tomorrow. Foolish in my misery, I hoped I could fill the void that Cara had left behind with the attention of other women.

I was desperate to regain control because Cara's presence in my life made me feel powerless. In her audience, it was like I no longer reigned over my own mind, much less my body, and if there was one thing that frightened me above all, it was to be rendered powerless.

And yet, despite this, I experienced an incessant need to see her again. It was entirely compulsive; I couldn't seem to resist it no matter how hard I tried.

Dinner couldn't happen soon enough.

§ § §

'I'm very sorry to hear about Andy and Chloe,' Mum said after a sip of her favourite red wine. 'I'm sure they'll get back together, though. This isn't the first time they've hit a bump in the road.'

'Yeah, I'm convinced it's only temporary,' I said.

'I trust you'll make sure of that,' Dad said and gave me a crooked smile.

'Alex and I are working on it at least.'

'Meanwhile,' Jason said, 'I'm just minding my own business.'

I chuckled. 'You've certainly got a knack for it.'

'How about you, dear?' Mum asked and looked at Cara. 'Do you have a special man in your life?'

I hadn't anticipated it, but my stomach sank when Jason wrapped his arm around her chair as if to mark his territory.

'Only me,' he joked.

'Yes, only you,' Cara said with a smile and reached for her glass of wine. 'But on a serious note, the answer is no. I'm very committed to my studies, so I'm not interested in dating anyone at the moment.'

The reminder irritated me. Hadn't I heard her pathetic excuses enough times by now? Would I ever see the day when she wouldn't rub them in my face?

'I'm sure a lot of men are very upset about that,' Dad flattered her amusedly. If only he knew he'd mocked his own son while he was at it.

As if his statement had prompted her, Cara's eyes slid in my direction, but she averted them as soon as they collided with mine.

'I hardly think they're missing out on anything,' she said, and I was surprised by her humility. Did she not know the extent of her power? How effortlessly she rendered men senseless with lust? How far they would go for a mere second of her time?

'I'm really quite boring,' she continued. 'They'd grow impatient with my thirst for knowledge rather quickly, I expect, as it would probably come at the expense of their ego.'

Dad leaned back, and I could tell from his expression that her reply intrigued him. 'With all due respect, dear, I think you underestimate men – the decent ones, at least. In fact I'm sure that spirit of yours is precisely what would attract your admirers in the first place.'

I almost said 'thank you' since he had spoken my mind, but I resisted because it would have exposed our secret.

A smile surfaced on Cara's plump lips. 'I hope you're right.'

'He's definitely right,' Jason said with a shake of his head. 'You're remarkable, and you ought to know it.'

His confidence led me to focus on my dish because I suddenly couldn't stand the sight of him. Since I had experienced it before, although never quite so intensely, I recognised jealousy when it unfurled within me, but never had my own brother been the target of it.

When I arrived here, I hadn't expected to feel so rigid, much less this momentary resentment toward my brother which, if left untreated, could easily fester. Their familiarity triggered my envy because I yearned to know her like that. I envied him for having the freedom to wrap his arm around her shoulders without her shying away from his touch, and I envied him for having constant access to the enigmatic alleys of her mind.

He had told me that he didn't fancy her that way, but he was still a man. He would have to be blind, deaf and lack a cock not to feel even the slightest twitch in his pants around her. He might not view her in a romantic light, but I had no guarantee he wouldn't ever consider her in a sexual light. A couple of pints in, he could easily make the mistake. He had done it before with my friend Harper.

Did I really have to count on Cara to retain the decency not to play us for fools? Did she even care about us being brothers? I knew she cared for Jason, but it wasn't with ease that I relied on her to do the decent thing. The impression I had was that she was perfectly – if not *too* – capable of separating sex from feelings. In light of that, there wasn't a doubt in my mind that she could sleep with Jason without giving further thought to it – unless he forced her to.

It was reasonable that I would experience discomfort at the thought of Jason entering her the same way that I had, but what didn't make sense was my jealousy. Why did I yearn so desperately for her innermost secrets, for her body to invite my caress? And why did it bother me that other men could have the pleasure?

I continued to ride on that train of thought for quite some time until the answer dawned on me all at once.

This wasn't mere lust. This wasn't about my vanity; I wasn't on a quest to repair a bruised ego.

I had fallen in love.

Under any other circumstances, I would have enjoyed the realisation, but since I knew Cara was far from interested in being with me, I was instead rather upset.

'He's signed out,' I heard Jason say just before Mum called for what I realised was the third time, 'William, darling. Hello?'

Like a deer caught in the headlights, I looked up.

'Are you all right, dear?' she asked worriedly. 'You're as white as a sheet.'

'What is it?'

'I wondered if you could fetch us another bottle of wine.'

Grateful for the chance to escape the table, I pushed my chair out and stood up. 'Ripasso?'

'That'll do.'

'He's been acting weird all day,' I heard Jason say as I left.

'Well, he's got a lot on his plate at work,' Dad said. 'The transaction he's working on between GreenPark and Lightning Charge is a considerable one. GreenPark has got one of the largest networks of charging points for electric vehicles in the UK. Lightning Charge has been one of their competitors. You can imagine there's lots to go over and consider to ensure that the transaction happens smoothly and that the acquisition won't breach competition law – and I know Fred's pushing him hard.'

While I appreciated his excuse, it wasn't the real reason. The transaction was indeed a considerable one, but unlike my feelings, I had it under control.

I sighed as I reached into the wine fridge. This was quite the conundrum. Given Cara's convictions, I doubted I stood any chance at all of earning her affections. It didn't help that she commanded the attention of every man present wherever she went. It was only a matter of time before my successor would come knocking on her door. In fact, it was obvious that even Dad had fallen victim to her charm. So why should she favour me? It was clear our circumstances stopped her from entertaining even the thought of me, especially romantically.

I wondered if she would have been more amenable had I not been her flatmate's brother and future boss. At the same time, I knew I could never offer her anything else. These were simply the cards I had been dealt, but could I still win with them?

I frowned as I reminisced about our night together. She had told me then that she considered me 'boyfriend material'. Surely she must have meant that I possessed qualities she deemed desirable in a lover? So my personality wasn't the issue. Our incompatibility wasn't based on a difference of character but rather on external factors. But surely those things could be overcome?

I remembered another obstacle then. Aaron.

The moment I thought of him, my jealousy found another target, because her reasoning didn't make any sense. She had told me she didn't harbour romantic feelings for him, that he might as well 'be air' to her. But now I suspected her of having lied, because nothing else could explain her desire to remain with him when she could instead have reserved that time for me. No one was that rational. No one had that much self-discipline. If she truly liked me as much as she claimed – if I were truly 'boyfriend material' – then surely she would have chosen me over him.

It occurred to me that she might just be pretending that she didn't have feelings for him because she was scared he would reject her – a defence mechanism, of sorts. Perhaps she actually loved him.

What made matters worse was that he didn't carry the same risks as I did. He wasn't her best friend's brother, and he wasn't her future boss. He was her lover. The advantage that gave him made me ill with jealousy and fear. Considering her threshold, the likelihood that she would date him was far higher than the likelihood that she would date me.

They were already sleeping together. That could easily advance into a relationship. It was evident that she harboured at least some version of love for him, or else she wouldn't have been so attached. What if, in a few months, they decided to get serious?

I stood perfectly still, my heart aching in a manner it had never done before. I stopped breathing for a moment, waiting for the pain to pass, but it didn't.

I grimaced and shook my head. It felt like my brain was overheating from all this thinking; I was hung up on the fact that she had described me as 'boyfriend material'. Unless she had no conscience to speak of, it seemed too genuine a statement to be a lie. Had she told me that merely to shut me up? It would be a questionable method, but then again, it had worked at the time.

Delving deeper into thought, I remembered the scene in my office when she had signed her contract. The memory of her hand within mine remained particularly vivid because she hadn't shied away from my touch. On the contrary, I was under the impression she had welcomed the intimacy. Moments before that, she had confessed she was guilty of sexualising me as well.

Suddenly my chest felt a bit lighter. Maybe I did stand a chance after all. The question remaining was how. How could I make her see that I would be worth risking her attention for?

I realised then that my strategy should remain the same; I would need to befriend her before anything else. While biding my time until she felt ready to settle down with someone, I would try to warm her up to the idea of being with me. I would show her that, rather than take from her, I meant to give to her – everything in my power to help her reach her goals. She was convinced she could manage it on her own, and while I was sure she could, too, my presence in her life would make it even easier, not harder. I meant to prove that to her – that I would be a convenience, not a burden.

But since the strength of her convictions was considerable, I expected the process would require patience. Fortunately, I boasted quite a lot of grit, and I would rely on that to achieve my goal.

I was going over the details of my plan as I returned to the dining room. When I walked in, I could tell from their expressions that my smile puzzled them.

'That's a different man to the one who left,' Jason said with a raised brow.

'I had a word with myself.' I walked over to where Mum sat and opened the bottle to pour her a glass.

'*Merci, mon chéri,*' she said and caressed my back.

'*De rien.*' I directed my gaze to Cara's. 'I'm sorry I've been such terrible company. I've had a lot on my mind, that's all.'

She smiled, and my heart palpitated at the view 'No need to apologise. You're always wonderful company.'

'Especially when he's quiet,' Jason joked.

'Work-related?' Dad asked me.

'Yes,' I lied. 'Anyway, I'm handling it.'

'You always do.'

Like I'd said, one can never choose with whom to fall in love. Now that I had been struck, all I could do was gear up for the hunt – of a lifetime.

12

FRIENDS

CARA

TUESDAY MORNING, I WOKE UP AT EIGHT AND DRAGGED MY WEARY BODY out of bed to have a shower. My first exam, which was in Advanced Contract Law, was coming up on Friday, so I had reserved every weekday till then for revising. Since Jason started work at two this week, I would have the flat mainly to myself, so I had invited Aaron and Livy over.

They wouldn't arrive till ten, however, and I was grateful for that because I was a fire-breathing dragon straight after waking, so I would have incinerated them in a heartbeat had they been here already. They both had first-hand experience with that idiosyncrasy of mine, so I supposed that was why they had suggested that we should meet at ten and that I should wake up at eight.

Half an hour later, I sat at the kitchen table. As I ate my breakfast and read the news on my iPad, Jason walked past the open door. He hadn't bothered to put on a pair of boxers, but he covered his manhood with his hand.

'Morning,' he murmured groggily, and I could tell from his hair that he had just removed the eye mask he always wore to sleep. In fact that was the only thing he wore while asleep, and I had learned that last summer when we had spent a week at his family's holiday house on the Isle of Wight.

'Morning.' I smiled at the sight of his taut bum before he disappeared from my view on his way to the bathroom. Men, in my experience, often had better arses than women, and it was something I frequently envied them for. Jason didn't train his lower body half as much as I did, but judging from his derrière, it looked like he trained nothing else. Aaron was no exception, either.

An outsider would perhaps have found it strange that Jason didn't mind if I saw him naked, but the truth was that Jason was a bit of a naturist. To him, the naked body was the most natural thing in the world and therefore nothing to be ashamed of. Given his course of study, I supposed he had a rather clinical perspective on the matter.

He came back a few minutes later with damp hair and a white towel around his hips. 'When are Aaron and Livy coming over?' he asked and went to the Nespresso machine to make himself a cup of coffee.

'At ten.'

He nodded. 'I haven't seen Livy in ages – not since she split from Colin.'

'Yeah, she became a bit of a recluse while she licked her wounds. She's over him now, though, so you'll probably see her more often, especially now that we live together.'

'She's over Colin?' He turned toward me. 'Proper over?'

I raised my cup of coffee. 'I think so. Seems like it. She barely ever talks about him anymore.'

Jason faced away and grabbed his fresh brew. 'Good for her. That bastard never deserved her in the first place.'

'No, he didn't.'

'Well, I'm looking forward to it. I've always liked her. I think she's my favourite out of your friends. Aaron is a close second, though.'

I smiled. Olivia was indeed adorable, and I had always been thankful for her presence in my life even though we were quite different personality-wise; however, we had known each other since we were only three, so our difference in temperament was something we had learned to appreciate over the years. She had been my partner in crime for as long as I could remember, and because our ambitions had always correlated, we had helped each other prosper. Our biggest difference in character was that Olivia was a hopeless romantic while I was more of a realist.

'She's fond of you too,' I said.

'Is she?'

'Isn't everyone?'

He chuckled. 'Stop. You're making me blush,' he joked.

'Just stating my view.'

He shook his head, grinning.

§ § §

We had been revising for nearly an hour when I received a call from Dad. To avoid disturbing Olivia and Aaron, I walked into my room before answering it. He mainly wondered how I was doing and whether I felt ready for my exams, so I complained about how stressed I was. When I was done venting, he asked me to come for dinner on Friday. I declined because Mary-Anne, Aaron's mother, had already invited me, so we agreed on Saturday instead. Then we hung up.

I stayed in my room, checking my social media accounts. When I opened Instagram, I froze with surprise. I had received a message request from none other than William Night. It contained a meme of Leonardo DiCaprio biting on his fist from the film *The Wolf of Wall Street,* with the text: 'When you see her loading up the barbell with forty-fives'.

I had to laugh. Of course he would opt for nothing less than a grand entrance. But, despite his impeccable humour, I didn't immediately accept. My first instinct was to decline, because I wanted to avoid interacting with him as much as possible. Still, I couldn't deny that I was curious.

I clicked on his profile, but it was private; stalking it brought me no satisfaction. All I could see was his default picture, and it looked like it had been taken during some holiday. He was wearing a white linen shirt, smiling at the camera with sunglasses on, his hands tucked in the pockets of his light-blue shorts. Behind him was a picturesque village that looked like it could be somewhere along the coast of the Mediterranean.

Probably France, I thought. Daphné, his mother, was a child of French immigrants, though she was born and bred in England. I knew Jason and William frequently went to France because of that, since their maternal grandparents now lived there.

My body grew hotter when I thought back to the dinner with Jason's family last weekend. I had heard William and Daphné speak French to one another then, and William's pronunciation had sounded fluent to my ears, even though I didn't speak a word of French myself. One way or another, hearing it had set my libido on fire, and I had despaired; whenever I thought William couldn't possibly get any more tempting, he proved me wrong.

I stared at his locked profile, wishing I could see his grid so I could learn more about him. What kind of stuff did he post? Did he update it frequently? For some reason I doubted it, but I would have to follow him to know the answer. My pride wouldn't let me, though, so I returned to his message request with some disappointment.

I had already acknowledged that I was drawn to him like a moth to a flame, so accepting his request would mean speeding toward my doom. Had I learned nothing from the mistakes of Icarus? Was I really going to fly too close to the sun?

As I reclined onto my bed, I wondered why he had reached out. A demon whispered in my mind that I ought to accept, if only to uncover his motive. Besides, if he proved troublesome, I could always block him.

I responded with a meme of a girl squatting, with the text: 'When I hear, "No man wants a girl that's stronger than him", and I'm like, "Ain't nobody looking for a weak ass man either"'.

I waited one minute for him to see it, but since he didn't, I locked my phone and went back to the others. I had only just sat down when a notification lit up my screen. I hurried to check it.

Haha that's the spirit

How's revising going? Getting frustrated yet?

His brilliant pun made me double-tap his last message, adding a heart to it. There wasn't a doubt in my mind that he had referred to the doctrine of frustration, which was a common law doctrine relevant to Contract Law. After last Friday, he was well aware that I was currently revising for precisely that module.

Frustrated indeed. Nice pun

I think having lunch with me today might help you out of said frustration

I rolled my eyes. So that was his motive, was it? I had to give it to him: the man had remarkable perseverance. How many rejections would it take for him to understand that it wasn't going to happen?

Do you? I am shocked

That would probably frustrate me more than revising ever could tbf

After I had pressed Send, I paused to reflect on what I had just done. Rejecting him was actually becoming a habit. I had hardly given a thought to it, and I found it fascinating. This was quite the contrast to the first time he had asked to meet me again. I vividly remembered how difficult it had been for me to reject him back then. I hadn't been entirely sure that it was the right course of action. Now, on the other hand, I took his offer for granted. I was expecting him to ask again, and again, and again, until I perhaps one day changed my mind. I couldn't be at all certain that his interest would be perpetual, and yet I conceitedly acted as though it would be. Maybe this had been the last time he would ask, and I had wasted my chance without a second thought.

You are ever pessimistic

I could take a look at your notes, for example. Help you get a first

All I'm suggesting is a normal lunch between two friends – nothing more, I promise

Friends. I stared at the word for a while. My heart took a deep dive in my chest, the beats growing stronger but slower. I read 'friends' as a rejection in disguise. The fall from my high horse was certainly a painful one. Was he seriously friend-zoning me?

We could never be friends, I thought bitterly, and we couldn't for the simple reason that I didn't lust after my friends the way I lusted after William. I would never be able to view him in a platonic light, and I was offended by the idea that it wasn't mutual.

Or was it? Maybe he was just being devious. I had already noted his sly tendencies.

What was his scheme? I couldn't read him. Was he writing to me in a genuine effort to befriend me, or was he looking to capture me once and for all? I really couldn't tell. It was plausible he sought to be my friend because of our relationships with Jason. In the end, it was inevitable that our paths would cross for the rest of our lives, so perhaps he was simply trying to make the best of it, and he thought pursuing a friendship with me would be the way to achieve it.

Since I didn't know what to think, I opted for an ambiguous, albeit humorous, answer inspired by one of my favourite comedies, *The Inbetweeners.* It was an image of the character Simon from the show, and he was holding his thumbs up while saying, 'Oh, friend.'

Haha Simon. What a legend

Not sure I can be friends with a briefcase wanker

Bus wankers only?

His wit really was flawless, and I was delighted he had caught the reference.

'Who are you texting?' Olivia suddenly asked.

When I looked up, she was studying me with an arched brow. Her question drew the attention of Aaron, who paused typing on his laptop and gazed in my direction. His kind eyes filled me with guilt. I knew I hadn't done anything wrong – we weren't a couple – but since it was novel to remain in touch with one of my previous bed partners, it seemed immoral even though it wasn't.

'Phoebe.' I said my sister's name as though it was the obvious answer.

'She's awake?' Aaron asked, surprised. Blood rushed to my face at his astute remark. 'Isn't it like six o'clock in New York?'

'She's just woken up,' I lied again.

'Right.' He frowned, and I knew he didn't believe me, but he refrained from probing me further. 'Tell her I said hi, then.'

'Me too,' Olivia said. 'How is she doing?'

'She's doing well,' I said dismissively and focused on my phone. I wanted to avoid further interrogation.

Lol maybe

Anyway, I appreciate the offer, but I honestly don't have time. Exam's on Friday

I'm hardly allowing myself toilet breaks atm

Christ

You clearly need training in stress management

I'd be happy to tutor you in that as well. You'd get a 100 % discount

Both Aaron and Olivia stole glances at me, so I pressed my lips together to hide my smile.

Full-on life coach, aren't you?

Accept and you'll find out

Limited offer

I need to get back to revising. Enjoy your lunch

Seen

Sighing, I put my phone aside and told myself not to check it again for the remainder of the day, but I failed every hour and was equally ambivalent every time I saw that he hadn't sent anything else.

§ § §

All through Wednesday, I checked my Instagram more than usual because I both dreaded and hoped to find another message from William. But, following my rejection yesterday, he hadn't initiated any contact. I opened our message thread several times throughout the day only to see that he had been active now and then, but it hadn't been to message me.

On Thursday, I managed to recover some of my self-control and hardly checked. He had been active a few times, but since I no longer expected to hear from him, seeing it hadn't bothered me that much.

When the clock struck seven, I closed my textbooks, every tab in my Chrome window, and my Word documents, to quit revising for the day. I was one of those students who always took the evening before my exams off to let the information process into my long-term memory, so I planned to do some wall-staring for the remainder of the evening before I would go to bed at nine.

Wall-staring was one of my favourite activities. I could lie for hours at a time just staring at the ceiling while I contemplated life. Consequently, boredom was an entirely foreign concept to me, and I had always been grateful for that. My mind entertained me endlessly, so I had never been one to depend on external stimuli. Being stuck in traffic or waiting for the Tube was actually something I enjoyed because of that. Dad liked to say: 'If you're bored, it's because you're boring,' and that statement resonated with me.

I wasn't sure what time it was when I reached for my phone to check it. My heart did a flip when my screen lit up.

William had messaged me again.

I sat up and unlocked my phone.

19:57

Good luck tmrw. Not that you'll need it

My emotions were conflicted. While I appreciated hearing from him and was charmed that he had remembered my exam tomorrow, I also wished he would leave me alone, because this was precisely what I had wanted to avoid: I had been thinking about him most of yesterday, and I couldn't remember having checked my social media this often before, and it was only because of him. He had become the distraction I had feared he would the first time we'd met, and seeing proof of it was only reinforcing my desire to avoid him.

Nevertheless, I decided to reply.

I do though, but thanks

Seen

A grin I hated surfaced on my mouth when he instantly marked it as read. He must have been waiting for my response.

You'll be fine

You can't know that

He sent an image of Bob the Builder with the text 'YES WE CAN' written across it. I laughed. His humour was frankly one of his most attractive attributes.

Omg

Make Bob proud x

I'll do my best

I chewed on my lower lip when I realised that his back must be starting to ache from always having to carry the conversation. On the one hand, that was what I wanted, because if all I offered were dry replies, he would be more likely to grow bored with me. But on the other, I felt I owed it to him to return at least a portion of his interest. I convinced myself that it was the polite thing to do, so before long, I started typing.

Have you had a nice day?

I groaned when he instantly saw it and proceeded to like it. Too late to unsend it, I thought.

What's this? Are you actually showing interest in my well-being?

I already regret it lol

Haha. My day was fine. Miss teasing you, though

He attached a cartoon of an adorable but angry chipmunk. I stared at it, nonplussed.

...

It's you whenever I tease you

I gaped. Was that really how he saw me whenever I got flustered? No wonder he couldn't stop himself from teasing me.

Omg

Anyway, I don't want to distract you right before your exam, so I'll leave you to it

Break a leg x

I wondered if he was actually busy with something else, or perhaps even someone else, and had said it only as a cover-up to put himself in a favourable light. After all, shouldn't *I* be the one to decide whether he was stealing my precious time or not? Knowing how many women he entertained, it was perfectly possible that one of them had either just arrived or returned from the bathroom or something like that.

Hearing my own thoughts, I frowned at myself. Why should it matter who he was with? He wasn't mine, and I had no intention of pursuing him either. Regardless of whether he was with someone else, he had set aside the time to send me this encouragement, and I ought to appreciate that gesture. One way or another, he was only being kind.

Thanks

Seen

By nine o'clock, he still hadn't sent me anything else, and I noted to myself that I disliked his habit of always letting me have the last word. For some reason, it made me feel inferior. So yes, he had explicitly said that he didn't want to disturb me, but he had done this last time as well. Was he doing it deliberately, as some sort of strategic retreat? Was he playing games? Trying to attain some sort of psychological advantage? Unsure of what to make of it, I decided I would now pay careful attention to whether he would repeat this pattern.

I put my phone on my nightstand and settled to sleep, but I didn't feel the least bit tired. In the darkness of my bedroom, memories of our sensual night together feasted on my mind. One by one, they marched into my thoughts, regardless of how hard I tried to suppress them.

My pulse spiked as I imagined him above me and within me, mouth forming dirty declarations while he stared intensely into my eyes. I couldn't breathe. Wide-eyed, I stared blankly ahead and felt an abundance of heat in my face. Full of tension, I writhed beneath the duvet.

'Jason!' I yelled when I had spent hours chasing sleep to no avail.

A few seconds later, he opened the door, wearing nothing but a pair of boxers.

'You called?' He rubbed his face and leaned against the doorpost.

'Could you sleep here tonight? I can't sleep. I need cuddles.'

He nodded and smiled softly. 'Sure,' he said and climbed into my bed.

'I love you,' I cooed.

'And I love you.' He hooked his strong arm around me and scooped me into his familiar embrace. 'When are you waking up?' he asked drowsily.

'Alarm's set for half six.'

'Okay, I'll make sure you wake up.'

'Thanks.'

'Sleep now.'

'Yes.' I snuggled closer and released a contented sigh.

§ § §

The next day, Olivia and I were having dinner at Mary-Anne's place along with Aaron and Tyler when I boldly confessed to seeing little point in the Royal Family.

'That's actual heresy,' Olivia said. She had always been of the opposite opinion and fancied the tradition it entailed.

'I appreciate their charitable and diplomatic work,' I said, 'but that, as well as everything else, can be executed by elected officials. I can't stand the idea that people are born into roles like that. And how can we improve in the future if we won't let go of the past? The monarchy has served its purpose. It's outdated now. There's no reason to keep it around. I mean, merely for the sake of history? Please.'

Olivia gasped as if I had just cursed in church. 'In times of need, we require one head at the top to gather the people,' she argued. 'One who unifies the people under a common goal. Politicians can't do that the same way the Royal Family can.'

'Listen, I regard the Queen with the utmost respect,' I said. 'Don't get me wrong, I think she's wonderful. What I'm questioning is the principle. I don't support the concept that people should be born into roles like that. And I also find it fairly ironic that they're not supposed to have a political opinion. They're supposed to be neutral. But isn't politics what royalty was built upon in the first place? Wasn't politics the reason monarchies came to be? I just think it's ridiculous. We can have presidents and elected officials. Look at France, for example, or Germany. They've managed superbly without a monarchy.' I shook my head. 'I seriously think it's only a matter of time before we'll move away from the constitutional monarchy as well. It's outdated, to say the least.'

Across the table, Mary-Anne smirked and raised a spoonful of ice cream to her lips.

'Quite the diatribe,' Tyler said and glanced at Aaron. 'I can see why you like her,' he joked.

I had always appreciated Tyler, and I could understand why he and Aaron had been friends ever since secondary school. They were quite similar. Both were shy of conflict and always preferred a conciliatory approach.

'I disagree,' Olivia said. 'I think the Royal Family serves a unique diplomatic purpose, as well as an important general role in society. When or if a new war breaks out, the whole nation will be looking to Her Majesty the Queen, not the Prime Minister.'

'Er, to be fair, I think they'll be looking to both,' Aaron intervened. 'They certainly looked to Winston Churchill during the Second World War.'

'It's irrational to think that we should keep the monarchy merely for the sake of tradition,' I said to Olivia. 'It must serve a practical purpose that will prove more lucrative than other alternatives. Imagine how we could administer the resources that go into maintaining the monarchy. It's also a matter of caution that the head of the nation should only be allowed to sit for so long. We've seen how totalitarian a ruler otherwise can become. Have you learned nothing from when you studied constitutional law?'

Soon after I had said it, I leaned back and blinked. I hadn't meant to sound so harsh. Fortunately, Olivia knew me better than most, so she took no offence. She merely shook her head and said, 'We will never agree on this. And the separation of powers guarantees that no such thing can happen, so I actually did pay some attention while we studied constitutional law, thank you very much.'

'Biscuits, anyone?' Mary-Anne asked and sent the dish around the table. I recognised them as my favourites. Mary-Anne made the best butter biscuits in the world.

'Oh, Mary-Anne,' I cooed. 'Butter biscuits.'

She smiled at me. 'I made them especially for you.'

'You shouldn't have.'

'Of course I should have.'

Tyler chuckled. 'That attenuated the intense debate rather quickly.'

'Cara is quite similar to a beast, actually.' Olivia laughed. 'Feed her her favourite treats and she'll be placated.'

'I'm sorry, I'm too opinionated. I just get so engaged,' I apologised.

'Never apologise for that, my dear,' Mary-Anne said. 'You're a delight.'

Tyler asked me, 'Have you considered going into politics?'

I scoffed. 'No. I imagine I'd have to sacrifice my values on several occasions if I had hoped to get anywhere.'

'The caustic tone.' He smiled. 'Did you vote leave or remain?'

'Brexit? Remain, absolutely, for an abundance of reasons.'

'Me too.'

'Let's not go into that.' Olivia shook her head. 'The whole thing still makes me angry.'

'I heard you received an offer to extend your placement at Day & Night this summer,' Mary-Anne said to me then.

If the mention hadn't immediately reminded me of William, I would have grinned, but instead, a shy smile was all I gave.

'I did.'

'That's something we ought to raise our glasses to.' She lifted hers.

'Aaron's placement at Dentons deserves the same,' I said.

'To Aaron and Cara, then.' She grinned.

'Meanwhile, my marks didn't make the cut,' Olivia murmured amusedly.

'Hey,' I said after a sip. 'Don't let that bring you down.'

'I won't.' She nodded. 'I'm honestly overjoyed on your behalf. Knowing how hard you and Aaron work, you deserve it. I wish I could say the same, but I'm much lazier than you. Now I'm paying the price.'

Mary-Anne reached over and squeezed her hand. 'Never give up. Perseverance is always rewarded in the end.'

Olivia smiled fondly at her.

§ § §

After dinner, I helped Mary-Anne clean the dishes while the others remained in the living room and watched TV. I was thankful for some quietness. My brain was exhausted after today's exam, and socialising was something I usually found taxing, so I didn't say much, but that was something I had always adored about Mary-Anne: just like Aaron, she was extremely comfortable to be around. I never felt the need to say something to break the silence because, around her, I always felt welcome to be myself.

'Aaron told me the exam was tough,' she said after a while.

'It was brutal.'

'And the next one is on Thursday next week?'

'Yeah. I'll start revising for it tomorrow. I need a day off.'

'Understandable.' She reached over and stroked my arm. 'I'm very grateful to you, Cara. Aaron's always been a bit of a loner, but I can tell he's thrilled with his life at UCL, and I suspect I have you to thank for it.'

I chuckled. 'Hardly. Between the two of us, he's the more likeable person. I've been told I tend to intimidate people. Aaron gets on with everyone.'

My phone rang in my pocket then. I dried my hands and pulled it out. Jason was calling.

'Hiya,' I answered.

'Hi, love. How did it go?'

'Okay, I think, but it's hard to say. I might have missed the target. Who knows?'

'I'm sure you nailed it. Anyway, I'm heading to Will's, so I doubt I'll be home when you get back. We're playing a game of chess, and it tends to last a couple of hours.'

'Right, sounds like fun. Tell him I said hi, I suppose.'

'Will do. Love you.'

'Love you too.'

I rang off and saw that I had a couple of notifications, but one in particular earned my immediate attention. It was a message from William.

> Congratulations on completing the first of your exams! I'm checking in to make sure you're still alive.

Sensing Mary-Anne's eyes on me, I looked up to meet them.

'That's a lovely smile you're wearing,' she said amusedly. 'Could it be due to a lucky man?'

I feared my blush exposed me, but I shook my head all the same.

'No, just a friend, and a funny one at that, hence the smile.'

'Mm-hmm.' She was evidently not convinced, but instead of probing me, she merely gave me a knowing smile. I wondered if she would have reacted the same had she known about my arrangement with her son. Probably not.

Turning my focus back to my phone, I replied with a meme of a man in seemingly impenetrable armour of the medieval sort, with the caption 'Me: fully prepared for exams'. But in the image straight below, an arrow struck through the slim gap in his helmet, with the text 'question number one' written along its shaft.

After that, I put my phone back in my pocket and promised myself not to look at it again before I left.

§ § §

Olivia and I had planned a sleepover at mine, so we headed home together shortly before midnight. By the time we parted ways with Aaron and Tyler, I had grown impatient, wanting to check if I had received any new messages. As we stepped onto the Central Line, which would take us from Wanstead to Notting Hill Gate, I took my phone out of my pocket. A smile lit up my face when I looked at my screen. William had replied.

Haha I'm sure you aced it

Ever the pessimist

I liked his last message but decided to wait with replying because Olivia wanted to talk about Colin. She had heard that he was seeing Alison now, the girl he had cheated on her with. Naturally, she was rather irate about it, and she had only found out yesterday, so she was worried the news had affected her performance in her exam today. Listening to her was a solid reminder of exactly why I would do best to avoid William. To find myself in her shoes, my attention divided between a man and my ambition, was a far cry from tempting.

'You need to put that arsehole out of your mind, Livy,' I said. 'He's not worth your attention. I know it's easier said than done, but if he's really seeing Alison now, it's just another reason never to give him a single thought again. He really doesn't deserve even a scrap of your time.'

'It just feels so unfair,' she whined.

'The world isn't fair.'

'Your realism is hardly what I need right now.'

'Sorry.' My lips protruded. 'I wish there were something I could do to make you feel better. I completely agree that you don't deserve this, but . . .' I shrugged. 'It is what it is. You've spent three years of your life with a man who didn't deserve it, but that can happen to the best of us. You ought to do yourself a favour and learn from it as you move on.'

'Yeah, it's just difficult to accept.'

'I get it. I'd probably feel the same way.'

'Urgh.' She tossed her head back. 'I can't wait for exams to be over so I can start dating again. The lack of male attention isn't helping me forget about him.'

'I'll gladly be your wing-woman again. That's if you would dare to entrust me with that task after it failed last time.'

She laughed. 'You'll be too busy working anyway.'

'Not at the weekends – I hope.'

'We'll see. Either way, I'd love that. Speaking of, how's that going? Have you met William lately?'

'Not since he helped me assemble my wardrobe and since dinner with his parents, but I've already told you about that.'

'He's not made any other advances?'

I could tell her that he had started messaging me on Instagram, but I hesitated. I worried it would make everything real to me. If I told her, he would inevitably become a recurring subject, and I didn't want that. I was struggling enough as it was with putting him out of my mind, so I couldn't see what good it would do. The constant reminder would only worsen the headache he was giving me.

'No.'

'Hm. Well, I hope you're pleased. I still think you made a mistake.'

'Whatever.'

As we walked along the pavement toward my flat, Olivia was busy messaging one of her other friends, presumably about Colin, so I took the opportunity to reply to William.

I wasn't all that frustrated tbh ;)

Should work out fine (I hope). Anyway, how's your Friday?

Spending it with this knob

He sent a photo of Jason. I chuckled at first, but my amusement subsided when it occurred to me that he was currently hanging out with my best friend, who had no idea at all that we were chatting under his nose. What had my life come to? All this secrecy wasn't something I was used to. I had always been one to favour transparency in my friendships, but now I had lied to Olivia and continued to withhold information from both her and Jason, not to mention Aaron.

Yes, he told me you're playing chess. Who's winning?

I am ofc. Always

But he'd never admit that

So I can expect to find him licking his wounds tmrw?

Probably

Have you played chess?

Only once or twice with my dad. Not my forte

I could teach you

Imagine his surprise when you suddenly defeat him

Haha that'd be something

Sold, then?

Enjoy your evening, Will. Glad you're having fun. Don't destroy your brother completely tho. I like him

Seen

Left on read. Again.

13

LIVERPOOL'S IN THE LEAD

William was strangely quiet. He hadn't sent me any messages since Friday last week, and it was Thursday now. As I sat on the train on my way to the exam in Company Law, I wondered what the reason was. Was it something I had done? Or perhaps not done?

I fixed my gaze on the floor, staring absentmindedly at the tiny black dots. I knew William was a busy man, so I tried not to take it personally. He probably had a lot on his plate at work.

Or maybe he's just bored with me, I thought, sighing. Whatever the reason, I appreciated that he hadn't distracted me while I was revising for my exam. Aaron and I had spent almost the entire week together preparing for it, but I was still nervous.

When it was finally over, I was relieved. It had been as difficult as I had feared it would be, but I had done my best, so now I just wanted to celebrate that I was finished with it. Aaron was in a splendid mood; he had done great.

'Have you got any plans?' he asked as we exited the building.

'What do you have in mind?'

'You, me and a bed.'

I chuckled. 'Yours or mine?'

He shrugged. 'Tyler's home, I think.'

'Well, Jason won't be home till five, so perhaps mine is better, then.'

'Yours it is.'

We hurried home, eager to take advantage of our few moments of privacy.

I had barely entered the flat when Aaron pinned me to the wall and kissed me. I groaned against his mouth and gripped his shirt, undoing the buttons with impatience. He closed the front door, not bothering to lock it, and shrugged out of his shirt, all while he kept kissing me. Reaching for my blouse, he pulled it over my head and undressed me until I was completely naked.

'Bedroom or here?' he asked breathily.

'Bedroom.'

He sank down, grabbed me below my bum, and lifted me up. I wrapped my limbs around him and kept kissing him as he carried me into my room.

Kissing Aaron had never felt wrong, but it had never felt quite right either – merely familiar. It had been weeks since I had experienced a kiss as entirely right for the first time – how consuming and intense it could be. Only one set of lips had managed to set my system on fire like that.

But they weren't present.

A few minutes later, I was moaning nonstop as I closed in on my peak, but a sudden thud made us both freeze before I could reach it.

We stared at each other, stunned. Was Jason home already?

'What was that?' I whispered, frightened.

Aaron snapped out of his paralysis and climbed out of the bed. 'Jason? Is that you?'

'Hello?' I called and heard subtle swearing outside my bedroom door.

'Aaron!' I whispered harshly when I saw that he was recklessly approaching the door. 'It could be a burglar! Did we lock the door?'

He turned the lock, eyeing me with a furrowed brow. Full of anxiety, I gripped the duvet and covered myself.

'Who's there?' Aaron demanded and lingered by the door.

I searched for my phone, wondering if I should call 999, but then I remembered that it was in my bag, which was still in the hall outside. My heart contracted with fear. What were we supposed to do now? Open a window and call for the neighbours?

'I . . . It's Will, Jason's brother.'

Even though it was barely audible, I recognised his voice immediately. Air stormed out of my mouth as if I had just been punched in the gut. How long had he been outside? Had he heard us?

This was the last thing I had anticipated, so I had no idea how to handle the amount of guilt I felt.

What was he doing here?

'Cara?' Aaron prompted.

'William?' I called, on autopilot.

'I'm sorry,' he replied, and his voice was a little louder now, but the tone of it penetrated my heart like a blade. He sounded so defeated.

Seeming to realise the absence of danger, Aaron bent and lifted his boxers from the floor. He put them on and reached for the door.

'Aaron!' I called impulsively. What was he doing? I wasn't prepared for them to meet, especially like this; I didn't want him to walk out wearing only his boxers when it would essentially mean rubbing our arrangement in William's face.

'What?'

'What are you doing?'

He frowned. 'I'm getting our clothes. They're outside, remember? Feels weird to leave them there when we're not alone.' He unlocked the door and opened it. 'Shit,' he said, and I could tell from his profile that the view was chaotic.

'I'm so sorry. It fell over as I came in,' William said.

Seized by panic, I stormed out of bed and grabbed my nightgown from my desk chair. I wrapped myself in the black satin and rushed to the door to observe their encounter.

The coat stand had fallen over. I squeezed past Aaron and bent to help William clean up the mess.

'I wasn't aware you were coming,' I said as I tossed Aaron's shirt to him, and I hoped William heard the apology disguised within my statement.

Without looking at me, William grabbed the coat stand and lifted it up. 'I arrived just now,' he said. 'Chelsea's playing at half four, and I didn't want to miss it even though Jason won't be here till around five. I sent you a message, but I guess you haven't seen it.'

I couldn't hide my distress. I hadn't checked my messages since this morning. I had been too distracted discussing the exam with Aaron as we went home.

'I haven't.'

'So you're Jason's brother,' Aaron said. 'I suppose that also makes you Cara's future boss. I'm Aaron.' He extended his hand, but when William only stared at it, he quickly withdrew it, probably remembering that his fingers had been inside me mere minutes ago.

Aaron looked mortified, his eyes fleeting. 'Sorry, I . . .'

'I appreciate the gesture, anyway,' William said gracefully. 'And I'm sorry, I didn't mean to interrupt.'

Aaron chuckled awkwardly. 'No worries. Sorry you had to walk in on that.' He looked at his watch. 'Anyway, it's past half four now.' He lifted his gaze to William's again, who was about three inches taller than him. 'Don't worry about this. Cara and I can clean up.'

'Thanks, but I was raised to clean up my own mess.'

'Right. Decent parenting. I'll find the match on the TV for you, then. I'd like to see it too, as it happens. They're playing against Liverpool, and that's my team.'

'Thanks.'

As soon as Aaron had disappeared around the corner, I searched for William's eyes, but they eluded me.

'I'm sorry,' I said, but he didn't reply. He merely reached for my beige coat, which had fallen to the floor along with the coat stand. We both froze when he lifted it. Underneath it lay the knickers I had worn today.

'Fuck.' I snatched them from the floor and tucked them into my palm.

'I'm leaving,' he said without looking at me and reached for the door. 'I'll tell Jason I went home instead.'

His decision struck me like a cannonball to the chest. A sharp breath escaped and I stared at him. I had obviously hurt him, and I hated myself for it.

'I thought you wanted to be friends.' I said it quietly so that Aaron wouldn't hear. 'Surely this shouldn't matter if friendship is all you want?'

Finally, he met my eyes, and his crestfallen expression clawed viciously at my chest.

'I thought I could manage it,' he said. 'But as soon as I heard you, as soon as I saw this' – he gestured to my clothes on the floor – 'I realised I can't. It's impossible, I'm sorry.'

Without further ado, he opened the door and left.

Trying to process what had just happened, I stared blankly at the door. He had actually heard us. My stomach churned, pushing the contents to my throat. I felt sick.

'Liverpool's in the lead,' Aaron said as he turned the corner. 'Er, where's he gone?'

I drew in a breath to compose myself. 'He felt too awkward to stay.'

I faced him.

Aaron grimaced. 'Shit. Really?'

'Really.'

He walked over and tilted my head back. 'Are you okay?' he asked worriedly and kissed my forehead.

I swallowed. 'I'm actually feeling a bit weird. That was very uncomfortable.'

He wrapped his arms around me, trying to comfort me. 'I'm sure he just needs a minute. I hardly think this will pose a problem once you start work.'

'I'm not really in the mood for sex anymore,' I said and pulled away. 'I'm sorry.'

He chuckled. 'I'd be surprised if you were. Don't worry about that. Let's watch the match instead.'

He knew full well that I wasn't one to watch football, but, right then, it was better than the alternative of hanging out in my room with nothing to do but talk.

'Sure. I'd like to shower first, though.'

'I'll just wait in the living room, then.'

§ § §

Half-time was just over when Jason stormed through the front door and into the living room.

'Fuck,' he grumbled when he saw the score. 'Not again. We can't afford this! What the hell are they doing?' He gestured to the screen, clearly vexed.

'I'm having a great time,' Aaron said amusedly, lying spread across the sofa.

'Yeah, fuck you,' Jason said with a laugh and folded his arms. 'By the way, heard you've had an awkward afternoon.'

I stiffened. 'Will told you?'

'Yeah.'

Aaron sighed and reached over to squeeze my thigh. 'Yeah, it was quite awkward. We tried to pretend like it was nothing, but he left anyway.'

'Can't say I blame him,' Jason said and walked over to claim the spot beside me, which forced Aaron to move his arm. 'You've had her all day,' he joked. 'My turn.'

I hadn't thought anyone could manage it, but Jason's comment actually made me grin.

'Sharing is caring, I suppose,' Aaron replied.

I glanced at him, and I could tell he was equally amused. That was something I had always been grateful for: Aaron had never felt threatened by my friendship with Jason. In fact the two of them had become good friends and sometimes hung out without me.

'Honestly, women smell so good.' Jason wrapped his arm around my neck and pulled my damp hair under his nose. 'So sweet, like dessert.'

Aaron burst out laughing, and the sound caught me.

'How long has it been since you got laid, Jase?' he asked.

'A millennium.'

'Your right hand must be growing sore by now.'

'You've no idea. So I've switched to my left.'

Aaron guffawed while I shook my head, chuckling. Men.

§ § §

I was grateful that Jason had come home because it was chiefly him who had entertained Aaron after William's abrupt arrival and departure. I hadn't been in the mood for socialising at all since then and had been counting the seconds till Aaron would leave. Shortly before midnight, he did, and the first thing I did afterwards was head into my bedroom to check my Instagram.

When I saw William's message, my heart stilled in my chest. Very slowly, I found a seat on my bed and grimaced.

11:09

> I'm coming over after work to watch Chelsea play. Hope your exam went well x

Brilliant. A reminder of his kind and decent character was precisely what I needed right now. It might as well have been a slap to the face or a punch in the gut. I knew I had hurt him, and the more I thought about it, the more it pained me to know. Eventually, tears welled up in my eyes, but they never coursed down my cheeks because I simply would not let them.

I was upset because I had hurt him, not because I felt I had done something wrong. I owed him no fidelity – we weren't even dating – and I hadn't known he would be here. He could hardly hold it against me that I would enjoy Aaron in my own home the way he probably enjoyed Francesca, Violet and Kate in his. The only difference was that he had a key to my flat, but that came with the risk of walking in on scenes like this.

Either way, he shouldn't have had to witness that. I couldn't imagine how nauseated I would have been had the roles been reversed – had I walked in on him and Violet, for example. There was something brutal about even just the idea. That sort of intimacy was unique, so to witness a person you had shared it with offer it to someone else, especially enthusiastically, seemed like a defilement.

I took a deep breath and focused on what to write to him. He hadn't answered my apology earlier, but since he'd had a few hours to recover his equilibrium, perhaps he would now. Regardless, I wanted to apologise again to show that I had thought about this since so that he would know that it had sincerely bothered me.

I'm genuinely sorry you had to witness that.
I don't really know what else to say

Seen

I hadn't anticipated that he would see it immediately, but he did. I sat there for quite some time, hoping to be told that he was typing a reply, but it never happened.

14

LIMBO

I WAS IN A PENSIVE MOOD ALL OF FRIDAY. WILLIAM HAD BEEN ACTIVE ON Instagram several times without responding to my message, but what was there to say? That I was forgiven? That would require something to forgive, but I had done nothing wrong, and he knew that as well as I did.

Since I didn't want to be a nuisance, I hadn't sent him anything else. Nevertheless, remaining focused on my exams was nearly impossible. While I no longer expected to hear from him and was finally free of that anxiety, it hadn't been half as satisfying as I had hoped, because I was left with the feeling that he was keeping his distance for the wrong reason; he was avoiding me because I had hurt him, not because he wanted to let me focus on my exams. In fact, it wasn't impossible that he was staying silent to punish me for the pain I had caused him. I understood his need for space, but what I didn't understand was his total lack of a reply. A simple thumbs-up would have sufficed.

I had no idea what was currently running through his mind, but thinking about it got me no further. I sat on all the questions while he sat on all the answers, and since we weren't speaking, I doubted I would ever know them.

Ultimately, I was unable to appreciate the revelation that he hadn't been able to friend-zone me either; it was no victory in the grand scheme of things. I had hurt a person I had started to care for, and that was nothing to celebrate. I worried he would only despise me from now on.

By Saturday, I had been able to work through some of my feelings, which had enabled me to revise for most of the day. Still, he disturbed my thoughts more than I appreciated, but at least I was able to be somewhat productive.

It was nearing six o'clock when I heard Stephen and Jonathan entering through the front door. They had been there when I first met Jason at the pub three years ago, and I had grasped early on that they were a trio that had lasted since childhood. Stephen was the one who had lived here with Jason before I had moved in.

'At last,' Jason said. 'Don't tell me you forgot the sushi.'

'I haven't got a death wish,' Jon replied. 'You ready to get robbed tonight?'

I assumed he was referring to the lads' night they made time for once a month. 'Poker night', they always called it. I had been aware of that tradition of theirs for several years, but it wasn't until this morning that I had registered that William was a regular participant. The same applied to his friend Andy from work, and another man named Alexander. Apparently, William, Andy and Alex were also a trio alongside Jason, Stephen and Jon. The six of them often interacted because of that, although Jason was supposedly an uncounted member of William's group as well.

Sensing that there was about to be some activity outside, I reached for my noise-cancelling headset. They had been covering my ears for no more than ten minutes when my chair was suddenly pulled back. Next thing I knew, I was dangling from Jon's shoulder while I rushed to save my headset from falling to the floor.

'Oh my God!' I shouted. 'Put me down! Immediately! I'm revising!'

All three of them guffawed at the frantic motion of my arms, and it increased in volume when I spanked Jon's arse.

'Jon! Put me down!'

After three pirouettes, he charged toward my bed and launched us onto it.

Dizzy, I struggled to fix my gaze on anyone at all, but once my vision settled, I stared at Jon's devilish grin.

'Hello, pet. Long time no see.'

It was impossible not to laugh. 'You twat.'

He ruffled my hair, lay down beside me and tucked his hands under his head. 'We got sushi for you. Dinner's served.'

'Oh. That was kind.'

'It was my idea,' Jason said proudly. 'You've hardly eaten the last couple of days. Don't think I haven't noticed. You barely touched my scrambled eggs this morning, and that's unusual to say the least.'

If only he had been aware that it was solely because the taste now reminded me of William and the morning in his flat.

'Everyone needs dinner, Cara,' Jon said strictly and ran a hand through his short, light-brown hair, trying to tidy it.

'How's living with Giselle?' I asked Stephen.

'It's great. I'd forgotten how nice it is to have a female round the place. Everything smells wonderful all the time, even the bathroom after I've had a shit.'

'Same,' Jason said and patted his shoulder. 'Moving apart wasn't all that bad after all. Cara keeps the place constantly clean. There's hardly a speck of dust anywhere, ever.'

I smiled amusedly. 'You clean just as much as I do.'

'Maybe.'

'That, he does.' Stephen nodded. 'But he's been scared of germs since forever. Occupational hazard, I guess.' After a visual sweep of my bedroom, he directed his brown eyes to mine. 'Love what you've done with the place. All I had in here was that wardrobe, a desk for gaming and a bed. I barely recognise it.'

'Agreed. It's strangely homey, but fashionably at that,' Jon said and reached for one of my beige decorative pillows to tuck it under his head.

'The rug is a nice touch.' Stephen stepped forward and rubbed his foot against the white fabric. 'Very soft.'

'Thanks.'

'Anyway, let's eat,' Jason said. 'I'm famished.'

§ § §

Poker night was being held at Alexander's place in Kensington, so the lads left around half six to be there by seven. Their friendly presence had helped me forget about William for a couple of hours, so the silence that ensued after their departure came as a bit of a shock. Suddenly it was just me and my thoughts again, and for once, it wasn't something I enjoyed. In an attempt to drown them out, I played music so loud that I couldn't process a single word on the page as I tried to revise. Finally, I abandoned revising altogether and allowed the music to consume me instead.

In the darkness of my bedroom, I listened until my ears ached. Only then did I turn it off and decide it was time for bed. It was nearly midnight when I did, but I didn't expect Jason home anytime soon, so sleep was my best option in the search for a distraction. As I closed my eyes, I hoped he would find his way into my bed instead of his own.

Though scarcely, I had managed to catch some sleep when I suddenly woke to the sound of the front door being slammed shut. Harsh whispers followed, but I couldn't distinguish the words.

Jason, I presumed, but he was evidently not alone. My pulse spiked when my thoughts settled on William. I hoped desperately that it was him because, if it was, I could force him to talk to me. Then again, I hardly dared to hope for it since I considered it highly unlikely that he would risk encountering me so soon after what had happened.

Pushing my duvet aside, I decided to find out. While I put on my nightdress, I heard the subtle sounds of retching. Jason must have had too much to drink.

I opened my bedroom door as quietly as I could and saw light streaming out of the bathroom. The door was open, and once the sounds of vomiting settled somewhat, Jason moaned, 'Shit, the world's spinning so fast. I think I should go home.'

'Shush, be quiet. You'll wake Cara.'

My heart jolted at the sound of William's authoritative voice. My prayers had been heard.

'Cara's not here. She's at home.'

'You *are* home, you fucking knobhead,' William said, his voice low. Under any other circumstances, that would have made me laugh, but William's presence had made me apprehensive, so not a sound made its way out of my mouth.

'Really?' Jason asked, sounding surprised. 'Ah, yes. This my beloved toilet, isn't it?'

'Yes.'

'God, I'm so drunk.'

'You really are.'

'How come you never get plastered, Will?' Jason asked, slurring his words.

'I don't enjoy being helpless.'

'Really? I find it fun sometimes.'

'That's 'cause you're fucking stupid.'

'Cunt.'

'Come on, wash your mouth.'

Jason released a surge of loud laughter then.

'Why the hell are you laughing? Turn it down,' William said aggressively, though he kept his voice down.

'You're telling me to wash my mouth 'cause I called you a cunt?' Jason replied.

'No, I'm telling you to wash your mouth since you've just vomited every meal you've had today.'

'Oh.'

'Fucking hell.'

I took a deep breath for courage and approached the bathroom. The instant I entered the doorway, William looked up and caught my reflection in the mirror. As soon as he registered my presence, his eyes frosted as though he had just come upon an internal ice age. His forgiveness seemed far from my reach.

'Is he all right?' I asked him, but he was spared from having to answer when Jason noticed my arrival.

'Cara.' Jason smiled affectionately. 'There are two of you now, but I love both of you equally.' I barely managed to understand him. 'Double the love.'

'Christ. Is there anything I can do?'

'No, go back to bed,' William said.

'How come you got this drunk, Jason?' I asked.

'I was sabotaged. Stephen and Jon kept pouring and mixing my drink. All of a sudden I was plastered.'

I sighed. 'I should've anticipated this.'

William shoved Jason's toothbrush into his hand. 'When are you going to learn that you shouldn't let them mix your drinks for you? This isn't the first time this has happened, and I'm sick of being your voice of reason and getting completely ignored.'

Jason looked at him, and it was obvious from his expression that he was too intoxicated to comprehend what he was hearing. 'You're always so strict.'

'Only when you're reckless,' William said. 'Cara, go to bed. He needs a shower.'

Disobeying, I waited outside the bathroom till they were finished, and William didn't bother hiding his annoyance when he discovered me.

'I told you to go to bed,' he said, his irritation scorching, but his focus diverged when Jason approached my bedroom. 'That's not your bedroom, Jase.' He grabbed Jason's shoulder.

'I know. I want to sleep with Cara.'

Wide-eyed, my gaze darted to William's, and the wrath it contained expelled my soul from my body.

'That's not happening,' he said through gritted teeth and tugged Jason harshly in the other direction.

'What?' Jason looked at him, nonplussed, and then writhed his arm out of William's hold. 'The hell's your problem, mate?'

'Will, it's fine, he does it all the time. It's only friendly,' I said, hoping it would reassure him.

'She's *my* friend. Not yours,' Jason said, sounding like a brat.

William's chest expanded with his deep inhalation, but it seemed to have no appeasing effect, because antagonism continued to swell in his eyes.

'Fine.'

In the dim light, I saw his jaw flex, and it looked like he had stopped breathing.

Jason gave him a snort and zig-zagged toward my room, where he went straight to bed. As I went to close the door after him, William charged toward the hall, but I stopped him before he could pass me. I had just managed to shut the door when I gripped his arm, and I was shocked at the way he jerked away from my touch.

Pure intimidation exploded in my chest when he faced me properly. Stepping forward, he trapped me between his huge body and the door.

He reeked of alcohol. He had clearly seemed soberer than he was.

My heart pounded as I looked into his blistering gaze. His menacing demeanour held me in a tight grip, paralysing me. I couldn't move a muscle.

'You are to stay the fuck away from Jason,' he commanded chillingly. 'Do you hear me?'

I swallowed, my stomach clenching in a knot. 'Of course. I haven't touched him, not like that. I'd never.'

He raised a brow, conveying that he didn't believe me in the slightest.

'I swear,' I said as unbidden tears surfaced in my eyes.

He glared at me for another while, assessing my sincerity. Then, without a word, he turned and approached the door.

'William, I'm sorry I hurt you,' I said, and I couldn't help the quiver in my voice.

He froze, hand lingering on the handle.

Seeing a chance to speak, I continued, 'Will, I'm not your girlfriend. I've got to be allowed to do this sort of thing in my own home, and it's not as if you haven't been guilty of the same.'

He whirled around with a look of scorn. 'What?'

'Yes.' I gestured to him. 'Francesca, Violet, Kate? How many are there, really?'

I tensed up when he moved toward me again. Halting only a foot away, he glared down at me.

'For your information,' he fumed, 'Kate is my ex, and I haven't spoken to her in well over a year. As for Violet and Francesca, I haven't seen them like that for weeks and had actually planned to end it with them because of *you*.'

My lips parted with shock. That was the last thing I had anticipated, so it took me several seconds to conjure up a reply. 'I . . . I'm sorry. I didn't know.'

He frowned and stared sharply at me. 'Of course you didn't. That's precisely my point. Stop assuming you know anything at all.'

My throat tightened. 'You're right, I'm sorry.'

He kept glaring at me, holding me still with his eyes alone, until his shoulders finally sank.

Sensing that he was calming down, I dared to say, 'I don't expect you to stop seeing them. I don't expect anything from you at all.'

His face twisted, his features emanating a vulnerability that made my heart contract. 'Why are you like this?'

I grimaced. 'I tried to warn you.'

'You're in love with him, aren't you? With Aaron?'

His question beat the air out of my lungs. 'What? No!' Was that really what he inferred from this? 'I've already told you, I—'

He clasped my head between his hands, and before I knew it, his warm mouth had moulded against my own. Instantly, my chest filled with delight and I rejoiced in the taste of him. Again, that uncanny sensation spread through my body, reminding me that this was how a kiss was supposed to feel – entirely right. I softened against him, yielding to the amorous motion of his mouth.

His tongue pushed past my lips for a dance with mine, obliterating what remained of my self-control. Swinging my arms around his neck, I pressed myself against him and returned every ounce of his passion. Groaning, he pinned me forcefully against the door to my bedroom, but I was so engaged in the moment that I gave no attention to the fact that we might wake Jason.

Hungry in their movements, his large hands explored my curves, squeezing and stroking, causing lust of a whole new level to override my reason. As his hand grasped my breast, I groaned into his mouth and shoved it deeper within his grip. His other hand trailed lower, sliding down my waistline until he clasped my nightdress and pushed it upward. He ran his hands across my bared skin, lovingly, then cupped my bum and lifted me. Locked between his body and the door, I wrapped my legs around him.

He thrust his hips forward then, making me gasp. His erection pressed against my bare entrance, evoking delicious memories of our night together. I desperately wanted to feel him inside me again, but I knew it would only make a bad situation worse.

At that moment, I caught myself wishing he were all I cared about, that nothing else mattered. If only he weren't going to be my boss. If only he weren't Jason's brother. And if only I didn't care so much about my career.

But I did.

'Fuck.' I pulled away from his mouth.

His jaw clenched. 'As I thought.' He put me down and retreated a pace.

His words struck me like a knife.

'I'm sorry,' I whispered, tears pricking my eyes again.

Contempt poured from his. 'Spare me,' he said and went for the door.

'No, you misunderstand.' My face contorted. 'I pulled away because I don't want to hurt you.'

'Don't patronise me,' he said venomously.

'Please, listen to me. I can't give you what you want.'

He paused in front of the door. 'You can.' He glanced at me over his shoulder. 'You just won't.'

Panicking, I rushed over to stall him. We couldn't part like this. It was paramount that we settled this once and for all, because it was crucial that we maintained harmony, especially for Jason's sake.

I stepped in front of the door to prevent him from leaving. 'Can we talk? Once you've sobered up?'

He refused to meet my gaze. 'Do you have any idea how frustrating it is to feel wounded by something when I have no right to feel that way?' he asked vehemently. 'There is no satisfaction, just an everlasting state of limbo.'

I realised he was referring to when he had walked in on Aaron and me, and to know that he felt that made my tears brim over. His misery was palpable, and I hated being the reason behind it. I wished I could make it go away. He didn't deserve to suffer like this.

'Perhaps if you allowed me to explain, you won't feel that way anymore.'

'Why are you so scared to be loved?' he asked and finally looked at me.

My breath rasped in my throat, a sharp pain searing into my chest. Was he implying that he was in love with me? No, he couldn't be.

Could he?

'I'm not scared to be loved,' I said, my voice light and shaky. 'You misunderstand. I'm scared to find my attention divided. I'm scared *to* love.' *And you most of all.*

He shook his head. 'I'd like to leave now.'

I remained in front of the door. 'I really think we should talk.'

'There's nothing left to say.'

'Please.' I grimaced. 'Are you free tomorrow?'

His jaw flexed as he glared away.

'William, please.'

'No,' he bit out and forced me to step aside. 'I'll see you in June, Cara.'

In June? He planned to avoid me until June? My heart shrieked at the idea.

'June?' I echoed stupidly.

He didn't respond. He merely opened the door and walked out.

'William, I'm sorry,' I said just before he shut door between us. He met my eyes through the gap, and the view burned into my memory as one of the more painful things I had experienced. Then he closed it.

I stood perfectly still, staring at the door with tears coursing down my face. But they were silent tears. Not so much as a sob escaped me.

I wasn't sure how long I stood there, but eventually I found the strength to lock the door and return to my bedroom. For all I knew, Jason could have woken up and heard us. If he had, I would have a lot of explaining to do, and I dreaded it. But when I entered my room, I found him comatose in my bed, dead to the world.

I lay down beside him and stared up at the ceiling, trepidatious about what the future might hold. Would William truly avoid me until June or was it just something he had said because he was drunk and emotional? I hoped with all my heart that he hadn't meant it. If he was that cross with me, I couldn't imagine that my placement at Day & Night would be a good experience.

My face contorted and I stifled a sob. This was exactly what I had feared; this was exactly why getting romantically involved with him was a terrible idea. If things ended on a bad note between us, like they had now, it would undoubtedly create a hostile work environment for me. I would be miserable and demotivated, working under the leadership of a man who couldn't stand me.

To make it worse, it could also affect my friendship with Jason. What if William, out of spite, decided to tell him about our past? And that I had wounded him badly? Would Jason cut me off for William's sake? Was our friendship that fragile?

I turned my head and saw only the vague silhouette of Jason's figure beside me. I didn't think our friendship could break so easily, but then I had also witnessed first-hand how close he was with his brother.

I wiped my cheeks and tried to tell myself that it was useless to worry about things that might not happen, that I should cross that bridge when I came to it, but it was easier said than done. I hoped desperately that William would move on and forgive me, that when I finally started work, we would treat each other professionally, our past forgotten.

Strangling another sob, I turned onto my side and stared into the darkness, shaking. Had I known things would turn out like this, I would never have gone with Olivia to that bar. I would never have succumbed to those spellbinding blue eyes or that enchanting, crooked smile. I would have been blissfully unaware instead, as I missed out on the most captivating man I had ever met. Then June would have come and I would only have fantasised about knowing him so intimately, not actually experienced it.

If only I hadn't gone with Olivia to that bar . . .

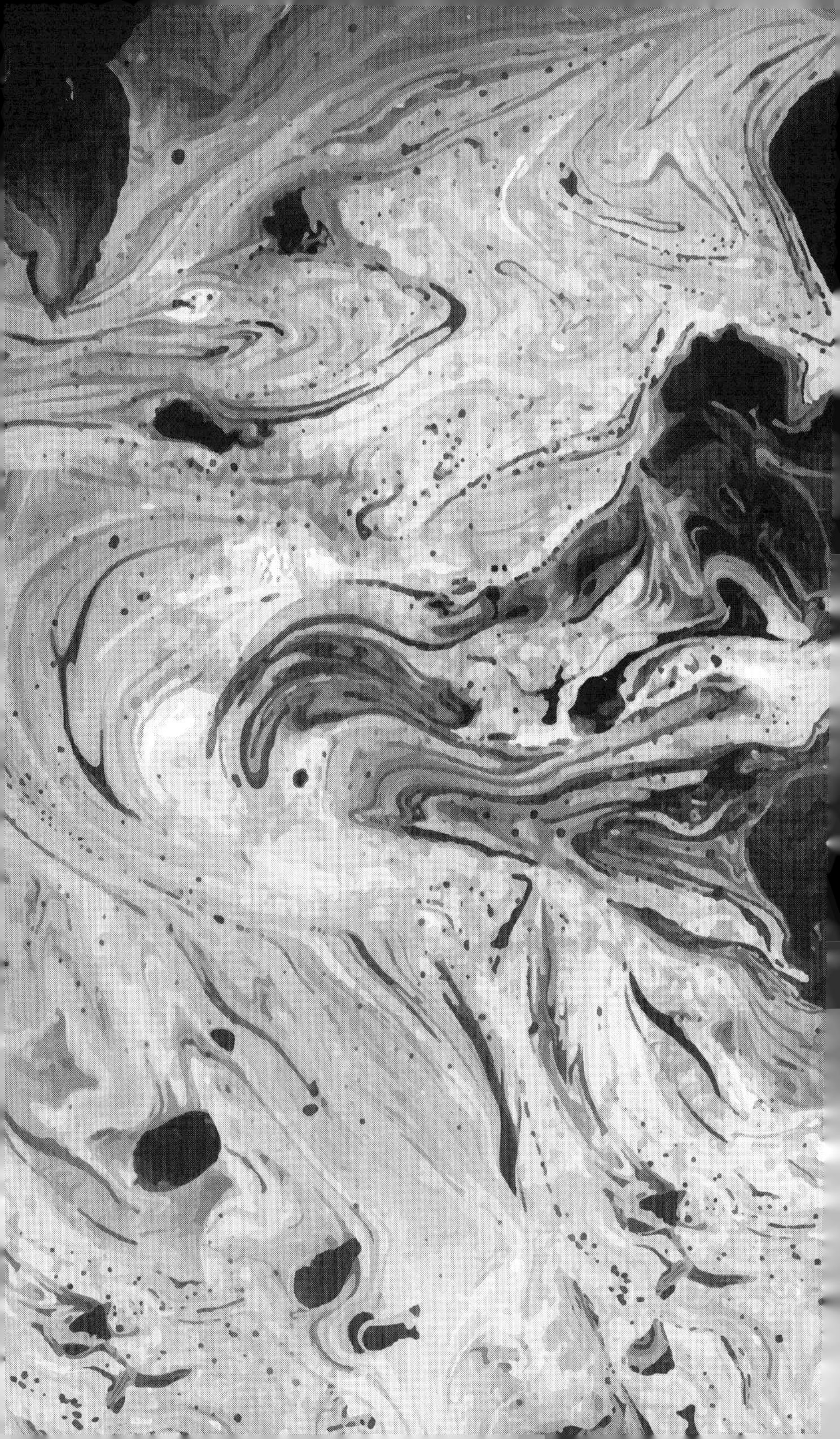

PART II

10 June 2019

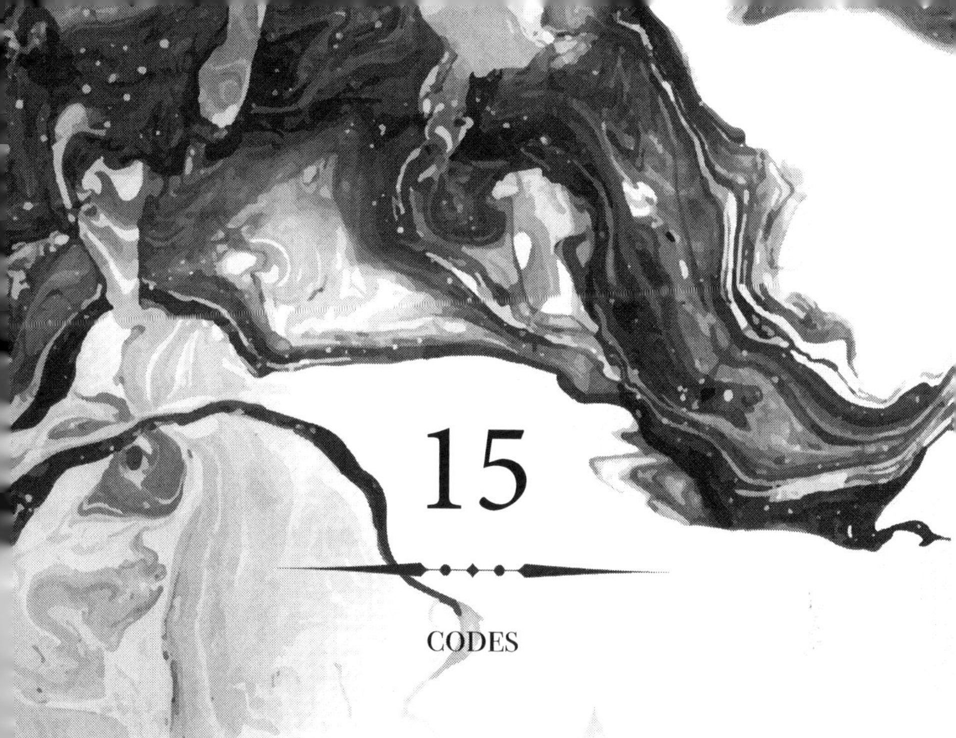

15

CODES

It was odd how having a degree to my name suddenly made me feel much older than I was. Wherever had my teens gone? I missed them. They had been such carefree days. All I thought about now was my career and how to advance it. At the moment, the way to do that was by showing up for my first day at one of the top City law firms, being Day & Night LLP, for my work experience placement.

I had woken up at six to prepare for it. I knew I would be shadowing none other than William for the span of the next three months, so I had been trepidatious while I completed my morning rituals and cooked breakfast for Jason and myself.

I hadn't encountered William since he had brought Jason home after poker night, and he hadn't sent me any messages either. I had frequently questioned if I had made the right choice, but upon receiving my exam scores back, I had been reassured. The exam that had suffered the most was Commercial Law, which was when my trouble with William had been at its peak.

To be as ready as possible for my first day, I had decided what to wear last night – a pastel blue pencil skirt with a white silk blouse to go with it. Low, white heels completed the outfit as I made my way through the revolving entrance door of the huge Day & Night building on Cannon Street.

At the reception sat a lady, brown hair tied into a bun atop her head. I halted before her pale marble desk, which was decorated with beautiful flower arrangements, and met her eyes. There wasn't a trace of a wrinkle on her face, though I suspected she was in her early forties from the experienced gleam in her eye.

'Hello, Miss,' she greeted. 'How can I help you?' She smiled up at me, baring white teeth behind rosy lips.

I swallowed nervously. 'I'm Cara Jane Darby, a new trainee.'

Nodding, she typed on her desktop Mac. Then she pressed the hands-free device attached to her small ear. A silver earring flattered the lobe of it. She had an excellent taste in jewellery. She presented herself as positively elegant.

'Hello, Ellie, it's Debbie. Miss Cara Jane Darby just arrived.' She paused, listening, and then nodded. 'I'll let her know. Thank you.' Hanging up, she smiled at me again.

'Elisabeth will be down in a moment, Miss Darby. Would you like any refreshments while you wait? A cup of tea, or perhaps some coffee?'

My eyes widened. Did I look like I needed refreshments? At once, I stifled my self-conscious thoughts. What was I thinking? She was only being accommodating, which I was certain was part of her job. Hold it together, I told myself, but I was extremely nervous about seeing William again.

'I'm all right, thank you.' I indicated with my hand a group of contemporary white armchairs at the far end of the lobby. 'I'll wait over there.' I went over to them.

I had just sat down when Ellie's round figure exited the lift and approached the security gates. While scanning her card, she gave me that enchanting smile of hers, and I was amused I still remembered the beauty of it.

'Hi, Cara,' she greeted excitedly. 'How are you?'

'Hi, Ellie.' I stood up and approached. 'I'm all right, thanks. How are you?'

'Excited to start your first day?'

'I am.' But also scared.

'Good. Will usually arrives at eight, so we'll have some time to get you settled before then.'

My heart raced at the thought of reuniting with William. How would he treat me now? Was he still upset with me or had he moved on?

'Great,' I said and took a steadying breath.

§ § §

Ellie had left my side for a minute while I was setting up the MacBook I would be using for work. Of course, that was when I saw him out of the corner of my eye.

I stopped breathing. My heart went berserk. It lashed out against my rib cage, beating so aggressively that I could feel my pulse thumping in my throat.

Inwardly I begged him not to notice me, as I could have used a few seconds to regain my composure, but judging from the direction of his travel, he already had. I turned my head to regard him properly, and I nearly sobbed at the view. My memory did him no justice at all. He was far more beautiful than I remembered.

For a moment, all I did was admire his elegance. Dressed in a beige suit, he carried himself so confidently, so gracefully, as if nothing could shake him.

He halted in front of my desk, his hypnotic blue eyes riveting me to the spot. I sat completely still, overcome with emotion. It was so strange to see him again.

'Good morning,' he greeted and gave a vague smile. I just barely managed not to shudder at the sound of his voice. I had almost forgotten how seductive it was.

I gulped, unsure if I could trust my vocal cords. 'Good morning.'

He glanced over my desk, setting me free from his paralysing spell. 'You're here early.'

I forced a smile. 'Ellie thought you might appreciate the efficiency, so she asked me to arrive at half seven.'

He nodded, his gaze elusive. 'She knows me well.'

As I lowered my stare from his handsome face, I noticed he was carrying two cups of Starbucks coffee.

'This one's for you,' he said and put the smallest on my desk.

I studied it, perplexed. He had bought me a coffee on his way to work? He had thought of me this morning? How often did I cross his mind? Part of me hoped it was often. Since he persisted in plaguing my mind, I wanted it to at least be mutual.

'That was kind.' I looked at him, uncertain. Had he bought me this to signify that he wanted to reconcile? Bury the hatchet and move on?

He shrugged his broad shoulders. 'Flat white is your favourite, right?'

Surprised he remembered, I stared at him for some time, gathering myself. 'It is, yes.'

He looked away, his lips twitching as if he was suppressing a smile. 'Makes sense. It's smooth, but powerful, just like you.'

My eyes widened while heat crept into my cheeks and crawled across my scalp.

Was he flirting? Or was he only trying to be nice?

He raised his coffee to his mouth and took a sip, still avoiding my eyes. 'I suppose regular black suits me similarly – conservative and bitter.'

My heart missed a beat. The man was communicating in codes, and I struggled to decipher them.

'A-about that,' I stuttered. 'I . . . Once again, I'm sorry about—' I stopped short when he met my eyes.

'It was just a joke – a bad one. Forget I said anything. It came out wrong.'

I swallowed. 'Still, I feel I—'

'It's in the past. I'd rather we left it there.'

I closed my mouth, nodding. Unsure of what to say, I glanced at the cup on my desk. 'Well, I appreciate the gesture. Aren't I supposed to be fetching coffees for you, though?'

He took another sip. 'As if I'd ever trust you to fetch my coffee for me. It'd be laced with poison, I'm sure. I haven't got a death wish.'

His banter caused an involuntary smile to bend my lips. 'So my boss is paranoid. Good to know.'

He smiled crookedly, and the view flooded me with emotion. That smile. It felt surreal to finally see it again.

'How have you been?' he asked and averted his eyes. 'How did your exams go?'

His questions helped me relax a bit. I was glad he was initiating small talk, because it gave me hope that we would at least be able to act civil toward one another.

'Really well, actually. Well, apart from Commercial Law, where I could've done better.'

He nodded and delved his free hand in his pocket. 'You must be relieved they're all over and done with.'

'For now.'

'For now?' He frowned and looked back at me.

'Plan is to start my master's degree after the summer.'

His eyebrows arched. 'Oh. Full-time?'

'Yeah.'

'I did that too.'

'You've got an LLM?'

'Yeah.'

'Oh.' I hadn't known that.

Ellie reappeared behind him. 'Morning, Will.'

He turned. 'Good morning, Ellie. Thanks for being here earlier than usual to help Cara get started.'

'Least I could do.'

'Still, I appreciate it.'

She gave him a knowing smile. 'I thought you might.'

'Anyway' – his gaze veered to the door to his office – 'I'll leave you to it.'

Hopelessly intrigued, I stared after him.

'No,' Ellie suddenly said. 'Trust me, love, you do not want a piece of that.'

It felt like somebody had just punched me in the gut. Had she seen me ogle him just now? She must have.

Breathless, I said, 'What?'

She eyed me sternly. 'Trust me.'

I cleared my throat and focused on my laptop. 'A piece of what? I wasn't—'

'You were.'

I pouted. 'Well, I'm sorry. I was only admiring the view. He's a good-looking man.'

She chuckled. 'He is, but don't fall for it. He's a complete workaholic and has absolutely no interest in relationships. Trust me, I've asked him several times, and it's always the same answer: "I'm single, but I'm not available." So don't fall for his charm, all right? I'd hate to see you mess this up.'

I didn't blame her for having that impression, but in this particular respect, I suspected I knew him better than she did. Nevertheless, her statement did make me wonder. What did he mean when he said he was single but not available? Had he abandoned the idea of relationships since we last met? The possibility intrigued me.

I gave her a warm smile. 'Ellie, I'm committed to my studies. Don't worry. Besides, I've already got someone to serve that purpose, but it's nothing serious.'

'Really?' She grinned. 'What's their name?'

I didn't fail to notice her gender-neutral phrasing. 'Aaron.'

'Aaron,' she echoed. 'Did he study law as well?'

'Yeah. We were in the same year.'

'I see. Well, I'm happy for you.'

'Thanks.'

I reached for the coffee William had given me. While lifting it to my mouth, I noticed the black ink of a marker on the side. When I turned it, I froze in my seat.

A peace offering, it read. My eyebrows curved and my chest filled with relief.

He had forgiven me.

§ § §

William remained in his office while Ellie and I covered some basics. She showed me how to fill in timesheets, which time codes to apply depending on the tasks I completed, as well as the difference between non-chargeable time and chargeable time. She also taught me the basics of 'WIP', which was short for 'Work in Progress'. Essentially, it translated to the total amount of chargeable time a team recorded against a time code on a specific client code. After that, she taught me the basics of billing and brought me to the finance team at Day & Night to show me how to send an invoice to a client. Once we returned, she taught me the firm's IT system, how to accept calls, where to store notes on clients, and how to set up appointments and meetings in the solicitors' calendars.

We were just about to head for lunch when an associate exited her office and approached Ellie and me. Looking up from my laptop, I stared at her, entranced. I remembered her vividly because she was one of those women you simply did not forget. Her eyes captured mine almost immediately, and below them, a slow smile made its way across her lips.

Violet.

I thought as I watched her that it was no wonder William had wanted her as a sexual partner. Her beauty was remarkable, and there was an assertive air about her that reminded me of William's. They had to be kindred spirits, so of course they would take a liking to each other. I wondered if she was still sleeping with him.

'Hello,' she greeted as she reached my desk. Now that I had the chance to look at her more closely, I assumed she was in her early thirties. 'I haven't had the chance to introduce myself yet, but I'm Violet – or Vi. Most call me Vi.' She extended her hand, and I admired her manicured nails before I took it. Her grip was firm, her smile bright.

'Pleasure to meet you . . . Vi. I'm Cara.'

She released my hand and folded her arms. 'Likewise. Will's told me a lot about you.' Her brown eyes gleamed, kindling a suspicion in me that he might have told her more than I would be comfortable with.

'Has he?'

She chuckled. 'Yes. Your dedication to your career has been particularly emphasised.'

Was she insinuating something? It was difficult to discern whether she knew about us or not.

'He knows me well, I guess.'

'Hearing it reminded me of myself.' She smiled and tilted her head. 'So I'm sure you'll manage brilliantly during your time with us.'

'I hope you're right.'

Her eyes narrowed faintly, and I got the feeling she was trying to get a read on me. 'Just be careful you don't sacrifice too much for it – your career, I mean. I've been there and done that, and if I could go back, I would have proceeded differently.'

Her warning confirmed my suspicion; William must have told her about us. Nevertheless, I was shocked. Was she implying that I ought to have given William a chance? She clearly wasn't a possessive type, and the reality of that made me realise that their arrangement was indeed only casual, if it even existed anymore.

'Consider me warned.' I nodded.

Just then, William exited his office. I looked at him, and Violet followed my gaze. He froze, eyes flickering between us, and his blank expression made it impossible to guess his thoughts. Seeming to recover, he walked over to us.

'Vi,' he greeted.

'Hi, Will,' she replied fondly. 'I was just introducing myself to our new paralegal.'

His gaze shifted from her to me. 'I hope she didn't scare you. She can be a bit intimidating, but she always means well.'

'I'm still here,' she said amusedly.

'She didn't scare me at all,' I said. 'She was just offering some words of wisdom to an aspiring solicitor.'

Sceptical, William knitted his brow and turned to her again. A message I couldn't decode passed between their eyes before she faced me and said, 'Anyway, lunch?'

'Sure.' I smiled.

§ § §

Lunch was an awkward event. Andy joined us for it, and re-encountering him was a strange experience, because I didn't remember him being so aloof. While he was polite when he greeted me, he didn't say much to me overall. I often sensed his eyes on me, but whenever I looked over, he averted them. He was obviously analysing me, and it made me feel slightly uncomfortable.

Ellie, who I was seated across from, initiated most of the conversations while Andy traded regular glances with William across the table. Neither Violet nor Ellie paid them any attention, so I assumed that they behaved like this on a regular basis. In the end, they were best friends, so it was to be expected that they would have secret and silent conversations that nobody else would understand.

Things took a turn for the worse when John Night arrived at our table, along with a few of his fellow partners. I met Mr Philip Day, for instance, who was John's first partner in establishing their empire. He was a nice man of short build, with a big belly that strained against his expensive suit.

While asking how my day had been thus far, John grabbed his son's shoulder.

'It's been amazing,' I said. It wasn't entirely a lie. The professional aspect of the firm had kept me on my toes all day, even if my boss had kept me on my toes for a whole different reason.

Looking John in the eye, while knowing I had slept with his son, was an unpleasant experience. Even though I had endured it before, it still unsettled me. I should not have been sitting on the knowledge of how William performed in bed, but I was.

I worried my gaze was a tad too fleeting, but I couldn't help it. What I had done was unseemly, and I was scared John would pick up on it somehow. Underestimating his perceptiveness was not something I intended to make a habit of.

When it was time for William's meeting with our client Clifford Paints, I was relieved. Finally, I would be provided with intellectual distraction.

Ellie was unlinking her MacBook Pro from her computer monitor when Violet caught my eye. She was walking beside Frederick Silverstone, a senior associate who was leading the team on the potential merger between Clifford Paints and Craft Interior.

The sexual power she wielded was outstanding. It was noticeable from her confident strut, which I paid keen attention to as she guided Mr

Clifford and his son, as well as their company's financial adviser, toward a conference room. Instead of watching where they walked, the three men kept their eyes glued to her firm bottom.

'Ready, then?' Ellie asked and gave me an encouraging smile.

'Yes.' I stood up and closed my laptop to bring it with me.

'Good. Could you let Will know that they're here?'

I nodded, a lump gathering in my throat. After a deep breath for courage, I turned for his office and scraped together what little strength I had left, but just as I was about to knock on his door, he ripped it open and nearly crashed into me. In my rush to dodge him, I tripped on my heel. As I was about to tilt backward, his hand shot forward and grabbed my arm, and then he yanked me toward him again with such force that I slammed face-first into his chest.

The irony of the situation was not lost on me. By trying to evade him, I had only ensured bumping into him. But since his intoxicating scent hit me before his muscles did, I didn't notice any pain.

My goodness, he smelled amazing. But his scent instantly evoked the memory of our sensual night together, causing a throb between my legs.

'Careful there,' he said when I tipped my head back and looked at him. Hyperaware of his closeness, I felt his thumb gently rubbing my arm. My skin tingled beneath his touch. No man had ever made me feel this way, where merely a touch could send my heart into overdrive.

Blushing scarlet, I cleared my throat and struggled to suppress the erotic memories his scent had triggered. Clutching my MacBook to my chest, I tried to ignore how hard my heart pounded against it.

'Your client is here,' I said.

'Vi's already notified me.'

I nodded. 'Do you always charge out of your office as though you're late for a flight?'

At the corners of his mouth, a smile threatened, but it never made it to full bloom. 'As a matter of fact, I'm nearly late for a meeting.'

'Right. Am I insured under the firm's policy if I end up seriously injured next time you storm out of your office like a bull? Because I didn't find that clause in my contract. "If your boss happens to run over you, you are entitled to compensation depending on the extent of your injuries",' I joked.

'I'll personally make amends if that happens,' he said, and his tone was loaded with something I couldn't distinguish. 'Though, for next time, try not to be such a slow turtle.'

I shrugged. 'Or, and hear me out, you could try walking next time, instead of bolting out like you're trying to outrun The Flash.'

'*DC Comics*?' His head tilted as he caught the reference. 'That was unexpected. Batman's my favourite. Which one's yours?'

I blinked. Was he flirting or just being friendly? I couldn't seem to read him today.

'Er, same actually,' I said as a new wave of heat coloured my cheeks.

He chuckled. 'Of course.'

I glanced down the aisle beside us. 'Weren't you running late?'

I detected a flicker of intrigue in his light-blue eyes as he stared down at me. Slowly, he released my arm and settled his hand on my back.

'After you.'

He ushered me down the aisle. Acutely aware of his hand on my back, I heard my pulse drumming behind my ears while my heart appeared to have relocated to my throat. I was tempted to ask him to remove it but, at the same time, I never wanted him to.

We were quiet as we went to the conference room. I was grateful for that, because I wasn't sure I would be able to string together any coherent sentences. His touch was far too distracting.

When we reached the door, I was about to open it for him, but he beat me to it. Pushing it open, he ushered me in first.

'Mr Night,' Mr Clifford greeted immediately, rising from his seat.

'Mr Clifford.' William smiled. 'This is Miss Cara Darby, a new trainee of ours. She'll be helping Miss Tallis with the report.' As he introduced me, his head jerked in Ellie's direction at the end of the table.

Violet studied me from head to toe from where she stood beside Mr Clifford, but I couldn't guess what her thoughts were.

'Hello,' I greeted and walked over to shake hands with them. As I escaped William's touch, I was struck by how cold my back felt without it. Odd. I had never noticed escaping someone's hold quite so consciously.

Once I had greeted Gerard Clifford, I moved to greet his son, Tom Clifford, and then finally their financial adviser, Bo Zhang. Then I grabbed a seat beside Ellie, put my laptop on the table, and huffed out a quiet, anxious breath.

The meeting was intense. Though Frederick was present, it was clear he had left William in charge. Was it normal for a junior associate to lead a meeting like this or was it a testament to William's competence?

Overcome with admiration, I observed as William led Mr Clifford and his son through the process of the congeneric merger and what it would entail. They discussed which information Day & Night would require to proceed, the specific technologies and sensitive information Clifford Paints had that required added security and which would also be included in the mutual non-disclosure agreement, as well as how soon we could pass said agreement to Craft Interior for signing. In the event that Craft Interior would sign, Clifford Paints would return to us with more information regarding the financial details for how they wanted to complete the transaction, as well as material for the legal due diligence process.

I didn't dare to question the state of my underwear while I watched William. He was in his element, and it was awe-inspiring to witness. I had never been so desperate for a man's sexual attention before, never been so aroused. I could almost hear my ovaries calling his name. Clever as he was, he was tantalising to a fault.

I could hardly fathom that I had managed to find my way into this astounding man's bed. His brain nearly gave me an orgasm in and of itself.

Tormented, I sat there till the meeting finally concluded. When it did, I remained paralysed in my chair, flabbergasted. My face had been constantly flushed. I felt out of breath, for heaven's sake. Under the table, I squeezed my thighs together, desperate for some friction, and shocked myself in the process. My fluids had not only drenched my knickers, but they had also lubricated the better part of my inner thighs. My skin was moist and sticky.

'Cara?' Ellie called when the solicitors had escorted our clients out of the room. My head jerked up, and I found her frowning at me.

'You okay?' she asked.

'Yeah.' I swallowed. 'Just a bit overwhelmed.'

She smiled reassuringly. 'Yeah, well, you'll get used to it soon enough. It's a fast-paced environment, but you shouldn't feel intimidated. It's always like that in the beginning. Everybody's been there.'

All I could offer was a nod.

'Well,' she said, 'now that I've written the first draft of the report, I'll have to do some polishing. We should probably do it together. Will, Fred and Vi are likely to want it on their desks by the end of the day.'

'Sounds good. Can I use the loo first, though?' My voice had a pleading tone because I was anxious to clean up the mess that William had unwittingly made. Would I have to bring spare underwear to work from now on?

'Of course.'

§ § §

When Ellie had read through my polished version of the report, she leaned back with a grin. 'This is actually really good work, Cara. Well done.'

I huffed with relief. Initially we had planned to do it together, but she had been called to attend another meeting with Frederick, so she had told me to attempt it by myself using her notes. I had appreciated that. I always learned faster when I was simply thrown into a situation and forced to sort it out on my own. Being guided was one thing, being micromanaged was another, and I was not a friend of micromanagement.

Her opinion made my day. It truly did. After all the chaos I had endured with regards to William being my boss, I was in dire need of positive feedback. During the meeting earlier, I had been genuinely concerned about my performance, seeing as I hadn't had the mind to notice anything but him. Thankfully, it would seem I had managed to compensate for what I had lost by completing this report.

'Thank you.' My shoulders relaxed, and so did my heart. Not even my final exams had left me as battered as my first day here. I was glad I had reached the end of it.

'Why don't you print it and hand it over to Will?' Ellie said. 'After that, I'm sure he'll let you leave for the day.'

'Sure.'

Nervous hardly covered how I felt when I stood outside William's door some minutes later, mustering up the courage to knock. My hand was trembling when I raised it to the dark brown wood.

'Yes?'

I sucked in a deep breath and opened the door. Poking my head through the gap, I said, 'I've finished the report.'

William ripped his gaze from the screen of his desktop Mac and gave me his undivided attention. 'Have you? Well done. Let's have a look, then.'

Stepping in, I closed the door after myself and approached him with some vigilance. I desperately wanted to impress him, so I hoped he would approve of the report.

Amusement crossed his face when I extended the document to him.

'Your hand is shaking,' he said, and I hated that he noticed.

'Caffeine overdose,' I lied.

He raised a brow as he grabbed the report. 'Perhaps you should consider reducing your intake.'

'I'm an addict.'

'Typical law student,' he murmured and fixed his eyes on the document. When his brows eventually furrowed, my heart clenched in panic. Had he spotted something? Taking his sweet time, he turned the page and slowly began nodding to himself.

'This is excellent. Great job.'

Air stormed out of my lungs, and I didn't care if he noticed. 'Really?'

He studied me with some surprise. 'Really. Are you all right?'

'I'm just a bit anxious. I want to get this right.'

His gaze softened. 'Cara, calm down. You'll do fine. I'll make sure of it.'

His calm demeanour was strangely contagious. 'Thank you,' I said, finally relaxing.

He dropped the report on his desk. 'You're free to go. I'll see you tomorrow.'

'Right, thanks. How long do you intend to stay? Just curious.'

He turned his attention to his screen. 'I usually leave at eight or nine, unless Chelsea's playing. But the season's over, so work has got my full attention now.'

I laughed. 'You are such a nerd about football.'

'I'm a nerd full stop.'

I giggled. 'And you should be proud of that.'

'I am.' He smiled crookedly, still looking at his screen.

'I'll see you tomorrow, then.'

'Yes. Tell Jason you did wonderful on your first day, or else I will.'

'All right.' I grinned, and I was still wearing it when I exited the building and walked out on the street. Maybe shadowing him wouldn't be as bad as I had feared. Thus far, we had managed to maintain a professional relationship impeccably, I thought.

16

CURIOSITY KILLED THE CAT

William and Ellie weren't here yet, which I was glad to see. To make a good impression, I had meant to arrive before them. It was Wednesday now, and my first two days at Day & Night had gone rather well. In particular, I had William to thank for that. I had been worried he would have difficulty treating me as a colleague, but his behaviour had exceeded my expectations. He hadn't sexualised me so much as once, much less forced me to remember our one-night stand. Instead, he had been perfectly professional and had taken me under his wing precisely the way he had promised he would when I signed my contract some months ago.

Finding my seat, I booted up my laptop and opened William's virtual calendar to get an idea of his day. I knew I had to visit Clifford Paints this afternoon to collect some documents on William's behalf, so I was trying to figure out when to complete the task. Shortly after lunch, he had a meeting with Violet, so I gathered I should do it then.

At five to eight, I heard the gates to the lift slide apart. A smile caught my lips when I turned my head. Wearing a navy suit, William was approaching me with two coffees in his hands. It amused me that he continued to bring me coffee every morning. He had done it yesterday as well. While I appreciated it, I wondered if it was special treatment because I was new and he wanted me to feel welcome, or whether he had been in the habit of doing it for Charlotte as well – the paralegal who had taken maternity leave.

'Morning, love,' he greeted. 'You're here early – again.' He surprised me when he proceeded past my desk. 'I thought you could work in my office today,' he said with a grin when he noticed my confusion.

'Your office?'

'Yeah. We've got plenty of things to go over today, so I thought it might be more efficient. Bring your stuff.'

Heeding his command, I charged up from my seat and gathered my things. Then I headed toward his office, where he stood waiting by the door.

The closer I drew, the more intense his gaze seemed, so a faint blush had smeared my cheeks by the time I reached him. Too shy to look up at him, I walked in while mumbling, 'Thanks.' My own shyness surprised me somewhat. I couldn't remember having felt this way around a man – ever. Too shy to look him in the eye? What on earth was going on with me?

As I put my things on one side of his desk, my eyes investigated the surrounding chaos. Myriad files covered nearly the entire surface of it, and it made me gulp. So this was what I had in store? How did he keep track of all this? Then again, he did seem like an organised man.

I thought of his flat. I remembered how tidy it had been. I hadn't noticed a speck of dust anywhere, but perhaps he had someone to do his cleaning for him. A maid, for example. With his schedule, I couldn't imagine he had time to spare for chores like dusting.

He shut the door and approached. 'I'll get this out of the way,' he said as he rounded his desk. 'Here.' He extended a cup of coffee to me.

Shyness still dominated my feelings, but I was able to meet his gaze and offer a smile of gratitude as I took it.

'You don't need to do this every day, Will. I appreciate it, but you know I'd be happy to do it instead, right?'

He chuckled as he dumped his brown leather bag in his office chair. 'I don't expect you to bring me coffee, Cara. The shop's in the same building as my flat. It's part of my routine to stop by every morning.'

'Expensive habit.'

He raised a brow. 'I can afford it,' he said, and from his tone, I was reminded that he didn't enjoy drawing attention to his wealth.

'Time-wise too?'

His lips twitched with amusement. 'It hardly takes a minute. Besides, by doing it, I'm helping the economy overall. I'm creating jobs.'

That was an excellent point. I hadn't thought of it like that before.

'If you insist.'

'I do.'

'Did you bring coffee for Charlotte every morning as well?'

He shook his head. 'Never occurred to me.'

My ego appreciated hearing that, as it made me feel special to him.

'I suppose I should start doing it when she comes back,' he said then, which punctured the boost my ego had just enjoyed.

Scared he would notice, I avoided his eyes and focused on setting up my laptop while he cleared his desk. 'I'm sure she'll appreciate that.'

He might as well have said 'enough small talk' when he proceeded to change the subject. 'Anyway, we've got quite a lot of work to do. As you know, you've got to collect the files from Clifford Paints later. In the meantime, I'll be working on the DD for the deal between Porter BioScience and Elixerion Pharmaceuticals. I've got a meeting with Vi shortly after lunch to go over it.

'Now, while I work on that, I thought you could have a go at drafting up the NDA for the merger between Clifford Paints and Craft Interior. I've got a few templates you can use to help you get started. I'll of course look over your work, but if you have any questions before then, don't be shy. Please ask, and I'll be happy to help you out.'

Nodding, I pulled a chair over so that I would be working across from him. 'Right, to summarise, and correct me if I misunderstood anything,' I said as I descended into my seat. 'First, I'll get started on making a draft of the non-disclosure agreement. While you're meeting with Vi after lunch, I'll head over to Clifford Paints to collect the files, and I suppose you'll want photocopies of those. Then, whether it's today, tomorrow or next week, you'll go over the draft of the NDA I've written?'

'Yes.'

'Okay. Why don't you email me the templates and I'll get started at once?'

'Great.'

One of several things I appreciated about shadowing William was that we worked exceptionally well together. In that regard, he reminded me of Aaron. We hardly ever talked while we worked, and whenever we did, it was always with a razor-sharp focus that intensified my excitement about getting things done. We seemed to speak the exact same language, perfectly synchronised. Neither of us were prone to beating around the bush. We were direct and efficient in our communication, and since neither of us were particularly sensitive, we never had to fear that our clipped tone would offend the other person. William was also remarkably pedagogical, so whenever I voiced any concerns as I worked on the NDA, his explanations were easy to grasp.

Overall, working with him was an exhilarating experience. I hadn't thought we would be so compatible in areas relevant to work, but we obviously were. To be perfectly fair, I couldn't remember having had such a good partner in anything before.

§ § §

It was nearing time for lunch when I received a call from the reception. Adjusting the hands-free device attached to my ear, I answered, 'William Night's office, Cara speaking.'

'Hi, Cara, it's Debbie. Could you please inform Mr Night that Miss Francesca Strafford is here to see him?'

The world crashed down on me all at once and I froze. Suddenly I lost every train of thought I'd had today and stared blankly at my screen.

Francesca? He was still seeing her?

For some reason I hadn't expected this, and the news struck me like a bucket of cold water. My whole body tensed. Breathing hurt.

I sensed William's eyes on my face. He must have noticed my stiffening figure.

'Cara?' Debbie prompted.

'Of course,' I hurried to say.

'Thanks.'

I hung up, trying to maintain my equilibrium. The idea that he was still seeing Francesca was more painful than I had anticipated. Then again, why was I surprised? I had rejected him. Of course he had moved on since then. I had no right to be upset about this; he wasn't mine. This pain was entirely self-inflicted.

'Everything all right?' William asked, and the sound of his alluring voice only intensified the sting of my loss.

'Yes.' I kept my eyes on my screen, feigning nonchalance. 'Francesca is here to see you. She's in the lobby.'

'Is she?' He sounded surprised, but I wasn't sure it was genuine.

I could feel his gaze on me, inspecting, and it bothered me. To be put under his microscope was the last thing I needed right now, because I was experiencing feelings I hadn't seen coming. I wished he would look away, and I also wished he would order me to call Debbie back and say to her that Francesca wasn't welcome.

After hesitating for some time, he asked gently, 'Would you mind collecting her for me?' By his tone, it was obvious that he was trying to show me consideration, as he knew full well that I was aware of who she was.

Exerting every ounce of my self-discipline, I nodded my head and refrained from exhaling the ton of air that I badly wanted to.

'Of course.' I stood up.

'You might want to bring your laptop with you,' he said, and I thought I detected a hidden message. Had he tried to say, 'I intend to fuck her, so you might want to step out for that bit'?

I frowned at the thought. He wouldn't go that far, would he? Surely he was above that sort of behaviour. No, I refused to believe he would do such a thing. He couldn't be that unprofessional.

'Right.' I grabbed my laptop and walked out without looking at him. It felt like I was in a trance as I approached the available desk beside Ellie. After leaving my laptop on it, I gave her a vague nod of acknowledgement and went to the lifts. As I waited for one to arrive, I tapped my foot, my arms crossed as if to protect myself from harm.

Francesca. Francesca Strafford, William Night's what? His girlfriend? His plaything? What was she to him? Were things getting serious between them?

I knew they had been seeing each other for months by now. While I was curious to meet her, I also dreaded it. Did she know that we had shared him once? That I had also seen him naked? Like her, I knew what his vulgar mouth could do. Like her, I knew how delicious it felt to have him buried within. But was she aware of that?

I couldn't imagine he would have mentioned me to her. Sure, he had clearly told Violet, but I suspected their friendship was to blame for that. William's conduct with Francesca didn't strike me as friendly in nature. Then again, what did I know?

My thoughts continued their unpleasant journey as I travelled down to the lobby. When the doors slid apart, my heart missed a beat. Beyond the security gates stood a tall woman with a slender frame and caramel coloured, wavy hair that was drawn back into a high ponytail. Her skin was light-brown with a golden shimmer to it, and she was immaculately dressed in a bright yellow and elegant summer dress of expensive fabric. It was undoubtedly a designer dress, but I had never cared for brands.

She turned toward me and my breath caught. She was nothing short of stunning.

At the centre of her face was a small, round nose, and her hazel eyes – set slightly wide apart – gazed curiously in my direction. Somehow, the distance between her eyes made her look even more attractive. She was an intriguing beauty – not the type you saw in make-up commercials, but rather that of Vogue.

Was she a model? She could be, I thought, if she wanted. She had the beauty, height and build for it.

'Hello,' I called and forced a smile as I went through the security gates. 'I'm Cara, a new trainee. Mr Night's assistant, of sorts.' I offered my hand to her. 'I'm here to collect you on his behalf.'

Not a trace of a smile was present on her face when her limp hand reluctantly reached for mine. 'I see. How's his mood?' she asked, startling me, and let go of my hand after a lazy shake.

Did he tend to be in a bad mood around her?

'He's . . . William?' I gave her a lopsided smile, but she was not amused.

'Shit.' She sighed and folded her arms.

'Something the matter?' I tilted my head.

'Well, he's not expecting me, so I'd hoped to find him in a good mood. I guess luck's not on my side today. It's just . . .' She waved a hand in the air. 'I'm headed for a job in Spain, so I wanted to say goodbye.'

It was tempting to ask if she was his girlfriend, but I refrained. It wasn't my place, regardless of how badly I wanted to know.

'Right. Well, he sounded happy when he asked me to collect you,' I said.

Hope ignited in her eyes. The same moment I saw it, I knew she was in love with him. Was he in love with her, too?

'Really?' she asked, and finally, a small smile flirted with her lips.

I nodded. 'If you'll come with me?' I ushered her toward the security gates. Her mesmerising legs moved with such elegance that I was further convinced she must be a model.

'Spain's lovely,' I said to create small talk while I scanned my card to let her past the gates.

'It really is, but it's sweltering during summer. Third time I'm there this year.'

My eyebrows climbed higher. 'Travel a lot, do you? I'm jealous.'

A smug smile decorated her mouth. 'Yeah. Occupational hazard, you might call it.'

'What's your occupation?'

She shrugged. 'I'm a model.'

And I was right.

'To be honest, I suspected,' I said amusedly. 'You're absolutely gorgeous.'

Her smile became a grin. 'Thanks, but you should take a look in the mirror.'

I chuckled. 'Oh, I do that every morning. Don't you?'

She laughed. 'You know what I meant.'

I grinned. 'I do. Anyway, so you get to travel for work. I'd have loved that, I think.'

She cocked her head from side to side while we headed for the lifts. 'It gets a bit tiresome. I sleep in hotels more often than I sleep in my own bed.'

'Really?'

She nodded. 'Makes it hard to maintain relationships – and friendships,' she said, and I found myself wondering if she was alluding to some sort of difficulty with establishing a relationship with William.

Once we were in the lift, she did a visual sweep of my body.

'So how long have you been on the job, Cara?'

'Two days.' I turned to smile at her. 'This is my third.'

'How do you like it?'

'I love it. It's hectic and demanding, but definitely riveting.'

'I bet. How's having Will as a boss?'

'It's amazing. I'm very lucky to be shadowing him.'

'I can imagine. He fits the role, doesn't he?'

I chuckled. 'He does.'

We continued to chat about William, and it was an odd experience because whenever I tried to change the subject, she kept making him the centre of our conversation. I got the impression she was a bit obsessed with him, but I could hardly blame her; he was certainly a captivating man.

Though, I did wonder if she persisted in talking about him because she felt possessive of him and perceived me as a threat. If she did, I pitied her. I had no plans to pursue him, so it saddened me to think that she might be worried about it. All the same, I thought she was a sweet girl, so I could understand the appeal. We were quite different, however, but maybe that was why William had chosen to stick with her.

'I suppose you know the way?' I said as we exited the lift.

She glanced in the direction of William's office, looking a bit nervous. 'I do.'

'Well, then. It was lovely meeting you, Francesca.' I offered my hand, and when she took it this time, her grip was firmer. 'I hope you'll have a wonderful time in Spain and that you won't melt in the hot weather.'

Her wide smile revealed her bright white teeth. 'Thanks, Cara. Best of luck to you.'

'Thanks. I'll need it.'

When I had found my seat, Ellie said amusedly, 'She stops by every Wednesday she's in town. She won't be leaving for at least half an hour.'

My brows knitted and I faced her. Quietly, I said, 'You sound like you think they'll have sex.'

She tittered and looked rather charmed, which bewildered me. 'Oh, you are *so* new to this.'

'New to what?'

'An actual workplace.'

'What do you mean?'

Her smile was patient. 'Well, I hate to burst your bubble, but do you really think people don't do questionable things while at work? People cheat on their spouses left, right and centre. Not everybody, of course, but definitely some. Sometimes, people have sex here too. I'm not saying it's acceptable, but it's absolutely to be expected.' She shrugged. 'Humans are stupid.'

I shook my head. 'It's not that I don't expect it. I just don't expect it from Will. It's not my impression of him.'

The curve of her brow disclosed her disagreement. 'Well, what do you think they'll do? Talk? They don't need to meet up in person for that, especially not during work hours. Besides, had you seen what I have – the state of her when she's left his office in the past – you'd suspect the same. It's clear as day they've had sex.'

Hearing that, I found myself quite appalled at his lack of work ethics. What sort of professional would have sex in their office? And furthermore in the middle of the day when they had work to do?

'Just seems a bit unprofessional. I hadn't thought Will was like that.'

'Hey,' she frowned, 'don't be so sanctimonious. Cut the man some slack. Honestly, he deserves it. He practically lives in his office – I'm sure that's the only reason. I've often wondered why he won't just invest in a bed. That way, he'd never have to leave. Though, on second thoughts, that's probably why he hasn't. If he did, he'd actually never leave. This way, he's got to.'

I didn't want to talk about this anymore, so I got back to work. Gossip was definitely not my thing, but it was clearly Ellie's. Still, she hadn't lied. Francesca walked out twenty minutes later, and the whole time she had been in there, I had struggled to remain focused. I had so many questions.

My eyes dashed to her figure. Her long, wavy hair cascaded down to her shoulders now. He had obviously made a mess of her ponytail.

Ellie struggled to stifle a giggle and shook her head, clearly humoured by William's lascivious behaviour. I didn't share her amusement. I was disappointed in him, and I was also slightly gutted that he had evidently moved on.

When he suddenly rang, my heart bolted to my mouth. After a moment's hesitation, I accepted the call. 'Yes?'

'You can come back now.' He sounded a bit strange, but I wasn't sure why I thought that. He didn't seem stressed, but he didn't seem calm either.

I swallowed. 'All right.'

He hung up.

I couldn't think of anything less tempting than returning to his office right then. I was certain I would imagine the two of them naked. The scene was already awakening in my mind. Had he fucked her on his desk, for instance? Where I was supposed to work? Despite how nauseated I felt, I closed my laptop to go back.

Since he was expecting me, I didn't bother to knock. Opening the door, I found him near one of the windows, facing away from me. It was open, probably to ventilate the room so I wouldn't smell the sex that had been in the air.

He turned toward me, eyes fleeting. His lips were slightly swollen and redder than usual, no doubt due to the things he had been using them for. The more I studied him, the surer I was that Ellie had been right. They must have had sex.

Unsure of what to make of the situation, I shut the door and approached his desk without a word. I was appalled he would fuck someone while at work, essentially right in front of me, and then order me to work in here straight afterwards. It was incredibly inconsiderate of him, not to mention insensitive.

First and foremost, I was upset at his lack of work ethics, but I felt too intimidated to speak up since it was only my third day here. I also didn't want him to think that I was only complaining because I was jealous. While it was true that a part of me was hurt, I wasn't jealous. I was upset only because it had been that easy for him to move on. By contrast, I wasn't over him at all. When he focused on me, I heard only him. When he walked into the room, I saw only him. And yet, despite this, I thought that if he was actually happy with Francesca, he deserved to be. Indeed, he deserved to be happy, and he deserved to have his feelings reciprocated by someone worthy of him – someone who wasn't me – because he was a wonderful man.

'Sorry about that,' he said.

I stared out of the windows behind him. The traffic of London droned in the background, and above the pulsating metropolis, I saw the smog, tainting the blue sky and reminding me why I had never really preferred cities. The summer breeze played with the white curtains, and I closed my eyes to savour its dance across my cheeks.

For the first time since I had started here, a moment of sadness gripped me. On the face of it, losing William seemed trivial, but I couldn't ignore the way my heart ached.

'No worries,' I eventually said and, somewhat reluctantly, put my laptop back on his desk. 'Do I need to clean this surface?'

He blinked at my bold question. 'No, that's not necessary.'

At least they hadn't fucked on his desk.

Giving him a vague nod, I found my seat again. As he returned to his own, I felt him peering at me.

One question kept bothering me while I tried to concentrate on my screen. To get rid of it, I might as well ask, I thought. Besides, it wasn't unusual for colleagues to discuss this sort of thing, was it? In the end, it was rather obvious what he had done. Even Ellie suspected, so would I be speaking out of turn if I asked?

I decided to bite the bullet. 'So, are you two seeing each other now or . . .?'

When I looked up, he was regarding me with an arched brow.

'With all due respect, Cara, I'm not inclined to discuss my love life with you.'

Since he immediately focused on his screen again, it was apparent that trying to dig further would get me nowhere.

'I'm sorry I asked,' I said embarrassedly. While I felt robbed of the satisfaction of knowing the answer, I returned my attention to my laptop to respect his boundaries.

'Why do you care?' he suddenly asked.

It was an excellent question. Why did I care? I had no right to. However, the fact remained, which was that I did care. Was it because of my supermassive ego? Was I so narcissistic that I couldn't accept his moving on? Did I want him to yearn for me eternally, despite my endless rejections?

No, it was really quite simple. I cared because he remained the only man who had ever captured my interest this way. He was the only man I had ever experienced butterflies in the presence of, the only man I had ever felt so connected with, and he was the only man it had ever felt right to kiss. So, it hurt me to know that it wasn't mutual.

While I had myself to thank for his moving on, it wounded me that it had been so easy for him, as I was nowhere near the same point. I still fancied him.

But that didn't change anything. My feelings were simply not justified.

'I was just curious,' I said.

He scoffed. 'Haven't you heard? Curiosity killed the cat.'

I looked away. 'No, I've heard. It's just . . .'

'Just what?'

I sighed. 'It's not my place, but I think she might be in love with you.' I said it because I wanted him to refute it. Nothing would have satisfied me more than to hear him ridicule me for even thinking such a thing.

'You're right. It's not your place,' he said and got back to work.

'Sorry.' I felt ashamed for prying into his love life – I had no right to be doing it – so I said nothing else until it was finally time for lunch.

When the clock struck half eleven, I stood up. 'Lunch?'

'In a minute. I need to look over a few more things before my meeting with Vi.'

'I'll join Ellie, then.'

He merely waved a hand in the air to indicate that I was free to go.

§ § §

Over lunch, Ellie and I exchanged some small talk, and I was grateful for the distraction. We talked about where we had grown up, what sort of party-scenes we were into, what interests we had in common, as well as romantic statuses. Ellie was engaged to a man named Brian, whom she had met four years ago. He was an economist, and their encounter hadn't been particularly unique, according to her. They had both been drunk at the same pub when Brian had decided to chat her up.

She was sharing stories about their relationship when I noticed William, but instead of joining us, he grabbed a seat at Andy and Violet's table. Part of me was disappointed, another thankful. My mood was still unstable after Francesca's visit, so I appreciated some mental room to sort out my thoughts, especially my feelings.

'But you're determined to stay single?' Ellie asked as we waited for the lift after lunch.

The doors opened, and I was just about to elaborate when a large hand landed on my back and ushered me in gently. As I tilted my head back, a spellbinding pair of eyes instantly hypnotised me.

'Please, don't let me interrupt,' William said and held my gaze. Speechless, I stared back.

'Mind your own business, Will. Nosy,' Ellie said. She wasn't one to talk, but I refrained from commenting on that.

'No, it's okay.' I smiled. 'I was only going to say that I'm committed to my career. That's the only thing I have the capacity to maintain at the moment.' I propped my back against the wall.

'She sounds like you,' Ellie said with a smirk and looked up at William.

He shrugged. 'In a way, yes.'

I frowned. What was that supposed to mean? Wasn't he seeing Francesca now?

Hearing my thoughts, I nearly groaned. I couldn't keep doing this. It would do me no good to wonder about his love life.

'I'll be leaving to collect the files from Clifford Paints,' I said to William.

'Good. You might get back while I'm meeting with Vi. If you do, just continue your work on the NDA.'

I nodded.

§ § §

It was almost three o'clock when I returned from my errand, and it took me another hour to make copies of all the files. I scurried back to William's office with the stack of paper in my arms and opened the door with my elbow, but he was nowhere in sight. Looking at his desk, I was inevitably reminded of Francesca's visit. Sighing, I walked in and dumped the documents on it.

As I stood there, I wondered what to do if William was currently seeing her with the intention of building something lasting. I would need to move on as well, that was for sure, but I was already trying and had been ever since we met, and it hadn't brought me far. But, given enough time, perhaps I would consider this a blessing in disguise. If he and Francesca were getting serious, perhaps I would come to realise that it was the best thing that could have happened. Perhaps I would finally be able to view him solely in a platonic light. Nothing would get in my way, then.

As for his beauty? Well, I would admire that in silence until it became like furniture – familiar and something I didn't give a thought.

Sinking into my chair, I got back to work.

I had been sitting there for a few minutes when my phone received a message, and it was from the single person I appreciated hearing from most right then.

Aaron.

> You available tonight? I'm curious to hear how your vacation scheme is going. Mine's chaotic but amazing x

> Yes! Mine? I finish at five x

Just after I had pressed Send, William came in, and his arrival jolted me. For some reason, the fact that I had just texted Aaron made me feel like I had been caught committing a crime. With haste, I put my phone next to my laptop and focused on the NDA.

'You're allowed to look at your phone,' William said with a tone of amusement.

'How was the meeting?'

'Efficient. Vi's not one to waste anyone's time.' He sat down in his chair.

I was just about to reply when the screen of my phone lit up. Aaron had replied. Immediately after I had read his name, I saw that William stole a glance at it. I tensed, feeling awkward.

Some silence elapsed before he said, 'I need you to stay for a bit longer today.'

I stared at him, but he seemed completely unfazed. Deciphering his thoughts was impossible, and I hated it.

'Would that be all right, or have you got plans?'

A vague frown crossed my face. While we definitely had plenty of work to do, I considered the timing of his question rather conspicuous.

'No, I can stay, but for how long?'

He shrugged. 'I'm not sure. Depends on how quickly we work.'

'Okay.' Suspicious, I wondered if he had asked me to stay solely to punish me for interacting with Aaron. Then again, it seemed unlikely when taking his relationship with Francesca into account.

We had been working for a few minutes when he suddenly said, 'By the way, on Fridays, we tend to go for post-work drinks at Disrepute – the cocktail bar where we first met. You should come. We'll celebrate your first week with us.'

Ellie had already mentioned it during lunch, but after today's events, alcohol and William didn't seem like company worth seeking out. Rather, it seemed like the recipe for a devastating night out. Under the influence, I didn't trust myself not to do something stupid, like act on my lust for him. Alcohol severely reduced my inhibitions, and I was struggling enough already. If I made a pass at him, I would never be able to live it down. He was my boss, and I had just been preaching to Ellie about maintaining professionalism. It would make me a hypocrite, to say the least.

Moreover, William was likely to reject my advances now, due to Francesca. Acting on my lust for him would also mean contradicting myself, and I wasn't about to allow that. I had chosen my career, and I intended to stand by my decision. In fact, I owed it to William to stand by it. I respected him too much to do anything else.

'I can't. I've got plans,' I lied. 'Maybe next week.'

'Next week it is, then.'

§ § §

William made me stay till eight. I was exhausted after spending more than twelve hours at work, so Aaron and I agreed to postpone meeting till tomorrow. I called Olivia on my way home, needing to vent.

'Seriously?' she gasped. I had just told her about Francesca's visit. 'No way he did that.'

'Right? I can't get my mind around it. But Ellie was convinced,' I said as I walked home from Notting Hill Gate station.

Olivia hesitated. 'Well, actually, when I think about it, didn't you say he was also sleeping with his colleague?'

I pursed my lips, the image of Violet popping up in my mind. 'Yes, but so what?'

'So he's clearly not opposed to pushing the boundaries. If he's been shagging his colleague, we already know he doesn't abide by standard professionalism, so maybe he did fuck Francesca in there. I wouldn't put it past him, at least.'

I frowned and kept my gaze on the light-grey pavement. 'I will be so disappointed in him if he did it.'

'You need to ask him, Cara. You can't just let this slide.'

'But then he's going to think I'm only jealous.'

'Do you really think he's that vain?'

I wrinkled my nose. 'I honestly don't know.'

'I seriously doubt it. He's your damn boss. It's a valid concern to bring to his attention. And if he decides to flatter himself with ideas about you being jealous, then that's on him, honestly.'

I slipped past an old lady walking her tiny sausage dog. 'I really don't want him to think that I'm jealous, though, Livy. It could make things awkward between us. And honestly, if he's moved on, I'm happy for him. He deserves to be happy.'

'Well, that makes one of us. I'm quite sad. I've had my fingers crossed for you two ever since you met.'

I rolled my eyes. 'That's ridiculous. I haven't given you any indication things would ever evolve between us.'

'It was enough just that you hesitated with rejecting him.' I could hear the pout in her voice. 'I really thought he was it. Fuck this Francesca girl. I hope he dumps her.'

It was difficult to stop a laugh from spilling. 'Okay, Livy, I'm nearly home now, but I appreciate the support. Talk to you later, yeah?'

'Hold on. Are you free on Friday?'

'Yes.'

'Then let's have a girls' night at mine.'

'I'd love that. Just the two of us, though, right? Or will Jess and Nora be there?'

'Just the two of us, don't worry.'

'Great.'

§ § §

When I got home, I quickly showered and settled on the sofa to watch TV with Jason.

'I'm knackered,' I groaned. 'Your brother is a force to be reckoned with. Fucking hell. I can't believe he works such long hours every single day. How does he stay so fit?'

'He trains before work.'

'Christ.'

Jason brought my feet onto his lap and started massaging them. 'He's a machine. Always has been.'

During a momentary lapse of judgement, I muttered, 'Well, that machine also has a sex drive.'

He stiffened, hands freezing on my feet. 'What?'

I blinked when I realised how that must have sounded. 'No, no, I didn't mean it like that. Sorry. This woman stopped by today – Francesca. I think he fucked her in his office, but I'm not sure.'

His jaw dropped and he stared at me. 'What?'

'Yeah, and he made me work in there right afterwards. I was really uncomfortable.' I wrinkled my nose.

'I can't believe he did that. Are you sure?'

I shook my head. 'No, but Ellie, another paralegal, told me Francesca tends to stop by on Wednesdays, and she's under the impression it's to have sex. Still, I neither saw nor heard them, so I'm not sure it's what happened, but the evidence is definitely compelling.'

He leaned back. 'What sort of evidence? Other than Ellie's impression?'

I regretted that I had said anything at all then. At the same time, maybe Jason sat on the answer that William refused to provide: was he serious about Francesca?

'Well, when Francesca walked out, her hair was down, and it had been in a ponytail when she walked in. And when I went back to his office, his lips were slightly red and somewhat swollen, probably from kissing. He'd opened a window as well, and I think it was to ventilate the room so I wouldn't smell anything. She was there for a while, too, and he also told me to bring my laptop with me before she came in, and there was something about the way he said it that I found . . . odd.'

Jason blinked, visibly appalled. 'Bloody hell, that's bang out of order. What's he thinking?'

I shrugged. 'Probably wasn't thinking, or at least not with the right head.' My joke earned a chuckle. 'Are they seeing each other?' I asked boldly. 'Like dating?'

He frowned. 'I'm not sure.'

'I thought he was interested in that girl named Sandra or something?' I could hardly believe my nerve, but my curiosity had got the better of me. I felt awfully fake, but I was just so desperate to know more.

Jason gave a vague shake of his head. 'Yeah, he's not mentioned her lately.'

'Really? What happened?'

'I don't know, I haven't asked.' He shrugged. 'He stopped talking about her about a month ago, though, so I think he's just moved on.' Suddenly he shuddered. 'Honestly, good riddance. I don't think I would have liked her much.'

I pressed my lips together and averted my gaze. What he had said made me wonder if he would change his opinion of me if he ever learned the truth. I feared he would, and because of that, I became all the more determined to keep him in the dark.

'Thanks for the massage, Jason, but I think I'll go to bed.'

'Yeah, get some sleep. But before you do – did you talk to Will about it? Did you tell him it made you uncomfortable?'

I looked at him. 'Well, I'm not even sure they had sex, and it didn't seem appropriate to ask.'

'Yeah, I get that.' He nodded. 'I'll have a word with him, then. If he actually did that, he needs to be reminded it's unacceptable.'

I tensed. 'What will you say?'

'I'll ask him whether he did it.'

I grimaced. 'But then he's going to realise I told you.'

'Well, would you rather ask him yourself?'

'I'd rather not ask at all.'

He knitted his brows. 'But then he might repeat it. Would you prefer that?'

What a dilemma. My lips protruded. 'If he does it again, I'll ask him myself.'

'Fair enough.'

'Thanks, anyway.' I swung my legs off his lap and stood up.

'I'm here for you, love.'

'You always are.'

'Always, Cara. Sleep well.'

But I didn't sleep well. I spent hours chasing slumber, and when I finally caught it, I tossed and turned like my worst nightmare was coming to life.

17

HAVE YOU EVER

Aaron and I were watching a documentary about white-collar crime when we heard the front door open and close. Sprawled across Aaron's body on the sofa, I lifted my head to welcome Jason's arriving figure.

'Hello,' I cooed. 'Did you have a nice day?'

Completely ignoring me, he flashed Aaron a fond grin. 'Aaron. Good to see you, man.'

Aaron saluted him with a jerk of his head. 'You too.'

'How's Dentons?'

'It's a dream come true.'

'I bet.'

When he reached us, he didn't hesitate to smother us with his weight. Squeezed into a sandwich consisting of two unfairly sexy men, I could hardly breathe.

'Jason,' I choked. 'Can't breathe.'

He squeezed me harder.

'Oh my God,' I mouthed as I lost my breath.

Laughing, he reclined toward the other end of the sofa.

'How's summer holiday?' Aaron asked him and reached for the remote to pause the documentary.

'It's great. When the sun came out after three, Stephen and I went to the park with Livy and Giselle to work on our tans. Played some volleyball, messed about.'

'I saw that on your Instagram story,' I said, my lips protruding with envy.

'Yeah. We missed you guys.' He smiled affectionately. 'Responsible twats that you are.'

Aaron chuckled. 'Stephen and a tan? I can't see it happening.'

'Me neither,' Jason said. 'Man produces more UV rays than the sun. I had to wear my sunglasses for that reason alone.'

They burst into laughter at his joke. I shook my head at them, smiling.

When they finally calmed down, Jason asked Aaron, 'Anyway, are you spending the night?'

'I think so.' Aaron turned his dark brown eyes toward me.

I hugged his warm body and smiled up at him. 'Of course you are. Why else would I tell you to bring a change of clothes?'

Grinning, he planted a kiss on my head and brought both arms around me, pressing me against him.

'Sweet,' Jason commented. 'Fancy a beer, then?'

Aaron shrugged. 'Suppose the one won't do any harm.'

Jason nodded and stood up. 'How was work today?' he asked me.

'It was good. Much better than yesterday,' I said, which was the truth. William and I had barely spoken, and whenever we had, we kept it strictly professional. He also hadn't fucked anyone in his office, which was where I had set the standard since yesterday. So, whenever William didn't shove his cock into somebody else in my presence, I was having a good day.

'William treat you well?' Jason asked as he turned for the kitchen.

'Brought me coffee, actually, so yes.'

Aaron tensed beneath me, and it confused me.

Jason halted and turned around. 'What?' he asked, puzzled. 'Isn't he your boss?'

'Yes?'

He looked stumped. 'Then aren't you supposed to bring coffees for *him*?'

'Oh, don't be so conventional.' I rolled my eyes.

He chuckled. 'Right.'

'I think he was just trying to make me feel welcome, or maybe he wanted to apologise for yesterday.'

'Yeah, you're probably right,' Jason said and disappeared into the kitchen.

'What happened yesterday?' Aaron asked.

'I'd rather not talk about it,' I murmured with a pout.

He hesitated. 'Is it related to him walking in on us that time?'

I shook my head. 'No, of course not. Why would it be?'

He looked sideways, and it roused some alarm in me. I wished I could hear his thoughts. Was he suspicious of William? Had he sensed something that awful day? Sensed my past with William?

'I was just making sure,' he finally said. 'I've been worried that incident would make things awkward for you once you started work.'

Touched by his concern, I smiled fondly at him. 'You're very sweet for worrying about that, but you don't have to. He's acting like it never happened.'

'Good.' He rubbed my back. 'I'm here if you want to talk about it, though – whatever it is.'

I hugged him tightly and drew his soothing scent deep into my lungs. 'Thanks, but it's really nothing. He just did something a bit insensitive, but it wasn't on purpose.'

'Was he too hard on you?'

'Aaron.'

He chuckled. 'Sorry, I'll stop.'

'Thanks.'

§ § §

Something tilted me to the side. When I opened my eyes, Aaron was smiling tenderly at me, and it was infectious.

'Morning,' he cooed and swept a lock of my hair behind my ear.

'Morning.' I rubbed my face. 'What time is it?' I rolled onto my back, spread my arms apart and relished how refreshed I felt. Sex last night had been exactly what I needed, and it had been *good.*

'Half six. I woke up half an hour ago. Made you breakfast.'

'Aw, Aaron.' I lunged forward and hugged his naked back. 'Thank you,' I said and covered his neck with soft kisses.

'Why don't you have a shower while I set the table for us?'

'Sounds wonderful.' Releasing him, I climbed out of bed. As I walked completely naked toward the door, I felt his gaze on my back, so with a crooked smile on my face, I turned my head to catch him in his ogling.

'We've got time for a quickie,' he said.

I chuckled. 'Have you showered yet?'

'No.' His usually calm voice was saturated with eagerness.

'Then let's spare the environment and do it together,' I said and walked out.

He charged after me without a moment's hesitation.

§ § §

Aaron resembled husband material as he placed a mug of coffee in front of me on the table. With a grateful look in my eye, I gripped the black porcelain and raised it to my mouth.

'How long are your days?' he asked, grabbing the seat opposite.

'Eight to five, but they may differ depending on the workload. You?'

He unlocked his phone and opened a newspaper app. 'Same as you,' he said, dragging his own mug of coffee to his mouth. 'By the way, are you free next Saturday? Not this one, but the next.'

I frowned in thought. 'I think so, why?'

'Tyler is celebrating his birthday. He said to invite you.'

I stiffened. 'Shit, when's his birthday?' I asked, worried I had forgotten to congratulate him.

He chuckled. 'Next Saturday. Don't worry. Can you make it?'

'Yes, of course. Any ideas for a present?'

'Boxers. He's in dire need of them, he said.'

A chuckle escaped me. Student life in a nutshell, that was. 'Sorted.'

'Perhaps we could sleep at yours then, so Tyler and Valentina can have the flat to themselves.' Valentina was Tyler's girlfriend of one year.

'Good idea.' I nodded. 'Let's do that.'

We had been sitting there for a few minutes when I suddenly started comparing him to William. They were so different, yet somehow so similar. Their drive and intellect were alike, though Aaron was much gentler. It made me wonder why I hadn't ever developed feelings for Aaron. A relationship with him would have made perfect sense. He was supportive, reliable and sweet, not to mention that he brought out the best in me. Without him, I doubted I would have reached as far as I had in terms of my career. So why couldn't this be love? Why had I never entertained the idea of pursuing a relationship with him?

We had been doing this for three years, yet I had never considered dating him. Meanwhile, William had made me consider dating him the same night I had met him and several more times since then.

I wondered if Aaron had ever been in my place, where a girl he was attracted to had made advances. Had he rejected her to maintain a strict focus on his career? Had he given it a go, but later discovered that they were incompatible? Or perhaps the opposite had happened. Perhaps he had fancied a girl and had pursued her, but she had rejected him instead.

I was curious to hear his perspective on this. We had never discussed it before, but I was about to change that.

'Have you ever considered dating someone while we've been together like this? Cassie, for example?'

Aaron froze, his cup of coffee remaining by his full lips for several seconds. While staring into my eyes, he lowered it slowly.

'What's brought this on?' he asked with furrowed brows.

I shrugged. 'Just wondering. I know we're not supposed to talk about others to each other, but it's been three years, so I'm curious to know if it's ever happened during that time. If it has, I obviously won't get mad.'

His frown intensified. 'No, it hasn't.'

'You've never considered it?'

He shook his head. 'Not at all.'

'Why not?'

He scoffed. 'You know why.'

'Do I?'

'Yes. It's because, like you, I'm not interested in anything romantic right now. I prefer just sticking to what you and I have got going on.' His eyes narrowed. 'Why? Have you?'

I tucked my cheek into the palm of my hand. 'No, not really.'

His head jerked back. 'That's not quite the answer I was expecting. What do you mean "not really"?'

I looked away and folded my arms. 'Well, there was one guy who wanted me to give him a chance, but I rejected him, so I was only curious about whether you've ever been in the same boat.'

'When was this?'

'Some months ago. Anyway, it's history, so you don't need to worry. I was just curious to hear your perspective, that's all.'

'Well, Cassie has asked me out, but I rejected her point-blank, so the answer is still the same – I've never considered it.'

I gasped. 'I knew it. When?'

He rubbed his neck. 'At the party after our last exam.'

I remembered Aaron and I had gone home together that night. Poor Cassie. It must have hurt to see that.

'See? I knew she had feelings for you.'

'Well, it doesn't change anything.'

When the satisfaction of being proved right subsided, my lips protruded. 'Poor Cassie. Was she upset?'

He wrinkled his nose. 'Of course. I don't think anybody enjoys being rejected.'

I sighed and raised my cup of coffee. 'I expect she hates me now.'

'It wouldn't surprise me, but it would be misplaced. In the end, I'm the issue, not you.'

'Good morning!' Jason exclaimed as he burst into the room. Aaron looked entirely unaffected, but I nearly fell off my chair.

'It's a beautiful day!' he sang, quoting U2.

'Bloody hell, Jason! Did you fire crack up your arse this morning?' I scolded.

He gave me a smile to die for, complemented by a wink, and moseyed over to grab Aaron's shoulders. Squeezing them, he leaned over him and then stole a piece of bacon from his plate.

'Haven't you made me breakfast, Cara?' he asked with a wounded tone.

'Sorry.' Aaron chuckled. 'I made it this morning. I wasn't aware you'd be up this early when you're on holiday.'

Jason raised a brow. 'Med student. Hello?'

'Right. Serious as they come.'

'Exactly.'

'His earlier show says otherwise,' I muttered. 'But you can have the rest of mine. He made far too much.' I pushed my plate toward him.

'Thanks, darling.' Jason smiled and went to the kitchen counter to toast some bread.

'Did you wake up by yourself today? I was going to wake you in a minute.' I turned in my chair and stared at his naked back. Like his brother, he was athletically built and very tall, with defined muscles that merited admiration.

'No, I was woken by the sound of your sexual moans arriving from the shower,' he said without looking at me.

My face paled. 'Oh,' I squeaked. 'Sorry.'

'Was weirdly erotic. I almost got a boner, but then I remembered that you're basically my sister, so it's all flaccid.'

Aaron guffawed while I sagged into my seat, mortified.

§ § §

Aaron got ready to leave before me, seeing as his workplace was further away. As I was seeing him out, he wrapped his arms around my waist and pulled me close. Descending onto my mouth, I felt him smiling against my lips. It was a sweet kiss, and it was likely to assist me through the day.

When he pulled away, he rested his forehead against mine and said with affection, 'Have a nice day at work, love.'

I grinned. 'You too.'

Leaning back, he called, 'Bye, Jason. Have a great day, yeah?'

'You too,' Jason replied from a closer distance than I had expected. Sure enough, once I had shut the door after Aaron, I turned to discover that he had been peeking at us from around the corner.

'Pervert,' I said.

Laughing, he walked into full view. 'Honestly, I'm only fascinated. How the hell have you managed to keep your feelings in check for three bloody years? You look like a couple! If I hadn't seen it for myself, I would never have believed it was possible.'

I shrugged. 'Well, aside from you and Livy, he's my best friend. I don't know how to explain it. It just . . . is.'

'I'm genuinely amazed. Where do I get one?'

I giggled and shook my head. 'I'd start by breaking up with your hand maybe.'

'Noted.'

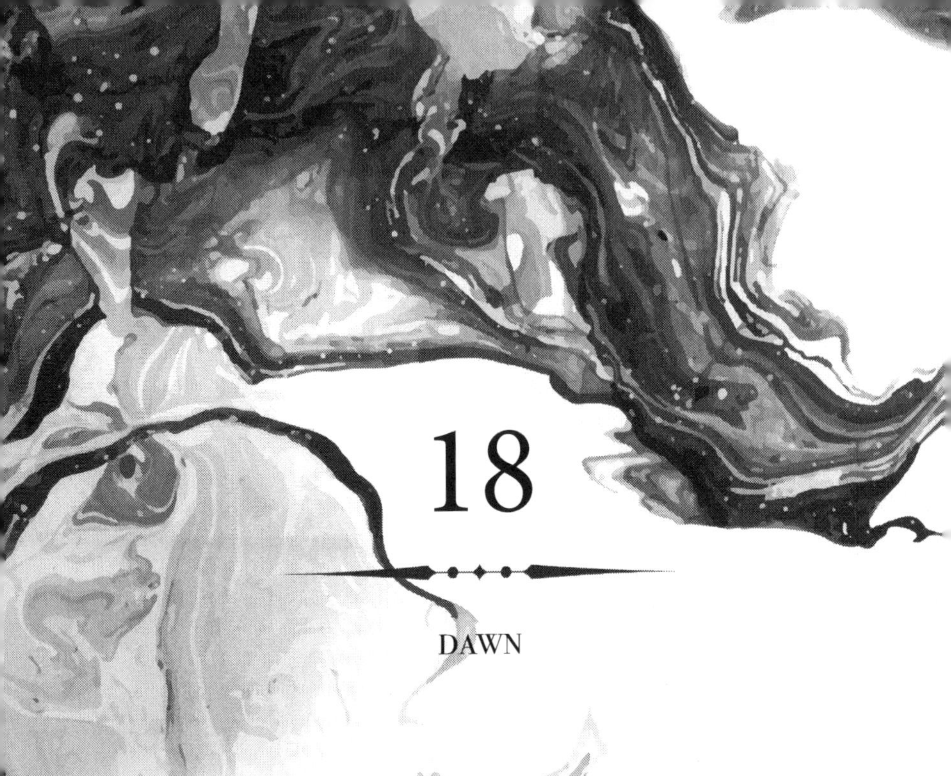

18

DAWN

'I'm going to take you now,' William warned, his warm breath spreading across my kiss-swollen lips. 'And I assure you, love, you'll be feeling me for a week.' A lecherous smile emerged on his mouth before he claimed mine. Powerfully seductive, he dominated me completely through a mere kiss.

I inhaled sharply, my chest tingling. My pounding heart was on the verge of bursting with excitement. Finally I would feel him enter me again, thrusting in to reach a depth no other man had. I had longed to feel him buried inside me for months now, and with each day that had gone by, my lust for him had grown more extreme.

He pushed in, his gaze searing while he elicited a long moan of pleasure from my mouth. I clawed his muscular back, my face contorting at the unmistakable sensation. God, he felt good, and he stretched me so far. Closing my eyes, I savoured how complete I felt. Caged beneath his strong, naked body, I marvelled. How had I ended up here again?

The same moment I thought it, I realised I was dreaming. I awoke with a gasp, my eyes opening. Rolling sideways, I propped myself on my forearm and grabbed my phone from the nightstand to check the time. It was six in the morning – too early to wake up, but too late to go back to sleep.

Groaning, I put it back and noticed how soaked I was. My juices covered the better part of my inner thighs, deriving from the cleft above which still throbbed and tingled from the illusion of William's touch. Clearly, they were called 'wet dreams' for a reason, but waking up from one starring none other than my boss was not an ideal way to start my day. What made it worse was that it was easily one of the most fantastic sex dreams I had ever had, and he hadn't even made me orgasm. Though, last week, he had managed to on several occasions, albeit in my dreams and fantasies of him.

This was getting out of hand. Not even during sleep did I manage to escape my lust for him. He was driving me mad. The past three nights, he had been present in all my dreams. My subconscious clearly refused to let him go, regardless of how much I wanted it to.

In an attempt to exorcise him from my mind, I had even gone so far as to masturbate to the thought of him, but it hadn't helped. All it had done was reinforce my lust for him. Sleeping with Aaron yesterday hadn't helped either. I had been distracted under his touch, comparing it to my memory of William's, which had ultimately led Aaron's to lose its impact. I hadn't even been able to reach orgasm – I'd had to fake it – which was surely a first for me. In the three years I had slept with Aaron, I had never been unable to climax – until now.

It infuriated me. William had clearly moved on, so why couldn't I? Why had my body latched on to the memory of him like this?

A few tearless sobs escaped while I rubbed my face. Pushing my duvet aside, I climbed out of bed and mentally prepared myself for another intense day under his spellbinding stare. I was still dazed by my erotic dream, so I showered for longer than usual, hoping the hot stream of water would cleanse my mind, too, and wash away my lust for William.

When I finished, I walked dispiritedly out of the glass cage and wiped a line of condensation off the bathroom mirror. Leaning toward my reflection, I saw how discouraged I looked. My freckles were fainter than usual, and purple bags had gathered under my eyes.

I watched as a frown surfaced. 'Stop thinking of him, Cara. He's your goddamned boss,' I scolded and opened the middle drawer beneath the basin to fetch my make-up kit.

I started by moisturising my face, hoping it would treat the symptoms of my exhaustion. Then I grabbed my corrector, applied it under my eyes, and covered it with my concealer. Eventually I had managed to hide any sign of sleep deprivation. Since I preferred a natural look, I didn't apply anything else on my skin. As I got started on my eyes, on a whim

I decided to add a very faint smoky eye. I would look fiercer like this. Ready to attack the day. Ready to fend off any daydreams about my tantalising boss.

§ § §

As intended, I arrived before William. Since he had wanted me to work in his office all of last week, I headed straight into it at ten to eight to clear his desk and organise the files on it for him. He would probably assume that I had done it as a favour to him, but I was determined to do it solely because I couldn't stand untidiness. Mum had always said, 'Order around you, order within you', and that statement had stayed with me.

A few minutes later, I heard the doorknob turn. My gaze dashed to it just as William came in, dressed in a light-grey suit. The smile he wore nearly made me sob. The fact that he looked even better in reality than in my dreams was hardly fair. Looking him in the eye right then, when I had just had a vivid and erotic dream about him, was mortifying. To keep from blushing was impossible, and I was certain he noticed, because his smile suddenly broadened.

'Well, good morning to you too,' he said amusedly. 'I don't think anyone's blushed so hard at the sight of me before.'

'Don't point it out,' I muttered and looked back at the files. 'And don't flatter yourself. I'm blushing because you caught me tidying up your mess, and I don't want you thinking it's to suck up to you.'

He shut the door, murmuring, 'Somebody got out of bed on the wrong side.'

I kept my eyes off him as he approached the desk, and my heart plummeted when he put a Starbucks cup in front of me. He had to stop doing this. I couldn't bear his kindness. All it did was remind me of how irresistible he was. If he carried on this way, I might as well wave my sanity goodbye.

'Perhaps this will help,' he said.

I couldn't bring myself to look at him. 'You need to stop bringing me coffee, Will.'

'Er, why?'

'Because it's unnecessary. I've got a machine at home.'

'So? I thought it could be a nice custom. Besides, you can't make flat whites at home, can you?'

I let out a loud breath. 'I don't need flat whites.'

'Well, I have to stop by the shop anyway. Might as well—'

'Fine.'

My hostile attitude made him pause. 'Are you all right?'

'Yes, I'm fine. Sorry.'

What he did next nearly made me smile. Very slowly, he pushed the coffee toward me as though I were a wild animal that would chew off his hand if he did anything too abrupt.

I grabbed it with a sigh and raised it to read the black ink.

True grit is what leads to success, it said, and my heart missed a beat.

I frowned. Was it a reference to our conversation the night we first met? I remembered I had pointed out his grit then. What else could it mean? Was it merely a coincidence? Or was he implying perseverance? Then, regarding what? Me? Was this his way of telling me not to give up on him? Or was he trying to say that he hadn't actually given up on *me*?

No, he wouldn't do that. He couldn't possibly be trying to flirt with me, not when he had Francesca.

Puzzled, I looked at him. 'What's this supposed to mean?'

'That you should never give up on your dreams despite the obstacles you might face.' He shrugged. 'Just some inspirational words. You've done an excellent job so far, and I wanted to motivate you to continue with it.'

My eyes narrowed with suspicion. 'Hm. "Grit" sounds familiar, though.'

His facial expression was blank. 'Does it?'

'Never mind,' I murmured, as I didn't feel like bringing up the night we met. Pretending that I didn't remember anything at all from our first encounter was much more tempting. 'Thanks.'

'I'll help you out,' he said as he rounded the desk.

I froze when he stopped right next to me. Delicious electricity seemed to charge between our bodies, and mercy was nowhere to be found when I caught his seductive scent.

'I can do it,' I said, because his closeness was clouding my thoughts.

His beautiful hands reached out to organise a stack of paper. 'I know you can, but four hands will get the job done quicker.'

I grew quiet.

'That's a lovely perfume you're wearing,' he said after a while, and it made me blush again. Could he stop being so goddamned charming? I had to move on, but he was making it impossible. 'What's it called?'

'It's called none of your business,' I said impassively.

He chuckled. 'Christ. It was only a compliment. What's got your knickers in such a twist?'

You.

'Sorry, time of the month,' I lied.

'Ah. I'll tread gently.'

'Do you ever?' I said under my breath, but when his hands froze, it was apparent that he had heard me.

After a brief pause, he leaned forward to lock eyes with me, and his glowed with a strictness that I found oddly arousing. 'I don't appreciate your passive-aggressive behaviour right now. If there's something you'd like to say, be direct about it.'

Ripping my gaze from his, I glared away and wondered if I should tell him that I hadn't remotely appreciated his conduct last week with regards to Francesca's visit. At the same time, I was reluctant to enlighten him.

'You're right, I'm sorry. You didn't deserve that.'

'Apology accepted.'

A period of silence elapsed, and I spent it dreading the rest of my day here. I hoped Francesca or another lover wouldn't make an appearance, but if it happened, I hoped William would retain the decency not to ask me to work in his office straight afterwards.

We spent another five minutes on the task before we got started on actual work, and we hardly exchanged a word until lunch, but I caught him stealing glances at me so often that my irritation with him continued to increase. I hated being scrutinised by him, so I didn't want to work in here. I wanted to work next to Ellie.

His presence was bothering me immensely – his whole existence was. He was my boss, and I was madly attracted to him. Watching him sit there in his light-grey suit with that olive green tie around his neck – a neck which I had lavished with kisses some months ago – was beyond frustrating. Though I had never been religious, I could relate to Eve's time in Eden. However, in my case, Eden was my job – my personal paradise. The serpent was my never-ending lust for William, always whispering at the back of my mind, trying to tempt me into tasting the forbidden fruit that was my boss – William fucking Night. Truly, the more we interacted, the harder it was to resist acting on my infatuation with him, and it pissed me off.

I would have to think of something to rectify this situation. Being in his audience was far too distracting. It was difficult to maintain a strict focus on work. So easily, my thoughts ventured into erotic fantasies about him. I could barely look into his eyes without seeing the sizzling gaze he had once trapped me with, when I had been spread flat across his dining table.

Groaning, I decided I would hit the gym after work. Maybe blowing off some steam would quell my lust for him, at least for a while. Indeed, to tackle this, I would make the gym my go-to place for therapy to cure my anger and frustration with myself. I would exhaust myself completely, to the point where I wouldn't have energy left to spare for anything other than breathing.

§ § §

Over lunch, I hardly shared a word with anyone. Violet tried to strike up a conversation with me, but I was dismissive in my replies because I was preoccupied with my thoughts. She didn't seem offended, though, for which I was grateful, but then she didn't come across as a sensitive person either. Besides, as she was talking to me, I couldn't help but think that she might be trying to play me for a fool. I knew full well that she had been, and perhaps still was, William's regular bed partner, so I was suspicious of her intentions. It was possible that her interest was innocent, but part of me wondered if it was based solely on the fact that we had once shared a man. I decided to give her the benefit of the doubt, though, because there was something about her character that I found rather agreeable. Perhaps it was her assertiveness, or perhaps it was her intellect. Regardless, she had acquired my respect, so while I was dismissive, I was still polite about it.

When Andy tried to get a word out of me, asking if my pasta salad was any good, I had enough.

'It is,' I said and stood up. 'Anyway, I think I'll get back to work.'

Without looking at me, William nodded and put his fork down. 'Me too,' he said and pushed his chair out.

I cursed inwardly. I had hoped to get some space from him, and now he was robbing me of the opportunity.

§ § §

At half three, I attended the meeting that William had with our client Clifford Paints to go over the draft version of the NDA. Ellie joined us for it to write the report, so I looked over her shoulder a lot while William discussed the specifics of the NDA. Fortunately, I managed to resist admiring him this time and instead remained focused on what was being said.

It was nearly five o'clock when the meeting concluded, and I caught myself hoping that William wouldn't ask me to stay longer to complete the report or polish the NDA. If he did, I considered whether to ask him if I could do it from home instead, as I was all too eager to depart from his presence and hit the gym.

'I'll walk you down in just a moment,' William said as Gerard, Tom and Bo left the meeting room. Closing the door, he turned around and answered my prayers by ordering Ellie to stay longer instead. But then he looked at me and said, 'You can go and wait in my office.'

I blinked. 'Er, because you need me to stay longer as well?'

'No, but we need to have a chat.'

My body turned rigid while a faint, 'Okay,' poured out of my mouth. Was I in trouble?

As soon as he had left the room, I met Ellie's eyes. 'Have I done something wrong? Do you know?' I asked worriedly.

She looked puzzled. 'Not that I'm aware of. He probably just wants to ask you about your experience so far.' She put her hand on my shoulder, squeezing it. 'Try not to worry.'

I huffed. 'Easier said than done.' Standing up, I closed my laptop and said, 'Well, good luck with the report. Hopefully I'll see you tomorrow.'

'I'm sure you will, Cara. Honestly.'

My heart was drumming to the beat of a dramatic orchestra as I waited for William. Minutes felt like hours as I sat in his office after having packed my things. Staring at my bag, I wondered if I had packed them for the last time. If he intended to dismiss me, I wondered on what grounds. I had done my absolute best since I started here, and I hadn't messed up a single thing as far as I was aware, so what could possibly be wrong? I knew I had been rude to him this morning, but we had already addressed that, so what was the problem now?

I sprang up from my seat the moment I heard him open the door behind me. My eyes wide, I watched him close it and delve his hands in his pockets.

'Thanks for waiting,' he said.

My heart was in my mouth. 'What did you want to speak to me about?'

'Well, something's clearly wrong,' he said. 'You avoided me all of last week, and today you've hardly said a word – and when you do, you're grumpy and rude.'

I pressed my lips together. Did he have any self-awareness? My tongue might have been sharper than usual today, but he was definitely rude too, albeit by his actions rather than his words.

'Rude? *I'm* rude?'

He frowned. 'Yes.'

His hypocrisy pushed me to the end of my tether. 'Well, at least I don't fuck someone in my office and then proceed to make my colleague work there right afterwards.'

His eyebrows leaped up his forehead. 'That's what's been bothering you?'

'Well, of course, Will!'

'Why didn't you tell me this immediately?'

'Why didn't I tell you?' I waved my arm in the air. 'Maybe if you used the right head for once, you'd know why.'

His lips snapped into a winding line upon my phrasing. He was clearly trying to hide a smile.

'Enlighten me, then.'

I gestured to him, vexed. 'I was worried you'd get the wrong impression. Moreover, you're my boss. In case you need your memory jogged, I'm brand new at this job, and I'm still trying to find my footing round here. Scolding my superior for his lack of work ethics isn't exactly a tempting thing to do on my third day.'

He nodded. 'Please elaborate on why you were worried it could give me the wrong impression.'

Frowning, I looked away and folded my arms. 'I didn't want you to think that I'm jealous because you're seeing someone else.'

'I'm not.'

My heart did a flip and my eyes flickered back to him. 'What?'

He shrugged. 'I'm not seeing anyone.'

I stared at him, my face flushed with surprise. 'Do you mean you aren't even sleeping with anyone?' Disbelief permeated my tone.

He raised a brow. 'Not that it's any of your business whether I am, but yes, that's correct.'

I blinked. 'Then why was Francesca here?'

He waved a hand in the air. 'She came to ask me for a second chance.'

Several seconds elapsed while I tried to make sense of the facts. 'But her hair,' I said in my confusion. 'The window, your lips . . .'

Surprise flashed across his face. 'You surely noticed a lot.'

'I . . .' The more I remembered the scene, the more severe my confusion became. 'But you even asked me to bring my laptop with me, and the way you said it . . .'

He regarded me with patience. 'I asked you to bring your laptop with you because I wasn't sure what to expect. She cried a lot when I ended things with her, so I wanted to make sure that you'd be able to keep working if she needed some time to collect herself.' He raised a hand and scratched his cheek. 'As for my lips . . .' He gazed away and shook his head. 'Well, she kissed me right before she left, and quite fervently at that. It made me feel a bit queasy, so I opened a window for some fresh air.'

A new wave of colour flooded my face. I was mortified. 'I . . . I'm so sorry.'

Grimacing, I averted my eyes and scolded myself for having been so bold as to accuse my boss, however indirectly, of something so outrageous without any firm evidence whatsoever. What had got into me?

'Please, forgive me. I don't know what came over me. I . . .' I hugged myself tighter and dropped my gaze to the floor. 'It won't happen again.'

'It's all right.'

I looked up, hot with shame. 'I really am so sorry.'

'Don't worry about it. I get why you'd assume that.' He nodded. 'And I also understand why you were reluctant to bring it up with me. Though, for next time, please just tell me straight away.'

'I will.' I nodded vehemently.

We were quiet for some time before a sigh travelled out of his mouth. 'Well, you're free to go,' he said and opened the door for me, but I didn't move. I stood glued to the ground, wondering if I could find the courage to ask him why he had ended things with Francesca.

Frowning, he scanned my body and slowly closed the door again. 'Is there something else?'

I swallowed and avoided his gaze.

Just do it, I told myself. Otherwise I'll go mad wondering about it.

'Cara?'

'Why did you end things with her?' I asked and bravely met his eyes.

He studied me, his jaw flexing. 'I really shouldn't be answering that.'

My eyebrows curved. 'Why not?'

'Because it's inappropriate.'

'The question? Or the answer?'

He knitted his brows. 'This whole conversation.'

I fell silent. I knew he was right – I was being extremely unprofessional – but I couldn't help my curiosity.

After some time, he sighed again. 'You really want to know, don't you?'

'Yes,' I admitted shamefacedly.

He blew his cheeks out. 'Fine, I'll tell you.' After a beat, he added, 'But only if you promise that you won't hold it against me.'

I locked eyes with him then, my whole body tingling with anticipation.

'I won't.'

Clenching his teeth, he gazed away and remained quiet for some time.

'It's because you're the only one that I want,' he finally said.

My breath caught. The shock brought my heart to a halt, and when it resumed beating, it hammered like never before. Rendered mute, I tried to swallow, but my throat was aching so terribly that it did little to ease the pain.

After all this time, I struggled to fathom that he remained devoted to me.

He looked back, his eyes glimmering with a dream unrealised. 'I am open to something more only with you.'

I couldn't find the words to say. I was completely stunned.

'I'm sorry,' he said then, and his tone was filled with remorse.

'F-for what?'

'For telling you this.' He grimaced. 'For making you believe I was with someone else. For making you believe I did to her what I would only do to you.'

It felt like my chest was about to explode with a million butterflies. Utterly dazed, I said, 'You're not mine, Will.'

'But I am,' he said resolutely. 'Even if you don't want me.'

Disbelieving of what he had just said, I started to tremble. Intense heat engulfed my cheeks, and when he saw it, a faint smile claimed his mouth, but there was sadness in it – wistfulness. His eyes wandered across my face, studying the pinkness. After a while, his smile transitioned into the crooked version I often saw in my dreams.

I didn't know how to react. The extremity of my feelings was drowning out every single one of my thoughts. All I knew was that I was desperate for some space. I needed time to process this.

Totally confused, I grabbed my bag and said, 'I should go.'

He nodded vaguely and opened the door. 'I want you to know that I won't let this affect anything in terms of work.'

I approached him slowly, too overwhelmed to look at him.

Just as I was about to pass him, he said, 'Hopefully you can just forget that we ever had this conversation.'

I looked up at him then, pausing. 'Why would I ever want to?'

His eyes widened, and I heard him take a sharp breath. Staggered, he stared back at me.

'I'll see you tomorrow, Will.'

He didn't reply.

As I walked away, everything seemed bizarre. My body felt like a gooey mess, all because of his romantic declarations. Had he truly meant it? He hadn't moved on?

Feeling his gaze on my back, I glanced over my shoulder, and my heart contracted at the sight. He was staring at me as if I were the dawn when all he had ever known was the dark of night.

19

JUST GIVE IT A THOUGHT

Because I'd had no idea what to wear, I had settled for a maroon-coloured Bardot dress that hugged my figure. I felt opulent in it – ready to seduce the night.

It was Friday now, and Ellie had begged me all week to go to a club with her, where we would meet Brian – her fiancé – after we'd had post-work drinks at Disrepute with our colleagues. That was why I had struggled with deciding what to wear tonight. It wasn't easy to find a dress that would be suitable for a posh cocktail bar as well as a nightclub, but I was pleased with my choice.

I had felt a bit hesitant about returning to Disrepute. It was where I first met Will, so I was certain the surroundings would evoke the memory of his skilful hands sliding across my naked body.

And I was right. Aroused, I inhaled sharply, my eyes searching for his presence, but it was nowhere to be found. Nevertheless, I could have sworn I felt him within me right then, hard and forceful as he rammed deeper than any other man ever had.

I had just arrived and was sitting with Ellie when I sensed someone coming through the door. Because I hoped that every person who entered would be William, I refused to look; I didn't want to betray my foolish expectation.

I had no idea if he would show up at all. Sometime after lunch, he had asked me whether I was coming today, and when I had confirmed that I was, he had fallen silent. I had asked whether he would come as well, but his reply hadn't been definitive. All he had said was, 'I'm not sure yet.'

Since it was only Lawrence who arrived, my heart sank with disappointment, but at least I could dare to look properly in his direction.

He wasn't the tallest man. I had noted the first time we met that we were around the same height – five-foot-eight. Despite this, there was something about his general demeanour that made him easy to notice in a crowd anyway.

I had barely spoken to him, but I liked him so far. He was a quiet type with a powerfully brooding air. His eyes were such a dark brown that they verged on black, and his skin was paler than even mine. The dark circles around his eyes made him look constantly sleep-deprived, but somehow it suited him. He seemed more mysterious that way – and he was mysterious. He had hardly said a word to me since I started. It was Ellie who had informed me that he was thirty-five years old and married to a male nurse with whom he had two young children.

Ellie greeted him while I considered my situation.

It was weird to be back. Last time I was here, I had been swept away by William's unconventional charm. My heart tingled at the memory. That night, he had nearly ruined my defences, and I still hadn't managed to restore them to their original strength. If anything, I was weaker than ever, especially now that I knew he still had feelings for me.

We hadn't talked about it since. The whole week, we had both been acting like his confession never happened, but I had seen in his gaze that he was wondering where things would lead from here, and I knew I had mirrored the same look back at him.

I was terribly conflicted. On the one hand, I was hopelessly infatuated with him, but on the other, he was still my boss and Jason's brother. In other words, dating him would still be incredibly inappropriate – and risky.

I often wondered if he shared my concerns since he hadn't made any advances. He kept treating me like I was merely a colleague to him and nothing more. But perhaps he was just waiting for me to give him the green light. In the end, he was my boss, so maybe he was worried about the power imbalance between us; maybe he wanted to be sure that, if I started dating him, it would be of my own volition, and not because I felt intimidated by his role as my superior – that he wouldn't merely be getting a date with me because I was afraid to say no.

I was still thinking of him when he suddenly walked through the door. Commanding and magnetic, he exuded a boundless kind of strength that petrified those contesting it. He was unbearably elegant and alluringly self-assured. I could see it in his deportment. He carried himself with pride and grace, as if nothing could shake him.

While he put the whole place to shame on his way to the bar, his captivating eyes scanned the room. Browsing, browsing, and then they met mine.

My breath abandoned me. Searching for friction, I pressed my thighs together beneath the table. Merely with a glance, he had dampened my underwear.

Trapped under his spell, I blatantly ogled him from where I sat. He was wearing a shirt that matched the colour of my dress, and it made his eyes sparkle. Matching his trousers, a grey waistcoat encased his powerful torso, and the sight made me wet my lips.

He was such a vision. It wasn't fair that he should be so tempting when he was both my boss and my best friend's brother. I didn't deserve to suffer like this.

Fingers snapped in front of my face, breaking me out of my trance. Blinking, I turned my head, and I was met with Ellie's frown.

'Shit!' I squeezed my eyes shut. She had caught me again.

'You're hopeless.'

'Sorry. Thank you for . . .' I shook my head. 'Helping me out.' My lips protruded as I dragged my espresso martini to my mouth.

She chuckled. 'That's what I'm here for, love. And I don't blame you. He's been keeping a keen eye on you ever since you started. Honestly, I feel bad for you. Had I not been happily in love with Brian, I would have drooled after him all day long too, especially if he gave me that sort of attention.'

Her words held comfort. I could always count on Ellie to offer sympathy. She might be a fan of gossip, but there was no doubt that she was an endearing sweetheart in spite of it. It just meant that I had to be careful with what I told her, but I could live with that, because she made up for it with her genuine kindness. Besides, it had become obvious to me that when she gossiped, she was simply trying to bond with the person she spoke to, which was why I forgave it. She never had ill intent.

That said, it was a shame that she didn't seem to realise that, by gossiping, she could come across as someone who wasn't trustworthy, which could ultimately make some people reluctant to confide in her the way a true friend would. In that way, her bonding technique was a bit counterproductive.

'Ladies,' Andy greeted us. 'You look ravishing,' he said and grabbed the seat next to mine. With a playful gleam in his warm brown eyes, he turned toward me. '*Cara*,' he emphasised. 'You look like you frequent this place.'

My eyes widened at his unexpected quip. What impeccably slick humour.

'That colour on you should be illegal,' he flattered, probably to conceal his inexplicit poke. 'William will be jealous – you suit it better.'

I chuckled. 'As if.'

'Why wasn't I told about your plans to wear matching outfits?' he asked and gestured to me. 'I'm made to feel like an outcast.'

Ellie laughed while I studied his own choice of colours. Wearing white, grey and beige, he looked enticing.

'You look dreamy just the way you are, Andy, don't worry,' Ellie said and cocked her head slightly to one side. 'Still single? Or has that changed since last?'

'Semi-single.'

What was that supposed to mean?

'Elaborate,' Ellie said.

Andy sighed and leaned back. 'Chloe's difficult. She wants children, but I'm not ready for that yet. So, because we're not on the same wavelength, she's told me to make up my mind. Either I have to let her go or go all the way with her. So, while I make up my mind, we're on a version of a break.'

I gaped with sympathy. What an ultimatum.

'You've been together for a decade.' Ellie shrugged. 'It's not surprising she's reached that point.'

Andy looked displeased as he stared at her for a beat. 'Well, when she puts it that way, I feel like my only purpose is to get her pregnant. It's not romantic. I don't feel seen, let alone heard. I just feel like a bag of sperm she desperately wants. And I've always been scared of babies. I'm not ready to change nappies and clean up spew, and I am definitely not ready to sleep three hours a night. I'm building my career, Ellie. Children will have to wait till I've reached a stable point in it.'

I was surprised to discover that I had so much in common with Andy. Suddenly I liked him much more, because he was finally starting to make sense to me. We were similar. I was certain I would have reacted precisely the same way if my partner had demanded we conceive when I didn't feel ready.

Ellie rested her cheek in her hand and continued to regard him patiently. 'Well, do you think she'll change her mind?'

A sigh left Andy's mouth, and I could hear that it had come from his heart. 'I'm negotiating it with her. I'm trying to make her give me a few more years. I started with seven, but she drives a hard bargain, so I'm down to five at the moment. She keeps going on about female fertility depreciation, and saying that our children are more likely to have biological problems the longer we wait, things like that.'

'But do you love her?' Ellie brought herself to ask.

He stiffened, and from his furrowed brows, I could tell he found her question ridiculous. 'Of course I love her. I can't imagine my life without her. We've been together for ten years, Ellie. I've forgotten what it feels like *not* to love her.'

'Well, at least you're sure about that,' she said, visibly charmed.

From behind, William's voice rang through me. 'Give her the damn baby, Andy. Hire an au pair if time's becoming a problem. You've got the money.'

I froze completely. How close was he?

I had my answer when he leaned over my shoulder and placed a gin and tonic in front of me. Then he relocated his hand to my naked shoulder. His touch burned like fire, sending a delicious torrent of heat through my body. Hyperaware of his hand on me, I didn't dare to face him. I was much too overwhelmed.

Andy bent his neck and looked up at him as he stood behind us. 'I've already heard your opinion, Will – ten thousand times. Give it a rest already. It won't be your baby to deal with.'

William gave him a smirk. 'No. But if I were in your shoes, I'd give her the baby. Andy, last time you and Chloe hit a bump in the road, you lost the plot. You can't manage without her. If you let her go, you'll regret it for the rest of your life.'

'I'm with Will on this one,' Ellie said.

I remained silent, pretending not to exist. This was not a discussion I wanted to get involved in. I knew too little to be able to form an opinion, but from the little I knew, I was honestly inclined to support Andy.

'How about you, Cara? Are you with me?' William asked and successfully ruined my effort to evade the topic.

Bending my neck, I met his smouldering eyes. I wanted to submerge myself in them, swim in the sensual pleasures they whispered of. Bewitched,

I watched him, and forgot all about his question.

Andy laughed softly when I failed to respond. 'I think you've dazzled her.'

His comment dragged me back. Straightening my neck, I looked toward the toilets. I had to escape William's presence somehow. He looked nothing short of devastating, and I was absolutely susceptible to his allure.

'I'm not dazzled,' I lied. 'I'd just rather not comment on something that is absolutely none of my business. I think we should let Andy decide for himself. Anyway, excuse me,' I said and pushed my chair out.

'Thanks, Cara,' Andy said, and the affection in his voice made me give him a smile.

As I approached the ladies' room, I felt William's stare burning into my back. I escaped it as I walked in. Looking at an empty stall, I decided that I might as well relieve myself. I needed a minute to muster my strength before I could dare to go outside again. Being in the presence of William was like high-intensity interval training – quick breaks to regain my strength before I would push myself to the limit again, and with each interval, my overall strength declined.

'Fuck,' I muttered and shook my head as I walked out of the stall to wash my hands. Violet was there, leaning over a basin and drawing on a thin layer of nude lipstick while she studied her plump lips in the mirror. In the reflection, I saw her brown eyes swivel sideways.

'Cara,' she cooed. 'You look lovely.'

I studied her from head to toe. She was wearing a beautiful black dress that clung to her curvaceous figure. She had such a beautiful bum, full and perky, and it was pointing straight at me. Between her incredible body and keen intellect, Phoebe would have lost her mind over Violet, and, frankly, my bi-curious side was too.

'Thanks, Vi, but so do you,' I said and approached the basin right beside her.

'How have you found your first weeks with us?' She put her lipstick in her purse.

'Amazing,' I said as I collected soap in my hand.

'I'm glad. I've come across some of your work. The NDA you drafted for Clifford Paints was excellent. I was impressed.' A sweet smile curved her lips.

She intrigued me. Did she like me, or did she not? I really couldn't tell. All I knew was that she didn't come across as a person who cared much about men. My impression of her was that she was not the type to grow bitter and petty just because I often interacted with her past lover. On the contrary, I found her integrity rather apparent.

'Well, you've impressed me during every meeting,' I said as I washed my hands.

'Have I?' She smirked. 'Has Will impressed you as well? I think he wants to.'

I froze. Was she jealous? When I gazed at her, she gave me a knowing look.

'Listen,' she said and brushed a lock of her raven tresses away from her face. 'He told me you know about us.'

My lips parted. Why had he done that?

'It's not my business,' I squeaked and avoided her eyes.

She grabbed my arm. 'Cara, don't worry. I just need you to listen for a second.'

I met her eyes, my throat feeling tight.

She sighed and shook her head. 'I can't believe I'm doing this,' she murmured.

Doing what?

'Just . . .' Her eyebrows curved downward. 'Please, give him a chance. He's completely besotted with you, I can tell. Aside from Andy and John, I know him better than anyone else in this firm, and I've never seen him like this.'

I stared at her with shock, my face prickling as fresh colour emerged on my cheeks. 'I . . . I appreciate your sentiment, but Will's my boss and—'

'I know, and I'm sorry for meddling.' She smiled embarrassedly. 'I just can't help but think you're making a mistake. If you actually have feelings for him, giving him a chance is the best thing you can do. I swear you'll be rewarded tenfold.'

A half-suppressed laugh escaped me. I was just so shocked. 'I hadn't expected you to be so supportive.'

She chuckled. 'Did you think I'd be bitter?'

'Not really, but I definitely hadn't expected *this*.'

'Well, he's all yours. I've never had feelings for him. Only respect and a friendly fondness.' Was William to her what Aaron was to me? 'And maybe a little lust, but honestly, he's a bloody gorgeous man, so who could blame me?' She shrugged. 'Anyway, I'll stay away from now on. I hope you're not angry with me for sleeping with him.'

'Vi, I'm not remotely angry with you. He's not . . . mine, for lack of a better word.'

'Oh, but he's made it very clear that he is,' she said with a shrewd smile. 'Give it a thought, Cara. You're just a trainee. It won't get in the way of you being hired later. People marry their colleagues all the time. As long as you conduct your relationship in an appropriate manner, nobody's going to care. Besides, I'm sure John would be delighted to have you on board regardless of you and Will. You're a clever girl. You'd be an asset without a doubt.' She folded her arms.

'And I'd love to see you make him happy,' she went on. 'I've had a few cocktails already, so excuse me for speaking out of turn about all this, but you know as well as I do that he is exceptional in bed. Why settle for any less when you can have him?' She sounded baffled. 'So yes, he's a bit of a challenge on certain fronts, but overall, he compensates for that with his intellect and personality. Honestly, he'll make you feel like a goddess if you just give him a chance.'

I could scarcely believe how candid she was being with me; I barely knew her. But I did appreciate it. She was authentic, real, and clearly a bit drunk, but at least her heart was in the right place.

'Just give it a thought,' she repeated and gave me a wink as she went to the door. When she opened it, she eyed me over her shoulder. 'Oh, and this conversation never happened. He'd break my neck.'

I swallowed the massive lump that had gathered in my throat and nodded. As soon as the door closed, I propped my hip against the basin and released a pent-up breath. She and William really were remarkably similar. Perhaps that was why I found myself slightly attracted to her as well.

Turning toward the mirror, I studied my reflection. I had gone for smokier eye make-up than usual, but it looked good. I hadn't overdone it. According to Jason, it didn't look like somebody had tried to punch me to death, which he had said as he drooled after my figure sauntering toward the front door. Like his brother, Jason was terrific at giving compliments – his body language even more so. I had felt like a million quid when I left our flat today, confident in my strut.

When another woman came in, I was dragged back to reality. It was time to step outside again. I was quite sure that a certain someone had been counting the seconds I had spent in here. So, with my chin raised, I returned to the bar, where I saw that a group of men had replaced William and Andy, and they were all chatting with Ellie.

Glancing around, I eventually spotted William and Andy at the bar. A herd of women surrounded them, circling the two lads like vultures. There were six of them, and they looked slightly older than me.

William's eyes caught mine across the room but I quickly looked away. After Violet's speech, I was more conflicted than ever, so I didn't feel like interacting with him right then.

My gaze settled on Ellie, and I decided to come to her aid. Surrounded by three strangers, she was visibly uncomfortable. I was certain she had already told them she was engaged, but not everyone respected boundaries.

'Hi,' I said when one of the men looked over. He wasn't particularly handsome. He had a pointed nose and mouse eyes, with thin lips and a narrow head, but his gawk made up for it because it boosted my ego.

Turning my attention to Ellie's desperate eyes, I gave her a fond smile. 'Gorgeous girls only or am I allowed?' I asked and gestured to the only vacant seat.

The lad that had noticed me first immediately stood up and pulled out the chair for me.

'Please,' he said and jerked his ginger head toward the seat. I smiled at him as I sat down.

'I'm Lewis,' he said as he descended beside me. 'Those things over there are James and Francis, but they're not worth your attention.'

'What the hell, mate?' James frowned. 'Killing the competition already, are you?'

'Like a true capitalist.'

'Fuck you, then,' Francis said.

I giggled.

'Can I buy you a drink?' Lewis asked me, brown eyes intense, like he wanted to suck out my soul.

'She's already got one,' Ellie intervened and pushed a gin and tonic toward me, which I recognised as the one William had put on the table earlier. He had bought it for me?

'All right, then. I'll still be here for the refill, hopefully,' Lewis said amusedly.

I gave him a lopsided smile as I raised the drink to my lips.

'So what's your name?' he asked.

'Jessica,' I lied. It was just so amusing. I couldn't shake off the habit. Out of the corner of my eye, I saw Ellie struggle to suppress a smile.

'And how was work, Jessica? Do you work?'

'Does it look like I don't?'

'You look like luxury, so you tell me.'

Slick.

'Got a taste for the finer things in life, have you?' I teased back.

His thin lips tucked up into a smug smile while a ravenous gleam entered his eyes. 'There's not a doubt in my mind.'

I soon realised I had become Ellie's entertainment for the night. She laughed nonstop while I teased the men accompanying us, and as though my attention was in short supply, they fought for it until they nearly surrendered their dignity. I knew the only reason they found me more interesting than Ellie was that I seemed available while she had a huge diamond on her finger, but I was having too much fun bantering with them to care about their intentions. For a good two hours, I kept them on their toes while they ordered round after round for Ellie and me.

I had almost forgotten about William when he suddenly grabbed my attention by putting his big hands on my bare shoulders. Startled, I nearly choked on my sip. Only one touch could make me feel this way, so I didn't need to turn around to know who it was. Besides, after a glance at his hands, I had enough proof to be sure. Those beautiful long fingers had once caressed my naked body, and they had done it so well that I couldn't ever forget their appearance, let alone the pleasure they had provided.

I tipped my head back and looked up at him, but he didn't meet my gaze. Instead, his eyes resembled two blue flames as he glared at the men around me.

'Gentlemen, I'm afraid I'll have to steal this one away from you. Considering how many drinks you've bought her, I doubt she can walk in a straight line anymore,' he said, voice composed, and squeezed my shoulders.

He did have a point. I felt quite drunk by now, but I wasn't completely off my face either. I doubted that I could walk in a straight line, but I could probably make some fancy zigzag pattern for him.

Lewis frowned up at him. 'I wasn't aware she had a boyfriend.'

'You don't strike me as being aware in general,' William riposted and pulled my chair back with surprising force.

I gasped at his insolent comment, shocked. Ellie pursed her lips so as not to laugh, but when James and Francis started guffawing, she lost control. Her laughter rumbled out of her until she snorted, and it made me giggle, so much so that I barely noticed William's hand around mine while he dragged me away.

He didn't stop until we had reached the bar, where Andy stood waiting. He released my hand and glowered down at me, but he said nothing.

Drunk as I was, I swayed a little under his stare. 'What?'

'Cara, not in front of me. Please.'

Andy sighed and shook his head while William clenched his teeth. Was he suppressing his anger? It looked like it.

My heart throbbed upon hearing his fears. Was that why he had been unsure about whether to show up tonight? Had he been afraid that he might witness me go home with a stranger?

'What? I wasn't even thinking of it. I was only trying to help Ellie out.'

Andy summoned the bartender's attention and asked, 'Sorry, could I have a bottle of still water, please?'

William kept staring at me. Why wasn't he taking his eyes off me? It unsettled me. Folding my arms, I leaned against the counter and turned my side to him.

'Thank you,' Andy said and walked to stand between William and me. After unscrewing the cap, he handed me the bottle. 'Drink. You've had more than a barrel of gin by now. It's going to hit you any moment.'

I scoffed. 'Christ, Andy, I'm not a child. I can manage my intake. But thanks, anyway.'

As I raised the bottle to my mouth, he gave me an affectionate smile and then turned to William.

'Calm down, Will. She's fine,' he said, patting his shoulder.

William shot him a glare, his Adam's apple ascending and falling. It dawned on me then that I had read him wrong. He wasn't angry. He was anxious, maybe even worried – about me. But why? Because I was intoxicated?

'Cara!' Ellie called then. I looked over. She had left the table and was beckoning to me.

Right. The club.

I had barely moved a pace when William clasped my arm.

'Where are you going?'

I gazed up at him. 'Ellie and I are meeting Brian at a club.'

His eyes flickered in Ellie's direction. Then they landed on mine again. 'There's not even a slim chance I'll let you go to a club right now. When the drinks kick in, you'll be up for grabs.'

'Excuse me? You are not my boss,' I said. 'Fuck,' I mumbled as soon as I heard what I had said.

His eyebrows arched, his head tilting as some amusement twinkled in his eyes. 'Actually, Cara, I am.'

'That's not what I meant. I meant you don't get to decide that.'

His chest expanded with his deep inhalation. 'Fine,' he said. 'But then I'm coming with you. Andy?'

Andy shrugged and tucked his hands in his pockets. 'Sure. But we aren't appropriately dressed for that.'

'I'm sure they've got a cloakroom,' William said and started toward Ellie, his hand on my back.

She blinked confusedly once we reached her, and it made me sigh. She wasn't an idiot. If William kept acting this way, it was only a matter of time before she would realise the true nature of our relationship.

'Mind if we join you, Ellie?' Andy asked.

A grin took over her mouth. 'Of course not!'

Always so cheerful. I wished she had said No. Then again, I doubted that William would have listened.

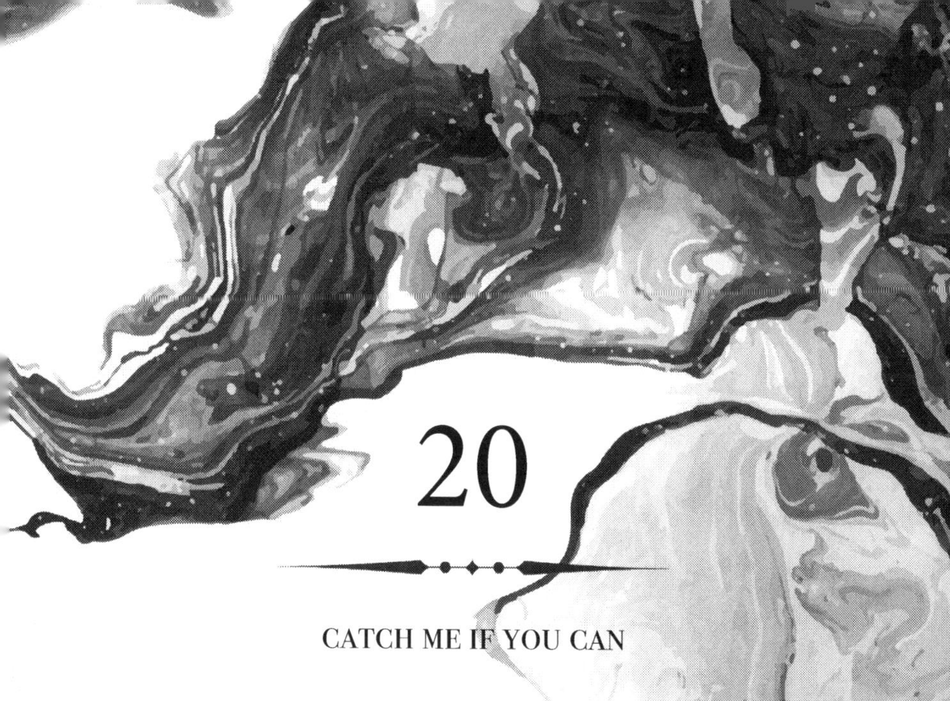

20

CATCH ME IF YOU CAN

THE PULSATING MUSIC POUNDED AGAINST MY EARDRUMS – THE KIND OF music that would transform even the most sensible person into a lustful animal. The club resembled a strobe light illuminated jungle, where the wild creatures unleashed their primal core. Still, there was a level of class to it. Spread over three floors, the whole area was quite impressive. The guests weren't casually dressed, but they weren't wearing much to cover their glistening skin either.

William and Andy had left their waistcoats and ties with the cloakroom staff. They still looked somewhat out of place, but they weren't a lost cause. Looking at William, I saw that he had already rolled up his sleeves, which was a nice touch of casualness. All that was required was a little tweak. I intended to put theory into practice when I raised my hands toward his collar, but when my fingers gripped it, he clasped my wrists. My breath hitched upon the contact of our skin and the ensuing current that charged through my bloodstream. Had he felt it too?

I looked up and found him glaring at me, his grip tightening around my wrists.

'What are you doing?' he asked.

'Damn.' I smiled. 'Who let you out of your cage today?' I twisted my wrists out of his grip and undid the top button of his shirt.

Andy laughed. 'I didn't,' he said. 'I'd rather he stayed in it all the time.'

'That makes two of us,' I joked back.

William was not amused, and I could tell because his glare shifted onto Andy instead.

After undoing a second button, I retreated a few paces to judge my artistry, and I immediately regretted it. Like this, he looked beyond tempting. The sight of him right then even made my vagina throb, and when I felt it, I nearly sobbed. How on earth did I manage to resist him? I deserved an award.

'Thanks, love,' William murmured and turned his profile to me. He delved his hands in his pockets, and his casual stance only made him more appealing.

I searched for his gaze, but I didn't find it. 'That colour really suits you.'

He scoffed and stole a glance at me. 'Hardly as much as you do.'

Taken aback, I gaped, my eyes flickering to Ellie to see if she had heard him, but her face was buried in her phone. Relief closed my mouth again.

'Nice one, Will,' Andy said with a smirk as he undid his top buttons, copying my work.

Suddenly Ellie exclaimed, 'He's texted me. He's in there, far end!' She pointed into the crowd. A heartbeat later, she had caught my hand and was dragging me into it.

Countless bodies ground against one another, and mine. Numerous eyes glanced in my direction, and most of them looked faded, drugs lifting them high above the clouds. Going in had been like sinking into quicksand – the more I shifted, the deeper I got. Andy and William charged after us, but the moving crowd swallowed us up until they were no longer in my view.

'Fuck,' I mumbled. William was not going to like this. 'Hey, Ellie!' I jerked her hand. 'We've lost the others!'

'They've got my number, and they know where we're going! We'll be fine!' she yelled back and carried on squeezing through the crowd.

Suddenly a pair of arms hooked around my waist and tugged me into a warm embrace, breaking my grip on Ellie's hand. Whirling around, I stared up at a face I had never seen before. I shoved him off and turned toward Ellie again, scared I had lost her too. Glimpsing the twists of her mane, I charged after her. She had stopped, her eyes searching for me.

'Cara!' she yelled as soon as she spotted me. She extended her hand, and I grabbed it firmly. 'Don't let go!'

She faced away and pulled me through the crowd until we reached a bar at the far end. Among the people around it stood a group of five men. One of them briefly met my gaze before his eyes darted to Ellie's person, and then to the man in front of him. As he jerked his head toward us, all five of them looked over.

Ellie released my hand and rushed toward them. A man of average height, with bronzed skin and dark brown hair, spread his arms to welcome her. She swung her arms around him and planted a firm kiss on his waiting mouth.

So that must be Brian, I thought.

I couldn't hear what they said to one another, but while they embraced, his friends blatantly ogled me. Feeling awkward, I gave them a wave.

Ellie pulled out of Brian's arms and motioned to me.

'Nice to finally meet you, Cara!' he yelled.

There wasn't much room for conversation above the pounding music, so introductions were swift, but I was too drunk to remember the names of Brian's friends. When one of them caught my hand and dragged me toward the dance floor, I looked at the bar, hoping to spot William, but I couldn't see him anywhere. I faced a dilemma then, because while I wanted to find him and Andy, I didn't want to be a killjoy, especially since the original plan had been to spend time with Ellie tonight. So, with some reluctance, I allowed myself to get dragged away, but it was only because Ellie and Brian were heading to the dance floor as well.

Like William and Andy had warned, the drinks suddenly kicked in. The room spiralled around me while I danced with this good-looking stranger. We danced until we were glistening with sweat. Even though we were out of breath, the music hypnotised us into continuing.

I had to give it to him: he was an excellent dancer. Did he have a single stiff bone in his body? I could feel a stiff muscle, but it contained no bones.

We had danced for a while when I sensed his mouth beginning to search for mine, clearly hoping for some action. Three months ago, I wouldn't have minded a random snog, but something prevented me now, and the reason wasn't present. I had lost him some time ago, and he still hadn't found me.

'Sorry, I need the loo!' I shouted and escaped out of Brian's friend's hold.

Staggering toward the edge of the crowd, I searched for the toilets.

When I found them, I sucked in a deep breath, determined to breathe only through my mouth to avoid the stench of the place. I hurried to finish because I despised toilets in clubs and pubs. Thankfully there was still a little soap left that I could wash my hands with.

When I came out I leaned against the wall. I was so drunk, and the thought of having to find Ellie again made me want to go home.

While standing there, I got the eerie feeling that I was being watched. I scanned the crowd, but I didn't register any familiar gazes.

Suddenly I saw Brian's friend – the one I had been dancing with – and the sight of him was like a light at the end of the tunnel. He was walking out of the men's room. Maybe he had some idea of where the others were.

Our eyes locked, and the smile that caught his mouth was infectious. The music was quieter here, so when he said, 'Hey, there. Cara, was it?' I could actually hear him.

'Yes.'

He came over, but when he put his hands against the wall on either side of my head, my smile faded. I froze in place, feeling intimidated.

'Well, then, Cara. How are you?'

'Quite drunk,' I said as I gazed into his dark eyes. His brown hair was longer than that of the average man, and, like Will, he had symmetrical features and neatly groomed stubble.

'Well, you're not alone.' Smirking, he lowered his head, his lips drawing closer and closer to my own.

I turned my head. My gut twisted with discomfort. This didn't feel right. I didn't want this.

'Oh, come on, love. Just a peck. I swear you won't regret it.' He clasped my jaw and turned my face toward him. Putting my hands on his chest, I wriggled against his hold.

'N-no.' I tried to push him away and was just about to thrust my knee into his balls when big, familiar hands gripped his shoulders. A split second later, William dragged him off me with violent force. He was fuming, his eyes ablaze as he glowered at Brian's friend, who had fallen to the floor.

Leaning down, William gripped his collar and held it firmly, pulling him up somewhat. 'Touch her again and I swear I'll rearrange your fucking face!' he hissed and let go with a shove, causing Brian's friend to slam into the ground again. 'She's made it abundantly clear she doesn't want you.'

William moved to stand in front of me. Peeking past his strong right arm, I saw Brian's friend scramble to his feet and leap into the crowd. A few people stared at us while William glared after him.

When he turned toward me, his eyes immediately softened. 'Are you all right?'

I swallowed, overcome with lust. I wanted him so badly.

The waves of his hair cradled his ears, and the bigger wave above his forehead made me raise my hands to run my fingers through it. My breath hitched at the feel of it. It was exactly how I remembered – thick, but velvety soft. With wonder in my eyes, I gazed up at him, captivated by his beauty.

'I'm sorry we lost you,' I said and dragged my hands to the nape of his neck to play with the strands there.

'That's not what I asked,' he said and lowered his head somewhat. I could smell the alcohol on his breath; he was intoxicated as well.

He stared into my eyes, intensely, and it made my chest flutter. Merely by looking at me, he made me feel more alive than I ever had. Caught under his influence, I bucked my hips forward, wanting to be closer to him.

His lips formed a brooding line as he locked his arms around my waist and pressed me against him.

'Cara, say something. Tell me you're all right.' He sounded unbearably sensual when he used that tone. I had never heard a voice more inviting in my life. I knew he was merely speaking to me, but I could have sworn he was singing, luring me to my doom.

'I'm fine.' It was almost a whisper.

He grimaced. 'I'm sorry I didn't intervene sooner. At first I thought . . .'

My eyebrows curved with surprise. 'You were watching me?'

He nodded vaguely. 'I thought you wanted him at first. I saw you dancing earlier.'

'You did? Why didn't you come over?'

'I wanted to, but . . . I wasn't sure you'd appreciate it.'

I frowned. 'That didn't stop you earlier tonight.'

'I know, but that wasn't right of me. I didn't want to repeat my mistake, so I left you alone. I have no right to interfere like that, and you looked like you were enjoying yourself.' Averting his eyes, he turned his profile to me, and he looked a bit sad. 'Frankly, I . . . I gave up for a moment.'

My heart palpitated painfully. Moving my hands to his jaw, I turned his face toward me.

'I wasn't enjoying myself – not really,' I said as I held his gaze. 'I'd rather it was you. In fact I've been looking for you, but since I was supposed to spend time with Ellie tonight, I didn't want to leave her side.'

Something bright shone from his eyes. 'Really?'

'Really.'

He smiled winsomely and glanced over his shoulder, but when he faced me again, he had knitted his brows. 'I have to say, though, I'm a bit disappointed. Of all women, I'd expect at least you to escape predators like that.'

I chuckled. 'Well, I was just about to kick him in the balls when you arrived.'

His lips stretched into another smile. 'Really?'

'Yes.'

He looked proud. 'Good. I'm almost sorry I intervened, then. A kick in the balls is what he deserves, and even that would be merciful.'

Nodding my agreement, I gazed at the crowd. I wanted to dance again, but with William – only him. Biting my lip, I looked back at him with a mischievous smile. His brows twitched faintly, revealing some confusion, but before he could say anything, I pushed him away. As I strode past him on my way to the dance floor, I wondered where Andy had gone.

'What are you doing?' William asked.

Eyeing him over my shoulder, I gave him a lascivious smile. 'Escaping a predator,' I teased with a wink.

His eyes grew darker as he followed me. I had barely managed to pass a few dancing bodies when he clasped my hand, and I nearly shuddered with desire at his touch. As he entwined our fingers, I took a deep breath to steady my rising pulse.

'I'm not letting you out of my sight,' he said. Good. I didn't want him to, and I let him know by squeezing his hand.

When we were further into the crowd, I turned to face him. 'Can you dance?' I asked above the music.

He grinned. 'With you, I'll do just about anything.'

A warm wave of colour flushed my cheeks, but I didn't think he could see it under the dim light. He moved closer and brought his arms around my waist, pulling me against him.

I had never felt so anxious before – not over a man. My blood simmered in my veins as I circled his neck with my arms. He was so fucking hot. All I wanted was to submerge myself in this moment with him.

Lowering his head, he paused by my ear. 'Stay close,' he said and began to move along with the carnal music. I followed his movements with my heart in my throat, feeling my arousal drench both my mind and my underwear. All I could think of was my intense yearning for his flesh, how much I wanted him – all of him.

I hadn't thought that a man like William could dance, but he was indeed proving me wrong. Then again, considering his skills in the bedroom, it shouldn't have surprised me. He practised perfect control over his body, and he seemed determined to make mine come undone.

And it was working. My hands were all over him, exploring and caressing.

We had danced for a while when he gripped my hips and whirled me around so that my back was facing him. Smoothing his hands down my arms, he didn't stop until they covered the back of mine. There, he entwined our fingers and brought our arms around me to form an embrace. My heart jolted when he hugged me tightly. Our new position was powerfully intimate, and it made me catch my breath. When he moved along with my body now, I could feel his erection straining against my bum.

Oh my God. I was going insane.

Resting my head on his shoulder, I closed my eyes and surrendered to the euphoric moment. He was seduction in the flesh. The longer he held me, the more unbearable my lust for him became. Eventually my desire for him grew so heavy that I knew I would be crushed under its weight if I didn't act on it.

All at once, lust capsized my good sense. I needed to kiss him. It felt as vital to my existence as oxygen did.

Opening my eyes, I saw an area deep in shadow at the far end of the room, and it became my quest to bring him there. I thrust my hips back to push him away. He let go of me, and I rushed forward immediately, but not before I had cast a lewd smile at him over my shoulder.

'Cara,' he called, though it sounded more like an order. He charged after me.

Giggling, I snuck through the crowd, always just barely escaping his grasp. Like a man possessed, he chased after me, eyes resolute.

'Cara!'

Twirling, I gave him another smile. 'Catch me if you can, Will!'

Still giggling, I manoeuvred past the dancing bodies toward my desired spot. It was just below the staircase leading to the second floor, and it was shrouded in beckoning darkness.

I had nearly reached it when I turned to wait for him. About three feet away from me, he stopped, his eyes flickering between my mischievous smile and the dark area behind me. Seeming to infer my intentions, he took a deep breath, his jaw flexing.

With a lustful gleam in my eyes, I offered my hand to him as a silent invitation. I couldn't quite distinguish the emotion that permeated his gaze. All I could tell was that it was intense.

He seized my hand and pulled me forcefully toward him. I slammed into his muscular chest, startled by his urgency. Before I could recover, he was moving forward, his hands on my hips as he steered me backward into the darkness. Veiled by shadows, he kept walking until I bumped into the wall behind me.

Suddenly his lips were right by my ear. 'You are such a tease.'

I wetted my lips and locked my arms around his neck. 'Am I?'

'I swear to God, Cara, you'll be my undoing,' he said gruffly.

'What, you can't handle me?' I purred and ran my fingers through his hair. Moving my leg between both of his, I started grinding against his thigh.

'Oh, I'll fucking handle you,' he said and thrust his hips against me to pin me to the wall. Air exploded out of my lungs at his lustful action. A heartbeat later, his mouth found mine, and my chest ignited with a passion I had only felt twice before.

Truly, he was the best kisser I had ever encountered. How I had managed to resist him before was beyond my comprehension. I must have been an idiot.

The mesmerising motion of his mouth sent a surge of excitement through me. Tender, yet still so forceful, it ravished my own. His tongue wasn't plunging into my mouth. It merely teased it, and it aroused me to an extent nobody but him had ever managed.

Dopamine raged through my system when the delectable taste of him detonated in my mouth. I had missed it more than I had been aware of. He tasted so good, and he kissed even better.

But his kiss was slightly different this time. It held such resolve that I was rendered powerless.

As his lips continued to slide against mine, my heart ached terribly. Pleasure tore at the very fibres of it. When William kissed me, I felt ecstatic. It was as though nothing else mattered anymore. Everything faded, everything but him. It just felt uncannily right; I felt complete, as though a vacancy I hadn't known I harboured had been occupied; as though our lips had been designed for each other; as though we had been fated to combine all along.

It was entirely liberating to finally allow myself the sin – to touch him, to taste him. I wanted the moment to last for ever. There would be no consequences, then. Just him and me, marvelling endlessly at our overwhelming chemistry, in a moment locked away in infinity.

He groaned into my mouth and cupped my cheeks in his hands. Pulling away, he rested his forehead against mine and heaved for air.

'Shit, Cara. What you do to me.'

'Less talk, more kissing,' I said on a ragged breath and brought his mouth back to mine. His stubble scraped my palms when I clasped his strong jaw, and I felt him smile against my lips. God, he was enticing. I wanted to devour the entirety of him.

He kept kissing me for minutes on end, and I never wanted him to stop. He was so damn good at it. I was addicted to his mouth, and all the things it could do.

My heart seemed to have caught fire, and his lustful hands on my body were adding fuel to it. Again, a most uncanny feeling poured into it, nibbling on the fibres.

What was it? It was so alien to me. So sweet, and yet so vulnerable. Delicate yet profound.

I frowned, trying to identify it, but when his hand trailed down my thigh, I forgot all about it. Groaning, I invited his touch to progress. Seeming to understand, he hooked his arm around my thigh and brought my leg around him. His fingertips travelled as light as a feather up my thigh again, then inward toward my dripping lips. He was barely touching me, yet a touch had never felt more powerful.

'Will,' I moaned and broke our kiss.

Chuckling, he reclaimed my mouth as his fingers drew closer and closer to my aching wetness. When they flirted with the soaked part of my thong, he pulled away and rested his lips by ear. I panted, trying to withstand the tingling sensation he was causing between my legs.

Suddenly he cupped my sex, making me gasp.

'Always ready for me, Cara.'

'Yes,' I whined. 'You drive me insane!' I gripped his collar to tug him back to my mouth, but he refused me the satisfaction. He stopped just before he reached my swollen lips, his breath breezing across them.

'Good.' He rubbed me gently and I shuddered, caught by the delicious friction he provided. Hooking his fingers into my thong, he pushed it aside and revealed my wetness. One finger lapped over me once. Then he dipped it into me, though barely.

I shuddered again, wanting him to continue.

'More?' he purred into my ear.

'Mm, yes,' I said, high-pitched, and curled my fingers in his hair. I dragged his mouth toward mine, and this time, he allowed it. He pushed his finger deeply into me then, making me groan into his mouth. It felt so good.

Using the thumb of his other hand, he rubbed my clit. The sensation rippled up my spine and made my head jerk backward. He seemed determined to make me come with nothing but his hands, and I marvelled at the idea of it. No man had ever managed to make me come this way before, but William was well on his way to becoming the first.

Adding another finger, he thrust them in and out of me, and he focused his point of impact on my front wall. Meanwhile, the thumb of his other hand continued to rub me.

My lips parted and my eyes grew wide. *Whoa.* This was nothing short of delicious.

The tension rallied in the pit of my belly. Growing larger and larger, it expanded until every muscle of my body tensed.

'Shit,' I breathed out.

I chewed on my lower lip, grimacing. Heat spread across my skin, burning. Everything was so *hot*. My heart accelerated with the speed of his fingers, my breathing growing louder, harder, ragged. The background faded. All I noticed was him.

His thumb struck my clit with perfect precision then.

I moaned, my eyes squeezing shut. Applying more pressure, he continued to rub my throbbing bud, making my thoughts scatter into dizzy elation. Inside me, his strong fingers kept stroking that susceptible spot.

'Will,' I wailed. Responding, he thrust his fingers harder into me. I gasped, my walls clenching around his digits. Shivers bolted through my system while my toes curled in my heels.

Oh no.

'Fuck!' I cried, hitting the peak. The dam inside me crumbled and a warm torrent of pure liberation flooded my body.

As I convulsed away from the wall, he rushed to cage me in his arms. Whether he remembered my tendencies was lost on me, but it was entirely plausible. I always quivered when I came, and he had experienced that first-hand before.

Finally, I went limp, drifting away on the blissful orgasm that stormed through my body. William's intoxicating scent filled my nose as I recovered against him. When I found the strength to lift my head again, he leaned down and nuzzled his nose against mine.

I couldn't see much, but I could make out the vague silhouette of his hand as he raised it to his face.

'What an appetiser, Cara,' he said then, and I realised he was licking his fingers clean.

Lost for words, I stared at him through the dark. He was so fucking erotic.

He took my hand with his other one. Moving next to my ear, he said, 'About time we leave this place, don't you think?'

'Y-yeah.'

He leaned away and turned his head, probably scanning the crowd. When he looked back, he said, 'I need to find Andy first, though.'

21

SWEET DREAMS

William pulled out a stool at the bar. 'Stay here,' he said, pointing at it. 'I'll come back for you as soon as I've found Andy.'

I hopped up on it and nodded. 'Okay.'

He leaned down and kissed me, making my chest flutter. It felt so strange to be lavished with kisses from him. Smiling, he pulled away and then looked at the bartender, summoning her attention.

'Give her a bottle of water, please,' he said, jerking his head in my direction, and reached into his pocket. He withdrew his wallet and left a tenner on the counter. 'Keep the change.' He turned, gave me a smiling look, and then left.

As I gazed after him, I sensed that I was starting to sober up. The gravity of what I had done with him was slowly beginning to dawn on me, but I wasn't ready to face up to it yet. I wanted the blissful ignorance to last just a little longer. Tomorrow, I would take accountability and weather the storm caused by my actions, but for now, I wanted to exist without thoughts, only feelings.

Turning, I said to the bartender, 'Could you give me three shots of tequila as well, please?' I opened my purse.

'Of course, love.' She smiled.

I necked them one after the other, feeling the heat slide down my throat and numb my panic.

I wasn't sure how long I had been sitting there when William came back alone, but somehow it felt like ages that had been wrapped up in mere minutes – a sign that I was drunk.

'Cara?'

I struggled to keep a steady gaze on him. The tequila had blunted my senses and slowed my reflexes.

'Are you all right?' he asked, furrowing his brows.

I narrowed my eyes, hoping it would make him stop spinning. Maybe three shots had been overdoing it.

'I'm a bit drunk,' I said. 'Where's Andy?'

'I haven't found him yet. Man's not answering his phone either.'

It took me a while to process what he was saying. 'Okay. I'll keep waiting.'

'No, we're leaving. You look like you're about to pass out.'

'Okay.' I slid off my stool and nearly lost my balance.

'Jesus Christ.' William rushed to grab my arms, holding me upright. 'What happened?' he asked, his eyes flitting to the bar. 'Did she spike your water or something? You weren't this . . . unwell when I left you.'

'I had three shots of tequila,' I confessed, unable to fix my gaze on his. 'Bad idea.'

'You what? What the hell did you do that for?'

'I was sobering up.' I shrugged. 'I just wanted to . . . not be doing that.'

He pressed his lips together. 'Well, you're a fucking idiot.'

'Yes.' I nodded.

'Come on, I'm taking you home.' He wrapped his arm around my waist.

As we were walking out – clumsily, thanks to me – William suddenly spotted Andy among a group of women.

'Andy!' he shouted, his body tensing against mine. He was fuming, I could tell. 'Put your dick away and get the hell over here!'

Resembling a scared dog, Andy moved toward us.

'Why weren't you answering your phone?' William asked. 'I've been looking everywhere for you.'

'It's probably on silent, I'm sorry. And I didn't think to check it because I thought you were still busy with Cara.' Andy looked at me then. 'Goodness, is she all right?'

'She's completely off her face,' William said and jerked me toward him when I nearly collapsed. 'I need to take her home, but I'm not leaving you here – I leave you alone for two minutes, and this is what happens. Have you got no self-restraint? If Chloe had seen this . . .'

'Chloe, Chloe, Chloe. I swear, sometimes, you'd think *you* were her boyfriend.'

William inhaled deeply. 'Well, sometimes, I think she'd be better off with a man like me.'

Andy shot him a baleful look. 'Careful, Will.'

'Sorry, tough love.'

My stomach turned, the contents rising to my throat. It demanded all my remaining strength to swallow it back down.

'Will,' I moaned.

'You – oh, for fuck's sake, Cara. Are you going to be sick?'

I shook my head. 'Just take me home, please.'

Dipping into his pocket, William produced his ticket for the cloakroom and handed it to Andy. 'Fetch our things – and be quick about it. I'll meet you outside.'

I had nearly passed out by the time William put me in a taxi. When he slid in next to me, I laid my head on his shoulder and surrendered to the darkness.

§ § §

I woke up to the sound of Jason's voice. 'Bloody hell, is she all right?'

'She's absolutely plastered,' William said.

I heard a car door close, and it felt like I was moving, but not by myself.

'Could you hold the door for me?' William asked.

'Yeah,' Jason said.

When I finally found the strength to open my eyes, I saw the underside of William's sharp, square jaw. He was carrying me across his chest, up a set of stairs. Where were we?

This angle made me feel sick again. It looked like the stairs above us were spinning. I wouldn't be able to hold it down for much longer.

'Will,' I whimpered. 'Toilet.'

'Shit.' He looked at me, grimacing. 'Just hold it in for one more minute. We're almost there.'

Jason rushed past us and opened the door to our flat, holding it for William.

The second William put me on the floor of the bathroom, I lifted the lid of the toilet and vomited.

'Cara' – William sighed as he gathered my hair to hold it for me –

'you really are an idiot.'

'Yes,' I squeaked as I retched and retched until nothing came out. Tears welled in my eyes from vomiting so hard. Leaning away, I rested my head against the cold glass of the shower.

'I can't believe she got that drunk, especially in front of her boss,' Jason said from the doorway. 'You might be my brother, but for heaven's sake. This is so unlike her.'

'We haven't exactly been together all night,' William said. 'She and Ellie were supposed to go to a club just the two of them, but then Andy and I asked to come along. We lost each other in the club. I suppose she didn't expect to find me again.'

He was sort of lying, but I appreciated it. I was certain I would wake up to proper angst tomorrow.

'*You* asked to come along? Wearing that?' Jason seemed flummoxed. 'And since when do you go clubbing?'

'That's enough,' William said, sounding like a parental figure.

'Are you drunk as well?'

'A bit.'

'Well, you can sleep here if you're too tired to go home. I'm sorry you had to babysit Cara, man. I'm embarrassed on her behalf.'

'It's all right. It's not the first time I've had to babysit a drunk idiot.' William shot him a look. 'But yeah, I'll sleep over.'

Jason rubbed the back of his head. 'Can I get you anything?'

'I think Cara could use some water. She's completely emptied her stomach. While you're at it, bring some for me as well.'

'On it.' Jason turned and left.

Sighing, William reached over and flushed the toilet after me. As he leaned back, his hand skimmed my cheek, brushing my hair away.

'Come on, darling,' he said. 'You need to brush your teeth.' He grabbed my arms and lifted me. Tearless sobs escaped while I grimaced in protest. Although I felt better after puking, all I wanted was my bed.

He managed to make me stand, though he kept his arm around my waist.

'Will, I'm so sorry,' I said, but I slurred the words and struggled to keep a steady gaze on him in the mirror. 'I didn't mean to ruin your night.'

He raised a brow and shook his head. 'We'll talk in the morning. Which one's yours?' he asked, indicating the two toothbrushes.

'Green.'

Jason returned, tossing William a bottle of water. As he undid the cap of another, he came toward me.

'Cara.' He sighed. 'This isn't like you. You're worrying me.'

I wrapped my feeble hand around the bottle. 'Well, I've had a rough couple of weeks.'

'Clearly.' He planted a firm kiss on my forehead and rubbed my arms. 'I'll make you a full English for breakfast tomorrow, yeah?'

'I love you,' I cooed and attacked him with a hug.

He chuckled and pressed me against him. 'Love you too, idiot.' He didn't release me as he turned toward his brother. 'Poker night still on tomorrow?' he asked while I raised my bottle to my lips.

'Of course,' William said after a mouthful from his own. 'Have you got a spare toothbrush?'

'Yeah. Bottom left drawer.'

After Jason and William had forced me to brush my teeth and rinse my mouth to get rid of my bad breath, they helped me to my bedroom, where I changed into my pink silk nightie. Jason tucked me into bed while William leaned against the doorpost with a brooding expression on his face.

When my eyes closed, Jason said, 'She's going to pass out any moment now. You know where my bedroom is.'

'You're sleeping here again? With her?' William asked, and his voice lacked any trace of emotion.

'Yeah.'

'Jason, is there something you haven't told me?'

'What?'

'Why do you always insist on sleeping with her?'

'We do it all the time,' Jason said, sounding confused.

'But you haven't had sex with her, right?'

'What? What the hell have you been drinking tonight, Will?'

'Fair question.'

'No, of course I haven't.'

'Ever wanted to?'

'Oh, piss off, Will.' I could hear that Jason was losing his patience. I had called it: if there was one person in this world whom I thought capable of stirring Jason's temper, it was William, and I was currently hearing it live.

'Don't,' William said.

'Don't what?' Jason snapped.

'Don't fuck her. I have.'

Complete silence filled the room for seconds that felt like hours. I had been close to drifting off, but now I was only pretending to be asleep. Although I was drunk, I wasn't so drunk that this didn't send my heart racing in panic, and vomiting had made me feel much soberer.

When Jason found his voice, it was low and cold. 'Are you taking the piss?'

'No,' William said. 'It was sort of an accident at first, but I've every intention of doing it again, so I thought you should know.' His voice was devoid of emotion. He might as well have been reading a sheet of instructions.

'What the hell, Will? That's my fucking flatmate! She also happens to be my best friend!'

'Yes, I know. I would say I'm sorry, but I'm not.'

Jason whirled around in my bed and grabbed my shoulders, and he shook them so hard that I would have been an idiot to pretend I was asleep.

'Cara! Tell me he's joking!'

'He's joking,' I said.

'Are you lying?'

'Yes,' I squeaked.

He quickly released me. 'What the actual fuck, Cara? And you haven't told me?' He was fuming.

Tears brimmed in my eyes. I was far too drunk to handle this right now.

'I'm sorry. I didn't mean to have sex with him.' My voice was light and feeble and broke at several points. 'I wasn't aware he was your brother at the time. Had I known, I would never have done it.'

'For fuck's sake, you guys. This is unbelievable.' Jason groaned and dropped his head between his hands.

'Jason, I'm really sorry.' My tears ran over. 'I didn't want to tell you because it was an accident, and it had only happened once. I thought it would be best to just leave it at that.'

Clearly despairing, Jason shook his head. 'I honestly can't believe this has happened.' He turned and glowered at his brother. 'You really are an absolute prick, Will.'

'Really?' William frowned. 'And how is that, exactly? It's not like my intention here is to make your life any harder. I can't help that she's . . . Well, that she's her.' He gestured to my figure in the bed.

I looked at William, my tears coursing down my cheeks. He had betrayed me, and for what? Why had he done this? I was so upset with him, so angry.

'Why did you tell him?' I asked. 'You promised me you wouldn't.' I snuffled and wiped my face. 'Don't you think you could at least have warned me before you decided to drop the bomb on him?'

Jason gaped at me. 'You made him promise not to tell?'

'I was scared of how you would react,' I said, my voice quivering. 'Jason, I was scared you'd be angry with me – that you'd stop being friends with me.'

Jason turned to William. 'Does Dad know about this?'

William raised a brow. 'Of course he doesn't, and I wouldn't tell him either if I were you.'

'When?' Jason asked.

William frowned. 'When what?'

'When did it happen?'

William shrugged and rubbed his neck. 'April.'

Jason gasped. 'April!'

'Yeah. She was at Disrepute, with Olivia. Remember I told you I'd met a girl named Sandra there?'

Jason was quiet for several seconds, seemingly struck by shock. 'Oh my God,' he breathed out. 'Sandra? That was *Cara*?'

'Yeah.'

'Jesus Christ, it all makes sense. Ah, shit. Fuck.' Jason raked his hands through his hair. 'I should never have recommended that bar to her. If I hadn't, we could all have avoided this.'

'Jason, we're brothers. It was only a matter of time before I'd meet her. You'd only be postponing the inevitable – we would have ended up fucking one way or another. Calm down.'

'Calm down? You're telling me to calm down when you've fucked my best friend behind my back, and she turns out to be the girl you were so hung up on?' He shook his head and turned toward me. 'And *you* – you've lied to me for months!'

'I didn't lie,' I said, but my voice broke again. 'I omitted, Jason.'

'The result is the same,' he said, smouldering with bitterness. 'Cara, I am so disappointed in you right now.'

'Jason, please.' I reached for him, but he writhed away from my touch. 'I didn't know what to do,' I explained, upset. 'I was afraid you'd pick him.'

'I don't want to hear it. I need to think. You've had some fucking cheek, asking me about Will and "Sandra".'

'Has she?' William asked, surprised.

Jason ignored him. 'How could you do that, Cara? How could you play me for a fool like that?'

I sobbed. 'Jason, I'm so sorry. I was only trying to find out what was going on. I never meant to hurt him. I really didn't. And I was scared to tell you because I didn't want to put you in a situation where you'd have to choose between us. I thought it would be best if Will and I kept it strictly between us and sorted it out like *adults*.' I glared at William upon my last statement.

He looked away, his face twisting with obvious remorse, but he said nothing.

Jason turned toward me again and stared at me for some time. Finally, his eyes softened. 'What about Aaron? Is he aware of any of this?'

'No.' I started bawling at the thought of Aaron. 'I-I haven't t-thought this through at all.'

Jason crawled over and hugged me. 'Oh, Cara, I'm sorry. I know you didn't mean for this to happen.' He squeezed me against him. 'I'm sorry I freaked out. I'm just a bit shocked, and I'm worried about how this will turn out.'

His compassion only made me cry harder. I felt so terrible for the position I had put him in.

'Good God, look at you two,' William said. 'This is ridiculous. I honestly don't understand what the problem is. I want her, she wants me. It really is that simple. So yes, we kept it a secret for a while, but the cat's out of the bag now. Isn't that just a relief?'

'Will, sometimes, I seriously think Mum dropped you when you were a baby,' Jason chided. 'She's upset. You don't always have to agree with the reason.'

'I clearly picked the wrong brother,' I said, sniffing. I didn't really mean it, but I was still so angry with him.

William's eyes turned steely. 'Oh, come on, love. What do you want me to do, then?'

'I want you to leave me alone.'

He looked to the heavens for aid. 'Why her?' he asked. 'Just . . . why her?'

When Jason saw it, he smiled widely.

William lowered his head again, sighing. 'All right. Get out, then, Jase. I'll deal with her.'

'No! I don't want you near me,' I said.

He shook his head and approached. 'Yes, you do.'

'You broke my trust!'

'Like you haven't broken shit yourself, Cara,' he said bitterly, and I gasped.

'Jason,' I called, for help.

'See, this is what I mean. Don't drag me into this. This is *your* mess. I'm not taking any sides in this – ever.' His brows curved with annoyance.

'Jason,' William said as he reached the bed, 'we can either sleep here all three, or you can get out. One way or another, I'm not leaving her side until we've reconciled.'

'I'll see you in the morning.' Jason released me and climbed out of the bed. 'Try not to kill each other.'

'No promises,' I said and folded my arms. Irritated, I watched him close the door after himself. He didn't so much as look at me, probably because the expression on my face would have changed his mind.

'Well, then,' William said and raised his hands to the line of buttons on his waistcoat.

I turned over and glared holes into the wall beside my bed. 'Could you sleep on the sofa, please?'

'No.'

'Then don't touch me. I will bite off your fingers.'

He chuckled. 'And here I thought you preferred them inside you.'

My cheeks boiled at his quip. 'William!'

'Cara.'

'Urgh!' I shuddered. I could tear him to shreds.

He sighed. 'You'll feel better in the morning. Jason deserved to know. You'll see that, eventually.'

'You could at least have warned me that you meant to tell him! Instead you made me look like the most deceitful wench on the planet!'

'Cara, I'll take care of it. I'll explain things to him in the morning, and I'll make sure he'll forgive you.'

A sudden rush of more tears sprang to my eyes. 'He was so hurt, Will. I really hurt him – my best friend.'

'He doesn't like being deceived.'

'But I didn't mean to. I just didn't want to—'

'I know, Cara, and I'll tell him that. Don't worry, I'll have your back.'

I closed my eyes and turned mute on him while he undressed, killed the lights, and then climbed into my bed.

'Give me at least a portion of your duvet, Cara.'

'No. You don't deserve it. I'm hoping you'll die of cold during the night.'

He sighed. 'It's summer. It would prove difficult.'

'Well, I feel like a glacier, so perhaps that might help.'

'More like a volcano, I think.'

'If that's the case, then I hope the pyroclastic flow of my eruption will kill you off,' I fired back with a frown, horribly annoyed.

'You are such a nerd, and I fucking love that about you,' he said, making my chest contract. 'Pyroclastic flow,' he echoed. 'Honestly, I am amazed by your flair for comebacks. You're fucking sharp. You're going to make an exceptional solicitor one day.'

My heart was acting strange, all tingly and light, when I was supposed to be pissed off, but the way he handled my blows only reminded me why I fancied him so much. He wasn't intimidated by me – at all. He stood up to me, and it turned me on like nothing else. I needed a man like him, or else I would grow bored within the span of a mere breath.

Suddenly he gripped my duvet. With brutal force, he dragged it off me completely and rolled himself into the entirety of it. He exhaled then, audibly satisfied.

'William!'

'Yes, darling?' he replied with a tone of infuriating contentment.

'I swear I'll kill you one of these days!' I whirled to face him.

'You'd regret it,' he said self-assuredly. God, he really knew how to stir my temper. 'If you give me a kiss, I'll share.'

'That's blackmail.'

He snorted. 'It isn't. It's bargaining.'

I folded my arms and realised suddenly that I didn't have to stay here. I could sleep in Jason's bed, or on the sofa.

I had crawled halfway over William's large body when he suddenly freed his arms and wrapped them around me. 'Where are you going?'

'Out!'

'Why?'

'To sleep on the sofa!'

'Don't be ridiculous. Here.' He rearranged the duvet so that it covered us both, hooked his strong arms around me, and pulled me toward his warm, naked chest.

Divided, I lay rigid against him, paralysed by my confusion. Part of me wanted to leave, another wanted to remain in exactly the same place.

'Cara,' he cooed and nuzzled his face in the crook of my neck. 'Just sleep. You can kill me in the morning.'

'I intend to.'

'Then you should make good use of my heat while you still can,' he said smugly and wrapped his leg over mine.

How had it come to this? This was not how I had anticipated my night would end.

'You're a bloody headache, but I do adore you,' he purred and kissed the slope of my neck.

'If I'm a headache, you're a tumour.'

He shook with mirth. 'That's an original way of saying you can't take your mind off me. I'm happy to know it's mutual.'

I moaned. He had an unmatched ability to twist my words.

He squeezed me against him. 'Drunk out of your mind, and still, you maintain your bravado. I take my hat off to you.'

Silence ensued. I was nearly asleep when he propped himself on his elbow beside me and leaned over my figure. As light as a feather, his fingers tucked my hair behind my ear. Then he lowered his lips to my cheek. He left a prolonged kiss there.

'I'm not going to hurt you, Cara. You've nothing to be afraid of. If you give me a chance, I'll take good care of you, I promise.'

Affection set my heart ablaze. I pressed my lips together, and it took some time until I was calm enough to reply.

'I don't want you to take care of me. I want to take care of myself.'

He hesitated. 'Cara, I . . . This fear of commitment, it's so extreme. Has someone hurt you? Is that why you're like this? Please be honest – help me understand.'

I sighed. 'No. You know I've never been in a relationship. They scare me.'

'Why?'

'The ownership,' I said. 'I can't stand the idea of it. I want to be free. I want to be free to do exactly what I want, when I want, without having to show consideration to anybody else.'

He fell silent for some time. 'I'll wait for you, then.'

My chest throbbed. 'What?'

'I'll wait till you're ready. I can't give you up – I just can't.'

Tears pricked my eyes. I was deeply moved. Turning, I raised my hand and stroked his cheek. 'Do you really mean that?'

'Yes.'

I snuggled closer and stopped only when our noses touched. 'You're such a romantic.'

'About you, yeah. You've driven me mad.'

'Well, you drive me mad too.'

'Do I?' He sounded surprised.

'Yes.' My lips protruded as I pouted, tickling against his. He must have thought I was searching for a kiss because, as I was about to pull back, his hand caught my neck and held me in place. Then his mouth was on mine again.

The beats of my heart had never been louder. My pulse drummed behind my ears, attenuating the sound of our lips moving passionately against each other. When he rolled onto me, my intense feelings overwhelmed my chest. For a moment, I couldn't breathe. It was like my lungs had ceased functioning to create space for that foreign emotion.

'Will,' I said on a loud breath. 'We shouldn't.'

His hands felt like fire on my skin, resolutely amorous and awakening the desire to sin again.

'We absolutely shouldn't,' he said, his hand sliding down my waist. Using his knee, he spread my legs, positioned himself between them, and lay down on me. His arms on either side of me supported the weight of his upper body, and I had never felt so safe.

His mouth dived for mine again, and I was instantly lost in its sensual dance. I knew I ought to pull away, but I couldn't. His magnetism was too powerful to resist, and our bodies communicated too well. They wanted each other desperately, and it seemed impossible to deny it.

'I want to be yours, Cara,' he whispered between lustful kisses. 'Say you'll consider it. Just one chance.'

Turning my head, I heaved for air to steady myself. I wanted him so badly. My body was beseeching me to surrender, to leap into sin.

His mouth landed on my throat, tracing the vein that revealed how hard my heart was beating just for him. I groaned and ran my fingers through his hair. An aching burgeoned between my legs, begging for his intrusion. I wanted to feel him within me again. If I didn't, I thought I would lose my mind.

'Will, we need to stop.'

'We do.' He claimed my mouth while his hands travelled hungrily across my body, and he knew exactly where to squeeze, where to stroke and where to pinch. 'But I can't,' he said. 'You'll have to push me away.'

I closed my legs around him and pressed him down on me. Another wave of arousal flooded my system when I felt his erection between us, pushing against my entrance. I kissed the crook of his neck, taking his scent deep into my lungs, and felt myself fade ever so slightly. His embrace was the closest I would ever come to experiencing heaven. I was sure.

'Say you'll consider it, Cara.' He folded his hand over my breast and squeezed the aching mass. I moaned against his throat. 'Let me pleasure you like this,' he purred and lowered his lips to my ear. 'Over, and over, and over.'

I huffed, wondering whether rejecting him was really the right course of action. If I wasted this chance and he moved on, I knew I would regret it. Moreover, the argument that I should avoid him so as not to get my attention divided was no longer valid; I had hardly thought about anything but him since April, so I didn't think refusing him would actually make any difference. One way or another, I would remain preoccupied with him for quite some time, so did I really have anything to lose?

I considered how it could affect our situation at work. Both Violet and William had provided strong arguments for ignoring our role as colleagues. It was true that I was only going to work under William for three months, and that I could always get someone else to write my reference – Violet, for example. And if we kept our liaison a secret, it wouldn't harm my chances of getting hired. However, if things ended on a bad note between us, working at Day & Night could turn out to be difficult. I might not even want to work there, and it didn't help that it would be a lot harder to find employment somewhere else; it was much easier to get a job where you completed a placement than at other firms.

I thought of Jason. Judging from his reaction earlier, he would probably prefer if I gave William a chance. Besides, things had reached a point between William and me where the damage, in regard to Jason, had already been done. I didn't think he would be any more likely to pick William in a couple of years than he was now. On the contrary, he would probably be less likely to abandon me then, because we would have even more years of friendship behind us.

There was also Aaron. I would need to end things with him, and I wasn't looking forward to it. Though I had never been in love with him, I was still attached to him. He had become a habit, and it was a habit I loved in my own way, because it offered freedoms that a relationship with William would not.

It was like my heart switched off my brain and took control of my tongue when I said, 'Okay.' I took a deep breath. 'Okay, I'll give you a chance.'

All at once, William stopped – stopped kissing, stopped moving, stopped breathing.

'Really?' Disbelief saturated his tone.

'Yes.' I grinned in the dark.

'Really?' he repeated, but he seemed sceptical now.

I giggled. 'Yes, Will. Really.'

'Oh my God. I can't believe this.' He sounded overwhelmed.

'That makes two of us,' I mumbled amusedly.

'You're – Cara – fuck . . . I'm honestly speechless.' His voice was almost a whisper.

'I should warn you, though,' I said and ran my fingers through his hair. 'I'm not familiar with dating. I've never really done it before, so you'll have to cut me some slack. You'll need to be patient with me.'

'I'll do my best,' he said and stole a tender kiss. 'You won't regret this.'

I hoped with all my heart that he was right.

Rolling off me, he pulled me into a spooning position. His erection pressed against my bum, but since he made no further advances, I was confused.

'What are you doing?' I asked, and I couldn't hide my disappointment.

'I don't fuck drunk women unless they're my girlfriend.'

An abundance of heat claimed my face. 'Seriously?'

'Yes. Why do you think I told you not to get drunk the night we met?'

'Will, you have my utter consent.'

'Not happening. Matter of principle.'

'But you'll take my word regarding whether I'll date you or not?'

'I'll take what I can in that regard.'

'But you fingered me at the club!'

'Yeah, but that was the exception to the rule.'

'Then make another exception.'

'No. The scene at the club was different. I was a bit drunk myself then. Now I'm essentially sober, so it wouldn't feel right. I don't like having sex with someone who's drunk. Just sits wrong with me – the consent is so blurry in a way, like I'm taking advantage.'

I frowned. 'So you never have sex with somebody if they're drunk?'

'Only if they're my girlfriend, because I feel surer about their consent, then. So, if you want drunk sex, you'll need to be my girlfriend. This is a boyfriend level request you've made. If you'd like to upgrade your subscription, you'll have to go on several dates with me.'

I moaned with frustration. 'You bastard. Do you have any idea how aroused I am right now?'

He laughed smugly. 'Don't worry, I'll make it up to you. Until then, you can dream about us having sex instead. I do it all the time.'

I blushed. 'Oh my God, Will.'

'Not even slightly ashamed of admitting that.'

'You're not right in the head.' I chuckled. 'Then again, I'm guilty of the same.'

He tensed against me. 'Have you dreamt about me too? Actually?'

'Far too many times. Night, Will.'

'Sweet dreams, then,' he said complacently.

22

BETTER LUCK NEXT TIME

Last night was a hazy memory, ripped into bits and pieces. The club. William. The spot under the stairs. Kissing. His fingers inside me. Tequila. Vomiting.

Jason.

'Jason,' I whimpered and opened my eyes. I was in my bed, alone. Sitting up, I pushed my duvet aside, and the sight of my nightie reminded me that William and Jason had put me to bed last night.

I looked around. William was gone, and so were his clothes. Had he left?

It felt like a hammer was bashing on my head. I closed my eyes, wincing. I was suffering from a tremendous hangover, but Jason and I needed to talk, and it couldn't wait. I was desperate to clear the air and make amends. I felt terrible, and it only added to my headache.

As I opened my bedroom door, the smell of bacon filled my nose, and it was sent directly from heaven. Was Jason making me breakfast? He couldn't be too angry with me, then – I hoped.

I decided to have a shower before I faced him. Walking across the corridor, I opened the bathroom door and froze.

There stood William, naked in all his glory and drying his hair with a white towel. What a beautiful backside he had. Prominent muscles hugged his long spine, and dimples carved into the flesh right above his taut bum. His biceps and deltoids, as well as the muscles of his hairless, broad back, rippled with his motions. Saliva accumulated in my mouth. What a bomb of testosterone. He was strikingly masculine. I wasn't even remotely prepared for the captivating sight of him.

I tore my eyes off him and stood perfectly still. As my eyes flickered around the humid room, I saw that his clothes from last night were dumped on the toilet seat.

His head turned toward me, and when our eyes locked, a roguish smile claimed his mouth. He looked elated. His eyes glowed with a joy I hadn't seen in them before.

'Morning, love. I'm flattered you wanted to shower with me, but I'm afraid you're a few minutes too late. Better luck next time.'

My cheeks turned rosy and hot. 'Are you finished?' I asked, slightly abashed, and averted my gaze.

'Oh, don't be that way.' He chuckled. 'Nothing you haven't seen before.'

My face grew hotter. 'Will.'

'Care for a look of the front? It's all yours.'

He turned slowly toward me, but I whirled around before I could see anything.

'Oh my God, stop it!'

He laughed. 'Sorry, that was inconsiderate of me. The view would of course only increase your current sexual frustration since I refused to fuck you last night.'

'That's not it, you conceited twat!' But it was.

He kept laughing, and I heard him turn on the tap. I dared a peek at him. He had wrapped the towel around his hips and was watching my reflection in the mirror, his lips bent with amusement.

'Could you hurry up, please?' I asked. 'I need to shower as well.'

'Then do.' He gestured to the transparent glass door. 'I don't mind – at all.'

My whole face flushed. 'Without you here.'

He rolled his eyes and raised a toothbrush to his mouth. 'Then you'll have to wait.'

Sighing, I folded my arms and looked away.

'William, come on,' I moaned when I had counted to a minute.

With white foam around his mouth, he grinned at me in the mirror and then spat into the basin. 'Patience is a virtue, darling.'

He rinsed his mouth and spat once more before he finally approached the door, still grinning. Just as he was about to pass me, he paused and curled his hand around my neck. Bringing me close, he planted a firm kiss on the top of my head.

'Enjoy your shower,' he purred as he pulled away. 'I'll see you in a bit.'

Paralysed, I heard him close the door. My body was complete chaos. I couldn't understand a single thought or emotion. Everything lacked sense. But there was one thing I knew.

He fuelled the fire of my soul and gave the beats to my heart. In his presence, I felt capable of glowing in the dark.

Shaking my head, I walked into the shower and lowered the temperature. After a dreadful night, my body was feeble, so I sat on the beige tiles under the stream of cold water, reviving. I had obviously had too much to drink. Those last three shots of tequila hadn't helped anything at all apart from offering a temporary relief from the panic I had experienced.

When I started shivering, I dragged myself out of the shower and dried myself with a towel. Then I put on my white satin robe and walked out. Jason and William were talking in the dining room, so I paused to eavesdrop, wondering if Jason was still angry with me.

'Yeah, we're quite compatible,' William said.

'I can't believe I never tried to set you up with her.'

'You should have.'

'I would have if she hadn't been so uninterested in dating. Plus, you weren't really that interested in it yourself.'

'I wasn't until I met her,' William said, and my heart throbbed.

'I suppose that's what happens when you find the right one.' There was a smile in Jason's voice.

'Yeah. You sort of did set me up with her, though – by sending her to Disrepute. You know I often go there on Fridays.'

'True.' Jason chuckled. 'But since you're not one to have one-night stands, and since you already had Violet and Francesca, it never occurred to me that you might end up interacting, let alone actually sleeping together. Honestly, when she came home the next day, I was sure it had to be someone else – perhaps a colleague of yours or something. I definitely didn't think it could be you, all things considered.'

'She never mentioned my name?'

'No. But, in hindsight, she did say you were really forthright and opinionated, so maybe I should have suspected at that point.'

'Very funny.'

'I'm actually not joking. Anyway, seems like you made up last night.'

'I'm not sure. She was very drunk, even at the end. Hopefully she meant what she said.'

'I'm sure she did.'

'Don't give her a hard time when she comes out, yeah? Please, Jase.'

'I won't. I can see why she would hide it from me.'

'Yeah?'

'Yeah. I'm only a bit upset because I really despised Sandra on your behalf. Safe to say I'm shocked it's been Cara all along.'

'Understandable.'

I blew out a breath of relief and went to the dining room. William had kept his word and had supported me, and I appreciated it immensely because, without his intervention, I was confident that Jason would have stayed angry with me for longer.

They sat at the dining table, where orange juice, coffee and a full English breakfast waited for me. I could have kissed Jason. This was exactly what I needed.

William appeared to have borrowed a pair of black joggers from Jason, and both brothers were shirtless. Had I not been so hungover, I would have appreciated the view more than I did.

They turned their heads to acknowledge me and, at that moment, I seriously wondered how I hadn't realised that William was Jason's brother when I first met him. While their hair colours were different, they had nearly identical eyes, although William's were slightly more piercing and somehow darker, even if their irises were exactly the same colour. However, William's eyebrows always formed a slight frown, as if he was sharply judging and examining everything he looked at. Jason gazed around with an innate desire to appreciate everything he saw for what it was. William's jaw was also a little sharper than Jason's, but even their noses and full lips were incredibly similar.

I was such an idiot.

'Morning,' I said and met Jason's gaze. He smiled faintly.

'Morning, love. How are you feeling?' He pulled out the chair beside him. My chest ached at his tone. I didn't deserve him. I hated that I had betrayed and disappointed him.

'I have an awful headache.'

As I sat down, my eyes zoomed in on the paracetamol beside the glass of orange juice. My heart melted. Jason would make a woman the luckiest in the world someday.

He smirked and pointed at the pill. 'I'm miles ahead of you, dear.'

Nodding, I swallowed it with a mouthful of orange juice and then faced him with a miserable pout.

'Jason, I'm seriously so sorry about everything. I hate myself for betraying you like that. I mean it. I—'

'I know, Cara, don't worry. Just don't do it again, all right?'

I inhaled sharply and nodded vigorously. 'I promise.'

'Apology accepted, then. I get that this was the exception to the rule since he's my brother.' He rubbed my back. 'Just eat, you must be starving.'

'I love you.'

He glanced at William, who was behaving like he neither saw nor heard us. 'I love you too.' Smiling, Jason stroked my cheek with the back of his fingers.

I grabbed my knife and smeared a thick layer of butter onto my toast. William's eyes looked about to fall out of his skull when he saw it.

'Damn. Would you like some more bread with your butter?' he joked.

'I like butter.'

Jason laughed. 'Correction, she loves butter.'

William's lips slid into a winsome grin. 'Yes, I can see that. Duly noted.'

I gave him a smile and topped my toast with a layer of scrambled eggs. As I was putting the spoon back, I sensed William's eyes on me.

'Weak for his scrambled eggs, are you, love?' he asked. 'Familiar recipe, perhaps?'

I froze.

'Right, what's going on?' Jason asked.

I sighed. 'Will made me scrambled eggs the morning after we . . . I thought they tasted familiar, but I . . . It just didn't strike me.'

'Oh my goodness,' Jason laughed. 'This is ridiculous.'

William captured my gaze, still grinning. 'I'd be happy to make it for you anytime you like.'

It was like something cut into my chest – how could pleasure feel so painful? I took a quick, quiet breath. 'Thanks. You're very sweet.'

He studied me as he reached for his cup of coffee. 'Am I?'

'Yes.'

'Then perhaps you'll have dinner with me today.'

My heart jammed in my throat. He obviously wanted me to confirm that I had meant what I said last night – that I would give him a chance.

Though it took me a moment, I managed to calm down and smile at him. 'I'd love to, but I can't,' I said sincerely. 'I've got plans.'

He cocked his head to the side, his eyes riveted on my features. 'What sort of plans?'

'A birthday party.' I struggled to hold his gaze. I wasn't sure he would appreciate that Aaron would be there, but I wasn't about to cancel my plans last minute. It was Tyler's birthday, and he was my friend too. I had to show up.

'Whose birthday?' William asked, and it sounded like he was faking nonchalance.

'Friend named Tyler.'

His features hardened. 'Will Aaron be there?'

My heart stilled and I swallowed. 'Yes.'

His eyebrows jumped. He looked disbelieving.

I rushed to explain myself before he could say anything. 'It's just a birthday party. Nothing's going to happen between us – I won't, you know . . .'

He knitted a brow. 'Fuck him?'

'Er, yes.' I wrinkled my nose. 'That.'

He frowned for a beat. 'Well, I've got poker night, so feel free to call me if you'd like some company after the bash.'

I bit my lower lip, smiling, and poured myself a cup of coffee. 'Thanks. I'll probably take you up on that offer.'

At this he visibly relaxed, his gaze softening. 'Good.'

'I'm going to have such an advantage tonight,' Jason said smugly, changing the subject. 'What with you being hungover for once.' He smirked at William.

'You'll regret saying that.' William chuckled. 'It will make things even more embarrassing for you when I beat you.'

'We'll see.'

23

IT'S A LONG STORY

At five o'clock, William and Jason were about to leave. William wanted to go home and change clothes before he and Jason would head to Stephen's together, who was hosting poker night this time around. As we stood in the hall, William wrapped his arm around me and pulled me close.

'Have fun tonight,' he said and brushed the back of his hand across my cheek.

I smiled up at him, my heart racing at his affectionate behaviour. 'You too.'

He leaned down and kissed me, and it felt like my insides were soaring. I loved how casually he did it, as if we were already a couple, as if kissing me was the most natural thing in the world to him.

As he pulled away, he rubbed his nose against my smaller one. 'Don't hesitate to call me, no matter how late it is.'

I nodded and stroked his chest, feeling the dent between his big pecs. 'Okay.' I glanced at Jason, who was looking away from us with a huge grin on his mouth. 'Look after Jason for me, all right? Don't let him get too drunk.'

'Don't worry, Cara,' Jason said, meeting my gaze. 'I learned my lesson last time.'

'He says that every time,' William told me flatly.

'Exactly.'

He kissed me again, longer this time. I smiled against his lips, savouring the way they moved.

Jason groaned. 'At this rate we're going to be late, Will. You'll only be away from her for a few hours. You can last that long.'

William leaned away with a sigh. 'I'll see you later,' he said and curled his forefinger under my chin, tilting my head back.

'Yes.'

Jason opened the door. 'Come on, then.'

'Yeah.' William followed him out.

Right after they had gone, I went to my room and grabbed my phone to call Olivia on FaceTime. I had so much to tell her.

'Hi, love,' she answered with a grin. Judging by the marble artworks on the walls, she was in her room.

'Olivia.'

Her smile faded. I hardly ever called her that. 'What?'

'I have *so* much to tell you. Remember I went out with my colleagues last night?'

'Oh my goodness, yes! Spill the tea, what happened?'

I sat down on the bed. 'Are you alone?'

'Yes!'

'Right, good. Well, there's really no way to say this, so I'll just put it plainly.'

My heart started pounding. For some reason, telling Olivia about this made the whole thing seem even more real. William was becoming a larger part of my life by the second, but bringing it to the awareness of the people I cherished seemed to grant him even more space, while simultaneously increasing the pace of things. Telling people about us was a manifestation of my choice, and with it came graver consequences. If things didn't work out, interrogations would ensue. People would inevitably care about the outcome. While I enjoyed the thrill of it, I also found the risk involved rather intimidating.

'I'm growing old here,' Olivia complained.

'Will asked me to give him a chance and I said yes,' I blurted out.

'What?' Her wide eyes told me she couldn't believe what she had heard. 'You mean you've agreed to go on a date with him?'

'Yes. We haven't decided when, though – just that we're going to give things a chance.'

She gawked for a good while and then finally gathered her wits. 'To be clear, you mean William Night, right? Jason's brother? Your boss?'

'That's the one.'

Her jaw dropped. Speechless, she only stared at me.

It felt like my face was about to burst. 'I know.'

'Oh my God! I knew it, I bloody knew it!' she exclaimed. 'You'd have to be a robot to resist that sort of chemistry. Cara, fucking yes!" she cheered. 'I am so happy for you! And for William. He must be over the moon. I'm sure he's been pining for you ever since you met!'

'I'm really happy,' I cooed.

'Tell me everything! What happened? What changed your mind?'

'It's a long story.'

'I've got time!'

Her excitement made me laugh. 'All right,' I said and began sharing the whole story, and her engaged responses charmed me to my toes. For the first time in my life, I felt like a proper teenager.

'I honestly can't believe this,' she said. 'You're really going on an actual date with somebody? Despite your reservations?'

I chuckled. 'Yes.'

'But you've always avoided romance as though it were a plague. William must be wielding some serious magic, especially when considering he's both your boss and Jason's brother. You've been crystal clear about how much those circumstances have bothered you.'

'I know. He really does.'

Looking sideways, she pondered for some time, and I spent it observing her with some curiosity. What was on her mind? Eventually she faced me again, and from her sober expression, I could tell something serious was headed my way.

'Cara, does this mean you're in love with him?'

Her question took me aback. I stared at her as blood warmed my cheeks, trying to think of what to say.

'Gosh, look at you. You're a tomato,' she remarked amusedly.

'I'm not sure,' I said. 'I've never experienced this before. But I think I'm getting there.'

Her smile was sympathetic. 'Do you think he's in love with you?'

I swallowed. I didn't want to entertain that thought. The mere idea that William's feelings might be that profound unsettled me, because if our chemistry failed to transition into love on my end, I would have to break his heart. I dreaded that possibility more than anything. Work would become a place worse than hell and Jason would be stuck in the middle. And, worst of all, I would be rejecting a man who absolutely deserved to have his feelings reciprocated.

'I don't think so,' I said. 'Like me, I think he's just curious to see where things lead. He's definitely optimistic, but I don't quite think he's in love.'

'I think he is.'

'Livy, please don't.' I shook my head. 'I'm uncomfortable.'

'Sorry.' Her face crinkled. 'I shouldn't have said anything. I got a bit excited.'

'It's okay.' I glanced away. 'One way or another, I'm not looking forward to seeing Aaron later.' I huffed. The thought of him made my glee plummet into anxiety. I would have to tell him that I had met someone, and I didn't know what to expect. How would he react? We had been doing this for so many years now; I was sure the news would strike him like a bolt from the blue.

'Oh, shit, Tyler's birthday,' Olivia said, remembering. 'What are you going to do?'

I sighed. 'Well, I'm going to have to end things.'

'That's bound to get a bit uncomfortable.' She grimaced. 'He's going to have a shock, at the very least.'

'Yeah, I know. Do you think I should wait with telling him? I don't want to ruin his night. I mean, the news might put him in a weird mood.'

'Yeah, at least wait until the party's over.'

Just as we were talking about him, Aaron called. My chest tensed up, my cheeks expanding with air.

'Shit, he's calling me right now.'

'You should probably answer. I'll wait.'

I accepted Aaron's call, putting Olivia on hold.

'Hello?' It was nearly impossible to prevent the stress I felt from seeping into my voice.

'Hi, love.'

'What's up?'

'Are you at home right now?'

'I am.'

'Good. I'll be there in about twenty minutes.'

My head jerked back, my eyebrows slanting downward. 'What? Why?'

'To drop off my things? That way we can just head straight to yours later.'

My heart clenched, my eyes widening. I had completely forgotten that he was supposed to spend the night at mine. What was I supposed to do now? I could tell him that he couldn't sleep here after all, but he would want a reason, and I didn't have one. Panicking, I racked my brain for a solution, but came up empty. Maybe Olivia would have one.

'Oh, right,' I said, trying to sound normal. 'Good plan. Have you had dinner?'

'No, have you?'

'No. Should we order a pizza or something, then?'

'Yeah, why not?'

'Okay. I'll place the order in the meantime. See you soon.'

'All right, thanks.'

Hanging up, I returned to my call with Olivia.

'Fuck!'

'What is it?' She looked alarmed.

'He's on his way here! I had completely forgotten that we had planned to sleep at mine so that Tyler and Valentina could have the flat to themselves. What do I do? If I tell him he can't sleep here, he's going to wonder why.'

She rolled onto her stomach, and her knitted brows told me she was thinking. 'Tell him he can't when the party's over. Yeah, it will be inconvenient for him if he's left his stuff at yours, but if you tell him now, you'll either have to explain things or come up with some lie. If you wait, you'll at least avoid ruining his night – well, most of it.'

I took a deep breath, nodding. 'Okay, yeah. That'll work.' I looked around my room, wondering whether William had left any traces behind.

'One thing, though, and I don't mean to make a bad situation worse, but . . .' She trailed off, grimacing as she chewed on her lower lip.

'What?'

She scratched her head, looking uncertain. 'Well, you know, now that you're ending things with Aaron . . . Has it maybe occurred to you that you might break his heart? I know we've had this conversation before but—'

'Oh, no need to worry about that,' I said with a faint smile. 'He doesn't want me that way. We actually talked about it quite recently, and he was very clear that he's not interested in anything romantic at the moment. So yeah, I am absolutely sure his heart will be completely fine.'

Olivia blew out a loud breath of relief. 'Oh, thank God. I'd hate it if you two fell out. I mean, I adore that guy, so I really don't want to be torn between you. Obviously I'd pick you, I'm just saying I'd prefer not having to choose.'

'Well, you won't have to – in any event,' I reassured her. 'You know I'm not one to tell you who you can and can't be friends with. Anyway, I'm hanging up. I need to order a pizza.'

'Right. Try to have some fun tonight, yeah? I'm just a call away if you need me.'

'Livy, you really are the best.'

'I'm sending you strength.'

'Thanks, I'll need it.'

§ § §

My pulse was pounding in my throat when I pushed the button on the intercom to let Aaron in downstairs. I knew I wasn't cheating on either him or William, but somehow it felt like it, and I hated it. I could hardly wait until the party was over so I could disclose things to Aaron. My conscience would finally be relieved then.

As I waited for him to arrive, I wondered what to do with myself. I was terribly scared that he would try to kiss me – or worse, try to have sex with me. We had a few hours to kill before we would head to the bash, and I hoped he wasn't planning on spending some of them in my bed. If I rejected him too bluntly, he could sense that something was off and ask me about it. I wouldn't be able to lie to him if that happened. My plan to maintain harmony, at least until tonight, would inevitably go up in smoke, then.

I can get ready, I thought. If I seemed busy when Aaron came in, he would probably be less likely to make sexual advances toward me.

I unlocked the front door and dashed into the bathroom. Just when I had plugged in my straightener, Aaron knocked.

'Come in!' I popped my head out of the bathroom and forced a smile. 'Hiya.'

He dropped his scarlet bag on the floor and smiled back. 'All right?'

'I'm just getting ready,' I said and escaped into the bathroom again. 'Feel free to watch TV or something while you wait.'

'What? Already? But we don't have to be there till eight.'

'I know, but I'm a woman, plus I've decided to straighten my hair.'

'But you're most beautiful with your natural waves,' he said and arrived in the doorway.

I looked at him in the mirror. 'Aw, thanks. But the look I'm planning calls for straight hair.'

He rolled his eyes and walked in. I stiffened for half a second, panicking. I tried my best to act normal as I opened the middle drawer to fetch my make-up kit, but when his arms came around my waist, I froze. He didn't seem to notice, but if he did, he ignored it.

'Where's Jase?' he asked and brushed my tresses aside to clear my neck.

'He's with his brother. They're heading to Stephen's for poker night,' I said, just barely managing to keep a steady octave.

He lowered his head. I tensed when his warm lips landed on my neck, covering it with soft kisses. Not long ago, I would have closed my eyes and submerged myself in the sweet feeling. I would have leaned against him and stroked his thigh behind me. But Aaron's kisses didn't feel good anymore – they felt alien. Wrong.

'We should take advantage, then,' he purred as his hand slid down my waist and gripped the hem of my white satin robe.

I shrugged out of his embrace.

'What's the matter?' he asked, and I saw concern in his eyes when I turned to face him.

'I'm not really in the mood for sex,' I said, stressing. 'I was in a bad way last night. I puked so much.'

He leaned back, looking surprised. 'What?'

'Yeah. I went out with my colleagues.'

'Oh.'

My face scrunched up for a beat. 'I'm sorry.'

He shook his head. 'Don't be. I'm only up for it if you are.'

I let out a sigh of relief. I didn't know why I had worried so much; I had rejected sex with him several times before, and he had never questioned me about it, so why would he now? It wasn't in his nature to push for sex if I wasn't in the mood.

'Did you have fun at least?' he asked.

I shrugged. 'For the most part, yeah.'

'You must be exhausted, though. When did you get home?'

'I don't remember. I blacked out.'

He gaped. 'You blacked out? How did you get home, then?'

I grimaced. 'Will took care of me.' My heart hammered as I uttered William's name. Even just mentioning him made me scared that Aaron would catch on to the truth prematurely.

'My goodness,' Aaron said, clearly shocked. 'Your *boss* had to take you home?'

'Please, don't. I'm still absolutely mortified.'

His handsome face remained straight for a split second, then he suddenly burst into laughter. 'Oh my God, that poor man. First he walks in on us, and then he has to babysit your drunken arse. He must think you're the apprentice from hell.'

A gush of colour spread over my cheeks. I hadn't thought of it like that. 'I've got a lot of redeeming to do.'

'I'm sure you're making up for it at work.' He kept laughing. 'Why did you get that drunk, though?'

'I don't know. It's not like I meant to.'

'So unlike you.' He shook his head, smiling. 'But all right, then. I'll let you get ready.' He turned around and disappeared into the living room.

I looked in the mirror, staring absentmindedly at my reflection and the sad shape of my mouth. Aaron was laughing now, but I doubted he would later.

§ § §

I wasn't sure if it was because I had got so drunk last night, but alcohol seemed to affect me differently this time. I didn't experience the usual buzz that gradually increased the more I drank; trivial things didn't excite me. Quite frankly, I was bored, and I missed William, which didn't help. I had seen him just a couple of hours ago, yet I already ached for his company.

As I sat next to Valentina on the sofa, I tried to picture exactly what William was doing right then. I imagined him holding playing cards in his hand, his eyes flickering around the surrounding faces as he tried to calculate what his next move should be. Was there actual money on the table or just poker chips? Was he winning or losing? I knew he was hungover, so I pictured Jason sitting opposite him, smirking nonstop as he saw victory on the horizon.

'Would you like some more to drink, Cara?' Valentina asked, jolting me out of my thoughts.

Valentina had moved to London from Italy two years ago, which was clear by her strong accent and captivating Mediterranean beauty. She had wavy, chestnut brown hair that reached her shoulders, and a strong, aquiline nose that suited her. But most arresting were her eyes, for they were such a luminous blue that they rivalled even William's, and because they contrasted with her olive skin, they constantly looked like they were sparkling.

'I can't get over your name,' she said then, chuckling. 'It means "dear" in Italian, as I'm sure you know.'

I smiled at her. 'Yeah, I know.'

'Is any of your family Italian?'

I shook my head. 'None – that I know of. My parents just love the name. They're quite fond of Italy, though, but who isn't?'

She laughed, her sharp cheekbones becoming rounder with her wide smile.

'As for whether I'd like another drink' – I looked at the empty glass in my hand – 'I'd love one.'

'Red?'

'Sure. Thanks, by the way. I can't believe I've already finished what I brought.'

'Have you?' She peered at me. 'You don't seem drunk.'

I made a face. 'Yeah, I went out last night, so it seems like my tolerance is slightly higher than usual today.'

'Ah.' She nodded. 'Aaron!' she called then.

He turned around immediately, and my heart sank. Wearing black trousers and a bright orange shirt, Aaron looked fantastic. He was standing in the kitchen with a group of mates. Tyler was among them, wearing a pink crown that Aaron had made for him.

'Can you bring us the wine that's on the counter?' Valentina went on. 'The one with the red and blue label.'

He grabbed it and came over.

'It's for Cara,' Valentina said when he was about to pour her glass.

He froze, his eyes flitting to mine.

'I should have brought more,' I said.

His eyebrows arched. 'You mean you've had four pints already? Did you down them or something?'

I chuckled. 'No.'

He was hesitant to fill my glass. 'Are you sure this is wise?'

'I'm not remotely drunk, Aaron. I'm tipsy, at best.'

'Your call, I suppose.'

'Thanks.'

When he finished filling my glass, he put the bottle on the coffee table in front of the sofa. 'I'll leave this here for your convenience,' he said jokingly.

'Thanks.' Valentina flashed him a grin.

As he walked away, she said to me, 'Thank you *so* much for taking him in tonight, Cara. I want to give Tyler some extra love on his big day, so I'm very grateful we'll have the flat to ourselves.'

My body went rigid. Fuck. How was I supposed to follow through with my plan now? It hadn't occurred to me that it would be inconvenient not only for Aaron, but also for Tyler and Valentina if I suddenly said that Aaron couldn't sleep at mine.

A row of curses streamed through my mind as I tried to think of how to solve this. I knew I could still refuse Aaron to spend the night at mine, but it seemed ridiculous when considering the implications. On the one hand, I desperately wanted to see William later, but on the other, Aaron, Tyler and Valentina had made plans that I would inevitably ruin if I didn't take him in. And it wasn't like I had to sleep in the same bed as him. If I brought him home with me, I would take Jason's bed. Besides, if Aaron stayed at mine, we could talk things through in the morning, and I liked the idea of that. He was already intoxicated, as was I, so I couldn't imagine that having the conversation with him tonight would be optimal.

But I want to see William, I thought with a pout. But I could see William tomorrow maybe, if he was free and wanted to.

'Of course,' I replied to Valentina. 'I like to think of it as a second birthday present to Tyler.'

'That's definitely how he sees it too.'

'Babe, come here! You have got to see this,' Tyler suddenly called, beckoning to his girlfriend. The lads around him were laughing, staring at the phone in his hand.

'I'll be back in a sec,' Valentina said and went over to them.

Sighing, I reached into my purse for my phone. I needed to tell William that we couldn't meet later after all, but I didn't want him to know that it was because Aaron would be sleeping at mine, as I was certain it would make him worry unnecessarily. At the same time, I knew I had to give him some kind of excuse, or else he would most likely get the wrong impression and assume it was because I intended to sleep with Aaron tonight. I wanted to avoid that, but how?

A white lie, I thought, grimacing. I didn't like it but, in this situation, telling a lie such as 'I'm too tired to meet up' seemed like the best option to spare William from worrying. It wasn't sufficient on its own, however. I would also have to reassure him that I was still interested in seeing him.

Shaking my head, I started typing. While it was a white lie, I would make sure to tell him the truth the next time I saw him. By then, I would already have disclosed things to Aaron and our arrangement would be over, which should help allay William's concerns.

Hi, I'm really sorry, but I'm too tired to meet up tonight. Are you free tmrw? x

Seen

I blinked when William instantly marked it as read. He must have been on his phone already. Feeling nervous, I locked my screen. My palms were clammy; I was so uncomfortable with how this evening was panning out.

I kept glancing at my phone, waiting for a reply from William, but it didn't seem to be coming anytime soon.

Fuck. Was he angry? Disappointed? What was running through his mind? Maybe he was just busy.

I was just about to send him another text when Aaron arrived in front of me.

'Look at you, sitting here all alone. Sad scene.'

I put my phone in my purse. 'You know I don't mind being alone.'

'True.' He smiled lopsidedly. 'Anyway, we're heading off.'

'To the pub?'

'Yeah.' He took my hand and dragged me up.

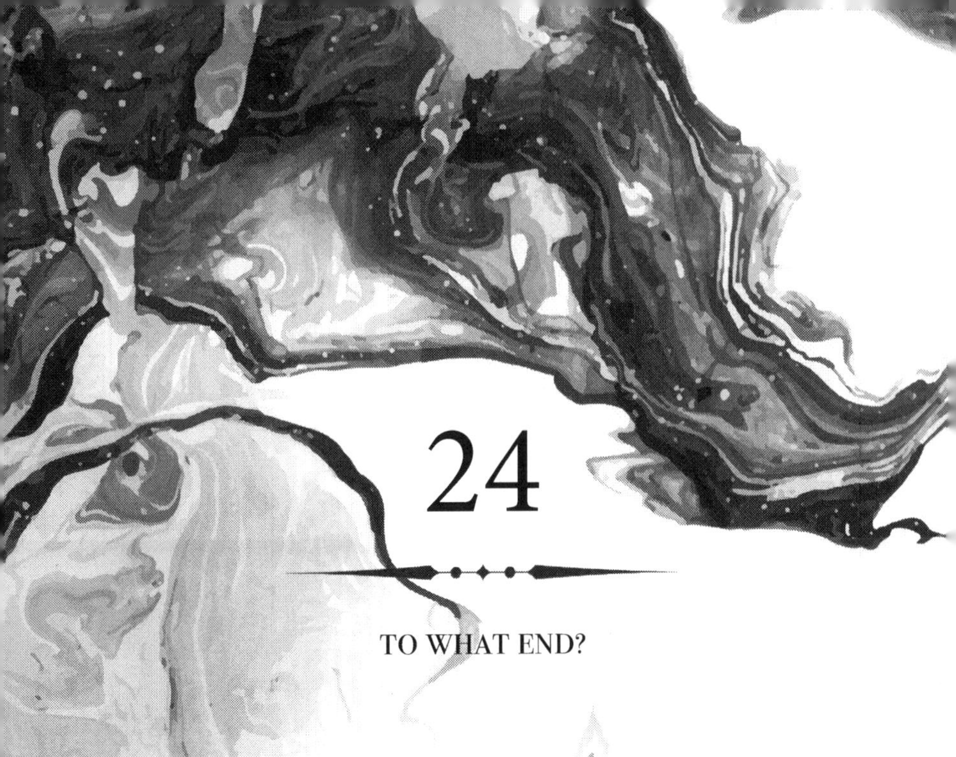

24

TO WHAT END?

Though by a slim margin, Valentina and I beat Tyler and Aaron at shuffleboard. After the match, Aaron proposed to take me home since I was exhausted after going out two nights in a row. I expressed concern about ruining his night, but he convinced me that I wouldn't.

'I've never been much of a party person,' he reminded me.

As we walked along the pavement toward my flat, Aaron wrapped his arm around my waist. It unsettled me, but I concealed it with a smile as I looked up at him. He smiled back, and I savoured the shape of it, knowing I had news to share that would probably make it disappear. I dreaded the moment we would enter my flat and I would have to tell him that I would be sleeping in Jason's bed. He would inevitably ask me why. What would I say then? That I would explain tomorrow? Or should I just tell him straight away? We were both a bit drunk, so I wasn't sure what was best.

Just go with the flow, I thought. I could say that I would explain things tomorrow, but if he asked me to do it tonight instead, I would.

It was nearly two o'clock when I opened the front door and heard music coming from the living room. Was Jason home already?

'Hello?' I called and stepped aside to let Aaron in. That was when I noticed five pairs of shoes on the floor that did not belong to Jason or myself, and one pair looked particularly familiar. They were formal brown leather shoes. An alarm went off in my head.

'Home already?' Jason yelled back.

'Hi, Cara!' Stephen greeted.

My heart faltered. Immobile, I stood next to Aaron while he kicked off his shoes. Panic swallowed me whole as I feared the worst: had their plans changed? Had poker night been moved to ours instead? The likelihood made me gulp with horror. I had Aaron with me, and if poker night was being hosted here, it would mean William was here as well.

I looked back at the brown leather shoes. They had to be his. *Shit!*

Colour drained from my face as I turned my head and saw Aaron delve his hands in his pockets. When he was about to move forward, my hand acted of its own accord and reached out to stop him.

What was I supposed to do now? I couldn't just kick him out without further ado. But I feared that if William saw him, he could get the wrong impression, and how was I supposed to make him believe my innocence? I had texted him that I was too tired to meet – I hadn't said anything about Aaron. What if he assumed the worst? It definitely looked like I had lied because I intended to sleep with Aaron tonight.

Was this why he hadn't replied to my text? Because he knew he would see me when, or *if*, I got home?

Shit. Another clusterfuck. I wanted to hide in my room and never come out.

'What's the matter?' Aaron asked and glanced at my hand on his arm.

My heart was running at a hundred miles per hour. How would I tackle this?

'I . . .' I couldn't bring myself to say anything coherent. I was too shocked. Why hadn't Jason informed me? Had he thought I would be home later than this?

'Cara, you're acting strange.'

'Sorry, I'm just surprised. I thought we'd be alone.' My voice sounded anxious even to my own ears.

Aaron's eyebrows knitted with confusion. 'I don't see the problem.' He shrugged his arm out of my hold and moved toward the living room.

Oh no. This was not going to end well. I could feel it in my bones.

I rushed after him and grabbed his arm once more, but just when I was about to speak, somebody exited the bathroom. A tall figure entered my peripheral vision, and I saw it freeze after a single pace. I turned toward them, barely hearing the music above my own heartbeat anymore.

Halfway out the door stood William, and he was staring disbelievingly at Aaron.

I wanted to cry. From the look of him, it was obvious that he had the wrong impression, and I was desperate to correct it. That was the only reason I didn't immediately seek shelter in my room.

'Hi,' Aaron greeted him.

William nodded back, but not a word escaped his lips. His eyes flickered in my direction then, and my heart skipped a beat.

I couldn't hold his gaze. There was so much hurt in it.

Fixing my eyes on the floor, I tried to think of a way out of this mess, but my panic was clouding my thoughts, and the alcohol in my system only made it worse.

'It's been a while,' Aaron said, 'but it's Will, right?'

'It is. And you're . . . Aaron?'

'Yeah.'

I felt William's subsequent glare upon my figure. I barely managed to glance at him. His jaw was clenched. He was seething.

'Would you mind giving me a minute alone with Cara?' he asked. 'I need to have a word with her.'

I was on the brink of bursting into sobs. As I peeked up at Aaron, his kind brown eyes stared back at me, full of confusion.

I gulped down a lump in my throat. 'Just give us a minute, please.'

His eyes narrowed and he looked briefly at William. Without a word, he gave me a nod and walked down the corridor, past William's rigid figure. Just as they overlapped, I saw them exchange a vigilant glance.

As soon as Aaron was out of sight, William turned toward me.

'What the fuck is this?'

My face contorted. 'I'm so sorry. I wasn't aware you'd be here.'

He moved closer, and I tensed. As he stopped in front of me, he bowed his head and glowered down at me. I stared nervously at his chest.

He was silent for such a long time that I dared another glance at him. The sight stabbed into my gut, filling me with pain. He looked so wounded.

'You lied to me,' he said, and he sounded so bitter that I winced.

'I'm so sorry.' My voice broke. 'I didn't want you to worry.'

'You didn't want me to worry? What kind of bullshit excuse is that? I'd definitely prefer to know that you're about to fuck another guy.'

'I'm not!' I met his eyes, hoping my sincerity permeated my gaze. 'It's not what it looks like.'

'Oh, really?' He lowered one brow, making his scepticism loud and clear. 'Then please explain what's actually going on here.'

'It's complicated, but we planned ages ago that he would sleep at mine so that Tyler and his girlfriend could have the flat to themselves.'

'So then why didn't you tell me?' He leaned back and gestured to me, maddened.

'Because I'd completely forgotten about it! I only remembered when he called me after you'd left earlier.'

He shook his head. 'That changes absolutely nothing. "Too tired to meet up" my fucking arse,' he spat. 'You knew when you wrote that text that he was coming home with you.'

My eyebrows curved and my lips quivered. Remorse clawed inside my chest, making it difficult to breathe.

'Will, I really am so sorry. I just didn't want you to assume wrong. I was going to tell you next time I saw you.'

He looked away, glaring at the front door with clenched teeth. Was he considering whether to leave? My heart palpitated at the mere thought, my throat tightening.

'Will,' I said, and my voice had a pleading tone. 'I swear I wasn't going to sleep with him. I was going to take Jason's bed.'

He shook his head again. 'How do I know you aren't just telling a lie right now because you were caught red-handed?'

Tears brimmed in my eyes, obscuring my sight. I didn't know what to say. How could I make him believe me?

Staring at him, I could feel him slipping from my grasp, and it was agonising. His demeanour radiated mistrust, his features spilling with wariness as he retreated a pace.

I had really fucked up.

'You lie and you lie, Cara, and I've had enough of it.' A thick layer of resentment swelled in his eyes, but it was the unmistakable vulnerability shining through that made my heart ache. He looked completely shattered.

'What do you want me to say?' My voice wobbled. 'How can I prove that I'm being honest?'

'I don't know,' he said, his face twisting with pain.

Agitated, I gestured to the corner Aaron had disappeared behind. 'Do you really think I'd be so stupid as to sleep with Aaron tonight when I live with your brother?'

He pressed his lips together, and I saw a vague spark of forgiveness in his eyes. My argument had pushed him closer to believing the truth.

'It's not like I would have been able to hide it from him,' I said, striving to bring him all the way there. 'He would have come home and seen Aaron's shoes in the hall, and he would have confronted me about it.'

'And you could have denied it.'

'To what end?' I gesticulated. 'One way or another, Jason would have told you that Aaron slept here. But if things had happened the way I intended, Jason would have found me in his own bed tonight, so he would have known that I didn't have sex with him. And in the morning, he would hear that I had ended things with Aaron because I want to be with *you.*' I wiped my cheeks, sniffing. 'I know I've made mistakes, Will, but not this time. Things may not look right, but I'm telling the truth.'

'Are you really ending things with him, though?' he asked sceptically.

'Of course I am. You're the only one that I want.'

He swallowed, but I could tell by his stare that he still wasn't convinced. I turned my face to the ceiling, exhaling deeply through my mouth.

Lowering my head again, I said, 'The only reason I haven't ended things with him yet is that I didn't want to ruin his night. I was trying to be considerate of him and Tyler, especially since it was Tyler's birthday. But I wish I hadn't. If I had prioritised myself, we would have avoided this. But it was his best friend's birthday, so it just seemed like it could wait a day.'

William's eyes were fixed on the front door, and it was clear by his expression that he was pondering. Sensing how conflicted he was, I reached out and took his hand. My chest stung at the contact of our skin. It felt so right, and I didn't want to lose it. Indeed, if I lost him over something like this, I would regret it for the rest of my life.

His gaze darted to our hands, then up to mine. I squeezed and stepped closer to him, staring at him with a desperate plea in my eyes.

'Please, Will. Say you believe me.'

His jaw flexed and he withdrew his hand from my grip. 'Have you kissed tonight?'

'No,' I said, high-pitched. 'I've treated him only as a friend would.'

He narrowed his eyes, scanning my gaze for lies.

'Is everything all right here?' Aaron suddenly interrupted.

I stopped breathing and turned my head. Aaron stood near the corner leading to the living room, and it seemed like he had just arrived. When he saw my face, his eyes widened.

'What the hell have you done?' he asked, looking accusingly at William.

'Nothing.' William frowned, his voice taut with irritation.

Aaron gestured to me. 'She's crying her eyes out, man!'

'Oh, piss off,' William snapped.

Aaron looked at me. 'Shall I kick him out?'

'No, it's all right.' I shook my head and dried my cheeks. 'It's my own fault that I'm crying.'

Aaron grew quiet then, studying me. A series of different emotions crossed his face, and he hesitated.

'Am . . . Am I missing something here?' The apprehension in his eyes struck my chest like a bullet.

'Yes,' I squeaked.

His lips snapped into a tight, straight line and his jaw clenched. Several seconds of silence elapsed.

'I thought he was just your boss,' he said. 'Nothing more.'

Guilt twisted my face and I started to tremble. A row of sobs threatened at the back of my throat.

This wasn't how I had meant for him to find out.

'Please, don't tell me you've slept together,' he said, grimacing. He tucked his hands in his pockets, and they formed fists there.

'Aaron, I . . . I'm sorry,' I said, my voice quivering.

His eyes were filled with hurt. I had never seen him like this, and it gnawed at my chest like vicious poison.

He looked at William. 'More than once?'

William merely glanced at me, keeping quiet.

I studied Aaron with wide eyes, desperate to soothe him, desperate to make amends, but I knew that if I reached for him, he would only shudder away. He always did when he was upset about something, and this time, he was upset about something *I* had done.

'That's strikingly unprofessional,' Aaron said as he surmised the truth from our silence. 'Aren't you supposed to be her boss?'

William's face crinkled with shame. 'It's not as simple as that.'

'Isn't it? And how is that?'

William hesitated. 'Are you sure you want to know this?'

Aaron gritted his teeth. 'Yes.'

William blew his cheeks out and rubbed his neck. 'We slept together several months ago, before we even knew I was going to be her boss, and then feelings got involved, so when she came on to me last night, I couldn't resist reciprocating.'

'Feelings?' Aaron echoed faintly, sounding both surprised and disappointed.

'On my part, at least.'

William had never said that explicitly before, and it made my heart pulsate furiously. Even despite how sorry I felt for Aaron, elation warmed my chest and cheeks.

Aaron gazed away, nodding. 'And let me guess – now you're being a dick to her because you're jealous of her and me?'

'I'm not being a dick,' William retorted.

Aaron watched him mockingly. 'Then why is she crying?'

'Because she was caught lying.' William changed his posture, his stance becoming hostile. Waving his hand, he said, 'Will you fuck off already?'

'No.'

'Aaron.' I grimaced, dreading what I was about to say. I took a deep breath, gathering my strength. 'You should leave.'

His eyes popped with shock. '*I* should leave?'

I winced. 'Yes.'

He stared at me for several seconds, disbelieving, but since I revealed no sign of changing my mind, he eventually seemed to grasp that I meant it. Fixing his eyes on his bag beside my feet, he strode toward us. When he reached my side, I held my breath. My conflicting emotions were so intense that I thought I would be ripped apart. I hated that I was hurting him, and the fact that he had been defending me only made it worse.

Eluding my gaze, he put on his shoes, picked up his bag and hoisted it on to his shoulder.

'Aaron, I'm so sorry,' I said.

He shook his head and ripped the door open. 'This is unbelievable. I hope you'll be very happy together,' he spat.

Without another word or so much as a glance at me, he walked out and slammed the door after himself. I flinched at the sound and stared after him, my tears coursing down my face.

'Hey!' Jason called. 'Everything all right out there?' The music grew quieter. 'Get a move on, Will! We're growing old waiting for you!'

I could hear that he was anxious. Aaron's presence must have unsettled him.

'Just continue without me!' William replied and reached for my hand, but I recoiled from his touch.

'Please, go back to the others,' I said and avoided his gaze. Snuffling, I wiped my nose. 'I'd like to be alone right now.'

He was quiet for some time, watching me intently.

'You're obviously not all right, but is there anything I can do? Other than leave you alone?'

I shook my head. 'Thanks, though.'

When he still hadn't left after several seconds, I looked up at him. 'What is it?'

His eyebrows twitched, and his lips were set in a grave line. Slowly, he raised his hands and dried the traces of my tears.

'I'm sorry I made you cry.'

I huffed. 'You didn't. This is all on me.'

He cupped my face in his palms, watching me soberly. 'For what it's worth, I forgive you.'

My breath rasped in my throat and I stared at him. 'Really?'

'Really.' He tipped my head back, his gaze set on my lips. 'They look so puffy now,' he said, running his thumb across them. 'Makes me want to kiss them. May I?'

I sniffed and shrugged my head out of his hold. 'No. Not right now. It feels disrespectful towards Aaron.'

He nodded vaguely. 'I get that,' he said and glanced at my bedroom door. 'Does that mean you'd prefer to sleep alone or shall I stay the night?'

I blew out a loud, long breath and wiped my eyes again; new tears kept coming.

'Do whatever you want.'

'Then I'll be staying the night.'

'Okay.'

He raised his hand toward me but stopped before he could reach my chin. Withdrawing, he delved his hand in his pocket.

'I – I'm sorry. I hate to see you like this.'

I shook my head. 'I thought you were supposed to be at Stephen's tonight?'

'We were, but Giselle had to take an early shift at the hospital in the morning. A nurse called in sick, so we thought we'd show some consideration and do it here instead.'

I sighed. 'Right.'

He looked around, probably wondering what to do with himself. 'Well, let me know if you need anything.'

'Thanks, but I'll be all right.'

Nodding, he turned away and left.

I stood there for another while, thinking about Aaron. I had to explain things to him, try to salvage our friendship, but would he want anything to do with me after this? I was sure he felt betrayed, and I hated myself for it. At the same time, we had never been exclusive, so he had undoubtedly been aware that this could happen – that I might meet someone I would want to be with.

I decided that I should give him some time to come to terms with everything. It wasn't like Aaron to stay angry for long periods of time, so I felt confident that he would reach out to me as soon as he had simmered down. We had so many years of precious friendship behind us. I doubted it had been lost because of this.

Huffing, I went into the bathroom and got ready for bed. As I walked out, I didn't bother greeting the lads. I didn't want them to see me like this: my eyes puffy from crying and my lips red and swollen. I didn't think they had heard anything, but I was certain they had realised something was off by William's prolonged absence earlier.

Entering my room, I went straight to bed, but I was too rattled to fall asleep. I kept seeing the hurt in Aaron's eyes whenever I closed my own, and it made my chest ache with suffocating guilt.

Sleep was still eluding me when I eventually heard voices in the hall outside, and I realised the guests were leaving. When all of them had gone, I strained my ears, expecting William to come in, but instead I heard him lingering in the living room. He was chatting with Jason, but their voices were so quiet that I couldn't distinguish anything they said. They remained there for quite some time until I finally heard a pair of feet drawing closer to my bedroom.

William opened the door. 'Still awake?' he asked, sounding concerned. The light from the corridor shone on his back, so I couldn't make out the details of his face.

'Can't sleep.'

He walked in and shut the door. 'Do you want to talk about it?' He moved over to my bed.

I exhaled slowly. 'Not really.'

He sat down on the bed, and his closeness made my chest feel just a bit lighter. I heard him take off his clothes, the articles landing on the floor one after the other.

Sighing, he lifted the duvet and lay down beside me. 'Come here.'

A vague smile curved my lips. Snuggling closer, I rested my head on his chest while he wrapped his arm around me. My eyes widened at the march of his heart. I could feel it thumping against my cheek, hard and fast.

'Are you okay?' I asked worriedly.

'I'm fine, why?'

'Your heart's beating so fast.'

'Well, I'm not used to this yet – being allowed to hold you.' He paused. 'Feels a bit surreal.'

I hadn't thought anything could manage it, but hearing that brought a genuine grin to my mouth. Wrapping my arm and leg over him, I kissed his chest.

'It does, but it also feels completely right,' I said.

He tensed against me. 'I'm glad to hear that,' he said and dropped a kiss on my head. 'I agree.'

I closed my eyes, soothed by his embrace. My thoughts quieted, the tension in my chest abated. All my muscles relaxed as I mellowed against his warm body. Finally I could breathe freely again. I inhaled deeply, relishing his pleasant scent and the peace I felt. His hand roamed up and down my back, stroking me gently.

'Are you falling asleep?' he asked after a while, his voice so soft it would suit a lullaby.

'Yeah,' I whispered drowsily.

He kissed my head again. 'Good.'

I gave his chest a lazy peck. 'Good night, darling.'

'Good night, sweetheart.'

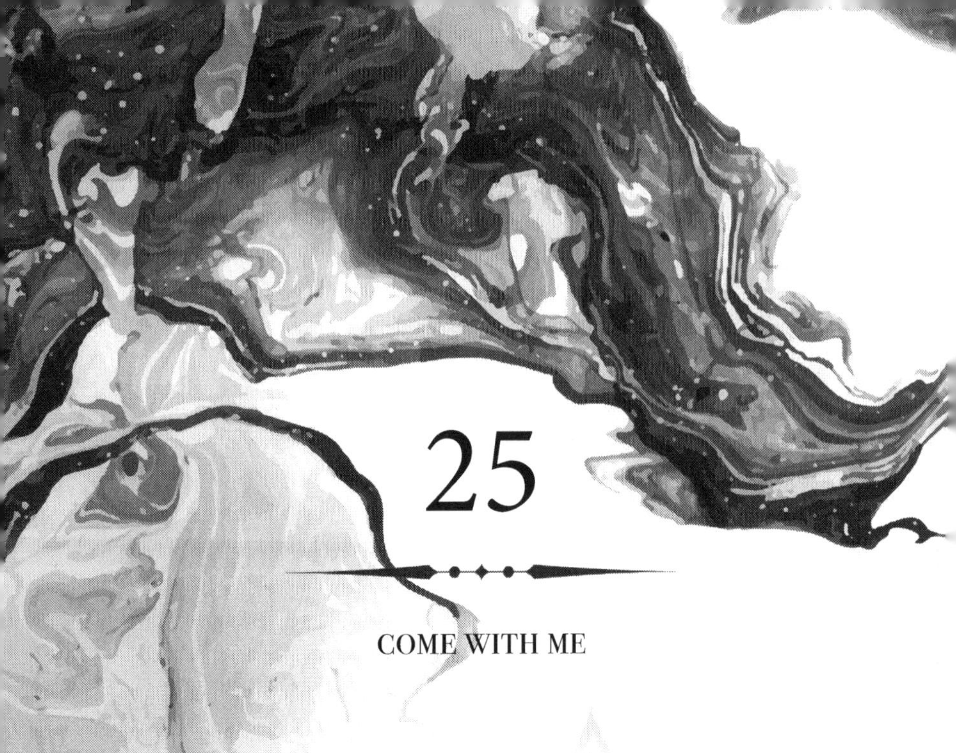

25

COME WITH ME

A FAMILIAR SCENT WAS THE FIRST THING I NOTICED. IT WHISPERED HIS name in the air around me, tempting me to wake up to a reality that was even better than my dreams. Slowly, I opened my eyes. Darkness shrouded his figure, and I noticed the surrounding silence.

My instinct was to wake him; to thank him for believing me last night; to apologise for the mistakes I had made; but when I saw the calm motion of his bare chest, expanding and deflating with his quiet breaths, I could tell he was fast asleep.

I snuggled closer and brushed my lips across the soft skin on the side of his chest, leaving a trail of feather-light kisses. When he stirred, I jerked away, worried I had woken him. Turning onto his side, he continued to sleep peacefully, and I owed him a moment of it – of peace. After leaving a last tender kiss of good morning on his back, I climbed carefully out of bed and went to the bathroom to have a shower.

As I sauntered into the kitchen later, I was grateful to see that Jason had already tidied the flat. I was also grateful to see that nobody had decided to sleep here. After last night, I was not in the mood to entertain any guests other than William.

I was sitting at the kitchen table, eating cereal, when Jason came in wearing a pair of navy boxers.

'Morning,' he greeted, groggy.

'Morning.'

'William still asleep?'

'Yeah.'

While pouring himself a glass of water, he shook his head. 'Listen, I'm seriously sorry about last night. Had I expected you to bring Aaron home with you, I would have refused to host poker night – or at least I would have warned you about it. But I didn't think it mattered since you and Will had already agreed to meet up.'

'It's all right.'

Turning toward me, he wrinkled his nose. 'I heard you fell out with Aaron.'

'Will told you?'

'Yeah.'

Sighing, I raised a spoonful of cereal to my mouth. 'Then I suppose he also told you about my text.'

'He did.'

I lowered the spoon again. 'I really messed up, Jason.'

He chugged his glass of water and then exhaled loudly, shrugging his shoulders. 'I actually took your side.'

My eyes widened. 'Did you?'

He nodded, putting the empty glass on the worktop behind him. 'I know you wouldn't have slept with Aaron. But I can still understand why Will doubted you for a minute, especially since you've got a terrible track record with him in terms of telling lies. I mean, even when you met, you were lying, and then you asked him to keep me in the dark about what happened between you . . . So you've come across as a tad deceitful to him from the outset, I'm sorry to say it.'

I grimaced, my stomach clenching in a knot. 'It sounds so bad when you put it that way. I don't understand where it's come from – it's not like me.'

'It really isn't.' Jason shook his head and crossed his arms. 'But in every case where you have lied, the common denominator is Will.'

I frowned, unsure of where he was going with this. 'Okay?'

'Well, what I'm trying to say is that you should bear that in mind – try to be more conscious of it. If I were you, I would stop lying wherever he's concerned.'

I folded my arms. 'It's not like it's been my goal to lie to him. Things have just kind of happened that way. I mean, when we first met, I lied about my identity because he'd acted like an arsehole. Then I decided to maintain the lie because I didn't want him to be able to find me. He seemed very interested, so I just thought it was the best way to ensure a clean break. And when it comes to you, I omitted, but it was only because—'

'I know all this, and there's no doubt you've had good intentions. But having good intentions doesn't necessarily mean you're doing the right thing. When it comes to Will, the right thing to do is always to tell him the truth. You don't have to worry about preserving his feelings – he's a grown man. He can handle that himself. What he can't handle, however, are lies.'

I pushed my bowl away. I had lost my appetite. 'Well, I certainly won't repeat it. I had enough of a fright last night. I really thought he would end things with me at one point.'

'Did you?'

'Yeah. In fact, after hearing this, I struggle to understand how he can still be interested in me. I mean, most people would have considered my actions to be a giant red flag, wouldn't they?'

His lips curved into a gentle smile. 'Will knows your reasons better than anyone, so he doesn't see it that way. He understands why you've done it, so he's writing it off as the exception to the rule.'

I let out a breath of relief. 'Good, because it was.'

'I know – I told him that.'

I looked at him with gratitude. 'Thanks for having my back, Jason.'

'Of course. Just please don't give me a reason to regret it.'

'I definitely won't.'

'Good.' He looked at the floor, seeming to contemplate something. 'Have you heard anything from Aaron since last night?'

I stared miserably at my bowl of cereal, my lips protruding. 'No.'

'I'm sure he'll get over it soon enough,' he said and walked over to me. 'Aaron's not the bitter type.'

'I hope you're right,' I said as he rubbed my back. 'I think he feels betrayed, though, and he's probably a bit disappointed since he'll have to find a new bed partner now.'

'I don't think he'll have much trouble with that. He's an attractive guy.'

I nodded. 'He is.'

He grabbed the seat beside me, and some silence elapsed.

'Cara, I've been wondering.'

'What?'

He scratched his cheek. 'It's going to sound very wrong, but I'm just so curious.'

'What?'

'Is Will really that good in bed?' he asked, a little intimidated. 'I remember you said he was the best you'd ever been with.'

I burst into laughter. That was the last question I had expected to hear.

'Sibling rivalry, Jase?'

'I'm just a bit impressed.'

I shook my head, grinning with amusement. 'Well, it's been months since we slept together, but if he's maintained his skills, then yes, he is outstanding.'

He fixed his gaze on the table. 'Any tips?'

'Why don't you ask him yourself?' Giggling, I stood up to put my bowl in the dishwasher.

'You know, I think I might.'

'Do. Men like William should spread their knowledge. It's not fair that such a small number of women get to experience sex like that. What I can tell you is that the woman's pleasure is his only focus. I've never met a man more attuned to the female body during sex in my life. Aaron's great, but William's another level.'

'Hm.'

I gazed into the living room. The sofa was tempting. 'I'm spending the day in today. Do you have any plans or shall we find a TV show to binge until William wakes up?'

'I'm in.'

'Can we still cuddle or is that off—'

'Hey' – he looked at me with a lowered brow – 'I've agreed to share you with him, not give you to him.'

Charmed, I gave him a smile.

§ § §

Suddenly I woke up from an accidental nap. Sprawled across Jason on the sofa, I turned my head and saw that he was fast asleep. What time was it? Was William still here? I had to find out.

As gently as I could, I pulled away from Jason and approached my bedroom. Very carefully, I opened the door and peeked inside. William was still sleeping soundly in my bed, and the view left a tender smile on my mouth. Closing the door again, I decided to make him breakfast.

I had just turned on the cooker when I sensed a presence behind me. Turning away from the omelette I was making, I nearly squealed at the sight of William. He raised his forefinger to his lips, commanding silence, and jerked his head in Jason's direction, who was still napping on the sofa.

Recovering from the jolt, I straightened myself and did a visual sweep of his body, which towered only a couple of feet away from me. His hair was in disarray, and he was only wearing a pair of white boxers.

Yet again, I was stunned by his beauty. Excitement prickled my face as my eyes traced the line of hair that climbed up from his boxers toward his navel. I knew where the strands began, and the thought aroused me.

Breaking out of my trance, I faced the cooker again, but I froze with tension when I sensed him moving closer. He stopped behind me, the heat of his body radiating against my own. Gulping, I looked at him out of the corner of my eye. He leaned over my shoulder, his eyes shifting between the frying pan and my profile. Very gently, he put his hand on my hip.

I stopped breathing.

Using his other hand, he reached in front of me and turned off the hob. Then he shoved the pan to the side and took the spatula out of my hand, letting it rest on the edge of the pan.

His lips drew nearer to my ear. My heart thundered.

He kissed my temple, his lips grazing my profile as he lowered them to my neck.

'Come with me,' he whispered, and I nearly shuddered at the sound of his seductive tone.

Taking my hand, he interlaced our fingers and led the way to my bedroom. My nervous heart was beating at a hundred miles per hour when he opened the door and walked in.

A small gap between the curtains allowed some light of day to illuminate the room, and through it, I saw heavy rain cascading from the sky. The sound of it tapping against the windows soothed me somewhat, as it summoned a sense of intimacy.

William pulled me inside and shut the door. Letting go of my hand, he gripped my hips and pressed me against the wall. I swallowed as I stared up at him, full of anticipation. His eyes radiated warmth as he held my gaze, his lips bending into an enchanting smile that took my breath away. Again, that sweet but foreign feeling crowded my heart, making it throb.

During that brief moment in time, I felt entirely alive. Dynamic and full of life. I could feel my blood coursing through my veins, feel the air as it passed through my lungs. All my senses sharpened. Suddenly, life wasn't just something I had been tossed into and emotionlessly endured. It was vibrant, it was vigorous, and it was magical. The present had never felt so real.

'I love seeing that colour in your cheeks,' he said, still wearing that captivating smile.

I hadn't noticed my blush until he pointed it out. My whole body felt hot, so I hadn't given a thought to the fact that my face would be too.

A coy grin spread my lips. Raising my arms, I wrapped them around his neck and pressed myself against him. His smile widened, and the tenderness that shone from his eyes set my body alight.

I longed to feel him again, both within and without. I wanted him to devour me the way the night consumed the day to reveal infinity. Like the night sky, I hoped his devotion would be infinite. There in the dark, I could strip to my core without fear of judgment, for eternity.

Hesitation emitted from him when he seemed to gauge the desire in my eyes. Slowly, he lowered his head to invite my lips, and I met him with full force. Jumping up, I hooked my limbs around him and returned his kiss with vigour.

His hands began to probe my body, worshipping what I had now devoted exclusively to him. Turning, he carried me to the bed and lowered us onto it, careful not to break our kiss. As he lay down on top of me, I smoothed my hands down his muscular back until I finally reached the band of his boxers. Sliding my fingers underneath it, I clawed his taut cheeks. His grin interfered with our kiss then, and it was contagious.

Pulling away, he propped himself on all fours. Then he grabbed my jaw and arrested my eyes. The heat in my cheeks mounted. Was he going to refuse me again?

Still smiling, he released my jaw and trailed his hand down my throat. As he reached the valley between my breasts, he dragged his finger to the left and drew a circle around my erect nipple. The tantalising feeling caused a throb between my legs. I could feel myself growing wetter, my vaginal walls tremoring with desire.

'Please, Will,' I begged in a whisper.

His smile turned crooked, his eyes glimmering with mischief. 'Please what, Cara?' He dragged his finger across my chest and circled my right nipple.

'I want to feel you again,' I said.

He abandoned my breasts and trailed his finger toward the sash of my robe. Then he proceeded past it, and my body tensed with suspense.

He lowered his head until not even an inch separated our mouths. His breath fanned across my lips, beckoning. 'Do you?'

Reaching between us, I responded boldly by gripping his hand and guiding it further down. Spreading my legs wider apart, I pushed my underwear aside and dipped his fingers in my arousal.

A grin spread his lips while ardent desire ignited in his eyes.

'Show me where it feels best,' he said.

Fresh heat painted my face as I raised his hand a little higher and slightly to the left. When his forefinger rested upon my most sensitive area, I released his hand.

'There,' I said vulnerably.

He applied pressure. Pleasure bolted through me at once, and my lips parted.

Suddenly he pulled away and retreated out of the bed. Dread made my chest contract, but it vanished when he reached for his boxers. Pushing them down, he revealed his erection, and the sight aroused me like nothing else. I could barely contain my excitement. This was really happening.

When I looked up, his gaze was sizzling. My breathing grew louder and faster, my heart hammering with anticipation. The magnitude of my feelings was overwhelming, and they seemed to have embedded in my chest, there to remain for ever; all of a sudden, my lungs were sharing the space with something entirely new.

He knelt beside the bed and left a trail of amorous kisses up my calves. I shuddered, my skin crawling with goosebumps. Teasing electricity charged between our bodies, intensifying my lust for him. At his touch, I felt powerful enough to shake the whole world, as though I had become divine.

He kissed his way upward, his big hands smoothing their way up my thighs until they snuck under the skirt of my robe and hooked in my underwear. His shoulders and back muscles rippled with his movements, and I savoured the view. He was exquisitely masculine. Compared with his robust physique, I was fragile, but it was something I relished. He seemed so much like a fortress – impenetrable and a source of safety.

My breath hitched when he tugged my knickers down my legs. As the cold air touched my nether lips, I realised just how ready I was –

completely soaked and just waiting to be claimed by none other than him.

Closing my eyes, I submerged myself in the blissful feeling of his mouth drawing closer and closer to my sex. His breath breezed across my thighs as he kissed his way inward. Fastening his arms around my legs, he yanked me toward him.

I gasped, my eyes shooting wide open.

A smirk dwelled on his mouth as he glanced back at me through long, dark lashes. 'The taste of you has been haunting me for months, so forgive me, but I demand my share.'

I could feel my face reddening. Immersed in expectancy, I ran my fingers through his hair and tugged at the strands. I watched as he leaned closer and pressed a gentle kiss directly on my bundle of nerves. Like a powerful strike of electricity, the delicious friction sent a current of pleasure rippling throughout my body, making me quiver in my desire for more. Cool air spread across my wetness as he chuckled at my reaction, and then his warm tongue lapped over my folds, collecting the arousal that kept seeping out of me.

Ah, that felt *so* good.

'Mm, Cara.' His voice was smoky. 'I want you to touch yourself while I make you come with my mouth.'

Erotic William Night. The thrill of experiencing his verbal ways of lovemaking again was wildly refreshing.

Yielding to his command, I caressed myself while his tongue drew slow circles around my clit, sensitising me and preparing me for direct impact. If he had learned this technique during his time with Kate, I felt incredibly grateful toward her, because I was the one taking pleasure from it now.

Groaning, I untied my robe and bared my breasts. Meanwhile, his expert tongue switched patterns, going round and round and then up and down along the sides of my throbbing clit.

This teasing was driving me mad. He was even better than Aaron, and it was nothing short of tormenting. I was desperate for his direct attention. More aroused than I had ever been, I knew what I had waiting, and I wanted it all. Now.

'Will,' I pleaded and pinched my nipples. 'Please, you're driving me mad.'

He swept his tongue over my clit then, and intense pleasure charged through me, making me stiffen. But then he proceeded to circle it again, making it clear that he wasn't done teasing me.

I moaned and tugged his hair, growing increasingly frustrated.

'Sorry,' he chuckled. 'I can't help myself.' Very gently, he pushed the tip of his middle finger into me, but it only flirted with my entrance. 'There's nothing I enjoy more than watching your body respond to me.'

'But I want you now,' I whined and clasped his jaw. I tried to lift his head away, but he refused. Wrapping his hands around my wrists, he locked them by my sides and gave me a roguish smile.

'Trust me, Cara, you've got me. Utterly.' He kissed my clit again.

Groaning with pleasure, I arched my back and closed my eyes once more. There was little use in protesting. Knowing him, he wouldn't stop until he had his way. He was easily the most stubborn man I had ever met, but I commended his self-restraint. Truly, he was remarkable in that he wasn't one to surrender to impulse. Delayed gratification was clearly something he practised religiously.

To my relief, he increased the pressure of his licks, and when his tongue swept over my left side – precisely where I had shown him – my breath caught.

'Ah,' I moaned, my brows furrowing. Shit, that felt fantastic.

Knowing that I was particularly sensitive there, he carried on, and I sensed him watching me as I writhed against his strong hold of my thighs and wrists. Slowly but surely, the tension amassed in my lower abdomen.

God, he was so damned skilled with his tongue. He wasn't even hitting my clit directly, and yet I was tensing all over.

'Will,' I whined and shook my head. Collapsing, I started to move my hips against him.

He flicked his tongue directly across my clit then, eliciting another moan from my mouth. At the sound of my pleasure, he gave it his full attention.

I failed to breathe. *Oh my God.*

At a rapid speed, he licked back and forth, up and down, fuelling the agonising tension. My eyes sprang wide open with shock.

This was fucking intense.

'Ah!' I cried out, my back arching off the mattress again. Only vaguely did I notice that he tightened his grip on my wrists.

The tension reached a new peak within me. Above it, I couldn't locate my lungs. The pleasure he provided was of such intensity and acuteness that I had to dedicate every single brain cell to withstanding it, and so I temporarily forgot how to breathe.

As I convulsed and writhed, he released my left wrist and pushed his middle finger deep into me. He curved it inside me, rubbing precisely against my front wall.

'Oh my God!' I wailed on my remaining breath and fisted the bed sheets with my liberated hand. I thought I would explode.

I climbed higher and higher, desperate for release. Determined to drive me over the edge, he persisted. When my shudders started and my toes curled, he increased the pace of his finger penetrating me.

Fuck!

Overwhelmed, I nearly shuddered away from him, but he was quick to prevent my escape. Withdrawing his finger, he locked his arm around my thigh, and his hold was so firm that I couldn't move so much as an inch. Grimacing, I struggled to contain the unbearable pleasure. Searing heat burned my cheeks. I felt so *hot.* Flushed, I panted his name. I would never recover from his impact. He owned me completely.

Suddenly his tongue hit me with clinical precision, causing the tension to unlock with extreme force.

'Ah, fuck!' I uttered, though barely a sound came out since I'd had no air in my lungs.

Like an avalanche, bliss flooded my entire body, and the sheer magnitude of it left me stunned. I could scarcely believe the level of pleasure he could generate in my body, and it amazed me that I had been able to endure it.

The moment I collapsed onto the mattress again, rapture stole me away. I closed my eyes, savouring it. My heart pounded against my ribs while I heaved for air. I hadn't felt this alive, yet simultaneously so faded, since the last time I had been with him like this.

'Mm, I love making you come,' he said as he kissed his way up my torso.

My hands found their way to his soft hair, where they lazily massaged his scalp. I heard him chuckle just before he grabbed my waist and flipped me over. Sliding his hands down along my curves, he gripped my hips and lifted me onto all fours.

'You're soaked, love,' he said and suddenly kissed my folds again. I jerked forward, overly sensitive now, but his strong hands stopped me from reaching far. Yanking me back, he made me kneel before he dragged off my robe.

He tossed it on the floor, and then his warm hands were all over my back, his nails drawing lanes of red before they travelled to my front, where he cupped my breasts. After squeezing them hungrily, he tugged my nipples. A smile formed on my mouth as his lips grazed my shoulder.

'You have the most beautiful shape,' he said and raised his mouth to the spot just below my ear.

I laid my head on his naked shoulder and circled his neck with my arm. 'You're rather stunning yourself, Will.'

Suddenly, music blasted from the living room, making us freeze.

'Oh my God,' I whispered, embarrassed. Jason had evidently woken up.

'Wise man,' William laughed before his mouth lavished my neck with kisses.

His hands felt like fire wherever they caressed me, hot and ardent. I loved his hands on me. They awakened parts of me that I hadn't even known I harboured until him. Upon acknowledging it, I considered myself either incredibly strong, or remarkably stupid, for having stayed away from him as long as I had. It was clear as day that this was what we were meant to be doing.

Yearning for more of him, I reached behind me and smoothed my hand along his thigh toward his crotch. His erection was rock-hard within my palm, and the feel of it left a lustful smile on my mouth. As I gave it a gentle squeeze, he groaned into my ear and tightened his embrace of me.

Suddenly he grabbed my shoulders and pushed me down on the bed. To ensure that I was pinned to it, he maintained a firm grip on my shoulders while he left hungry kisses down my spine. When he reached the dimples on my back, he gave each of them extended kisses. Finally, he released my shoulders and scraped his nails down my back till he settled his hands on my bum.

'Where do you keep your condoms?' he asked, his fingers clawing my lower cheeks.

'Nightstand.'

His hands abandoned me. I took a deep breath, mentally preparing. Out of the corner of my eye, I saw him lean over and withdraw a foil packet from the drawer. My heart missed a beat when he tore it open and leaned back.

At last, I would feel him within me again. I had never wanted anything as much as I wanted him right then. It was imminent, and it was intense.

When I heard him sheathe himself in the latex, I bit my lower lip and toyed with the bed sheets.

At first, his hands smoothed over my bum, but then he spanked me – fucking *hard*.

I winced, certain his palm had left a mark on my skin.

'That's for lying to me when we met,' he said roughly and lifted my hips to raise my bum in the air. Then he spanked me again, just as hard. Whimpering into the mattress, I fisted the sheets to counter the pain. My vagina throbbed in spite of it; his harsh treatment excited me.

'That's for fucking with my head ever since,' he said before he struck me once more. 'And that's for lying to me yet again last night, you unruly woman,' he scolded, and then thrust into me without a single warning.

The fulfilment shocked me. He was so fucking big. I had forgotten how deep he reached. Gasping, I clawed the sheets.

'Ah, Cara. You feel so fucking good.' Groaning, he leaned forward and coiled my long, brown hair around his wrist. 'The way you're gripping me, just barely letting me in . . .'

His sharp inhalation echoed in my ears as he pushed himself further into me, slow and steady. Using his hold of my hair, he dragged me up until I was on all fours again. Then he tugged me backward to pull himself even deeper. At this point, he was buried so deep within that it was on the verge of being painful.

'Shit,' I mouthed, out of breath, and shook my head. This was overwhelming. He felt so good, stretching me to my limit. It bordered on unbearable.

Upon his gentle retreat, he released my hair and grabbed my hips. Then he started a most staggering rhythm, shocking me again. I had never experienced more sensual thrusts in my life, and I had slept with my fair share of men. Each one was slow at first, but he picked up the pace the deeper he got. As he went, he focused his point of impact on my front wall.

I wished I could have seen him move like that as a mere spectator. I was sure it would have been the most erotic thing I ever saw. How he thrust toward me, while his big hands held onto my hips, was devastating. If he kept this up, I would be coming in no time, although it was obvious that he was in no rush to finish. He wasn't looking to blow his load. On the contrary, he was looking to make me come undone for him time and again, as though it was his sole purpose in this.

What a man. From the way he praised and tended to the female anatomy, keenly attuned to every response, he did indeed make his lovers feel like goddesses. In bed, he behaved like his main objective was to provide divine pleasure. Perhaps that was why he had a proclivity for dominance; he knew he could deliver heavenly gratification if he was in charge.

'Fuck,' I breathed out as I savoured his dick sliding back and forth across my front wall, which he repeatedly struck just perfectly. In and out – so fucking delicious. My fluids trickled down my thighs while the pounding sound of our flesh meeting over and over again drove me wild with desire. I couldn't remember having been so wet before.

My vaginal walls began to quiver around him. He crouched over me then, gathering my breasts in his hands. Struck by the intimacy of our new position, I moaned his name and thrust against him, aching for more of him. I just couldn't seem to get close enough. I wanted him to consume me – the entirety of me.

'Enjoying me, Cara?' he asked, and I could hear the smile in his voice. Across my upper back, he planted several wet kisses.

'Mm, yes. Don't ever stop,' I said breathily and turned my head in search of his lips. Realising what I wanted, he carefully folded his hand over my throat and guided my mouth to his. Dopamine flooded my brain upon the enchanting motion of his kiss. I never wanted him to stop. I loved kissing him. It was one of my favourite things to do in this world, as well as experiencing his exceptional lovemaking.

He kept kissing me as the tension accumulated within me, dense and heavy. My shudders started again – a warning of my looming climax. Immediately, he tightened his embrace and smothered me against him.

Seeming to sense that I was close, he accelerated his thrusts, hitting me faster, deeper, harder.

Fuck!

He held me tightly, trapping me in his embrace – trapping me in a state of complete pleasure. In and out. Back and forth. I would detonate like never before.

I moaned against his mouth and reached for something to hold on to. Gripping the arm of his hand around my throat, I clawed his skin; I had to release at least a portion of the agonising pressure that mounted within me.

'I . . . coming,' I warned breathlessly, my face crinkling.

'Yes. Let go for me,' he demanded and ploughed powerfully into me, knocking the air out of my lungs. I tried to pull away from his kiss, but he wouldn't let me. Like a famished man, he continued to kiss me while I trembled in his hold.

He fucked me so hard then that I promptly succumbed to yet another orgasm.

'Ah!'

I went limp in his embrace, held up solely by his arms around me. My walls clutched his dick, quivering and overly sensitive, but he kept pulling slowly in and out of me, allowing me to ride my orgasm for longer. His mouth remained on mine as I surrendered to oblivion, lost to the world and lost in the feeling of him.

He lowered me carefully onto the bed then, where he turned me onto my back. An abundance of kisses landed across my torso while I recovered beneath him. Eventually his kisses targeted my mouth again, and I felt him smiling against my lips. Still panting, I opened my eyes and looked at him. The sight melted my heart. Bottomless affection exuded from his light-blue eyes. Chuckling, he nuzzled my nose with his.

'Sorry.' He grinned. 'I just can't believe we're doing this again. Feels like I've waited an eternity.'

A coy smile teased my mouth while I chuckled too.

'I'm glad you swayed my mind, Will,' I said hoarsely, and then moaned when he pushed deeply into me again.

'I've sincerely missed the sound of your moans,' he said and brought my legs around his waist. 'Most beautiful thing I'll ever hear.'

My cheeks warmed at his carnal declaration. 'Well, you're the one eliciting them.'

His gaze was smouldering. 'And I intend to keep it that way.'

He lay down on me and positioned his forearms on either side of my head. Then he lowered his mouth to mine and kissed me so tenderly that my heart thundered, all while he continued to thrust gently into me.

Marvelling, I closed my eyes and I wished to myself that we could do this for ever. Nothing would ever feel as good as this – as right as this. I was certain.

26

NO MORE LIES

Sinfully later, William was finally reaching his peak. Merciless as he was, he had withdrawn every time he had been close to coming and given me head instead. By now, I had lost count of the number of orgasms I'd had.

This was reclaiming, and it was fucking intense.

In our current position, he was holding me up against the headboard of my bed so that I was essentially seated against it. With his hands under my thighs, he held my legs in place around his waist. Between them he was kneeling, charging savagely in and out of me. Our bodies were damp with sweat as I crouched over his broad shoulder, close to fainting. I couldn't make so much as a sound anymore. I was completely sapped after my streak of countless, mind-blowing orgasms. All I wanted was for him to finally allow himself to come.

'Ah,' he groaned. Burying his hand in my hair, he tugged my head back. My eyes were barely open as I watched him, saw how his square jaw clenched while his features twisted with carnal pleasure. His pupils were dilated as he ground his teeth and stared intensely at me.

He was close.

Just as he performed his hardest and deepest thrust yet, he placed his mouth on mine and kissed me fervently. Shocked by the fulfilment of such a powerful shove, I whimpered against his lips and clawed down his back.

'Please,' I begged, out of breath.

A crooked smile crossed his lips as he slowed his thrusts but increased their force.

'Nearly there,' he consoled me, and then he kissed me again.

One hard thrust. Another. Another again.

'Fuck, Cara, I love how you feel. I want to fuck you for eternity.'

Pulling me away from the headboard, he laid me down on the bed without withdrawing. As he put his forearms on either side of my head, I stared up at his striking beauty and gulped, momentarily overwhelmed by the sheer view of him. His eyes softened as they locked with mine, and a gentle smile took over his mouth. Clasping my jaw, he kissed me as though he were running out of air and I was oxygen.

Gently, he withdrew from within me only to push forward again, but fast this time. He moaned against my lips, and I knew from the sound that he was finally reaching it.

Retreating again, he pushed a little harder into me, sliding further and further until he reached the very end of me. Fuck, he reached deep. He lingered there, his kiss growing harder against my mouth before he groaned once more and repeated his thrust one more time.

Finally, he stilled, and a smile formed on his mouth as he pushed himself up.

'You okay?' he asked hoarsely.

I huffed out a loud breath, utterly destroyed.

'I'm dead,' I whispered. It was all I could manage. My sore vagina was pulsating as though my heart had relocated to it.

He chuckled. 'Sorry, but you've got yourself to blame. You're irresistible, and I love watching you come.'

I shook my head and wondered if this was what it was going to be like – crazy sessions every time we got down to business. Would I survive a relationship like that?

'You're inhuman,' I said.

Grinning, he withdrew from within me. Then he froze, his smile fading while his eyes widened. A look of panic crossed his face.

'What is it?' I asked, my stomach tying in a knot.

He leaned back and steered his gaze to his dick. 'Shit. The condom's broken.'

My lips parted. 'What?' I looked at his dick, and indeed, the condom had ruptured. It was barely on him anymore, and it looked as if it had burst at the top. 'Didn't you feel anything?'

'I . . .' His face crinkled. 'For a moment I felt a slight change in sensation, but I thought I was just nearing the edge. I'm sorry, I – it's been so long since I've had sex. I didn't realise—' He stopped short and met my eyes, his features spilling with self-reproach.

I swallowed, trying to remain calm. 'Are you clean?'

'Yes.'

'Are you sure?'

'Yes. I took a test shortly after I ended things with Vi and Francesca, and I haven't been with anyone since then.'

I sighed with relief.

'Are you?' he asked, his eyebrows furrowing.

'I should be,' I said. 'I mean, I've only slept with Aaron without a condom, and he's supposed to use protection whenever he sleeps with anyone else. He's never given me anything before, so I trust he's been careful about that.'

'When did you last get tested?'

'After I'd slept with you. Result came out clean, and you're my most recent one-night stand. I doubt Aaron has given me anything in the meantime.'

He blinked. '*I'm* your most recent one-night stand?'

I frowned. 'You sound surprised. Is that so hard to believe?'

'No.' The corner of his mouth curled up briefly. 'But for some reason I find that fact rather flattering. I feel special.'

I repressed a smile. 'You are special. But you know, frankly, I'm the one who should be surprised between us. Last time we had sex, you said you only had one partner. Was that Violet?'

'Yeah.'

'So Francesca came after that?'

'Sort of.'

I tilted my head. 'Elaborate.'

He sighed. 'Francesca and I were undefined at the time. There was always a question over whether we'd meet again. Violet was a stable, regular thing.'

'Right.'

'Anyway, are you on contraceptives?'

I nodded. 'I've got an IUD.'

'Right. No need to worry, then.' He pulled the broken condom off his dick. 'Have you got a bin in here?'

'Under the desk.'

He climbed out of the bed.

'Bloody hate these,' I heard him say in an undertone as he discarded the condom.

I chuckled. 'Are you trying to say that you'd prefer not to use a condom when we have sex?'

'Heard that, did you?' Facing me again, he rubbed the back of his head. 'Not really – unless you're comfortable with it.'

I shrugged. 'I am if we're exclusive.'

His eyebrows jumped. 'Oh, we are most definitely exclusive if I have any say.'

I bit my lower lip, smiling. 'No more condoms, then.'

'Great.' He smiled back. 'But I'd still appreciate it if you took a test, just to be sure. I realise the chances are slim, but . . . if you happen to have anything, it's better we pick up on it sooner rather than later in terms of getting treated.'

I nodded. 'Yeah, you're right. I'll get myself checked later this week.'

His eyes glimmered with affection. 'Thanks.'

Moseying over, he climbed into the bed again and lay down on his side, facing me. Taking my hand, he raised it to his mouth and kissed the back of it.

I stared at him, mesmerised by the chemistry we shared. I had been so blind, but he had pierced the darkness like a star upon the sky. While I was trepidatious about what awaited me, I trusted him completely to be my guiding light. There was no other man I would follow into the unknown – only him.

Moving closer, I kissed his lips and rubbed my nose against his. I couldn't remember having felt so content before.

We lay there in silence for a while, caressing each other. My eyes flickered around the room as I basked in the delight of our reunion. Eventually I stole a glance at William, and I noticed that he was looking at my wardrobe – the one he had helped me build. It seemed so long ago now.

'No more lies, Cara,' he suddenly said.

My heart skipped a beat and my eyes flitted to his face. His lips were set in a straight, sober line, and his brows were corrugated in a frown.

My face crinkled. 'I promise,' I said quietly and squeezed his hand.

'If you lie to me again, about anything, that's it – it's over.' His tone was so strict that I gulped.

'I promise,' I said again, my heart racing.

Retrieving his hand from my grip, he laid it on my cheek and kissed my lips. 'I know your heart was in the right place, but when you told me that lie last night – in fact, whenever you lie, you're depriving me of the chance to make the best decisions for myself. You're choosing for me and, frankly, that offends me. Do you have such little faith in my ability to think for myself?'

My breath hitched in my throat. I hadn't thought of it that way. 'No, not at all. As I've said, I just didn't want you to worry.'

'I would have worried,' he said, his face grave. 'But I would have decided to trust you all the same.'

Unbidden tears clouded my vision. I hadn't expected to get so emotional, but I was awfully ashamed of myself. 'I won't do it again – ever,' I said, my voice brittle. 'I truly am so sorry.'

'You're forgiven, don't worry. I just wanted to make it clear that I won't tolerate it happening again.' He leaned in and left a slow, tender kiss on my mouth.

'I need a shower,' he said as he pulled away. 'And so do you. We're covered in sweat.'

Sighing, I gazed down the length of my body. He was right. It looked like we had been in a steam room.

'You go first. I can't move yet,' I said and closed my eyes. I was going to be terribly sore tomorrow. He was abnormally large, and he had been at me for ages. I already dreaded having to sit. As if I required a reminder of him . . . Lately, he was all I thought about, and now I wouldn't be able to sit anywhere without feeling his phantom cock within me.

'Why are you blushing?' he asked then.

I looked at him. 'Because I'm not looking forward to sitting tomorrow.'

He laughed wholeheartedly, his eyes gleaming with mirth. For a moment, he looked years younger than he was.

'Might as well get used to it,' he said as he pushed himself up and moved out of the bed.

When he opened the door, the music pounded into the room.

'Jason!' he shouted. 'Turn down the bloody music!'

'Finally!' Jason roared back. 'Took you long enough! Jesus Christ, man! How long do you last?'

The music stopped.

'Why? You jealous of my stamina?' William replied, poking his head out the door.

'Piss off.'

'Unless you want to see my cock, you should look away. I need a shower.'

'Fucking animal,' Jason muttered. 'Is she even still alive in there?'

'Barely,' William said as he headed into the bathroom, audibly smug.

I giggled at the sound of them. They were definitely siblings.

William had been gone for a few minutes when Jason announced his approach. 'Incoming.'

I dragged the duvet over myself and faced the door. Reaching the doorway, Jason leaned against the doorpost and folded his arms. A look of great amusement covered his face as he scanned my lazy figure.

'Are you hungry?' he asked. 'I saw you'd started on an omelette, so I finished cooking it.'

'Aw, thanks, but I was making it for Will. I'm sure he's starving.'

'William!' he shouted.

'Yeah!'

'Are you hungry?'

'Famished!'

'Shall I order sushi for dinner?'

I heard laughter coming from the shower before it was switched off. Opening the door, William said, 'Go ahead. Why not move to Japan, Jase?'

'I'd love to.'

'I'd love it if you did too.'

Jason frowned in his direction. 'Cunt.'

Chuckling, I stretched my arms. 'What time is it?'

'Nearly three.'

I gasped. We had been at it for ages! 'Oh my God.'

'Yeah.' Jason nodded, seeming to have heard my thoughts. 'I thought you'd never finish.'

Heat mounted in my face. 'I'm so sorry.'

He tipped his head from side to side. 'Was a bit of a shock waking up to that. Then again, I might as well get used to it. Next time, I'll use my headphones. Unfortunately for me, they were out of battery this time around. So, if we receive complaints from the neighbours, it's on your shoulders, because there wasn't a chance I was going to listen to that.'

'Yeah. I accept full responsibility.'

He chuckled. 'Anyway, I'm happy for you.'

My heart tingled.

'Cara, I'm done using the bathroom,' William said then.

'Right.' I sighed. 'Unless you want to see me naked, close the door,' I said to Jason.

He scoffed. 'As if I haven't seen you naked countless times before. Guess you dating my brother changes things, though,' he said amusedly and shut the door between us.

'You've seen her naked?' William asked, sounding appalled.

'Cry me a fucking river, Will,' Jason replied, his voice flat.

'How did this happen?'

'Skinny dipping. Next time we'll do it in your tears.'

That made William laugh.

As I was climbing out of the bed, he opened the door.

'Are you busy on Friday?' he asked.

I frowned, thinking. 'I don't think so, why?'

'I'd like to take you out to dinner.'

A big smile lit up my face. Buzzing with excitement, I felt as though my insides were melting into a gooey mess. 'Oh. Then yes, I am busy on Friday – busy spending time with you.'

He chuckled. 'Great.'

'Will you stay the night today?' I asked, and my question appeared to take him by surprise.

'Would you prefer it?'

'Yes.'

He nodded. 'Then of course. But I haven't got any clothes here, so I'll have to leave earlier in the morning to fetch my things before work.'

I hesitated. 'I'd hate to inconvenience you.'

He shook his head. 'I'm an early riser.'

'Are you sure?'

'Yes. I'd love to stay the night – really.'

I smiled. 'All right, then.'

'That'll be the third night in a row,' he remarked with a grin. 'I'm obviously doing something right.'

I laughed. 'You really are.'

§ § §

Live at the Apollo was on the television while William, Jason and I slouched on the sofa as we recovered from our food coma. Jason's favourite comedian was on stage, and I suspected he was William's too after hearing him guffaw several times. I had always found their favourite comedian rather hilarious myself, and the chance to laugh was exhilarating after all the chaos of the weekend.

Unfortunately, my good mood was interrupted when Olivia sent me a text, asking how things had panned out with Aaron last night. I huffed as I started typing a wall of text to explain the situation, and how I hadn't heard a word from him since last night. It evoked the memory of how wounded Aaron had looked, and it made me squirm against William's side, as I lay cuddled up between him and Jason.

William cast me a worried glance, his arm tightening around me. 'You all right?'

'Yeah, sorry.'

His eyes homed in on my screen, and when he saw the wall of text I was writing to Olivia, his eyes noticeably widened. 'Wow. If I were you, I'd open with telling them to have a seat.'

I pressed my lips together, slightly amused by his joke. 'She'll want all the details.'

'Who? And of what?'

'Livy. I'm explaining what happened last night.'

His lips twitched. 'Right.'

I focused on my text again, picking up where I had left off. William could definitely read everything I wrote, but I didn't care to keep my screen out of his sight, because I had nothing to hide. Nevertheless, I was surprised that I didn't sense him trying to spy on my screen even once after that. He must have been curious, but he seemed to respect my privacy too much to do such a thing.

Olivia was quick to reply after I had sent the message.

> Oh wow. I am so, so sorry, Cara. I don't even know what to say. That did NOT go according to plan...

Do you think I should send him a message?

> It can't hurt. I would have

I'll do it rn. Will you let me know if he reaches out to you?

> Ofc. I doubt he will tho – not before he's talked to you. I mean, he knows we're best friends, so I don't think I'm the one he'd choose to confide in about this

Yeah, true.

Sighing, I scrolled down in my messages app to find my thread with Aaron. As I opened it, I wondered what to write. We had never fought before, so I had no idea what to expect. Would he reply at all? I couldn't guess what his thoughts were, but I hoped he would find it within himself to forgive me. After all, the only reason I hadn't told him about my liaison with William was that it was part of our agreement. Surely he had to see that.

I'm sorry about last night. I really am. Call me when you're ready to talk, yeah? x

My hand was shaking as I pressed Send, and my heart did a flip when the app informed me that the message had been delivered. I hoped with all my heart that he would reply soon, because I couldn't stand this silence between us. He was one of my best friends, and our argument made me more anxious than I could bear. I hated the possibility that I might have ruined our friendship.

'Right, Will,' Jason suddenly said as he leaned forward and poured himself a glass of water. 'This is going to sound really odd, but after hearing about your performance in bed from Cara, and witnessing the duration of it first-hand, I have got to know – how the hell are you able to last that long?'

I was grateful he asked while I was present, because I was curious to know too. Smiling with some amusement, I looked at William to see his reaction. He grinned from ear to ear.

'Why, are you a three-pump man, Jase?'

I rarely saw Jason blush, but his face turned completely pink.

'No, but I'm not a perpetual-pump man either.'

William shook against me, trying to stifle his laughter.

'Come on, Will,' Jason prompted. 'What's your secret?'

'What, aside from rubbing one out beforehand?'

I gasped. 'You did that today?'

He chuckled. 'No, not today.'

'Then there's clearly more to it,' Jason said and scrutinised William. 'Come on, then. Spill it. Help a man out.'

'I want to know too,' I said.

William wrinkled his nose. 'I'll probably sound insane.'

'We already know you are,' Jason said amusedly.

William smiled crookedly. 'Well, there are a few things you can do

– aside from rubbing one out beforehand, that is. Personally, I find it helpful to pull out every time I'm close to coming and proceed with going down on her instead. Then, once my arousal recedes somewhat, I carry on. You can also try squeezing the head of your penis if you feel like you're about to ejaculate. Sometimes that postpones it. There's one more thing I tend to do, though, which I doubt most men do in general, but it certainly helps my endurance overall.'

'And what's that?' Jason asked.

'Kegel exercises.'

I tittered. 'Kegel exercises? I thought only women did that?'

Condescension was written across the arch of William's brow when he looked at me. 'That's stupid. They're a great exercise for men too. They can help treat several problems, like erectile dysfunction, overactive bladder, premature ejaculation, the list goes on.' He looked back at Jason's gawk. 'But this requires that you do it frequently, which I do. Consistency is key here.'

Jason shook his head, looking impressed. 'Cara, you ought to appreciate his dedication.'

'I do,' I squeaked embarrassedly.

'Well, then. Cat's out of the bag,' William said with a grin. 'Happy wanking, Jason.'

'Fucking hell.'

'Do you guys talk about everything with each other?' I asked. 'I hardly ever talk to my sister about sex.'

'Yeah, everything,' Jason said.

'Yeah.' William nodded. 'Well, not everything,' he corrected with a frown, 'but if asked, always.'

'That's what I love most about us,' Jason said as he raised his glass of water to his mouth. 'The full transparency.'

'I love you too, Jase,' William said, clearly charmed, and reached over to ruffle Jason's hair. 'Glad I can help you improve your sex life. Though, to put it to good use, you'll have to start actually having sex.'

'Yeah, yeah.'

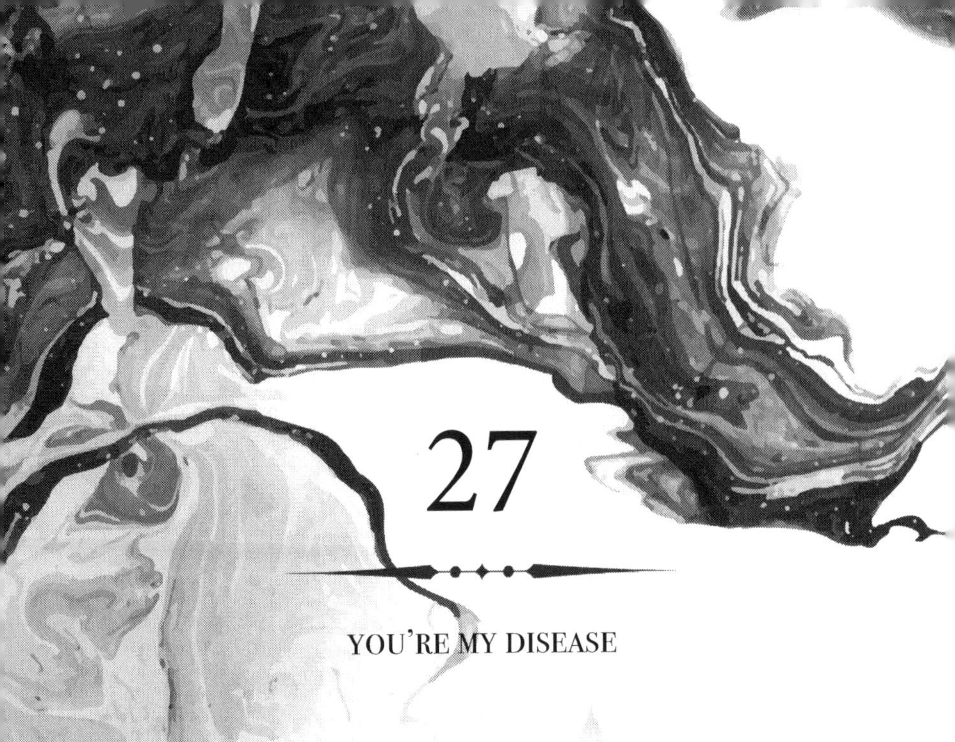

27

YOU'RE MY DISEASE

William left before my alarm rang the next morning, and while I had been asleep when he did, I had a vague memory of his lips on my cheek, and the sensation of it stayed on my mind all the way to work. It was a lovely feeling, but it also made me nervous; it was a reminder that everything had changed over the weekend. I was now seeing my boss, which meant that I was sailing into unchartered waters – I had no idea how to navigate it. But at least I was sure about two things: when at work, I expected us to behave professionally toward one another, and I also expected us to keep our relationship a secret from our colleagues – with two exceptions, being Andy and Violet. Since they were among William's most cherished friends, I expected he would tell them, but it didn't bother me all that much because I had faith in their loyalty to him.

However, in light of last Friday, I feared Ellie had her suspicions too, but I would confirm nothing if she did. While I truly appreciated her as a friend, I knew she was prone to gossiping, and I wasn't interested in being a subject of it, so as soon as William and I were alone, we would need to discuss how to proceed with our relationship at work. I would ask him to request Violet and Andy's silence, and I would also ask him not to tell anyone else till I had finished work in September.

'Morning, Cara,' Ellie called just as I was about to enter the lift.

'Morning, Ellie.' I gave her a smile and pressed the button to hold the doors for her.

'What happened to you on Friday?' she asked as she walked in. 'I got worried. Sent you a text, but you never replied.'

'Shit, Ellie, I'm so sorry.' I grimaced. 'I had such a rough night, and plenty of plans the day after, so it honestly slipped my mind.' I hoped my sincerity showed in my voice, because I truly felt sorry for making her worry. Knowing her, it wasn't something she said only to be polite.

'Rough night? What happened?'

'I got far too drunk. Will found me and took me home. It was awful. I'm still absolutely mortified.'

She gaped. 'What?'

'Yeah. After I lost you, I ordered a few shots of tequila and, you know, things just got a wee bit out of hand.'

She pursed her lips, trying to repress a smile. 'Your boss had to take you home? Good thing he's your flatmate's brother, eh? Goodness, Cara.'

'Please don't tell anyone. I'm still so embarrassed.'

'Of course I won't. Has Will given you a hard time for it? I know he tends to look down on people who don't drink responsibly. Either way, it was after hours. Might be unprofessional, but you had every right.'

I tipped my head from side to side. 'He wasn't exactly impressed. Anyway, on another note, one of Brian's friends tried to force me to kiss him.'

She gasped, and a look of horror crossed her face. 'What? Which one?'

'I don't remember his name, but he had somewhat long, brown hair and neatly groomed stubble. Brown eyes too. He was about the same height as me when I was wearing heels. He was quite handsome, to be honest.'

Her nostrils flared. 'Fucking Guillaume. He's such a cunt! I don't know why Brian hangs out with him. Then again, he's more Jake's friend than Brian's. I am so sorry you had to go through that, Cara. Trust me to have a serious word with him.' She was fuming, reminding me of a lioness. I had never seen her like this.

'Yeah, his behaviour definitely warrants a rebuke,' I said with a nod. 'But in Brian's defence, I suppose most squads have got an uncontrollable idiot among them.'

'Did Will see it?' she asked worriedly.

'Yeah, he came to my rescue like a knight in shining armour. But I didn't tell him that the guy was Brian's friend.'

'Thank God. Will would have given me a thorough earful had he known, and it wouldn't have been necessary. He has no patience with that sort of thing. But trust me to deal with Guillaume.'

I smiled. 'Thanks.'

The doors slid apart at our floor, and we had walked a few paces when another lift opened. I looked over my shoulder, and my gaze was immediately captured by William's. My heart leaped to my mouth.

'Ellie, good to see you,' he greeted, and I noticed he was carrying two cups of coffee, one in each hand. 'How are you? We lost you on Friday.'

She halted and turned with a smile. 'Yes, I heard about your adventure. Sorry about that. I did text you where we were located, but I suppose we moved before you had a chance to find us.'

He frowned, his eyes flickering in my direction. 'Adventure?'

'I heard you had to take Cara home.'

His eyebrows arched. 'Right. Yes, she was a bit drunk.'

A bit. That was an understatement, but I appreciated his grace.

I wrinkled my nose and regretted the fact that he'd had to see me like that. I didn't want to imagine how dreadful I must have looked, puking my guts out while he held my hair.

Ellie chuckled. 'Well, you're a gent for helping her home.'

'Just doing my part as an upstanding member of society.' He shrugged. 'Anyway, we need to get to work, Cara,' he said and walked past us. 'We've got a tight schedule today.'

'I'll see you for lunch, Ellie,' I said fondly and proceeded after him.

He opened the door with his elbow and jerked his head to indicate that I should enter first. I gave him a shy smile as I passed him.

'This one's for you,' he said and handed me one of the coffees. I turned it to read the writing on the side.

Behind every great man is a great woman.

I grinned. 'Aw, how sweet,' I said as he closed the door after us.

'Obviously I don't mean "behind" as in you're less important. I find that a lot of people often misinterpret that phrase. What it actually means, at least from my understanding, is that it takes a great woman to make a great man – we'd be nothing without you. To draw a parallel, you could say: behind every building is an architect. The message is the same.'

I laughed. 'I appreciate the clarification, but there's no need. It's clear as day that you don't have a trace of misogyny in you. To be honest, it would say more about me if I thought anything else.'

Smiling, he lowered his head to invite my lips, but I hesitated. Then

I remembered that nobody could see us, so I dared to take the risk. Stretching up on my toes, I gave him a peck.

'That was a reluctant kiss,' he said as I pulled away.

'Yeah, we need to talk about this.'

He nodded. 'I already know what you mean to say.'

'Don't you agree, though?' I walked over to his desk.

'For clarity's sake, tell me anyway.'

'That we should remain strictly professional while at work?'

'No, I agree, but a kiss now and then can't hurt, can it?'

I smiled at him. 'All right, how about this? At work, you get two kisses per day. One for hello, and one for goodbye, but it's a requirement that they are shared in secret.'

He walked around his desk with a vague smile. 'I can work with that.'

'Another thing,' I said.

He dropped his bag on the floor and met my eyes. 'Yes?'

'Violet and Andy know about us, don't they?'

He looked slightly ashamed. 'They do.'

'I'm all right with that,' I said, 'but can you please ask them not to tell anyone?'

'That's not even necessary, but since you want me to, I'll do it anyway.'

I released a sigh of relief. 'Thank you. I just don't want to take any chances.'

'Reasonable as ever.'

'As for Ellie, I think she's starting to suspect.'

'Me too.'

'Still, can we agree not to confirm anything to her?'

'I never tell Ellie anything at all regarding my private life,' he said. 'She's a darling, but her tongue is a tad too loose.'

'My thoughts exactly. Glad we're on the same page.'

Descending into his chair, he smiled up at me. 'Was that all?'

I paused for a moment, thinking. 'Yes, I think so.'

'Right. Let's get started on work then, shall we?'

'Yes.'

§ § §

At quarter past five, I had finished everything on my to-do list.

'I've done everything you asked me to,' I said to William. 'Am I free to leave or do you need me to stay longer?'

Glancing in my direction, he smiled. 'You're free to leave. Though, before you do . . .'

'Yes?'

'Practical question,' he said while his gaze remained fixed on the screen of his desktop Mac.

'Yes?'

He tilted his head from side to side, and I marvelled at how handsome he looked even while doing normal human things like that. What was wrong with me? The sight of him cocking his head from side to side shouldn't send my heart racing like this. This was becoming ridiculous.

'Well . . .' He tucked his chin into his hand so that his index finger repeatedly tapped on the cupid's bow of his lip. All the while, he was wearing an awfully sexy frown on his face. I wanted to slap it off him, just to spare my ovaries the grief.

'Yes?' I prompted.

Sighing, he reclined in his seat, his big hands gripping the arms of his chair. When he finally looked at me, his jaw flexed, his fingers tensing around the material of his chair.

While blatantly ogling me, he asked, 'Do you *have* to look so appealing, Cara? Couldn't you wear hessian sacks or something like that, just to spare me the pain? I mean, honestly, wearing a dress like that, you're an occupational hazard.'

Confused, I blinked back at him before I dropped my gaze to my outfit. I was wearing a grey dress, and while it did cling to my curves, it was a sophisticated dress, like that of a secretary during the sixties, and it showed no cleavage at all. It was square at the top, hiding the golden necklace Mum had gifted me for my eighteenth birthday.

'Is that seriously your question?' I asked disbelievingly. 'If you can't control your erection, that's not my problem.'

He chuckled and spun his chair around. 'It's going to become your problem, I assure you.'

I rolled my eyes. 'I will not change how I dress.'

He kept spinning his chair around as he gazed up at the ceiling, and it caused a smile of amusement to bend my lips. Carefree William Night was a sight to behold.

'It wasn't actually a request. It was a cheeky, indirect compliment, nothing else. As for my question – practicalities. We could be traditional for our date on Friday, meaning I'll take you to some expensive restaurant, or we could settle for something more . . . casual. Which do you prefer?

And I won't let you pay for a single thing. I'm not budging on that. Call me old-fashioned if you want, but I intend to uphold the traditions of a gentleman.'

'Interesting. "Gentleman" implies a man of gentle nature, but you're hardly gentle in bed,' I teased.

His feet charged down to the floor, halting his spin. With a roguish gleam in his eyes, he watched me with a wry smile on his tempting mouth. God, that mouth, and all the things it could do.

'Well, pardon my manners, but something about you turns me into a caveman.'

I stifled a giggle.

'So, then. Which is it? Stiff or casual?' he asked and propped his head on his fist.

'I like you stiff,' I smirked, 'but for a date, casual first, then stiff once we get home.'

Sparks of lust flashed in his eyes as he chewed on his lower lip. 'Sounds perfect.' Chuckling, he spun his chair again. Once he had gone full circle, he put his long legs on the desk and crossed them at the ankles. Entwining his fingers across his torso, he watched me for a few breaths.

'I've got time for a snog,' he teased. 'I'm spending the entire evening here. Consider it my goodbye kiss.'

I laughed. 'You idiot,' I said, but I ascended from my chair to oblige anyway. 'Is the door locked?'

'Yes. We should make a habit of that.'

'Agreed.'

I walked over and gripped his silvery tie. Pulling him toward me, I straddled his lap and kissed his perfect mouth. Though I had yet to grow used to the unique motion of his lips, I smiled at the fact that it was slowly becoming increasingly familiar. One day, I hoped it would feel as familiar to me as my own skin.

I had only intended to give him a quick kiss, but before I knew it, I had lost myself in the taste of him. I struggled to restrain myself – his expert tongue was seducing me. It moved so skilfully, casting a spell that confined me to him, trapped me in this moment with him.

His hands roamed across my body, worshipping every curve while he pressed me tightly against him, his mouth dispatching passion that made me feel light-headed. I yearned for more. I wanted to feel him within me again. Between my legs, I could feel him growing harder, his erection straining against the material of his trousers and poking my entrance. My vaginal walls were throbbing for him, begging for his intrusion, begging for his clothes to be gone so he could slide right in and complete me again.

Dizzy with arousal, I inhaled sharply, taking his seductive scent deep into my lungs. I felt my fluids trickle out of me then, generously saturating my underwear. He slid his hand from my hip to my thigh, then inward toward my wetness. I groaned when his fingers skimmed across my soaked thong, gently brushing over the area where he knew I was the most sensitive. The acute sensation made me break our kiss with a gasp.

As I looked at him, I suddenly remembered that we were still in his office.

'Oh my God!' Mortified, I stared at his smug expression. He looked so pleased with himself that smacking him was tempting.

'"God", what a mess I've made,' he said with a smile. 'Allow me to clean that up for you.' He pressed the pad of his thumb precisely against that awfully susceptible spot. The sensation bolted up my spine, making me stiffen. Intense heat slapped my face as another gasp leaped out of my mouth.

Panicking, I clasped his wrist. 'Will,' I pleaded, out of breath. 'Don't.'

He grinned, his hand remaining in place. 'I could.' Sudden pressure on my clit made me catch my breath. 'So easily,' he purred.

Digging my nails into his skin, I watched him beseechingly. 'Don't.'

Laughing, he withdrew his hand and ran his palms over my bum instead. 'Meet me at Leicester Square on Friday, at seven.'

The excitement for our date left a joyful smile on my mouth. 'Sounds good. Will I see you out of your suit?'

His brow curved while a crooked smile flickered across his mouth. 'Why, Cara, you've already seen me out of my suit.'

Another wave of heat hit my face. 'I set myself up for that one, didn't I?'

'You did,' he said amusedly. 'But rest assured, you're welcome to help me out of my suit at any time.'

'You're incurable,' I moaned and retreated from his lap.

'And you're my disease.'

28

INTO THE NIGHT

With a sense of foreboding, I stared at the brickwork of the building where Aaron lived. Initially, I hadn't planned to go this far, but since I still hadn't heard from him, I had decided to stop by after work. We needed to talk, but I had a feeling that it wasn't going to be pleasant.

As I gazed up at the second floor, I glimpsed a silhouette moving past the windows. Somebody was home, but I didn't know whether it was Tyler or Aaron. It could also be Valentina.

Huffing, I adjusted my bag on my shoulder and mounted the steps. I knew it was a bit extreme of me to show up unannounced – part of me wondered if it would be best to just leave Aaron alone until he reached out to me – but I hoped the gesture would help him see how precious our friendship was to me, and how desperate I was to save it.

My hand was shaking as I raised it to the intercom and pressed the button next to Aaron's surname.

'Hello?' Tyler answered.

'Tyler, it's Cara. Is Aaron in?'

He hesitated. 'No, he isn't, but have you tried calling him?'

'I've tried texting him, but he hasn't replied.'

'Maybe there's a reason for that.'

I took a sharp breath at his insinuation. 'Is he angry?'

'Cara, please leave me out of this.'

I took that as confirmation, and it made me grimace with misery.

'Right, sorry. Could you let me in, though? I'll just wait for him to come home.'

Silence.

'Tyler, please. I'll either wait here outside or you can let me in. One way or another, I'm not leaving until I've talked to him.'

I heard him groan before the door buzzed.

I dragged it open. 'Thank you.'

When I reached the top of the stairs, Tyler stood in the doorway, leaning against the doorpost. His short, curly hair was damp, and his brown skin glistened. It looked like he had just come out of the shower. Despite this, he was fully dressed, wearing grey joggers and a plain black T-shirt. Perhaps he had just come home from the gym?

'Don't ask me anything,' he said. 'This is between you and him. I don't want to get involved.'

I nodded faintly. 'I'm sorry if I messed things up for you on Friday. I know Valentina had planned something for you.'

He shook his head. 'Aaron didn't come home that night. He went to Mary-Anne's.'

'Oh.' My heart clenched at the thought of that. If he had told her what had happened between us, I hoped he hadn't blackened my character too much, because I adored that woman. I didn't want her to think badly of me.

'Anyway, I was just about to order a pizza,' Tyler said. 'Have you had dinner?'

'No, I've come straight from work.'

He stepped aside to let me in. 'Right, should I order for you too, then?'

'Yeah, why not?' I walked in and took off my shoes.

'Fancy a beer while you wait?' he asked and sauntered into the kitchen.

'No, I'm all right, thanks.'

Leaving my bag on the floor, I went into the living room and sat down on the grey, second-hand sofa that Aaron and I had spent so many hours talking and kissing on. As I gazed around, my eyes landed on the bonsai tree I had gifted him two years ago, which was thriving on the small, black table next to the television.

'What pizza would you like?' Tyler asked as he walked in, scratching his black stubble.

'Have they got diavola?'

'Yeah.'

'That one.'

Nodding, he focused on the screen of his phone.

Suddenly I heard a key being inserted into the front door. My whole body tensed. I stopped breathing.

Tyler cast me a worried glance. Turning, he looked into the hall and jerked his head. 'Cara's here.'

A bag dropped on the floor, and a loud, disembodied sigh followed.

'I'm ordering pizza for us. What would you like?'

'Diavola,' Aaron said quietly, and I squirmed at the sound of his voice.

Tyler's eyes flickered to mine when Aaron echoed my order. 'Right. Well, it should arrive in about thirty minutes. I'll leave you two alone in the meantime.'

He went into his room and shut the door.

My throat tightened as I heard Aaron's feet travelling toward me. When he arrived in the doorway, my heart twitched with anxiety.

'Hi,' I said in a quiet voice.

His gaze eluded mine as he walked in and slumped down in the black armchair opposite the sofa. I studied him intently, trying to gauge his mood. He still seemed angry, and it only made me more nervous.

'How was work?' I asked, unsure of where to start.

He raised a brow as he looked out the window behind me. 'Fine. Why are you here, Cara?'

I swallowed. 'Well, you've been dead silent ever since Saturday, and you left me on read after I texted you last night. It's not like you.'

His jaw flexed, but he didn't say anything.

'Listen, I know I messed up, but you know I didn't mean for that to happen. I didn't know he was going to be there, and—'

'Yes, I know that,' he interrupted and finally met my eyes. His stare was hard and bitter, and it sent a torrent of panic through me. I had never seen him like this.

'Th-then what's the problem?' My pulse pounded in my throat while I fidgeted with my fingers on my lap. I was so anxious that I felt like I was about to vomit pure emotion.

'I don't know. I'm still trying to figure it out,' he said, his eyes darting away again.

My stomach sank while my chest filled with tension. It was difficult to breathe normally. I could feel him withdrawing, and I hated it.

'You're still trying to figure out why you're angry with me? You don't know?'

Annoyance twisted his features, but he didn't answer.

'I don't get it,' I said, and I couldn't help the frustration that permeated my tone. 'I know it was awful how you found out, but I really didn't mean for it to happen that way. I had planned to tell you once we got home, but I thought we'd be alone. I wasn't aware that William—'

'Cara, it's not that! It's the fact that you've fucked him that's bothering me!'

His brutal tone struck me like a cannonball to the chest, making me jerk into the back of my seat. Staring at him, I could feel the colour draining from my face.

'Because it's him?' I asked quietly.

He leaned forward and rubbed his face 'Yes. No. I don't know.'

What did he mean he didn't know?

'Aaron, we had an open arrangement.'

'Yes, I know that.' His eyebrows knitted and he shook his head. 'And that's why I find this so hard to deal with, because I know my anger isn't justified.'

I didn't know what to say to that.

'Cara, was he the guy you mentioned?' he asked then. 'That man who wanted you to give him a chance a while back?'

I hesitated, my throat feeling tight. 'Yes.'

He looked at his hands, nodding, and the sight of him right then made my eyes grow moist with tears. He looked so defeated.

'I thought as much. When did you first sleep together?'

My face crinkled. I knew it would hurt him to know these things, and I wanted to spare him from it. But, at the same time, I owed it to him to be honest, and if it could help him reach closure, I would find solace in that.

'In April.'

His brow arched again, but still he didn't look at me. 'That time you went for drinks with Livy?'

I released a heavy breath, but it didn't lessen the ache in my chest. 'Yes.'

'So, when he walked in on us, you'd already slept with him.'

I covered my face with my hands and nodded.

'That makes a lot of sense,' he said. 'I always had a weird feeling about him.'

I lowered my hands and looked at him, just barely seeing him through the tears that brimmed in my eyes. 'Aaron, I would have told you, but we agreed not to tell each other about things like this.'

'I know.' He rubbed his neck. 'Regardless, I think you ought to know that during the three years we've spent together, I've only slept with one other girl.'

My stomach coiled. I didn't like where this was going. 'I see.'

He folded his hands between his spread thighs and pressed his lips together. 'It happened about three months into our arrangement, and it was fucking awful. It felt completely wrong, and that feeling has prevented me from doing it again ever since. And it wasn't the girl, Cara – she was perfectly sweet.' He raised his gaze to mine. 'It was because of you.'

My breath rasped in my throat. Realising what he was implying, I couldn't bear to hold his gaze anymore.

'I see,' I mumbled. 'I'm sorry, I . . . I haven't meant to . . .' My lips quivered, and it took all my strength to keep my voice steady. 'I haven't meant to affect you like that.'

'But you have all the same.'

A tear spilled down my cheek, and I hurried to wipe it away. I could feel him watching me, but I just couldn't return his gaze. I knew it would break me to see how hurt he was.

He sighed. 'Cara, what I'm trying to say is that during the three years we've been sleeping together, I've essentially been monogamous. I haven't minded the idea of you with other men before because I haven't really known that it was happening. And, every time we've met, you've been so attuned to me that I've found it hard to believe that you could have been like you are with me with somebody else.'

He paused. 'But I can't . . . I can't overlook this, I can't ignore it. I can't pretend like I don't know this happened the way I could with others, because I've seen him, and I know it's happened, and I can't get the images out of my head!'

I flinched at his last shout. Was this truly happening?

'And what makes it even worse,' he went on, his voice ringing with resentment, 'is the fact that he's your fucking boss! You'll be seeing him nearly every day for the next three months, and from the sound of him on Saturday, he has no intention whatsoever of letting you go. I mean, he said it himself – he's got feelings for you. I can't stand that, Cara, I really can't, and I especially can't when knowing you've fucked him before! More than once, too! You're obviously attracted to him!'

A sob leaped out of my mouth. Trembling, I screwed my eyes shut and shook my head. I didn't know what to say. How could I possibly fix this? The future of our friendship looked so bleak suddenly.

'I don't think I can do this anymore, I'm sorry,' he said then, his voice calm and quiet.

It felt like my chest cracked. I couldn't breathe.

'The way I see it,' he continued, 'we can either upgrade this to an actual relationship – exclusive at that – or we'll have to settle on being platonic. And, if you decide on the latter, you should know I'll require some time to move on, so we shouldn't be in touch for a while.'

Choking with emotion, my whole body shook. I could scarcely believe what I was hearing. He was giving me an ultimatum, and I hadn't seen it coming. And the worst part was that I didn't return his feelings. I would have to break his heart, and by doing it, I would break mine too.

'I-I t-thought you said you w-weren't interested in relationships right now?' I said in my confusion. In my mind I was going back to our conversation that day, trying to understand how I could have been so blind as to not foresee this.

'I said that because I was worried I'd scare you away if I said anything else. I mean, you've always been quite vocal about your thoughts on romantic relationships.'

I snuffled and wiped my eyes. I didn't know what to think, let alone what to say.

I sensed him watching me for a long while until his sigh broke the quiet.

'Right, you don't have to say it. If you wanted to be with me, you would have said it by now, so just get out, Cara. Please.'

I shook my head, disbelieving of reality. It was evident that my obliviousness might have cost me one of my dearest friends, and I was terribly scared our friendship had been broken beyond repair. And to know that he had been in love with me this whole time – it made me question whether we had ever truly been friends at all. Had he always had an ulterior motive?

'Cara' – his voice had a pleading tone – 'I don't want to be mean, but I'd really appreciate it if you left. Looking at you right now is making me want to cling to you, and that's not good for me in the long run. I'm running out of strength here.'

Sniffing, I stood up and went straight to the hall without looking at him. I couldn't bring myself to say a single word. I was far too upset, and I worried it would just make me sob uncontrollably.

I put on my shoes and grabbed my bag. As I opened the door, I could feel his stare on my back, and it made me hesitate. Part of me hoped he would say something that could give me hope for a future reconciliation. But when several seconds had ticked by, I knew he wasn't going to. Drying my face, I walked out and closed the door.

I moved slowly down the stairs, wondering if this was the last time I would descend them. He had said he would need some time to move on and that we shouldn't be in touch for a while, but how long was that while going to be? Months? Years? What if, by the time he had moved on, he would feel no desire to rekindle our friendship? Would we inevitably drift apart in the wake of this? Would he become nothing but a cherished memory?

My heart brimmed with regret as I considered that. Whenever I had imagined my future, Aaron had always been part of it. Now I wasn't so sure anymore.

I started bawling once I stepped out on the street, and I didn't care that people could see it. Reaching into my bag, I grabbed my phone and called Olivia.

'Hello?' she answered.

'L-Livy,' I sobbed.

She took a sharp breath. 'What's happened? Are you crying?'

'Y-yes.'

'Why? Tell me what happened.'

'I went to see Aaron a-and . . .'

She waited a few seconds before she prompted me. 'Yes?'

'He g-gave me an ultimatum.'

'What? What sort of ultimatum?'

'He said that we could either try an exclusive relationship, like a romantic one, or we couldn't be friends for a while.'

She gasped. 'What? You mean he basically confessed he's got feelings for you?'

'Y-yes!'

'But I thought you said you'd talked about this recently!'

'We did, but he essentially admitted he'd lied when we had that conversation. He said he was worried he would scare me away if he said anything else.'

'Shit.'

'I know!'

She paused. 'Well, this isn't your fault. He's a grown man. He had a responsibility to tell you – there's no way you could have known this.'

'I don't care whose fault it is – I don't want to lose him as a friend!'

'Oh, darling, I'm so sorry.' Her voice quivered with sympathy. 'Where are you now?'

'I'm on my way home.'

'Is Jason there?'

'No, he's with Stephen and Jon.' I wiped my eyes and saw spots of black on my fingers. My mascara was probably all over my face at this point.

'Would you like me to come over? I don't want you to be alone right now.'

I inhaled deeply, trying to calm down, but my chest kept trembling. 'I love you for that, but I'd actually like to see Will,' I said, my voice wobbling.

'Then go to him!'

'I can't.'

'Why not?'

'Because I'm currently crying over another guy! I hardly think he'll want to see that.'

'I really don't think he's going to care. I'm sure he'll just be grateful for the chance to comfort you.'

I huffed. 'He's probably still at work anyway.'

'Cara, call him. Please.'

I stopped walking and looked sightlessly around, hesitating.

'Do it, or I'll do it for you,' Olivia said strictly.

'All right, all right.' I shook my head. 'I'll call him.'

She sighed with relief. 'Good. Ring me back if he's busy and I'll come over instead.'

'Okay. I love you,' I said, high-pitched.

'I love you too.'

I hung up and searched for William's name in my contacts. I had never called him before, so it felt a bit strange. Nevertheless, I dialled his number and raised the phone to my ear.

He answered after a single ring. 'Hello?' He sounded puzzled. It must be a strange experience for him too, I thought.

I swallowed a lump in my throat and hoped my vocal cords wouldn't fail me. 'Hi.' My voice cracked.

He was quiet for a beat. 'Cara? Is everything all right?'

'N-no.' I sniffed.

'What's going on?' His tone was loaded with worry.

'I-I went to Aaron's after work and . . .'

He waited.

My face twisted. 'Basically, we're not friends for the time being.'

Silence.

'Will?'

'Sorry, I just . . . Is there anything I can do?'

I bit my lower lip, trying to find the courage to ask. 'Are you busy after work?'

'No. Would you like me to come over?'

'If it's not too much to ask.'

'Of course it isn't. But I've got a few things I need to finish first. Will you be okay in the meantime? It'll take me two hours tops.'

'That's fine.'

'Is Jason at home?'

'No, he's with Stephen and Jon.'

'Right. I'll work as fast as I can.'

A vague smile flickered across my lips. 'Thank you.'

'Anything for you, love. I'll see you later, then.'

'Yes.'

He rang off.

Sighing, I resumed walking and opened my front camera to check my make-up. As expected, it was a whole mess. I did my best to remove the lines of mascara that had stained my cheeks, but I still looked as if somebody close to me had just died. In a way, it kind of felt like it, too.

§ § §

Olivia kept me company via FaceTime as I waited for William to arrive. For the most part, we didn't really talk; she watched TV while I lay on my bed, staring up at the ceiling. Now and then I would repeat myself, asking her how I could have been so blind, but she always gave the same answer: I couldn't put the blame on myself when Aaron had intentionally misled me.

It was nearly eight o'clock when I heard somebody unlock the front door. I thought it was Jason at first, but then I remembered that William had a key.

'Cara?' William called, and the sound of his voice made my chest tingle with relief.

'I'm in my room,' I said as I sat up and grabbed my phone. 'William's here,' I told Olivia.

'All right, good.'

'Thanks for keeping me company in the meantime.'

'Of course, love. I hope you'll feel better soon.'

'Me too.'

William arrived in the doorway just as I rang off. When he saw how puffy my face was, his eyebrows curved with compassion, and the corners of his mouth dipped downward.

'Tell me, what happened?' He moved over and sat down on the bed.

His question triggered a new chain of tears to surface in my eyes, as it forced me to remember the painful details of my conversation with Aaron.

'Basically, he gave me an ultimatum,' I said, my voice brittle.

William raised his hand to my face and wiped a fallen tear away. 'What sort of ultimatum?'

'He said we either had to try a romantic relationship, or we couldn't be friends for a while.'

William grimaced. 'Did he?'

'Yes.' I started sobbing again. 'I just don't understand – I was so sure he didn't want me that way.'

William's eyes darted around the room, and I could tell from his expression that something was on his mind.

'What is it?' I asked, sniffing.

He shook his head. 'It's nothing.'

'Tell me.'

His eyebrows furrowed as he took my hand and squeezed it. 'Well, I'm just not really that surprised. When I saw him on Saturday, I thought it was obvious that he is in love with you. I'm sorry to say it.'

My breath hitched. 'What? How was it obvious?'

'The way he was defending you – it was excessive. It just kindled a suspicion in me.'

I looked away, thinking back to the scene he was referring to. I hadn't thought it was suspicious at all, because Aaron had always been protective of me. But maybe that was the problem. I had thought it was just who he was – I hadn't realised it stemmed from his feelings for me.

'But I'm sorry it turned out this way all the same,' William said and released my hand. Wrapping his arm around me, he lay down and brought me with him. I snuggled closer and rested my head on his chest. His lovely scent drifted into my nose, slowly calming my troubled heart.

'I just feel so . . . deceived,' I said after a while, my voice light and feeble. 'I mean, the whole thing makes me wonder if we were ever actually friends, or whether he's always had an ulterior motive.'

He kissed my head and rubbed my back. 'I'm sure there's been genuine friendship at the root of it all. He just wanted more, and I can't say I blame him.'

I let out a loud breath, wondering whether all casual sex arrangements were doomed to end this way. Then I remembered that William and Violet had had a similar arrangement, but as far as I was aware, the outcome hadn't been the same at all.

'What was it like for you and Violet?' I asked. 'Did she react like this?'

He brushed his hand over my hair. 'Far from it. Vi was actually the first to suggest we should end things.'

I stiffened. 'What?' That wasn't the impression I'd had.

'Yeah, but hold your horses. It was because I told her about you. To put it this way, she beat me to it. Right after I told her I had feelings for you, she suggested that we should go back to being strictly platonic. She was worried that if we kept sleeping together, it could ruin my chances with you. The irony is that I obviously brought it up for a reason – I had already planned to end things with her. Anyway, the answer is no. Vi did not react like Aaron did.'

I was surprised at that. I knew Violet was supportive of William and me, but I hadn't thought it went this far. 'I am continually impressed by this woman. How come you never developed feelings for her? She seems incredible.'

He kissed my hair. 'Because she's not you.'

'Will, be serious.'

'I am.'

I huffed, my lips protruding.

'To be honest, I'm not entirely sure,' he said, and there was a note of amusement in his voice. 'Maybe it's because she's too different from my mother.'

I gasped as I caught the reference to the Oedipus joke I had made when we first met. A giggle snuck out of me then, and it amazed me that he was able to make me laugh under these circumstances.

He chuckled at the sound of my laugh. 'On a serious note, I think it's because we're just too similar. It would be like dating myself, and I'm not really interested in that. There needs to be some friction, something to make it stimulating.'

'Hm.'

'And that's where you come in. Yes, we're similar in a lot of ways, but we're also different in a lot of ways – in the best ways if you ask me.'

I looked up at him then, and for the first time since my conversation with Aaron, a wholehearted smile claimed my lips. 'I'm glad you see it that way. I do too.'

He squeezed me against him and pressed a kiss to my forehead. 'Good.'

'I'm surprised Violet never wanted more with you, though. I mean, you've definitely changed *my* mind about romance.'

'Just how the world works, I guess. One man's meat is another man's poison, as they say.'

My stomach rumbled then, and I flushed with embarrassment at the loud sound. 'Sorry. You shouldn't have mentioned food.'

'Have you eaten anything since you left work?' he asked, audibly worried.

'No. I kind of lost my appetite.'

'I really think you should eat something. I can cook for you if you like, or would you rather we order something?'

I hugged him tightly, utterly charmed by how attentive he was being. 'I don't want you leaving the bed. I'm dependent on your cuddles right now.'

He smiled winsomely. 'We can order something, then. What would you like?'

I frowned, thinking. 'Indian. It's my comfort food.'

'Good to know. Indian it is.' He dipped into his pocket and withdrew his phone.

Just then, the front door opened and closed.

'Oh my God,' Jason said. 'You again!'

Had he seen William's shoes in the hall?

'You know, Will,' Jason went on, 'if you wanted to move in with me, you could've just asked. You didn't need to seduce my flatmate to make it happen.'

William grinned from ear to ear. 'Plan is to slowly force you out of your own home.'

'You cunning bastard.'

'Anyway, we're about to order some food. Are you hungry?'

'Yeah, I could eat.'

'Cara wants Indian.'

'Chicken biryani specifically,' I said.

'Oh, I'd like some dal makhani, then,' Jason said, 'and perhaps some king prawn dish.'

'How spicy do you want it?' William asked as he opened an app on his phone.

'Medium plus would be good,' Jason replied.

William smirked suddenly, looking highly suspect.

'What are you smiling at?' I asked, squinting my eyes.

He shook his head, his smirk stretching into a grin. 'Nothing.'

'Is it safe to come in?' Jason asked then, and it sounded like he was standing near the door to my room.

William looked at me, making it clear that he thought I should be the judge of that.

'Yeah, you can come in,' I said and wiped my cheeks in a last effort to look somewhat presentable.

But it didn't help. As soon as Jason entered the doorway, his eyes popped.

'What's the matter?' he asked. 'Have you been crying?'

I took a deep breath, my shoulders sinking. 'Yeah. I went to see Aaron after work, and it didn't end well.'

Jason walked in and sat down on the bed, his light-blue eyes oozing concern. 'What happened?'

Sighing, I started recounting my conversation with Aaron, but this time, I didn't cry; the sheer comfort of having William near kept them at bay.

'I'm so sorry, Cara,' Jason said and reached for my hand. 'I'm sure he'll move on soon enough, though. Just give him some time.'

'Yeah.' I nodded. 'I hope you're right.'

He squeezed my hand before he let go. 'I'll leave you two alone. I need a shower.'

As he walked out, I cuddled up to William again, and we lay there caressing each other until our dinner arrived.

When we came into the dining room, Jason had already set the table.

'Fancy a beer, anyone?' he asked.

'I'm good, thanks,' I said.

William nodded. 'I'll have one, thanks.'

A brief while later, we were loading our plates with the flavourful dishes. Jason was the most eager; he seemed ravenous.

'It's been ages since I've had Indian,' he said as he tore off a piece of naan. He soaked it in the dal makhani on his plate, added some rice, and then stuffed as much as he possibly could into his mouth. His cheeks were so big right then that he reminded me of a chipmunk.

'What?' he asked when William raised a brow at him. 'I'm fucking starving.'

'Good thing Mum isn't here. She'd have paled if she saw your lack of table manners.'

Jason rolled his eyes. 'Sorry, have I offended your grace with my peasant behaviour?'

William shook his head. 'Close your damn mouth. I don't need to see the food turning into porridge in it.'

Suddenly Jason stiffened, his eyes springing wide open. 'Shit!' Hunching over the table, he spat out his mouthful.

I grimaced with disgust. What the hell was he doing?

'Oh my God!' He stuck his tongue out and snatched his pint from the table. My lips parted as I watched him chug the whole glass. What was going on?

'William!' Jason charged up from his seat and tugged at his collar, and I noticed that his skin was becoming moist. His whole face was flushed. 'That is *not* medium plus!'

William burst out laughing then.

'What the hell did you do to my food?' Jason dashed into the kitchen. 'Cara! I'm eating your Greek yoghurt!'

I looked at William beside me. Tears leaked from his eyes as he shook with mirth, but he was laughing so intensely that he was barely making a sound anymore. The more I watched him, the more contagious his laughter became. Suddenly I was laughing my head off as well while Jason panicked in the kitchen.

'I swear I'll get you for this!' Jason roared with anger, but that only made William laugh harder.

All of a sudden the doorbell rang.

'Cara, are you expecting someone?' Jason shouted, and I could hear that his mouth was full of the Greek yoghurt.

'No,' I said, though I couldn't stop guffawing.

'I-it's me,' William said then, wiping his cheeks. 'I'm expecting someone.'

'Then you can get the fucking door!' Jason barked as he returned to the dining room. When he looked at his brother, his nostrils flared. His face was bright red.

William rose from his seat, his lips twitching while occasional bursts of laughter escaped his mouth.

When he came back to the dining room, he was carrying a new dish.

'Here,' he said and put it in front of Jason. 'That should be medium plus.'

Jason cast him an irritated look. 'You're a fucking dick, do you know that? What a waste of precious food.'

Descending into his chair, William reached over the table and grabbed the spiciest dal makhani. 'No, I'll eat it.'

'You can't eat that. Nobody can eat that.' Jason shook his head.

'Then I suppose I am nobody.' Wearing a grin, William grabbed a piece of his naan and dipped it in the brown lentil dish. Jason and I watched him with awe as he raised it to his mouth, and we waited in suspense for a reaction. But barely any came. William merely nodded and tore off another piece of his naan.

'I'll admit it's quite hot.' He shrugged. 'But it's perfectly edible.'

'You're not normal,' Jason grumbled.

'You're just a wimp. Haven't you lived in Mumbai? What have you got to show for it if not this?'

Jason rolled his eyes. 'You have to maintain a tolerance like that.'

William shrugged again. 'Well, you should have. You're missing out.'

'You just lack taste. Make of that what you will.'

William glanced at me. 'How rude of you to insult Cara like that.'

Jason snorted. 'Not counting Cara. She's the only choice you've ever made where you've shown good taste.'

I couldn't help giggling. Their antics were so entertaining that it distracted me from thoughts of Aaron, so much so that when William and I finally settled to sleep, the main thing on my mind was how happy I was to have both him and Jason in my life. I hated to think I might have lost a cherished friend, but at least I had gained William, and I wouldn't change that for the world, because something told me he would be there for the rest of my life, making my days brighter and happier than ever.

Snuggling deeper into his embrace, I smiled in the dark. He was so warm and big, and he smelled so good. Nothing could beat this feeling. I had never felt so at home in an embrace before – like I belonged.

'William?' I whispered, unsure if he was asleep.

'Mm?'

'Thank you.'

'For what?'

'For being there for me – for being you.'

He squeezed me against him and nuzzled his nose in the crook of my neck. 'I'll always be there for you.'

My chest brimmed with rapture as I closed my eyes and reminisced about the moment when we first met. Thank goodness I had gone with Olivia to that bar, and thank goodness I had succumbed to those spellbinding blue eyes and that enchanting, crooked smile. When the present was this promising, I could only imagine what the future held.

Riding on that train of thought, I finally fell asleep, drifting into the night on dreams of our future.

SEQUEL

Stay up to date on *Heart of the Night*, the next instalment in *The Night* series, by signing up for C.K. Bennett's newsletter on her website

https://ckbennettauthor.com

or follow her on Instagram

@ckbennettauthor

ABOUT THE AUTHOR

C. K. Bennett is a #1 Amazon bestselling romance writer, best known for her series *The Night*. If you would like to interact with her, don't hesitate to reach out to her on Instagram, where her username is **@ckbennettauthor**.

Made in the USA
Middletown, DE
01 September 2023

37743009R00213